The Hugh Kerr Mystery Series

" The Conundrum of the Vanishing Cream"

Book XVI

Ahead of the Press

St. Louis MO

Library of Congress Cataloguing-in-Publication Data

The Conundrum of the Vanishing Cream
The Hugh Kerr Mystery Series Book XVI
/ S.L. Kotar and J.E. Gessler

ISBN   KINDLE Mobi   978-1-950392-38-4   (ebook)
ISBN   PAPERBACK   978-1-950392-37-7

Ahead of The Press Publishing
St. Louis, Missouri

Table of Contents

THE HUGH KERR MYSTERY SERIES

"The Conundrum of the Decapitated Detective"
Book I

The corpse in the morgue had been beheaded, the hands severed and the bottoms of the feet scorched, making identification next to impossible. The man's identity hinges on personal belongings found near the body, and the formality of having his two best friends view the remains and agree with the name on the driving license. Failure to do so would consign the mangled body to a nameless grave; begrudging a positive I.D. would be admitting the detective was really dead. Neither option is acceptable. Not to Hugh Kerr, the criminal lawyer who had risen to fame on his Harvard education, his cunning and his almost magical reputation of pulling rabbits out of hats to save his clients from almost certain conviction. And not to Ellen Thorne, Kerr's private secretary and confidant. The two, having worked as a team in Los Angeles during the first half of the 1950s, reject both options. Rather than accept the obvious, they agree to cling to the belief their friend is alive, to discover his whereabouts, track down the perpetrator who had taken such pains to make it appear the detective had died a horrible death, and to properly identify the victim in the morgue. With some ingenuity and more good fortune they find their kidnapped friend barely alive and help him escape. Fearful their enemy's men have infiltrated the police department, they are unable to ask the authorities for help and go on the lam in an attempt to hide from both the long arm of the law and their adversary's grasp. Finally constructing a plan he hopes will prove their innocence, the Gang returns to Los Angeles and confident in the law, they turn themselves in. After enduring exceptionally insensitive interrogations by professional associates they supposed to be friends, the three are reunited in a hunt that ultimately culminates in the elusive justice Kerr sought, but with dire and unexpected consequences.
haring

The Hugh Kerr Mystery Series
"The Conundrum of the Absconded Attorney"
Book II

The story begins with defense attorney Hugh Kerr pondering his fate. Stinging from the loss of a murder trial he believes he should have won, and still emotionally shattered from his own recent brush with the law that saw him and his private secretary, Ellen Thorne, running from the police on an elaborate and grisly homicide charge, he questions the foundations upon which he has based his life. This takes him to a subject rarely broached, even to himself: the fact Christmas always conjures up tragic memories from his past. This particular holiday, the remembrance has come back to haunt him with virulence.

Trying unsuccessfully to rid himself of the darkness that envelops his mind, he comes to a grim decision. Making elaborate plans to send Ellen, the woman he loves, away on a holiday trip, and anonymously hiring his best friend, detective Jack Merrick, to work a case in Mexico, Kerr begins a long journey that takes him back to his childhood home where a series of events twenty years ago created a mystery he must now unravel to save his sanity.

The story follows Ellen and Jack as they trace Hugh's flight, following him from Los Angeles to Harvard, where he attended law school, and finally to St-Raymond, a small, rural town outside Quebec, Canada. Arriving just in time to prevent a tragedy, the three begin putting together the pieces of Hugh's troubled childhood.

With unanticipated help from Lieutenant Hank Wade, a policeman the attorney had often crossed swords with in Los Angeles, the four make several stunning discoveries.

With some answers finally resolved, there is hope Hugh will finally be able to restore his shattered psyche, but the "Kerr Gang" eventually realize the whole puzzle must be solved before any of them will have peace.

The Hugh Kerr Mystery Series
"The Conundrum of the Sins of the Fathers"
Book III

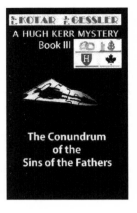

If Dale Kerr, attorney Hugh Kerr's older brother, did not commit suicide on Christmas Eve, 1938, who murdered him? That question remains to be answered if Hugh, his private secretary, Ellen Thorne, his best friend, detective Jack Merrick and Los Angeles homicide detective Hank Wade, are to reestablish any normalcy in their lives.

For the past eighteen years Hugh believed he was responsible for Dale taking his own life. Their suspicion that his death was actually linked to the rum-running operation the boy's father was involved in during Prohibition takes them in a far more ominous direction: one that points to Mrs. Marie Kerr, the boy's mother, and Dale being mixed up in the heroin trade. Vehemently denying his brother would ever become involved with the illegal drug business, the Kerr Gang is forced to confront unnerving evidence such was the case. Making matters worse, charges have been alleged that as a youth, Hugh, himself, was involved in selling heroin.

Putting together the facts behind a nearly twenty-year-old mystery proves difficult, especially when Hugh's memory of that time is clouded with misinterpretations, and the outward lies from Mrs. Cowan, a family friend of the Kerr's who clearly knew more than she was telling. It is not until Ellen and Jack break into Mrs. Cowan's home and discover several revealing photographs from Hugh's past that tie together his convoluted family history can they prove his innocence on the drug charges, but only at the cost of destroying his image of Dale.

The Hugh Kerr Mystery Series
"The Conundrum of the Two-Sided Lawyer"
Book IV

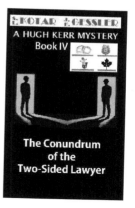

The "Kerr Gang" is back in Los Angeles where it falls to Ellen to try and reestablish Hugh's shattered self-image so he can go back to practicing law. One of the first items on the agenda is to re-address the murder case Hugh lost before he fled to Canada on what could have been the final trip of his life.

Hugh's client, was convicted of the murder of a man by bludgeoning him on the head with a rock. The D.A., Bartholomew Bond, argued it had been a robbery gone bad and called on two eye-witnesses to substantiate his conclusion.

Ultimately, the jury believed the eye-witnesses and convicted his client for a term of life imprisonment.

Believing the eye-witnesses had lied and that they, or in conjunction with two other men who fled the scene, were the real culprits, the Kerr Gang begin their re-investigation.

Hugh realizes the little black book his father and then his brother kept, detailing the names and dates of all the rum-running and heroin transactions they were involved in, was behind the murder. The men of his childhood home town believed the book contained directions to where his father hid the mob money he stole, had finally been stirred to action. Believing either Hugh had the book or knew where the money was, they had come to get what they considered their due. A falling out among thieves had led to one death. Proving that would not only exonerate his client but would possibly help Hugh solve the conflicts of his childhood which had plagued him for so long.

The Hugh Kerr Mystery Series
"The Conundrum of the Clueless Counselor"
Book V

After the attempted kidnapping of his wife, Ellen, Los Angeles attorney Hugh Kerr realizes the murder case against Daniel Jenkins is inextricably mixed up with his own tortured youth. In order to exonerate his client and clear up the twenty-year old murders of his parents and brother, he must turn to district attorney Bartholomew Bond for help. The idea of laying bare his past is not an easy one, but after confessing some details that link him to the four Canadians who actually perpetrated the crime, the prosecutor agrees to keep his secrets as long as justice is served.

Cleverly deducing the real names of the murderers, the Kerrs, detective Jack Merrick and police lieutenant Hank Wade, manage to trace their whereabouts before the crime was committed. In doing so, they not only discover evidence that will prove Daniel Jenkins innocent, but manage to track the men back to Kerr's childhood home of St-Raymond, Quebec. The information also provides details of the development of the post-World War II heroin trade in the province and explains why his parents and ultimately his brother were killed.

Traveling back to Canada on a treasure hunt to discover a fortune in buried money, they all risk their lives to solve the mystery that has haunted Hugh nearly all his life. In so doing, he is finally able to reconcile his personal history, as well as that of his beloved brother, whose death he has blamed himself for since Dale fell down a cliff the week before seventeen-year-old Hugh left for college in the United States.

The group return to Los Angeles where Kerr and Bond – longtime adversaries – are drawn closer by the shared secrets, but when it comes to facing one another in court, they are ready to resume their antagonistic battles with one another.

The Hugh Kerr Mystery Series
"The Conundrum of the Loveless Marriage"
Book VI

This sixth book in the Hugh Kerr Mystery series, takes a dark turn to touch on some very sensitive topics, especially for the newlyweds. Hugh and Ellen are trying to start fresh following their recent marriage and several highly emotional personal and professional events. The first day back in the office they are confronted with an unscheduled client asking very real questions about her rights as a married woman with respect to boundaries of the marriage bed. The law with respect to marital relations falls strongly in the man's favor, and Hugh could not offer much positive advice. Unfortunately, events rapidly progressed from extremely unpleasant discussions to shortly later discovering the husband of their prospective client murdered.

The ensuing murder case against Hugh's client brings many twists and turns. The discussion of appropriate behavior between married couples, and unconventional sexual explorations cause unexpected and sensational personal and court room drama.

The Hugh Kerr Mystery Series
"The Conundrum of the Executed Defendant"
Book VII

Hugh Kerr, famous Los Angles defense attorney, his new wife and longtime personal assistant Ellen, their "adopted" parents, Lt. Hank Wade and his wife Mary, Hugh's best friend and private investigator, Jack Merrick, along with the LA District Attorney, B.B. Bond all belong to the exclusive "Hugh Kerr Gang". Good times or bad, the gang members all support each other.

The Conundrum of the Executed Defendant pushes the boundaries of both good times and bad. The Gang has some fun designing a fixed raffle, so one of their own will be the predetermined winner of a much-needed home improvement without feeling obligated to the others. The fun ends quickly when Hugh takes on the case of a lower middle income black man accused of killing a police officer in cold blood. Defending a cop killer is extremely difficult in any situation. This case places several gang members on completely opposite sides, straining friendships and shaking the trust they have with each other. Twists and most unexpected turns in the case lead to life changing circumstances no one could have predicted.

The Hugh Kerr Mystery Series
"The Conundrum of the Jettisoned Jury"
Book VIII

The perfect, if delayed, honeymoon of famous Los Angeles defense attorney Hugh Kerr and his wife Ellen Kerr nee Thorne, is abruptly shortened when tragedy befalls the Kerr Gang. Lieutenant Hank Wade, the newlywed's adopted father, is shot in cold blood directly outside the police station.

Hugh is literally forced into the center of this very personal nightmare when Richard Baldwin, the man accused of the heinous crime, demands Kerr take his case or he threatens to defend himself. This puts district attorney Bartholomew Bond on the spot because Baldwin is a wealthy, influential man and his superiors worry such an individual, crying to the newspapers he is being denied his choice of attorney, will generate negative press. Although it is apparent Baldwin's arrogance stems from his desire to generate publicity for his toy manufacturing firm, rather than his concern over the possible repercussions of a conviction, Kerr reluctantly accepts the case. The disturbing conclusion of the Gang's investigation and subsequent trial will forever alter the lives of many innocent people.

The Hugh Kerr Mystery Series
"The Conundrum of the Perjured Pigeon"
Book IX

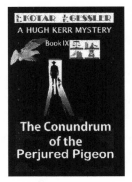

The theme of this novel focuses on the tragic, near fatal shooting of police lieutenant Hank Wade which was developed in the previous book, "The Conundrum of the Jettisoned Jury." Interestingly, when attorney Hugh Kerr accepts a completely unrelated case, a severe conflict develops within the Kerr Gang. The strain of the unresolved shooting of their adopted father and his slow, complicated recovery, combined with the uncertainty over the "jettisoned jury" create tensions which finally threaten to fracture the close relationships established between Hugh, Jack Merrick and the Wades. The separated gang members are forced to reevaluate their relationships while attempting to work outside their well-established support system. Not until the team manages to sort out the many divergent angles of both cases are they finally able to solve both and repair their friendships.

The Hugh Kerr Mystery Series
"The Conundrum of the Haunting Halloween Party"
Book X

Hugh Kerr first Halloween party was not what anyone had anticipated.

The excitement, planning, shopping, decorating and set up for the Halloween extravaganza was nearly enough to guarantee a successful event. Unfortunately, just not nearly enough. The treats were completely forgotten, leaving only a trick which was so horrific many lives would be forever altered, and not for the better.

Hugh Kerr, his wife Ellen and the whole Kerr gang would have to rely on and believe in each other more than they ever thought possible to solve this ghostly mystery.

The Hugh Kerr Mystery Series
"The Conundrum of the Tuneless Tunesmith"
Book XI

Shy to almost disabling, Nox, the eldest son and heir to his late Mother's fortunes, had to prove he was successful in his chosen career as a musician by age 30 to inherit the bulk of her estate. The young man started well enough as a virtuoso in a major orchestra however a series of untrue rumors caused him to abandon that position. A growing lack of confidence left him living the life of a recluse, rarely leaving his small apartment. He continued composing but fear prevented him from showing his work for years, and very nearly ensuring his future poverty with his lackluster career.

Hugh Kerr, prominent LA attorney was hired to represent this young near do well by his step-father. The step father most interested in preserving the estate for himself, hired the prominent attorney hoping his reputation would add credibility to the claim the young musician was a failure. The first meeting with Hugh and his wife and personal assistant, Ellen did not bode well for the step father's future fortunes. Both Hugh and Ellen were quite taken with the unassuming, nearly paralyzingly reserved musician and composer.

An unexpected turn of events, and extremely incriminating evidence, leads to the shy composer's arrest and trial for second degree murder of his step father. It takes Hugh and the entire gang to decompose the events and bring harmony and justice for all.

The Hugh Kerr Mystery Series
"The Conundrum of the Meddling Motorcar"
Book XII

The car rally was to be the height of the Christmas season, with the winner receiving an exotic sports car. All the "best people" were invited, including the Kerrs and the Bonds, pitting Los Angeles' premiere defense lawyer against the city's district attorney in an exciting and challenging venue outside the courtroom. That, by itself would have been enough to attract attention, but the car rally and its "treasure trove" unwittingly provided the two men with an unusual conundrum: working the same side of a case. Their unholy alliance lasted just long enough to provide sparks in the courtroom as they faced off in more traditional fashion: Hugh Kerr defending the man B. B. Bond was prosecuting for murder.

The Hugh Kerr Mystery Series
"The Conundrum of the Blundering Bear"
Book XIII

Tragedy strikes while Hugh and Ellen Kerr are on a working holiday in the Big Bear region of California. While returning to the lodge late at night, Ellen swerves to avoid what she believes to be a bear standing in the road. The car plummets down a gully, trapping her inside. She manages to escape with the assistance of a stranger but then faces criminal charges from the local sheriff. Complicating matters, when a child is reported missing, Hugh and Jack are called upon to help search for her. This entangles them in a murder case when the young man who saved Ellen becomes the primes suspect.

The Hugh Kerr Mystery Series
"The Conundrum of Shooting Fish in a Barrel
Book XIV

This adventure begins with Ellen's best friend's request for help. Judy's phone call alters the couple's plans for the weekend. Instead of relaxing and preparing for the expected arrival of their first child, Hugh, and the very pregnant Ellen Kerr rush to northern Los Angeles County where a major Western movie location is situated. The excitement of being on an actual production set is seriously hampered by the unexpected and tragic death of one of the picture's headliners.

Lieutenant Hank Wade is already at the Calderson Ranch when Hugh and Ellen arrive, and his investigation quickly moves the star's death from unfortunate circumstances to murder. Hugh is at the right place at the right time to offer his services to defend the deceased actor's stunt double who is quickly accused of the crime.

Hugh's determination to find the true murderer uncovers several revelations, and with detective Jack Merrick's assistance, the case quickly proceeds to trial. The inside workings of motion picture production are part of the defense, providing both fascinating revelations and difficulties in determining the true culprit. Complications abound and time becomes an enemy as a mistrial may be a real possibility.

The Hugh Kerr Mystery Series
"The Conundrum of The Girl with the Emerald Eyes" Book XV

With the arrival of a new addition to the Kerr family, both Hugh and Ellen pledged that they would take three months off to spend time with the baby. That promise did not last one week.

Although officially on maternity leave, when a schoolteacher appears at the office asking for her help in making a decision on whether or not she should use her retirement money to invest in a flower shop, thus fulfilling her lifelong dream, Ellen agrees to accept the assignment with the assistance of Mary Wade. Hugh's involvement in deciding to take on a new client comes against his better judgment and is destined to involve him in ways he finds difficult to explain.

While half the Kerr gang works on the viability of a flower shop, the other half finds themselves in investigating the murder of a once-famous architect. His granddaughter, Evelyn Wentz, whom Hugh had previously met while unwisely pursuing a whim, is charged with the crime. With motive, means and opportunity, her case is complicated by two disparate factors: her alluring emerald-green eyes and the fact a priceless collection of emeralds has disappeared from her grandfather's safe. Discovering the theft, district attorney B. B. Bond quickly assumes the synthetic emeralds left in place of the real ones were placed there by Miss Wentz, whom he unhesitatingly charges with second degree murder.

In an investigation that proves unusually complex, supplemented with details concerning the propagation and sale of orchids, the appearance of ghosts, mistaken identities, the threat of retribution and fireworks in the courtroom, the young woman's fate hangs on the jury's decision of who and what to believe.

The Hugh Kerr Mystery Series

" The Conundrum of the Vanishing Cream"

Book XVI

Ahead of the Press

St. Louis MO

DEDICATION

This book is dedicated to Amy Zimmerman, who will be the first to tell you, and the first to believe, "All things are possible." That may not be true for a normal human being, but it is with Amy. I know of no one who is more extraordinary than she. Not only have I known her all her life, Joan and I have personally witnessed her magic – magic, by the way, which she freely and graciously dispenses to anyone who asks. Research scientist, warden in the Episcopal Church, wife, mother – and sister – we have all been blessed by knowing her. She is, incidentally, our publisher, editor and greatest supporter. Without her, Hugh and Ellen and the rest of the Kerr Gang – as well as Rudy and Rose in the RB Saga, and all those others who people our books – would be consigned to a computer, rather than published for us to share. It is therefore with honor, pleasure and devotion we acknowledge "The Conundrum of the Vanishing Cream" was written for Amy.

SLK

And JEG, always

P. S. In this novel, the names have been altered to protect the innocent – and in some instances, the guilty

CHAPTER 1

"Are we certain this was a good idea?"

Addressing the question to Ellen, his wife looked up at him, eyes sparkling.

"Of course we are, dear."

Her use of the word "dear" at the end of the sentence was a clear warning: *Shut up and put up.*

When she added for good measure, "Smile," he knew his goose was cooked.

Figuratively and almost, but not quite, literally. That would come later.

Backing away with some trepidation, Hugh Kerr's eyes snaked toward the stove as a sharp, piercing sound caught his attention.

"Your kettle is boiling."

Mary Wade, his adopted mother, rested a hand on his arm.

"Kettles whistle, son; water boils."

"Yes, of course," he nervously laughed.

"Just relax," she encouraged. "It'll all be over before you know it."

"Move out of the way, bub!" a voice imperiously ordered. Head snapping in that direction, the lawyer scowled. Hardly intimidated, private eye Jack Merrick, who incidentally happened to be his best friend, nodded upward, toward the ceiling. Or, on second thought, considering the circumstances, Hugh decided the detective might have been indicating just a tad higher: toward those regions traditionally designated as the habitat of God. "You're blocking the light."

Hugh back-stepped in a legal maneuver that might have been termed "retreat" by a prosecuting attorney. Unfortunately, he bumped into Hank Wade, husband of Mary, and in a strange turn of events, his adopted father. The homicide lieutenant smiled. He was at his most dangerous when he smiled.

"What's a matter?" he cracked in a rhetorical snarl. "You'd think all this fuss and preparation was about you." His eyes narrowed, causing the erstwhile suspect to sweat. "It's not, you know."

"Yes, sir. I'm aware of that."

The falsehood of his statement was palpable.

"Good. I wouldn't want your head to swell."

"Oh, never that," piped up a staunchly-supportive voice coming from behind them. As everyone turned to her, Geraldine Sterrett, the receptionist at Kerr's law office, grinned in embarrassment, unused to being the center of attention. "Mr. Kerr never lets anything go to his head. He's as level-headed as any man I've ever met."

Jack snickered at the unintended double-entendre, hand jerking out at a right angle. A potato peel went flying from the paring knife he held. It landed with a soft plop on the floor. One-Eyed Jack, the black pigeon who happened to be standing at his feet, tilted his head to favor his good orb, then pecked at it. The peel twitched as though it had feelings.

"He thinks it's a worm," Geraldine interpreted.

"Pigeons don't eat worms," Judy Viele, who incidentally happened to be Ellen's best friend, scoffed.

"Anyone will eat a worm if they're hungry enough," Jack sniffed. The tension between the two was palpable.

"Let me see you eat one," Judy challenged.

Reaching down, Jack grabbed the potato peel and shoved it into his mouth. Giving it a quick one-two chew, he made a show of swallowing it.

"That wasn't a worm," Hank smugly pointed out.

"Baby Jack thought so and us 'Jacks' have to stick together." On cue, the infant and newest member of the Kerr Gang, Jacqueline Thorne Kerr, gave out a loud yowl. "See what I mean? You got it, babe."

"Don't call my daughter a babe," Hugh warned. The threat fell on deaf ears.

"Babe: baby. Ellen didn't name her 'Hugh,' you know. She's mine; we have *simpático*," he added, winking at the tiny form lying comfortably in a basket on the table.

Hands akimbo, Hugh demanded, "How could she name her 'Hugh,' when she's a girl?"

"She managed a way to name her 'Jack,'" he snickered.

"Jac-que-line," he emphasized.

"That's what I said."

"All right, *Mr. Merrick*," Mary, who served as mother, and thus the voice of reason to them all, including, on occasion, her husband, interrupted. "What is your contribution to the baptismal lunch?"

"Geez," it was a tough choice, Jack admitted, staring at the pile of potatoes yet to be peeled. "I'm not a gourmet cook, you know."

"Chef," Hugh muttered under his breath.

"The biggest feast I ever indulge in is carry-out pizza; or, maybe boxed fried chicken, if I have reason to celebrate," he added, purposely avoiding Judy, whose relationship as boyfriend-girlfriend had soured of late. "Asking me to prepare a dish gave me fits. I had to go back to my service days."

"Navy beans and hot dogs," Hank supplied.

"Something a little better than that. I hope. Hash."

"If hopes were horses, we'd all be eating out this afternoon."

"Be nice, Dad," Ellen pleaded. "I thought it would be a wonderful idea. All of us contributing to a special meal. A 'pot luck' celebration if you will."

"And I seconded it," Mary cheerfully informed the group. "A beautiful outdoor blessing and then a gathering of family. What could be more appropriate?"

Hating to be outdone, Hank reached for a fat pamphlet on the kitchen counter. Holding it up, he asked, "Who's using this?"

"That's mine," Ellen waved. "*The Joy of Jell-O.* I picked it up at the grocery mart the other day. It was free; well, not exactly free. It was either ten cents, or free if you purchased three boxes of Jell-O. I bought six," she added.

"Did you get two books?"

"No. I thought that would be cheating. I haven't had a chance to make any of the recipes but I thought the party would be a good time to experiment." She winked at Hugh. "Something old, something new. Something borrowed, something blue."

He rolled his eyes.

"Something old: Mom's family dish. Something new: the recipe. Something borrowed?"

"The gelatin mold."

"Something blue?"

"Your expression."

"Thank you," he pouted.

"Why don't you go practice the blessing you're going to deliver? The kitchen's getting crowded."

"Thank you," he repeated in precisely the same cadence, stepping aside, pausing to offer his daughter a tender squeeze of the hand before abandoning the field of contention. Everyone heaved a sigh of relief at his early dismissal.

Jack returned to peeling potatoes, Ellen turned the gas jet back on to reheat the water for her Jell-O, Mary checked the cast iron frying pan she had on the stove and Judy settled down by the baby. That left Hank and Geraldine standing.

"I made mine at home," she timidly offered to the officer. "It just needs to be warmed up before we eat. What are you making, sir?"

"Sauerkraut," Jack called over his shoulder.

"Shut up." To Geraldine, he added, "Worms."

She thoughtfully nodded.

"Is it an old family recipe?"

The innocence of the question forbad further elucidation.

Jack issued a sincere wolf-whistle as he beheld the sleek stretch limousine pull up outside the Executive Residential Hotel.

"Oh, wow. Getting a lift in this beauty is worth the trouble." Turning to Judy, he made an effort at civility. "Sort of like riding to the Academy Awards."

"It sure is. And how appropriate: our little girl is destined to go *Around the World in 80 Days*. Best picture for 1956," she elucidated to the Wades, "announced in March of this year." Nodded toward Ellen, who was holding the Baby of the Hour, she added, "Imagine the wonders she'll see. Jackie is a lucky child. The best parents in the world –"

"And the most wonderful family who loves her. If I hadn't said so before, Judy, Hugh and I very much appreciate you joining us."

"You made me part of the Kerr Gang. The honor is mine, kiddo. Besides," she added, elbowing Jack. "I want to see this big ol' galoot start bawling when he accepts responsibility to be Jacqueline's godfather."

"Not me," he sniffed, pretending to be offended. "Come on, let's get in the car. The sooner this is over, the sooner we can eat. And I'm starving."

Taking the baby from Ellen, Hugh waite morningd until she was settled inside before returning the precious bundle to her. He got in beside his wife and the others piled in afterwards. With a wave at Forsch, manager of the Residential, who had come out to see them off, the driver directed the mammoth vehicle down the driveway and into the street.

The drive to Griffith Park proved uneventful and they made good time in the early Sunday morning commute. Entering through the main gate, the chauffeur took them to the appointed area without direction, having been briefed earlier. As the limo rounded a corner into a privately reserved area, gasps of surprise were elicited from all within to see it decorated with dozens of pink and white helium-filled balloons.

"Hugh!" Ellen gasped. "You arranged this –"

"No," he demurred in even greater astonishment. "I didn't."

"Who, then?"

She turned to question the others, but none offered to take credit.

"Whose car is that?" Jack asked, pointing to a van parked to the side. "I don't recognize it."

Stifling a groan, Hugh cast a nervous glance at Ellen.

"Your mother and brothers didn't get wind of this, did they?"

Looking nearly as horrified as he, she shook her head.

"Impossible. I never breathed a word. You know what she wanted: a baptism at the Episcopal cathedral in San Francisco with my brothers and their wives as godparents. Balloons," she underscored, "are not her idea of proper decorum."

"Then, who?"

The answer became self-evident as a man and woman emerged from a particularly large bouquet of balloons to greet them.

"B.B. Christine!"

"And you thought I'd be fashionably late," Bartholomew Bond waved, a huge smile spreading across his face. "That's for the courtroom, Mr. Kerr. I'm always the first at a party."

Allowing the redoubtable district attorney to open the door and take her hand, Ellen stepped out. Mrs. Bond immediately joined them, holding out her arms. Lightly hugging her, she kissed the baby's forehead.

"B.B. and I wanted to surprise you."

"You did that and then some," Hugh admitted, joining them. "You did all this decorating yourselves?"

"We picked up the balloons this morning; fortunately, the shop opens on Sundays for weddings and ceremonies like this. You should have seen us," she laughed. "I'm afraid we got a little carried away. They wouldn't all fit into our car, so B.B. had to go over to the car rental agency across the street and hire a van. And at that, they barely fit. I had to keep batting stray ones away so he could drive. I'm surprised he didn't get a ticket for driving with an obstructed view."

All eyes turned to Hank.

"If I had known," he suavely replied, "I would have put out an alert to have the boys give you an escort. Now, if Kerr, here, had been driving, that would have been a different story. Since we all heard him testify in court about his deplorable driving record, I'm afraid I would have him pulled over and arrested. You get just so many points on your license, Kerr, before you're clapped behind bars."

"Those tickets were spurious!" he sputtered. "And besides, I paid the fines. No points," he added with a certain smugness meant to incur ire.

"You get 'points' just for breathing," he quipped.

Hugh groaned as Bond pulled Wade off to the side.

"What are you doing here?" he whispered in annoyance.

Hank Wade could deadpan with the best.

"They invited my wife and she threatened bodily harm if I didn't come. And she knows where I keep my service revolver," he added with such sincerity no one in their right mind could disbelieve him. "What are you doing here?"

"We got an invitation in the mail. What was I to do – tell them we were busy? On a Sunday morning? Besides," he added, "I'm not the one who hates Kerr's guts. Outside of court, he's a decent fellow. Besides... Christine wanted to go. She wanted to see how they'd handle it."

Hank wisely nodded.

"On the cheap because they had a girl and not a boy?"

"What else?"

"I approve. Scouting out the enemy."

Bond squeezed his arm.

"Good man."

They returned to the gathering, well satisfied the lines had been drawn in the correct places. In their absence, they noted, to their chagrin, Jack had taken control of the proceedings.

"All right, everyone," he ordered. "Hugh, you're the one who's giving the benediction, so you stand over here," he directed. "Ellen, you and Miss Jackie stand before him; Geraldine and I will be to your side, slightly behind, one to the right, one to the left. The witnesses and family members will form a semicircle behind."

Greatly pleased, Ellen moved forward.

"A very nice arrangement, Jack."

"I read up on it. And I had a long conversation with the monks up at the monastery. It turned out swell that I went up there."

"For a lot of reasons," Hugh agreed.

"I told them the whole story and they got it. Imagine that?"

"Before or after you asked about Addison Wentz?"

Jack cleared his throat.

"Well, sorta before and after."

"I see."

"I figured it was important. Besides, the Father knew something was on my mind. He opened the gate, so to speak."

"As it was meant to be," Ellen interjected before the conversation went off-track.

The group gathered into their appointed places, leaving it up to Hugh to begin. During the few seconds the arrangements took, he had paled considerably.

"Good morning," he began, eyes going from one face to the other before lifting his eyes upward toward the sky. "And it is a good morning. A morning in which to share with you our gladsome tidings: the birth of a baby: Jacqueline Thorne Kerr. While I realize you've all met her, we're gathered here today to share our happiness with one another and to announce our joy to the Universe.

"Men and women hold different beliefs about that universe we live in. Over the course of human history, we have worshipped fire, the sun, the stars; we have created ancient and modern gods, adorned them with magnificent raiment, told stories about their lives and their powers, their words of wisdom and their tragic fates. What ties these deities together is an innate sense of some higher power watching, and in some cases directing, our actions. The expression, 'God is in his heaven and everything is as it should be' has sustained many a broken or questioning heart. That, I think, is the key to understanding: the human heart. Not the organ which circulates our shared blood, but that serving as the ethereal concept of soul."

Stepping forward, he accepted the infant from Ellen's hands. Cradling her to his chest, Hugh smiled broadly as he continued.

"A soul, that unique concept which fosters love. Love of one another, not only on a small scale but a universal, all-consuming passion for what we know and what we don't know; love of children; a divine sense of what is pure and just. Love, in its unadulterated meaning, is the inspiration for exploration, for dreams, for creativity and faith; for hope and charity. We, in this small gathering, represent that love, and with that understanding, Jacqueline's mother and father bless this baby and ask you do the same."

Stepping forward, he offered the baby to Jack.

"According to tradition, Ellen and I have chosen Jack Merrick and Geraldine Sterrett as surrogate parents, also known as godfather and godmother. By which we ask that you hold her as your own, keeping in your hearts her wellbeing and her developing mind. Instill in her your own goodness; teach her to walk in your paths. Cherish her in what manner you hold sacred. Love her as Ellen and I love you."

Accepting Jacqueline, as tears ran down his face, Jack kissed her on the forehead.

"I will," he vowed, then stared into Hugh's eyes. "May I —?"

"Of course."

Taking in a deep breath, he made the sign of the cross over her before passing the child to Geraldine, who likewise had tears streaming across her cheeks. Taking the small, delicate hand, she squeezed it, then reverently kissed the five fingers.

"I will. I love you so much, baby."

Indicating Ellen take Jacqueline, Hugh addressed the others.

"Extended family – drawn, so to speak, from all corners of the courtroom," he grinned, "Ellen and I ask your blessing on our child, so that she may carry your devotion in her heart... not for the longest day she lives, but for all eternity, for we are all ripples on a pond, and each of us has influence on the everlasting wonders of the universe."

Turning to Mary and Hank, Ellen held Jackie out to them. With a cry of joy, Mary took her, kissed her half a dozen times, then prayed, "God bless you, granddaughter," before allowing her husband to take her in his arms.

"My job, Jackie, is to sit you on my knee and straighten you out about a lot of things you'll hear from your mother and father. You and I will be best friends and here's a little something to keep you on the straight and narrow." Taking a shiny object from his pocket, he placed it in her hands. "This is the first policeman's badge I ever wore. It's kept me on the side of right all my life. Now, I bequeath it to you. It's not a cross," he added, nodding approvingly at Jack, "but it's faith in doing what's right, even if the choices are hard. I hope it reminds you, as it has me, that life is hard and things don't always work out the way they should, but you stand by your principles and carry on, hoping to make the next day better."

"Thank you, Dad," Ellen whispered, deeply touched. Moving to the Bonds, she waited expectantly for either to make the first overture. B.B. surprised her by taking the baby in his arms.

"Jacqueline," he choked, "you've already had an impact on life. You've made me want to go home and hug my own children. Once in a while we all need a reminder of what's precious to us."

As he sniffed away a tear, Christine bent down and kissed the baby.

"A lesson we all need. Bless you, little one. And bless your parents for inviting us here to share their love."

Touched by the sentiments, Ellen received Jacqueline back from Bond and returned to Hugh. Before she could speak, the baby let out a loud cry.

"Oh, good!" Everyone turned to Jack. "She's hungry. So am I. I've been so nervous, I haven't been able to eat for days. Maybe a week. Let's go back and chow down."

A perfect ending to a perfect morning.

CHAPTER 2

As so often happened at the point between night and day, the change of seasons and the resumption of play after the All Star break, 11:59 slipped across the dial into 12:00 and "perfect morning" metamorphosed into afternoon, crossing a metaphysical barrier.

The baby began fussing, kicked her legs, then as her face turned red, started screaming in such a piercing wail Jack London might have retrospectively used it as an inspiration for the "call of the wild." Clutching her closer, Ellen attempted a quick fix then abandoned the idea as hopeless.

"I'll have to get her into the car."

"That's all right," Hugh reassured. "We're done here."

"I was going to help you clean up."

"No need for that," Christine offered, stepping forward with a smile that did testimony to the many hours she watched her husband practice his concluding remarks to a case he was sure to win. "B.B. and I will take care of that."

"But, you are coming back to the house? You were invited to lunch."

"Of course. And I've brought our contribution to 'pot luck.' I wouldn't miss it for the world." Relieved that Jacqueline's sudden squall had not ruined the event and thus prevented the Bonds from joining them at the Residential which was not necessarily the same thing, Ellen nodded in relief. "Babies cry," Christine continued. "For the first year, that's what they do best. Having been through two, I can assure you that you've already come out ahead. Your little darling was a perfect angel when it counted. Anything that comes after can be managed without apology."

"Thank you. We'll see you in a few minutes, then."

Guiding the way, Mary led mother and child to the waiting limo. As the others hesitated, Mrs. Bond shooed them away.

"Hugh, take everyone with you." When he hesitated, she directed the order to Hank. "Lieutenant Wade, go with your wife. Keep everyone calm. You know how to do that. Mr. Bond and I will pack everything up. It shouldn't take us more than half an hour."

Fully aware the formality was meant to keep everyone in their places, he grunted at Jack before assuming his police tone.

"Let's go, you. And Miss Sterrett, if you'll kindly follow me?"

Jack gulped in what might have been exaggerated terror.

"Geez. I thought you were gonna add, 'I've got a few questions I'd like the answers to.'"

Wade accepted the statement for the praise it was.

"Get a move on."

Slipping his arm through Geraldine's, either to protect her or himself, the detective hurried toward the waiting car, Wade following cautiously behind. Once the Kerr Gang was loaded and settled in, the driver gunned the engine, made a U-turn and stepped on it, possibly intimidated by the presence of his betters. Once the vehicle passed from view, Bond pouted.

"Why did you send them away like that?"

"I was as friendly as I could be."

"I don't mean that," he dismissed out-of-hand. "You could at least have ordered Wade to stay."

"What-for?"

"To help us pack. You could see he'd rather have stayed with us."

"Your point being?" Shriveling under the direct interrogative, he shrugged. "He's on our side."

"I hardly think so. He's a policeman. He works for you. Besides," she pursued, hands on hips as she surveyed the large accumulation of balloons. "I'm still steamed over the fact he didn't tell you about Addison Wentz wearing a suitcoat and shoes. That made you look like a fool."

"Thank you for that." He kicked the dirt. "Anyway, it was my fault."

"It's never your fault when your minions don't supply the requisite information. That's what they get paid for."

"Maybe he didn't know, either. We all supposed the man to be a cripple."

"Then Grindley should have told him and he should have told you. I don't see any reason to split hairs. Kerr figured it out. That woman was guilty as sin."

"You still think so?" he asked in astonishment.

"Your presentation convinced me. The jury only sided with the defense because of Kerr dumping the clothes on the floor. That damn shoe dropping turned everything around. I don't like to see you lose."

"I don't like it any more than you do. Less," he mumbled, reaching out for a bouquet of balloons. Tugging on the strings in a vain attempt to untangle them, she stopped him with a curt stomp of her foot.

"What are you doing?"

"I'm going to put them back in the car so we can take them up to the party."

"We've made our statement. You were right about that; they did go over well. But, now we're through with them. We're going to pop them all."

"Why? We paid good money for them. We might as well at least save some. They're... festive," he tried, puzzled and slightly saddened by her attitude.

"Do you have a pocketknife with you?"

Patting his trousers for no other reason than to have some action to perform, Bond shook his head.

"No."

"Go to the van and get my purse. I have a nail file there that will serve."

Following her instructions, he did as ordered, returning with the pointed steel instrument. Handing it over, he watched as she began a systemic destruction of the helium balloons. Bouncing on his toes, he offered an observation.

"At least that seems to be highly cathartic." When she didn't reply, he asked, "Let me try."

She surprised him by turning over the murder weapon. As he jabbed it at the latex, requiring several tries before it burst, she pursed her lips.

"What was this all about, anyway?"

"What do you mean?"

"This ceremony. It certainly wasn't a baptism. It was more like some sort of pagan ritual. How could Ellen have allowed it?"

"Oh, that," he laughed. "You know how peculiar Hugh is. I suppose she was just humoring him. She has a mother up north – in Lodi, if I remember correctly. And brothers. Since none of them were here, I'm sure they're going to hold the ceremony somewhere more convenient for the family. This was just for us."

"Us?" she asked, taking back the nail file and pursuing her work.

"Us. The locals," he tried at a loss for a better description. "The people he works with. His secretary; Merrick. The Wades."

"He doesn't work with the Wades," she announced through gritted teeth, delivering a particularly vicious blow to a pink balloon. "Wade works for you. And for that matter, you don't work for him, either. Although sometimes it looks like that."

Wincing under the blow, he wandered away, collecting a stray bouquet that had become detached from its mooring and started to blow away in the wind.

"That hurts."

After destroying two more balloons, she softened her tone.

"I'm sorry, Bart. I don't mean to take my frustrations out on you."

"We didn't have to accept, you know."

"It was actually gracious of them to invite us. Why did they?"

"So we wouldn't have to go to the expense of flying to San Francisco for the real christening?"

She conceded the point before pursing the question.

"Because you threw him a bachelor party?"

"Are you asking me or telling me?"

"Tit for tat."

"I think you were right in the first place."

"What's that?"

"They're gracious people. Besides," he added in an undertone, "I think they like us."

"God forbid," she responded, although he read a slightly less damning statement.

Will wonders never cease?

Which made him happy he had rescued the last bouquet of balloons for the celebration to follow.

Spreading the pink tablecloth over the formal dining table, Ellen smiled in pleasure.

"It looks right, doesn't it, Hugh?"

"Baby girl," he grinned. "Did she drink a quart of milk?"

"Two quarts, and then some. Followed by a diaper change and a new outfit. Just in time. Rubber pants only protect so far. I was afraid the christening gown Mom gave us was going to be soiled."

"No worry about that, dear," Mary called from the kitchen. "A good christening gown is made to withstand the rigors of a special day. And generations to follow."

"Something borrowed, something blue," Hugh grinned. "Not so blue, now, am I?"

"No, my love. You were wonderful."

"I had the worst case of shakes I've ever had."

"Ever?"

"Ever," he vowed. "A lawyer's first address to the jury is one form of terror, but speaking on the subject of love and eternity is something else, again."

"I'm glad to hear you say that."

"Yeah, pal," Jack sang from the other room. "I caught a quiver here and there. With practice makes better."

"Then you better start saving for two ponies."

Without seeing him, the Kerrs imagined Jack "quivering."

"Well, OK, not anytime soon. Unless you give me a raise."

"You're already the best-paid private 'dick' in the state."

"And worth every penny, too."

They grinned as he joined them from the kitchen.

"My special dish is ready. Where do you keep the ketchup?"

If anyone shivered, it wasn't apparent.

"In the fridge."

Jack gave her a quizzical look, then shrugged.

"That's the last place I would have looked."

Rather than go into a long explanation, Ellen smiled.

"We found our cabinets were too full, so I started storing bottles in there."

"Interesting. My problem is just the opposite."

Stooping down to pick up Law Book, which had planted itself by his feet, Hugh cuddled the Siamese in his arms.

"That's odd. Whenever we've been there, both your icebox and your cabinets have been bare."

"That's because he's always hoping you'll fill them for him," Wade chipped in.

"Not true! I'll have you know there's plenty of food in the apartment."

Detecting an unexpected note of sincerity, Hank frowned, glanced at Hugh, then immediately made the connection.

"With cat food!"

"So? I want something to eat, I call out. Goldie can't do that."

"She'll be able to, in time," Hugh chuckled. "I suspect our animals have us wrapped around their... tails."

"Speak for yourself," Hank huffed. "For myself, I believe in discipline. That's the only way to raise a pet – or a child," he added as an afterthought, scowling at the detective. "Something you didn't get enough of. Neither did you," he added to the lawyer. "You're both incorrigible."

"That's only because you chose the wrong occupations, boys," Mary explained, moving between them with a large casserole dish in her hands. "Jack, go look for your ketchup and set it on the table beside your hash. Hugh, what did you make?"

"Maple-walnut fudge."

"Oh. Then, that can wait until after dinner. If you're not helping, go sit at the table. And put that cat down. She may be part of the family, but she's not a dinner guest."

"Yes, ma'am."

Allowing Law Book to drip languidly from his hands, then crossed to the bar. Jack went in search of ketchup in unlikely places and Ellen scurried into the dining room with her contribution. When the doorbell rang, Judy raised her hand.

"I'll get it."

Crossing to the door, she opened it to admit the Bonds. Laughing at the sight of the district attorney holding a string attached to a dozen balloons, she bade them pass with a sweep of her arm.

"Enter as friends."

Stepping back to avoid being struck in the face by a wayward balloon, B.B. and Christine accepted the invitation. Amid sundry greetings, B.B. asked, "Where do you want me to put these?"

Coming to the rescue, Ellen untangled the line from around his hand and deftly tied it to a leg of the coffee table.

"I was hoping you would bring some back with you. They're so cheerful."

"What did you do with the rest?" Hugh asked, crossing to Bond. Shifting the wine bottle he was uncorking to his left, he extended the right and the two men shook.

Hardly expecting to be quizzed, the D.A. deferred to his wife.

"We popped them, of course."

"Good. If they get loose they may get tangled in the trees or the high wires. It disrupts the beauty of nature. You did pick up the shards, didn't you? Birds or little animals see the bright colors and think they're food. If they swallow them, the material gets caught in their throats or their stomachs and may cause harm."

Proving she was as adept as her husband at delivering a dubious statement as obvious fact, she smiled.

"Of course we did."

"Thank you." He smiled and held up the wine bottle. "Since we're having a mishmash of foods, I hope you don't mind a burgundy. But, if you'd rather, I can open a bottle of Riesling, as well."

"Now that you mention it," Bond eagerly accepted the offer, "I'd love to have a look at your wine collection."

Smiling in pleasure, Hugh took him away with the general approval of the rest. Making her way to the kitchen, Christine held out the covered dish she was holding.

"I brought mac and cheese. I hope that suits. Anything fancier and I was afraid it wouldn't travel well. And as I didn't know how long the ceremony was going to take –"

"Just perfect!" Ellen praised, taking it from her. "The oven is still hot. Shall I put it in there to warm?"

"I wrapped it in a blanket to keep the heat in, but it seems to have cooled, so I wish you would."

Ellen quickly complied, then indicated the dining room.

"Please make yourself comfortable; we're almost ready. The powder room is over there off the hall if you'd like to wash up."

"I'll just be a minute, then."

She disappeared as Geraldine hurried past with her own contribution.

"I hope you like this, ma'am. It's my celebration dish; the one I make when I have company over. It's also my... comfort food. It can be used as either a main course or a side dish. I wasn't sure what everyone was making, so I thought it could be used as either."

"It smells wonderful. And please, Geraldine: it's Ellen. You're among family."

"I know, but..."

"But, nothing. Hugh and I are so very grateful to you. Not only are you the best receptionist in the world – someone we couldn't do without – we've entrusted our child to you."

The woman bowed her head at the praise.

"I wanted to say... I don't know if it's appropriate, but if you ever need a babysitter, I'm always available."

"That's wonderful!" Ellen cried, clasping her hands together. "Eventually, we're going to have to let Mom and Dad Wade go home. I'll be sure and call you. That will be a great relief to both of us."

Making a small curtsy, Geraldine hurried into the dining room. Watching her go, Ellen finally turned her attention to the boys at the bar.

"Are you two almost ready?"

"Not yet," Bond called. "This is fun."

Allowing them another ten minutes to ruminate over the vast collection of wines, she joined Mary in the kitchen. Precisely fifteen minutes later the gang was rewarded by hearing four corks being extracted from vintage bottles and the reappearance of two grinning gentlemen.

"Two wasn't enough," Bond explained, eyes sparkling in anticipation. "There are, after all, nine adults here. Hugh and I felt four would be a more adequate number."

Hank caught their attention by tapping his knife on his wine glass.

"Oh, good. That will make us all eager to cap the luncheon off with the bottle of Irish whisky I brought."

Amid loud, if not somewhat hesitate cheers, they all settled around the table. With heads bowed, Ellen gave a simple grace then looked around the table.

"I think you have all done a wonderful job with your potluck contributions. I wasn't sure if I should have asked everyone what they were bringing beforehand to avoid duplicates." Catching Hugh's eye, she winked. "Too many desserts and not enough entrees, but I see I needn't have worried. It's fun to be surprised and we have a marvelous feast. Let's go around the table and explain what each of us made. Jack?"

"Corned beef hash," he grinned. "A recipe I picked up in the Navy. Filling, and it tastes good. And besides, we always had canned corned beef and potatoes in the mess. And onions, too. It goes better with ketchup."

"I thought you Seabees ate chipped beef," Hank snorted.

"That was for you trench-diggers," he scoffed.

"Geraldine?"

"I made a potato Spam casserole. You can actually make it as a soup, too, if you add extra milk, so that's what I did. With chunks of Spam and potato."

"Yum!" Jack declared. "Spam is on my top ten favorite foods."

"After steak, ribs, chops and anything free," Wade ad-libbed.

Going around the table, Ellen was next.

"I told some of you earlier I got a new recipe book at the store the other day: 'The Joys of Jell-O.' I was going to make my usual dish of layered flavors with fruit cocktail, miniature marshmallows and topped with whipped cream but I thought I'd try something different for the party. Especially suspecting we might need something along the lines of vegetables. So, I made what they called a Vegetable Trio: lemon gelatin made with water, two tablespoons of vinegar and a tablespoon of salt. With shredded carrots, cabbage and spinach."

"That's for me!" Hugh declared, well-satisfied. He reached for the dish but Ellen slapped his hand.

"I appreciate the enthusiasm, but we're doing round-robin, dear."

"I'm sorry," he apologized in embarrassment. "I made maple-walnut fudge which the men can eat at lunch and the ladies may partake with tea."

"Next!"

Mary look up the story.

"Since Hank has already told you he brought Irish whisky – made, in the sense he claims it by heritage if not actual distilling – it's my turn. I made an old family recipe: chicken and dumplings. So, please everyone hurry, because I don't want the dumplings to get soggy."

The choice was unanimously approved of as Christine took her turn.

"Another favorite, this one from the Bond family: mac and cheese, with three different types of cheese and a breadcrumb crust, lightly browned under the broiler."

"Boy food," Jack agreed. "Getting better and better."

Bond nervously laughed.

"I brought the helium balloons… which the birds and animals in Griffith Park won't eat."

"Fair enough," Hugh nodded.

"That leave me," Judy spoke, taking her turn. "My first thought was to bring a rich devil's food cake, but considering the occasion, I brought peanut butter cookies, instead."

Amid chuckles around the table, Jack demanded, "Where are they?"

"I put the box on the coffee table: for after lunch."

"Oh. Right. Are we ready?"

"We are."

Hugh poured the first bottle of wine to those interested in burgundy, then allowed B.B to pour the rest. He made his offerings with pleasure, extoling on the virtues of his selections as though he had supplied them. Which, in the company of friends and family, did serve as an additional contribution.

An hour later when nothing remained but empty casserole dishes, drained bottles and empty plates, the Gang considered themselves "full" and retired into the living room.

"Here's the deal," Jack began as everyone settled. "Before the ladies offer coffee or tea, I have an alternative to suggest."

If he had come in dressed in a grass Hawaiian skirt and dancing the hula, no one could have been more surprised.

"Do tell," Hank growled. "We're all going to have a shot of my Irish whisky, finish gorging ourselves on Judy's cookies, then separate to private bedrooms and take a nap."

"That sounds good. What I have to offer doesn't interfere with that plan." Taking a brown paper sack from the pocket of his suitcoat, he held it out. "In here is catnip —"

"Catnip? What are you going to do with that? Throw it up for confetti? Or, are you feeling sorry for the cat being left out of the celebration? What did you bring for the pigeon? A packet of sunflower seeds? He's not a garden, you know."

"No, Dad. You make tea out of it. It's supposed to be soothing and aid digestion."

Hank shot an annoyed expression toward Hugh.

"Kerr, that – employee of yours – has gone bonkers. What kind of assignments have you sent him on? Investigate those odd little shops with a five-pointed star hanging in the window? The ones that poison the air so that when you step inside you breathe in a nose-full of noxious odors that make you light-headed? Tarot cards; spirit readings?" Turning back to Jack, he shook his finger at him. "You're too old for that sort of thing. Grow up, will ya?" As Jack started to reply, Hank spoke over him. "Besides, those type of parlors are always up to something. One gets raided and you're inside, don't come crying to me to get you out. It's up the river and good-bye, so long and farewell."

Having completed the thought in one breath, he stopped to pant for air.

Jack offered him a wry expression.

"Listen, smarty-pants: I bought the catnip for the cats, see? And inside the package was this short history on the uses of catnip and one of them was its usefulness as a beverage for people. I figured it was just a gimmick to sell more merchandise but it sounded interesting, so, I went to the library and looked it up. It was true."

"You have a library card?"

"No," Jack deadpanned. "I borrowed your wife's."

Craning his neck, Dad looked over his shoulder at Mom.

"Be sure and wash it off. Merrick has been known to carry cooties."

"That's ladies' pocketbooks," she corrected.

"He's right," Hugh interrupted, holding up his hands before the conversation degenerated further. "The properties of catnip have been known for centuries. It's been used to relieve stress and anxiety and when taken as a tea before bedtime it can aid in sleep."

"Just the thing for your nap," Ellen helpfully offered, taking the bag from Jack. "I will most certainly make a pot of catnip tea."

"I wanted to… it's a present from the cats," he tried. "I didn't figure you'd want all of 'em over here for the ceremony, but they wanted to be part of it. So, we came up with this idea."

"Thank you, and please tell them I appreciate their sacrifice."

Digging a finger in his ear as though to clear it, Wade declared, "The most spoiled animals on the planet –"

"And Irish Rover isn't?" the detective countered, as though he had been accused of a nefarious deed.

Mary had had enough.

"Stop it, both of you! Hank, while it appears you two don't need the additional stimulant of that whisky you brought, get up, open the bottle and pour each of us a few drops. No more, or we'll all be too tipsy to stand. This is supposed to be a christening, not a rowdy New Year's Eve party."

Ellen went to make the tea while Judy opened the box of peanut butter cookies and passed it around.

"You know I don't cook, but I bought these at Ridley's, which is the most exclusive bakery in town. Caters to all the bigwigs." That impressed the Bonds, who each helped themselves to the saucer-sized cookies. Reading their expression, she readily encouraged them. "Take some home for the kids. I bought two dozen."

"Did you get a discount?" B.B. inquired, mouth full of cookie. "Being in the business?"

"No," she laughed, "but I did run into Ray Milland there and we had a nice chat."

"Did you get his autograph?" Geraldine hopefully demanded.

"No. But if you want a photo, I can always get one from the studio."

"Make that two," Ellen called from the kitchen.

"That's right. I forgot: Hugh and his collections."

"No. For me. I'm going to kiss him the next time I see him."

Not having been privy to a previous conversation, Judy grinned.

"The next time I'm over at Paramount, I'll look him up. He's always working. I don't suppose he'd mind a good-looking brunette coming up and landing a big wet one on his cheek."

"Oh, no. On his lips. Then Hugh and I will be even."

Even more puzzled, she naturally fell in on Ellen's side.

"In that case, I'll have to arrange for a cocktail party."

"And be sure and invite his wife," Hugh pouted.

"She's a lovely woman. Shall I have a photographer handy?"

"That might be a little much." They laughed as she changed the subject. "How do we prepare this tea, Hugh? Or is it just taken plain?"

"Usually with a bit of honey and a slice of lemon. The taste is bland but some people find it woody."

A moment later she returned with a tray, cups, saucers, a pot of honey and a plate of sliced lemons. When no one offered to be the first to try it, Wade nudged Jack.

"Go ahead. This was your idea."

Without hesitation, for despite what may have been said of him, Jack Merrick was no coward, he poured himself a full cup, added honey, squished a lemon slice into the mix, stirred it with a spoon, then made a show of sampling it. When his face remained expressionless, Judy demanded, "Well, what does it taste like?"

"Honey and lemon."

Unintentionally bringing down the house, Hugh was next up, followed by Ellen, Mary and Geraldine. Savoring the concoction, Ellen was the first to speak.

"I see your point, Hugh: I do taste the woodiness but it's actually very pleasant."

"And soothing," Geraldine agreed. "Thank you for bringing it, Mr. Merrick. It was very thoughtful of your cats."

"Wouldn't like one, would you? They're old enough now to be adopted."

"Yes," she surprised everyone by admitting. "I would. If I can get permission from the landlord."

"Oh, I can fix that. Just give me his name. I'll go over and inspect the place. You can always find something wrong. A little tit-for-tat and he'll be glad to give you permission."

"Yes," Judy agreed. "To keep a baby elephant."

"That's illegal," Wade interrupted. "Going around impersonating a safety inspector."

"I'll make a citizen's arrest." Turning to Bond, he poured him a dram of whisky from the bottle Hank set out. "I'm sure the prosecutor will go along with me."

Taking advantage of the fact the prosecutor had freely imbibed at lunch, Bond's reply proved Jack knew his man.

"I don't see anything wrong with it." Downing the drink in one swallow, he cleared his throat and addressed the policeman. "Excellent. Good to know we're on the same side."

"If that side includes Merrick, I'm out."

Pouring himself a drink, he took his in like manner.

"What do you say we all share a toast to Jacqueline and then make ourselves comfortable to let our –

stomachs – settle." Hugh poured the drinks and distributed them to the illustrious group. Holding up his hand, he offered a proud smile. "To Jacqueline Thorne Kerr –"

"Our most precious baby," Ellen added.

Jack eagerly added the last.

"To Her Ladyship – long may she reign!"

They touched glasses all around in honor of the sleeping baby, then Christine turned to Ellen.

"Thank you for a lovely party, but we really must be going."

"You're more than welcome to stay. We have many available rooms –"

"I think not. We have to get back to the children."

"We're sorry to see you go, but if you insist, accept our appreciation for the wonderful balloon display and the pot luck dish you brought. Let me clean it for you," Ellen offered but Christine shook her off.

"It can wait."

"I'll send it to the office then, with Hugh. I'm sure he'll have occasion to drop in on B.B. sometime soon."

"That's more than gracious."

Leaving Hugh to make the final announcement.

"If you won't stay, I've arranged for a driver to take you home." Before they could protest, he hurried on. "Just to be on the safe side. He'll take you in the van so you can return it to the rental agency. That way, you can retrieve your own car and he'll drive you home in that."

"How will he get back?"

"Someone will follow and pick him up. Everyone stays safe and there's no chance of an accident."

Remembering the last time they refused the offer of a ride, Christine quickly agreed.

"How thoughtful of you, Hugh."

"It's my pleasure."

Seeing them to the door, the Kerrs waited until the elevator arrived before waving good-bye. Emerging on the first floor, the Bonds found their driver waiting. Getting into the rear seat of the van than had been brought around, they gratefully settled into the long seat.

"How'd we do?" Bond asked as the vehicle rounded the driveway and entered the street.

"It went better than expected."

"I'm glad to hear you say that." After a pause, he probed, "Why?"

"Giving them the balloons and the mac and cheese was considerably cheaper than buying a fifty dollar savings bond as a gift for the baby."

Easily agreeing, he lapsed into silence before she added, "That Merrick creature addressed Wade as 'Dad.' Did you catch that?"

"As a matter of fact, I did."

"What do you make of it?"

"He was drunk."

"I think they're all a bit too chummy." Poking her husband in the arm, she demanded, "And why did you agree with him about prosecuting the apartment manager on a trumped-up charge?"

"I thought it was amusing. Besides, he didn't mean it."

"Oh, yes, he did."

He comfortably patted her hand.

"Christine, you take things too seriously. Be content we had a good time and saved eighty dollars."

She stiffened in shock.

"Why? Before we decided on the balloons and the potluck dinner you planned on giving them a hundred dollar savings bond?"

"What do you think?"

She gave the matter too much consideration.

"Because they had a girl? If it had been a boy, you would have given fifty?"

Bond smiled and rested his head against her shoulder.

She had come up with a better answer than he had.

CHAPTER 3

"You know, old man, I think you've come down with the mange."

Waiting until the "old man" had finished his business at the fire hydrant, Jack bent down to examine Irish Rover's coat. Running his hand over the dog's hair against the grain, he observed several bald patches. Clucking his tongue in disapproval, he got up, stretched, then shook the leash.

"What do you say another lope around the block, then home? I bet Mary's got a nice biscuit for you as a reward for being a good boy."

The dog hopefully wagged his tail then started out at a trot. Although in possession of only three legs, Rover managed forward progression at a good clip and in another ten minutes the pair presented themselves at the front door of the Wade's house. Politely knocking to announce their presence, he opened it with the familiarity of a friend and they made their way inside.

"Is that you, Jack?"

Irish Rover answered for him with an eager bark. Snapping off the lead, the dog preceded him into the kitchen where the odor of freshly-made cookies filled the air.

"Something smells good."

"I thought you might be in the mood for some ginger snaps."

"Oh, yum." Smacking his lips he followed her hand signal to sit, watching contentedly as she offered the dog his biscuit. Two crunches later the treat was gone.

"He eats like a boy," she grinned.

"Yes, ma'am. We appreciate the finer things in life." Peering past her to the row of still-warm cookies on the cooling rack, he offered her a wink. "I'm starved. The walk stimulated my appetite. Bet I can eat them all before Dad comes home."

"There are more in the oven."

"Oh. Too bad."

"But still plenty to wrap up a dozen for you to take home with you. It's so nice to have someone to bake for. When it was just Hank and me, we could only eat so many and the rest went into the freezer. The freezer is full of cookies and cake. Eventually, they get frosted and I crumple them for the squirrels. I don't mind sharing the wealth, but it's sad. I want them to be enjoyed by... my family. Now, with all you fellows around, nothing ever goes to waste."

"Yeah. I like the idea of ol' Crabby Face dropping by the Merrick Detective Agency with a bag full of goodies. Gives the mistaken impression cops are human."

"I don't think *Lieutenant Wade* is ever going to do that, unless by 'goodies' you mean an arrest warrant, but it does paint an amusing picture. Would you like a cup of coffee to go with your cookies?"

"How 'bout a glass of milk?"

The expectation in his voice was palpable and as she retrieved the glass jug from the refrigerator, Mother Mary wondered if anyone had ever supplied the young Jack Merrick with a plate of home-baked cookies and a tall glass of ice-cold milk. Or if, as she suspected, he were only trying to fill in the empty spaces of his childhood with memories of what might have been.

"It was awfully good of you to drop by to walk Rover," she said on the same tract. "You have a way with animals."

"I don't know why. I never had a pet growing up. Then it was the war and the Navy and drifting around until I settled here. Although I've been on a first name basis with a lot of 'rats.' Does that count?"

"No," she tersely stated, placing a large glass and a plate of cookies before him.

"Oh, well, Rover likes everyone. And he's just an excuse to come over and see you."

"The dog does not like everyone and he's especially fond of you. And I appreciate you taking him for a walk. Hank and I haven't been home much these days and I just came back here, really, to tidy up. Do the dusting, that sort of thing. Ellen said she'd be fine with the baby and it's good to give them some privacy, too. Mr. Forsch brought Rover over this morning and I took him home with me. I hate to impose on him, he's such a nice man. And it's good to remind the dog where he lives. I wouldn't want him to think we'd abandoned him."

Idly scratching the dog's head, Jack broke off a piece of ginger snap and offered it to him.

"We all need to be reminded once in a while where the heart is." Picking on a scab by Rover's ear, Jack caught Mary's eye as she sat beside him. "He's got some bald spots. Must be getting old."

"It's actually a skin condition. The vet called it something or other, I've forgotten what. It looks like dry skin to me and it must be terribly itchy because the poor beast is always scratching. I think that's why the hair has worn away in some spots. And then it bleeds, which only makes it worse.

But, I have something for it. He's actually much better. You should have seen him before."

Getting up, she hurried into the bathroom and came back with a small spray bottle which she handed to Jack.

"Is this medicine?" he asked, curiously inspecting the container.

"Yes. It works wonders; almost a miracle, really. If I use it regularly it cures the itch almost immediately. The dog stops scratching, the wounds heal and the hair grows back. But we've been away so much I haven't kept up with his treatments."

Squirting some on his hand, Jack sniffed the contents.

"Looks like water."

"It does, but it's very powerful medicine."

"Get if from the vet? Must have come dear."

"Actually, the vet didn't have any answer for the dog's itching. Oh," she dismissed, "he made a few suggestions – change of diet, baths with special soaps, that sort of thing, but none of them worked and some made the condition worse. I'm afraid we were at our wits end when a neighbor of ours gave us that... I guess you could call it a sort of lotion. You could almost hear the dog sigh in relief the first time Hank applied it."

"Really? What's in it?"

"I don't know. It's a special formula. Created just for Rover."

Jack whistled in appreciation.

"Nice. The guy must be a scientist or something."

"A research scientist, actually. And she's a lady."

"Oh, wow. Brainy types make me nervous." Realizing how that statement might be taken, he hastened to amend it. "I mean, Pop is as sharp as a tack and you're well on your way to becoming my top operative, but –"

"I understand what you mean," she laughed, delighted at the compliments. "She is 'brainy,' as you say, but she wouldn't make you nervous. She's an incredibly nice lady. Always smiling and always willing to help anyone. She saw us out walking one day and came out to say hello. When she asked about the dog I just casually mentioned the problem we were having with Rover and a week later she gave me that spray bottle with what you're holding there. She developed the formula, herself. Right out of her head and then made it up in the laboratory she has in her basement. Wouldn't take a dime for it."

He stared at her a moment in wonder.

"That's not nice, it's crazy."

"It's crazy nice. Go ahead – put some on Rover's bald spots."

Directing the spray on the dog's bald spots, he rubbed it into the dog's skin. True to Mary's word, he seemed to shiver in relief.

"Look at that!"

"In a few days the sores will be gone and the hair will start growing again. I'll have to remember to take some with me when I go back to Ellen's. When Mr. Forsch brings him over I'll keep up the treatments. I believe it's saved the dog's sanity. Itching all the time is a terrible thing. And then the open sores. They must hurt terribly."

"I'll say," Jack agreed, scratching his head. "Does it work on people?"

"It works on all skin," she agreed. "Amy says the formula was designed to penetrate the outer layer of skin and heal from the bottom up, if I understood her correctly."

"Neat. Well, I better be going. All play and no work means Jack doesn't pay the bills."

"Wash your hands in the sink, young man."

"Why? Will the spray hurt me?"

"Not at all. But you've been touching Rover's sores. I don't know if what he's got is contagious but I don't want you to go home and infect the cats."

"Oh. I thought you were worried about me."

Popping up, Mary engulfed him in her arms. After eliciting a "Humph!" as the air was squeezed from his lungs, she planted a kiss on his cheek.

"I worry about you night and day. And if that isn't enough, I worry about you afternoons and evenings. Is that worry enough?"

"You don't have to worry about me," he stated with a straight face, unconsciously denying that which he had asked for. "I'm a big boy. I can take care of myself."

"Big boys are the ones most likely to get themselves in trouble." Reluctantly letting him go, she placed a baker's dozen ginger snaps into a brown paper sack and handed it over. "One to grow on," she added before he could remark she had given him one extra.

"Oh, good. As long as it's up and not across," he winked, patting his stomach. "See you."

"Love you, son."

She did not see, as much as feel, his knees shake.

The office was humming as he entered. Taking a look around, he smiled in satisfaction. It might have been otherwise. That had been his concern. But, Jack reminded himself striding down the corridor, not all of his clients were referrals from Hugh Kerr. He did a lively business on his own.

The point that conclusion was debatable only to himself was moot. The rest of the world, including competing detective agencies spread out across Los Angeles county; other referring attorneys and occasionally those boys in blue who felt a case or a concern was better addressed by "those fellas who hang a giant eye on a shingle outside their door," and the ever successful word-of-mouth, were well aware the Merrick Detective Agency was a far-reaching and "damn successful" operation.

While the other private eyes were jealous of Jack's close-knit association with the top defense lawyer in the state, if the bulk of his caseload had come from Kerr, they would have been satisfied. That would have left collecting dirt on roving husbands, investigating missing persons who had left Ohio for their Big Break in Hollywood, and tracking down the who-what-where-when and how of myriad crimes, to them. Such was not the fact. With a sprawling empire that included not one but two offices, the first in a small building just across the line from respectability called "The Place," and a second in the highly prestigious and correspondingly expensive Conner Building where Hugh Kerr, Esquire, held figurative if not literal court, Merrick and his hand-picked team of trained operatives, were, as the owner, himself, might say, "the pick of the litter."

It was only Jack, out of the millions of people living in Los Angeles in 1957, who questioned his success. Too often he had stared into the mirror after shaving off a two-night stand of stubble and wondered. Honestly obtained by bone-jarring, mind-numbing snooping that would provide the last piece for an otherwise unsolvable puzzle Hugh would present in court the following day, he questioned if all the trappings of glitter and pseudo-gore that filled his offices were solely attributable to those big paydays he received. Knowing beforehand that some of this money came from the attorney's own pocket did not improve his self-image.

"It all spends the same," the tall, blond, broad-shouldered, good looking guy in the mirror would state with calm, almost flippant assurance, but the three-dimensional detective was not convinced.

"With the dough he just paid me, I could buy a yacht."

The fact he did not want one was inconsequential.

"So what? Buy one, then. You earned it."

"He didn't get two thin dimes outta this client."

"That's his business. He can afford to take on the destitute and the riff-raff."

"For the sake of justice."

"That's his bag. He pays you what you earn. How many times have you nearly gotten busted performing some shady work for him? When he pulls his rabbit out of a hat in court that wins the day, it's your rabbit. He gets the credit for being a genius: you get the financial reward. All's fair in love and the legal system, pal. If he doesn't recover his time from one client, he gets it twice over from the next. That's how he stays in business and drives a Lincoln Continental."

"That's my point. I could drive one, too, on what he pays me. The rest of all this −" he added, waving his hand to indicate the uptown suite he was not standing in, "comes from him, too. What I make on the side is peanuts."

"Then, you need a new accountant, bub. You've got ten fulltime detectives working for you and three dozen stringers across four states, not including Mexico. Your agency handles hundreds of cases a year, only a fraction of which comes from the illustrious Hugh Kerr."

"Yeah, but all the serious moola comes from him. And," he tried, torn between conflicting stories, "the publicity. That's what brings 'em to my door."

The face in the mirror scowled.

"What's your problem?"

"Without him, I'm just another P.D."

His second-self laughed at the joke. "P. D." Private dick. Funny in more ways than one. Fame had its rewards.

"So, you tool around town in a beat-up hack and live the celluloid image. He wears three-piece suits and you got on a sports jacket. You could have been an engineer if you wanted to be."

"Woulda-coulda-shoulda," Jack retorted to the looking glass occasionally used as a crystal ball, crunching his blue eyes until faint laugh-lines appeared at the corners. "The Navy and the Big One got in the way. Besides, workin' in a big, fancy office isn't my thing."

"All right: go out and buy an upgrade on your surfboard and stuff the rest of your money under the mattress."

Which finally made Jack smile at his other self.

"Nah. That's the first place any Tom-Dick-and-Harry-thief looks. I make it even easier for 'em. I got my wad stashed in the Kerr jar. On the kitchen table."

Just like Hugh. Only, mine's a savings account for my goddaughter.

To buy her a pony.

"What you're saying is, it's all in the family, Merrick. So, what's your beef?"

"Ain't got none."

Which made the reflection in his mind guffaw and disappear as he figuratively brought a white towel to his face to wipe away the excess lather. A towel pilfered from some gym that he had stuffed into his bag after taking a shower. No crime there; it came, he reasoned, with the dues. Management expected towels to disappear. The same way diners helped themselves to silverware and cops got free doughnuts. All part of doing business with the great unwashed. Or, even of serving those with silver spoons up their derrieres. He had once seen one of Hugh's clients swipe the linen napkins off a dining table at an upscale restaurant. Jack still cherished the memory, not the least of which because Hugh had left an overly-generous tip and added ten dollars to the client's legal bill.

It was good to be part of a gang and maybe not so bad if all his silver-spoon clients came from His Lordship.

"Mr. Merrick?"

Stopping his forward progression, Jack suavely turned around with the grace of an athlete, taking in the smiling countenance of Marie Sanchez, his secretary. Raising an eyebrow, he silently conveyed the question, "What's up?"

"I've got a client in the waiting room. She was supposed to see Bill Blaine but he got caught up on a case he's working and none of the others have time to see her. I was wondering if you might –?"

"Sure."

Having already assumed his positive response, she held out a manila folder.

"This is her paperwork. Nothing much but a few details –"

"No problema." Accepting the offer, he resumed his journey down the corridor. "Give me five and then send her back." On second thought, he added, "Who am I going to be this time? Mike Hammer or Mr. Suit-and-tie?"

"Just be yourself. That always works."

Taking the statement for the compliment it was, he whistled and finished the brief trek to his private office. Opening the door, he habitually lit a cigarette, glanced briefly at the folder, then checked the coffee pot. Noting it held the remnants of yesterday's java, he poured the black liquid into the trash can, then set about refilling the bin with fresh grounds, performing the action by rote rather than counting the scoops. That task completed, he shook the kettle, determined it contained just enough water for a pot of coffee and placed it on the stand-alone electric burner to boil. He had finished one smoke and started on the second before hearing a timid knock on the door.

Had the client been a man he would simply have called "Come in," but knowing beforehand she was a woman, he opened the door himself, then stepped back for her to enter.

"I'm Jack Merrick," he introduced. "Please come in."

Politeness, he fully comprehended, cost him nothing. What he didn't comprehend was why so many others in the business failed to realize that.

Without being overt, he sized her up with a professional eye. Late twenties, slim, she had a plain face augmented by a layman's hand at make-up. She wore a spring coat that reached to her knees. Not stylish, but probably her Sunday best. Ruling out "wanna be," he guessed she was looking for a lover who had jilted her, or a brother who had disappeared.

"Won't you take a seat? I'm just making coffee. Would you like some?" When she didn't answer, he added, "Won't cost you anything. Goes with the service."

"I've... never been to a private eye's office, before." Staring around the room, her eyes fell on the lower shelf. "So many books. I wouldn't have guessed."

Playing to his audience, already aware he did not have to impress or give the hard sell, he smiled.

"You'd be surprised how much of our work is nothing more than dull research. When a man comes in here asking for a job, the first thing I ask is if he has a library card. If he says no, he's out the door."

"Really?"

"You bet."

"I... don't know if my problem can be solved by reading."

"The second thing I ask is if he can stay awake for two nights running; doesn't mind getting soaked in a good rain, has the gift of gab, ask questions like nobody's business and can leap tall buildings in a single bound."

He made her smile.

"Yes, I'd like a cup of coffee."

On cue, the kettle whistled. Jack poured the boiling water into the bin, stood a moment to watch it drip through, then pointed out the chair in front of his desk. As she sat, he inquired, "Black? Cream? Sugar?"

"Black is fine."

"Good girl."

She appreciated the statement and took the mug he offered. Filling one for himself, he settled into his chair. With other clients he might have perched on the edge of the desk or remained standing, leaning against the wall, but one choice was too familiar and the other too intimidating.

Assuming she required the professional touch, he leaned forward, eyes alert.

"What can I do for you, Miss Dwight?" Noting her expression of surprise that he knew her name, Jack tapped his forehead. "All good detectives can read minds. You can't imagine how handy that comes in." When she let the comment pass, he tapped the folder on his desk. "My secretary clandestinely passed me the form you filled out when I came in."

"Oh," Miss Dwight realized, making a small cough to cover her embarrassment. "I'm Dana Dwight. D-a-n-a, pronounced 'Danna,' rather than Day-na. It's an English pronunciation."

"Got it. I like people who instruct others in how to say their name. It means they have a strong sense of identity."

She considered and then agreed.

"You make an interesting point. I never thought of it like that."

"I have a friend with an odd last name. It looks as though it ought to be pronounced 'Car' but it's actually 'Cur.'"

It was her turn to surprise him when she readily identified the person in question.

"That would be Hugh Kerr; the lawyer."

"How did you know that?"

"You have two offices, Mr. Merrick: one in the Connor Building and a second one here. Before I made an appointment, I went into the lobby of both places. In the Conner Building I saw that name – spelled with a 'K' – on the same floor as yours."

"Did you wonder how it was pronounced?"

"Actually, no. Being English on both my mother and father's side, I naturally presumed the British pronunciation. Is he English?"

"Canadian, actually, but that's a secret."

"Same difference," she smiled. "'We' still claim them. I say 'we,' of course, but I'm an American."

"His wife is trying to get him to change his nationality so he can run for governor, but he won't."

"I think a Canadian governor of California would be a novel and exciting idea. It certainly couldn't hurt."

"But Hugh's a good guy and neither of us would wish him mired into the dirty world of politics. So: tell me what I can do for you."

"I invested some money…"

Which fell somewhere between the jilted lover and missing brother of his first impression.

"With a man who told you he had a sure-fire scheme for doubling or tripling your investment."

He spoke without using a questioning inflection and she nodded.

"Yes."

"And you never heard from him, again."

"He did called me several times —"

"Telling you how swimmingly things were going and asking for more."

"You've heard this before."

With the comment, "Too many times to count," on the tip of his tongue, Jack gave a non-committal shrug. There was no sense making her feel worse than she already did. Instead, he replied, "Con men are good at what they do. They could fool a priest."

"I appreciate you saying that. I'm so... angry at myself."

"No need to be. I'll require all the details, but first you need to know what I charge."

"Are you... more expensive than the other detectives? I mean, you're the boss —"

"Not a bit of it. You just lucked out. I'm the best," he winked, "but considering you were supposed to see one of my agents and he's involved elsewhere, you get me for the price I'd normally charge for his services."

"I... don't usually have that sort of luck, Mr. Merrick. You were saying?"

"Let's begin with one detail: how much did you lose?"

"Two thousand dollars."

"All right. That makes it worth your while to seek redress. But, you understand, even if I find him, he may not have the money you invested. Those types spend it pretty fast. Have you been to the police?"

"Yes. They said it isn't their concern. If I gave him money on speculation, it's a bad business deal, not a crime."

"It's a grey area," he conceded.

Moving forward, she quickly demanded, "How so?"

"If he had a legitimate plan for increasing your investment and it didn't work out, the police are right. But if his sole aim was to take your money and run, that's against the law. Which is it, in this case?"

"He said he had a... system."

Despite himself, Jack rolled his eyes.

"Ok, now we're looking at a scam. Go on."

"He told me he came from Kentucky; knew all about horses. He knew the ones which were likely to win. He only bet on the long odds; that way, the 'turn-around' was bigger."

"I can go down to the track and ask around. That would be twenty dollars a day. I'll give it two days, so your risk is forty dollars. But even if I find him, there's no guarantee I can shake any money out of him."

"How do you mean – shake?"

She made him laugh.

"Oh, you've seen all the movies. I, tough-guy him, grab him by the lapels and rattle his teeth. Turn him upside down and see what falls out of his pockets."

She matched his laughter.

"Now, you're teasing me."

"Let's just say I'll practice some of the tricks of the trade on him."

"Will you arrest him?"

"I'm not a cop, honey."

"I'd like him to face restitution, somehow."

"You want me to give him a fat lip?"

"Something like that."

"Assault and battery is a crime. Believe it or not, private detectives are not above the law. But, I'll see what I can do. If I find him, which is no sure bet. You understand that?"

"Yes. I know it's a long shot but if I don't try, I'll never be able to regain my dignity. I don't like being played for a – dupe, Mr. Merrick."

"I don't blame you."

"Then, I will hire you for two days." Reaching into her purse, she took two twenty-dollar bills from her pocket. "Payment in advance."

"You were reading my mind." Jack filled out a receipt and handed it to her. "Now: for the details. What name did he give you?"

"Jim Ewell."

Taking out a pencil, Paul hesitated.

"Spell it."

"E-w-e-l-l. It's an unusual name. Do you think it's his real one?"

"Fat chance." On her reaction, he added, "It's one of the more common tricks of the trade. If he called himself 'Smith' or 'Jones,' most people would be suspicious right off. But if he has, as you say, an unusual name, you're more tempted to believe it's real."

Leaning back in the chair, she made a small gasp.

"That's precisely what I did think. 'Ewell' is the name of a Civil War general."

"I know," he surprised her again. "Southern: lost a leg in the war but he came back to command his troops until the end."

"You're a student of history, Mr. Merrick."

"I have a lot of time on my hands," he easily dismissed. "Standing under windows –"

"– in the rain," she finished.

"Sure. How did you meet him?"

"In the library."

Jack's eyes sparkled at the coincidence.

"As I was just saying."

"Yes," she agreed. "I have a library card. Does that make me a candidate for a sleuth's job?"

"That's a Sherlock Holmes' word," he identified.

"I suppose it could be. Do you read fiction as well as history, Mr. Merrick?"

Shrugging off the hopefulness in her voice, he got up and added more coffee to his mug. Silently questioning whether she wished her mug refilled, she shook her head.

"I read the magazines. You know: *Cops and Robbers; Real Crime Stories.* That sort of thing."

"And are they real stories?"

"Real enough to cure insomnia in a real 'sleuth,' and to keep five-year-olds and businessmen renewing their subscriptions. So: what was Mr. Ewell doing in the library?"

"He said he was looking for a book that was out-of-print: a Victor Hugo classic."

"Which one?"

"*The Man Who Laughs.*"

"Is it? Out of print?"

"It's from the last century," she admitted, "so I suppose you could say that. Very difficult to find, more's the pity."

"Good."

"Good that it's unavailable?"

"That he did his homework. He chose a book that would clearly impress a librarian and one that was actually hard to find."

"I didn't say I was a librarian."

"I read it in your file."

"No, you didn't. The form didn't ask my occupation. How did you deduce it?"

Jack hesitated then lit another cigarette as a means of occupying his hands.

"Con men look for certain types of 'marks,' depending on their line of work. Librarians are typically women; bookish, studious and unmarried.

Which means they don't have husbands to ask about whatever yarn he's going to spin. They also make a decent salary and tend to save their money: two things absolutely required to make his time and effort worthwhile."

"You mean, if I were wearing a wedding ring he wouldn't have approached me?"

"I doubt it. You can be certain he'd cased the joint –" He waited for her reaction to his lingo before continuing, "and checked you out before he ever approached. He can probably tell you what kind of car you drive and where you live. Probably even what bank you go to when you cash your check on paydays."

"That makes me feel soiled."

"It ought to. After determining you fit his requirements, he came up with a story. He's obviously got some education, himself, because I assume he threw in a few ten-dollar words and he knew what book to ask for. One, you'd have to order for him. Which gave him an excuse to come back: once to pick up the book, a second time to discuss it with you – over coffee?" he guessed and she nodded. "And then a third and fourth time as your relationship developed. One of those times he talked about himself – at your urging, of course." On a roll, for the scene played out in his mind as clearly as though he had been an eye-witness, Jack finished the scenario. "He's from Kentucky; a second son, let's say. He grew up around horses; loves horses."

"Yes," she whispered. And then, to cover her shame at being a "mark," she asked, "Why that story?"

"First, because everyone loves horses. So, he immediately caught your attention. Second, because betting on horse races has an immediate reward."

"If they win."

"Sure. That's where his fake background comes in. His 'system.' He knows all about racing; he understands how the odds can work in his favor. Not all the time, of course; that's his excuse to come back asking for more... investment capital."

This time, Miss Dwight slapped her hand on the desk.

"Yes," she ground out. "That was the expression he used: investment capital."

"That's because you're a lady. Sounds more legit and more profitable than 'betting money.'"

"All right. I was a fool. A walking, talking mark."

"We all get taken at one time or other in our lives. No shame there. The tragedy is if we don't do anything about it. You've come to me. I'll see if I can help. And maybe I'll just accidentally-on-purpose land a fist on his nose. Describe what Mr. James Ewell looks like."

She shot out the information as though she were going to explode.

"Five-foot-eight; light brown hair, neatly cut. A thin mustache, no beard. Wears reading glasses. Black frames. Well-trimmed nails; shoes not new but shined. He had on a business suit the first time I met him; when we met at the coffee shop he wore a sport jacket with a hat. There was a ticket – his lucky ticket, he said – tucked into the ribbon around the crown. Well-spoken; brown eyes. Oh: and he had a silver mechanical pencil in the breast pocket of the sport jacket."

"That's a honey of a description," Jack praised. "What was the name and address of the coffee shop?"

"Second Cup Café; 1452 LaCienaga. Does that tell you anything?"

"I'll check it out. It may be that he uses it for all his business endeavors. If the proprietor recognizes his description, I'll have it staked out. Operators of this type usually string along two or three marks at the same time. You might be able to help a few more unlucky ladies. And if he does show, we've nailed him. Otherwise, I'll go down to Santa Anita and sniff around."

Realizing the interview was at an end, Miss Dana Dwight gathered in her purse and stood. Waiting for Jack to do the same, she offered her hand.

"Thank you, Mr. Merrick. I've learned a great deal today."

"That's what I'm here for."

They shook and he escorted her down the hallway, leaving her at the door. She departed without looking back. As he caught Marie's eye, she shook her head.

"There's one born every day."

"That's what keeps us in business, honey."

That, Jack Merrick's best friend with the "odd" name might have added, *and the pursuit of justice.*

CHAPTER 4

"Why are you dressed like that?" Hugh gasped, putting down the evening newspaper to stare at Hank Wade. The fact he asked had nothing whatsoever to do with his desire for elucidation. It was more the type of compulsion that forced a person to stare at the wreck of a car without really wanting to know whether anyone died in the crash.

"To see whether or not it fits," came the logical reply.

"Well, go away. I don't want to watch."

Too late he realized he spoke too loudly. Coming in from the bedroom, baby in her arms, Ellen glanced at Hugh. Although his expression conveyed concern, the explanation was readily apparent and she beamed with delight at Dad.

"Overflowing pantaloons in red-white-stripes, a blue jacket, white vest and, I presume, there's a top hat lurking somewhere nearby."

"I've been asked to play Uncle Sam in this year's Fourth of July Parade." he proudly admitted. "An honor not casually bestowed."

"How did you merit it?" she asked, all ears, as Hugh covered his.

"Being injured in the line of duty never hurts," he guardedly admitted. "Length of service; heroism in the face of grave danger – and legible penmanship," he completed with a wink.

"I think that's wonderful. Congratulations."

Realizing he had to say something, Hugh pointed to the pant legs.

"Someone's going to have to turn them up for you. Or, are you going to parade down Main Street on stilts?"

"There is no Main Street in Los Angeles. Right down Hollywood Boulevard. This Thursday," he added. "Afterwards, there's a big picnic."

"I'm working that day," Hugh sniffed.

"It's a holiday, dear. Which you would know if you were a *citizen.* You're *not* working. The office is closed. We'll be there, front and center," she promised.

"It'll be too hot for Jackie."

"I'll dress her accordingly. As an *American:* in patriotic colors."

"As a citizen of the United States," he growled in correction. "We're all Americans; as in North Americans. It's arrogant that you people assume the word refers solely to –"

"– the country in which you live. The country in which you were educated; the country in which you practice law. The country in which your daughter was born. Shall I go on?"

"Not, however, the country in which we were married."

"Oh, Hugh, you really don't want to go there. Do you?"

He pouted and pretended to go back to reading the newspaper. Ellen turned back to Hank.

"I'm terrible proud and excited for you. And I'll be glad to hem the pant legs and sleeves for you. What about the hat?

Crossing back into his bedroom, Hank returned with the traditional top hat designed with red and white vertical stripes and a wide blue band sporting large white stars.

"It's too big."

"Never mind. We can adjust the band. By the 4th we'll have you perfectly attired. I'm so excited. And now that I'm thinking about it, there is a big city-sponsored barbeque –"

"Police sponsored," Hank clarified.

"All the prisoners receive a 'Get out of Jail free' card for the day so they can attend," Hugh sourly observed.

Ellen was ready for him.

"Jackie would like to know the date of Canada's Independence Day."

"Ha ha. Very funny."

"You can stop all this ribbing, you know, by applying for your citizenship."

"What about this picnic, Dad?" he asked to change the subject. "I seem to recall something about children?"

"Orphans. The police cars go around to the local orphanages and bring the kids to the park where we set up dozens of grills. Peanuts, hot dogs and ice cream. It's a day out for them: we try and make them feel like everyone else. Part of the greater Los Angeles family. It's a good reminder for them they're not forgotten and it's also good PR for us. A lot of kids in those homes tend to look down on the police. This is a good way to start them out on the right path. Surely even you can't object to that."

"I don't object to any of it. I happen to believe patriotism is the mark of a good citizen."

"Good. Then you won't mind coughing up a hefty contribution for the party."

"Oh. I thought the money came out of the police retirement fund."

Hank turned to Ellen.

"I told you to marry a cop."

"I'm afraid. I was in love with him before I ever met you. To get your good advice," she added with a wink.

Jackie reached up and grabbed a strand of Ellen's hair.

"Too late to back out, now," Hank sighed. Fussing with the coat sleeves, he finally removed it. "Mary can pin them up," he decided. "The outfit has to be used next year and the year after. Most Uncle Sam's are taller than I am."

"Oh, no, not pins. They'll work their way out and scratch you. I'll use a baste stitch – one that's easily pulled out after the party. Put it back on and let me measure the length."

Unceremoniously thrusting the baby to Hugh, Ellen went to get her sewing kit.

"You did this on purpose, didn't you?" he demanded, shifting Jacqueline from one arm to the other. "In legal terms, we call it collusion. It's illegal."

"Only when the intent is to commit or cover up a crime, Mr. Lawyer. No such thing here. And it is an honor to play Uncle Sam," he added.

"Dad, I know it is. And I'm very proud they asked you. Of course we'll go. And don't think for a minute I take this country for granted. I don't. In fact, I love it. I've spent half my life here. No one appreciates or defends 'liberty and justice for all' more than I do. And I take very seriously Ellen's desire for me to become a citizen. But, it's hard to give up the country of your birth. I owe the people of Canada my education."

"Seems to me they owe you something, too."

"There are evil, greedy people everywhere, Hank. You don't give up on a land or the bulk of its population because of a few."

"Would you go back there?"

"Jackie was conceived in Canada."

"That was Ellen's gift to you. I mean, to practice law. Take up permanent residence?"

"No. This is where I belong. I knew that the minute I crossed the border on that rickety old bus. It gave me goose bumps. But, in many ways I'm still an outsider. I think that's the way it was meant to be."

"All right, Hugh. I'm only giving you the hard sell because, well, you know. I think Ellen understands, too. It's more of a tease than anything else."

"Call it a prod and I'll agree with you." Offering the baby to Hank, Hugh crossed the living room and took up his wallet. Taking out a bill he returned and tucked it into the pocket of the older man's over-large coat. "Here's my donation." Poking him in the chest, he added, "Hail to the Chief."

Hank grinned but refused to let him take back the baby.

"This little 'American' belongs to her grandpa, now. We have lots of things to discuss." Taking her with him, he went to the large picture window. "Let's see how many felons we can count."

Which followed in the good ol' American tradition of leaving 'em laughing.

"Respectable looking; five-foot-eight, sport jacket; brown-on brown. Pencil mustache. Usually with a girl."

"That fits a lot of joes."

"Maybe has the racing forum under his arm. Might even place a local call to his bookie."

The owner of Second Cup Café eyed the Lincoln Jack had set on the counter, blocking its easy transference by keeping a finger on the $5 bill.

"Sounds familiar," he guardedly admitted.

"What name does he go by?"

"Jack."

"Yeah, there's lots of us Jacks. What name he go by?"

"I heard the dames call him Jim. Once, when he was on the phone he called himself Whitaker."

"What else?"

"Look," the man complained, "I ain't the *Sportin' News,* for cripes' sakes. Them reporters get paid."

"What do you think the fin is for? Not the lousy coffee you serve. And the sinker was stale," Jack added in disgust." Repositioning himself so he stood in what the proprietor could have taken for a threatening boxing stance, he pressed the issue. "I don't print Uncle Sam's wallpaper in my basement. I gotta work at it, just like you. My jalopy was the first that came off the assembly line after the Model A. I served in the Navy," he added as though in afterthought, "and fought Japs in the Philippines. I know how to make a guy talk. So, the money is 'cause I'm a polite boy. But that ain't my nature. Got it?"

"Look, he blew in here about six or eight months ago. Never seen him before that. He was down-and-out, looked like a bum. Tried to pass an out-of-state check on me. The name on it was Paul Ryan."

"You didn't accept it, did you?"

"Whatta you take me for?" He turned an indicated a hand-written sign over the counter.

NO CHECKS.

"So? The guy's good at sob stories," Jack countered.

"Do I look like a dame?"

Jack shrugged, conceding the point.

"Out of state check, you say?"

"Sure. What else?"

"Don't happen to remember which one?"

"Drawn on the Bank of Louisville."

His finger snapped up from the $5 bill and Wiggins greedily took it.

"I'm impressed." The compliment brightened the informant's expression. "How come you remember? Must see a million of 'em."

"Louisville: home of the racing ponies. That's why it stuck in my mind."

"Who's his bookie?"

"Someone who's making a good living off him, if appearances are any indication."

Jack laughed.

"There's nothing I like better than a sucker's sucker bein' taken." Relaxing his posture, Jack paused to look around the café. The tables were clean and covered with red-and-white checkered tablecloths, the counter boasted full sugar and creamer bowls and the pies in the circular glass holders appeared appetizing. "Actually, this ain't such a bad place, after all. You do all right for yourself?"

"Not bad. The neighborhood's looking up. I run a deal for the locals: buy five cups of coffee, they earn a free one on the sixth. Give 'em a little card and punch it after every sale. You'd be surprised how many of the bigwigs really go for that."

"No, I wouldn't."

"Keeps 'em coming back. They buy a coffee and I remember how they like it fixed earns me a nickel tip. Adds up. And then mebbe they buy a doughnut to take with 'em." He leaned closer to Jack. "The sinker wasn't stale, was it?"

"Nah," he dismissed. "It was OK. Not bad, actually."

"'cause if it was, I'd make it good."

Jack perched on the bar stool, not quite ready to leave.

"Get much foot traffic?"

"It's been pickin' up, lately. There's some new 'boo-tiques' goin' in down the street. And an upscale office building. I picked this spot years ago; had an idea the area would get classier."

"Might drop by myself, when I'm in the area. What about the cops?"

"For protection? Or, lookin' for trouble?"

"That fella I'm lookin' for – he told my client his name was Jim Ewell – is running a 'scam.' But, you knew that." Before Wiggins could squirm, Jack held up his hand. "That's not your business. All you're doing is serving him and his unsuspecting lady friends coffee and pastry. Who pays, by the way?"

"He does."

"Smart. He comes in here because the place is nice; puts ladies at their ease. That's smart, too. I was just thinking, if the flatfoot on the beat – and maybe some of the other blue boys – put you on their list, they'd drop in more often. For a gratuitous cup of coffee and a fresh doughnut right outta the fryer. Nothing gives a place a sense of respectability like having cops come in regular. And everyone knows they're the best judge of java and sinkers. I could put a word in."

"That'd mean a lot to me."

He started to push the five back toward Jack but he shook his head.

"I'm not trying to cut a deal with you. That's for free."

"You know the local boys?"

Jack's shoulders shook with genuine good humor.

"You ever read the name Lieutenant Henry Wade in the newspapers? He's the chief homicide detective. He's arrested me so many times we're best friends. Honestly," he added with a wink. "I'll tell him and he'll spread the good news." Unwinding his long legs from around the bar stool, he got to his feet. "I'm not helping you to encourage more schemes going on here, mind. They'll come, anyway. But it might happen one day that a lady finds herself... in trouble and seeing a policeman might just encourage her to go over and ask for help."

"That's one way of lookin' at it."

Reaching into his pocket, Jack withdrew his business card and handed it over.

"In case Mr. Jim Whatever Name He's Using comes in, you might give me a call. He hit my client up for her life's savings and I'd like to 'hit him up' for whatever he hasn't squandered on the nags."

"I'll do it."

The men shook hands, then broke off as two customers came into the café. Taking several coins from his pants pocket, Jack held them out.

"For the coffee and sinker."

"It's on the house."

As tempting as it was, Jack dropped them on the counter.

"Save your charity for the cops." Laughing mirthlessly, he sauntered off. "I'll put the tab on my expense account."

Collecting the money, Wiggins glanced at the card.

"Come again, Mr. Merrick."

Politely tipping his hat to the women, Jack stepped outside, a legitimate smile curling his lips. He had gotten more information with sugar than he would have with vinegar, he had arranged for Wade to be a big man down at the precinct and he had earned himself a "Mister Merrick" rather than any number of far less respectable names an irate proprietor would have called him.

Altogether, well worth the price of coffee and a doughnut he would not put on his expense account.

Unless, he decided, he had been working for Hugh Kerr. Then, the notation on his invoice would have included a full course meal.

Or. maybe not.

The vast parking lot was empty and the betting windows closed as Jack made his way down toward the field. While he appreciated a good crowd, the cheering, hand-waving and consequent confetti thrown in the air – not in celebration but in loss as shredded tickets floated down on unsuspecting heads – he also liked the track when there was no one about but the horses, trainers and men with stopwatches. It was the time when anticipation ran highest and before dreams were shattered.

One might have called him a romantic. But not to his face.

Hours before the first gate lifted and the announcer's voice boomed over the loudspeaker, "They're off!" was also the best opportunity for racetrack junkies and PIs to gather information not readily available to the general public.

Pausing on the descending stairwell to watch a horse fly around the track, he removed his hat, using it as a shield against the slanted rays of the eastward rising sun. Casually timing the ride with his interior clock, he nodded in satisfaction.

Good for a third place finish; maybe second depending on the field. Nothing to write home about.

If he had a home, which he didn't. At least not in the traditional sense. A mother "passed on," and a father dead to him from a time before he was born. This morning, that made him feel lonely.

"Shake it up," he grumbled aloud. "I got parents; one I just did a big favor for. Pat Jack on the head and move on."

He did, in fact, pat himself on the head before replacing his hat and sliding, eel-like down the remainder of the steps. Three men were standing at the rail, apparently keeping their own council for none were speaking. He sidled in-between the second and third, surreptitiously appraising them. One was a trainer, the other two betters.

"Fast, but not spectacular," he observed to break the ice.

The man to his left, short, sunburned, wearing a tweed coat that had seen better days, shot a quick glance at the newcomer.

"Didn't see you timing him," he observed in a scratchy voice that reeked of long tobacco use. The statement proved the detective was not the only one with clandestinely-sharp powers of observation.

Eyes carelessly dropping, Jack observed a pair of $50 sunglasses in the breast pocket of the man's jacket. He wasn't what he seemed, either. The awareness added to Jack's comfort level. It felt good to be among those operating on the fringes of society.

"Don't have to. A trained eye can tell."

"He's racing on the third card. What are you betting?"

"Show."

"Place," the man countered.

Jack shrugged.

"Either way, it's pennies on the dollar."

"There's no big killings to make today." Jack brushed a fly off his sleeve. "I don't know you. If you're hoping for a big win, you'll be disappointed."

"That's the nature of the game. In fact," he added non-committedly, "it's like life. Your big losses always trump your little triumphs. But that doesn't stop us from dreaming."

"Dreaming is for sissies. Racing is a science."

"I'm afraid I have to disagree with you, my friend. It's about big hearts and Lady Luck."

"It's about breeding and track conditions."

"I've heard it said show me a man with a 'system' and I'll send a cab for him."

The man took the statement for the insult it was. Taking a step back, he ran his eyes suggestively over Jack's tall, athletic frame.

"You bet with your heart, you lose to Lady Luck every time. And by the looks of you, you can't afford to do that, too often."

"Bet I go home more satisfied than you do. I love horses; gonna buy my kid a pony," he added, annoyed at himself. He hadn't intended to make an enemy of the man. He was just looking for information, after all.

"What good is a pony?"

"It's all part of 'heart,' bub."

The man made a low, disparaging noise under his breath and walked away, diminishing the number at the railing to three. He wasn't through, however, as he shot one last barb over his shoulder.

"You want a nag for your kid? Drop by the claiming auction tomorrow. You can pick up Brass Buttons – that bag of bones –" he added, pointing to the horse being walked to cool down after its workout, "tomorrow. For a song."

"Go to hell," he mumbled, dropping his head.

The man to his right, whom he had appraised as being the trainer, surprised him by moving closer and touching his arm.

"Don't let him get to you. He bets with other people's money."

"Don't it figure?" Jack responded, eyes taking on a new intensity. "A heathen. A scumbag."

"They make the world go 'round."

"Nah. The world'd go 'round without him. Without a lot of 'hims,'" he added in bitterness that came upon him in a flash.

"You thought second, did you? About the horse? Brass Buttons?"

Inwardly struck that he had considered a third place finish, he shook off his doubt.

"He had a fluidity of movement. Horses," he added, completing the thought on a more generous basis, "Don't understand losing. They believe they can win every race. I like that about them. It's an optimism I relate to."

"You don't look like a soft touch."

"Yeah, well, I don't like to think I am." He turned and stared after the better who had disappeared. "But I don't go around tryin' to impress with $50 sunglasses. That's more phony than a counterfeit winning ticket."

The trainer held out his hand and they shook.

"You have a sharp eye. I'm Bill Boerner. You pass many of those 'winning tickets'?"

"Jack Merrick. Nah. But, I've seen it done. Slick." His eyes sharpened. "I've also seen guys get their heads handed to 'em when they're not so slick. They hollered like hell. I hate a 'sore' loser. If you play a dirty trick, you'd better be able to accept the price of getting caught."

His grin proved infectious.

"You think our friend that just left was one of those?"

"Without a doubt. In fact, I'm lookin' for one like him, now. Five-eight, easy-talking, pencil mustache. Newish boy around town; claims to be from Kentucky. I'd like to shake him down a bit. He preys on women."

"I might have seen him around."

Jack handed him one of his cards, glad that he had offered the trainer his real name.

"If he shows up again, give me a call. The world'll keep on spinning but it'll be, maybe, a little faster."

Tucking the card away, Boerner came up with two dollars which he handed to Jack.

"Put it on Brass Buttons to win. He won't, but it'll make you feel a little better. Maybe make Brass Buttons feel a little better, too. Horses know."

"I'll do that. Thanks, but —"

"Keep it. 'B.B.' is mine. By that," he clarified, "I trained him. I... sorta liked him, too. More than I should have. He'll be in that claiming auction tomorrow."

Jack thoughtfully nodded.

"Keep your chin up."

"You, too."

He took the two dollars and made a bet on Brass Buttons to win. He didn't stick around to watch the race and didn't check with his own bookie to find out the result. It was enough to know "B.B." ran his heart out.

"B.B." was, after all, a member of the Kerr Gang, if only a distant cousin.

CHAPTER 5

"Are you coming to bed?"

"Just let me finishing brushing my hair."

Mary came out of the bathroom, brush in hand. The light summer nightgown flattered her and Hank's eyes shone with appreciation.

"You're looking prettier every day."

Caught off guard, she turned to him in surprise.

"Why do you say that? I'm old and frumpy and I think my hair is thinning."

"Is that while you're brushing it at this time of night?"

"Yes. Judy told me that's what movie stars do — men, mostly, but she said women tend to lose more hair as they grow older, too. It's just not as noticeable because they have more of it. First, you spend several minutes trying to pull it out by the roots —"

"That would seem the opposite of what you want," he observed, straightening up and leaning against the backboard to watch the operation.

"It's supposed to stimulate blood flow to the head. The more blood flow, the greater the oxygen. Hair, apparently, likes oxygen."

"So don't we all."

"Then you brush it out so you don't look like a fright," she added with a grin. "Why did you say I look prettier?"

"Because that's what I thought when I saw you silhouetted against the bathroom light. Anything wrong with that?" When she didn't answer, Hank tenderly placed a hand on her arm. "I think it a lot, you know."

"No, I didn't know. You never say."

"That's because I'm a crusty old man. Cultivating the image." He kicked his feet and the top sheet and blanket jumped. "It occurred to me... maybe I play it too hard at home."

Considering his words, Mary rested her hand on his, securing their contact.

"Are you only saying this because we're home in our own bed? Are you more comfortable here? I thought we ought to give Ellen and Hugh some privacy for a few days. They seem to have settled in with the baby. They don't need us around-the-clock, anymore."

"Oh. You didn't say. I wondered."

"I'll go over in the day, of course, to help her. She's gotten her strength back and I imagine she'd like to start making the meals, running her own house, again."

"Oh."

"Of course, there will be sometimes they'll need us to stay: when Jackie gets colicky, or he goes back to work fulltime and the baby cries all night. I'd just as soon Ellen stayed with him and we took the little precious one in with us."

"Does that mean I don't need my beauty sleep?"

Her grip on his arm tightened.

"You're beautiful enough as it is."

"A night of compliments," he grumbled, acutely embarrassed.

"Or, if they want to start going out on a Friday or Saturday night. I don't want to lose touch with them. I want both of us to be a part of Jackie's life."

"Me, too," he admitted, catching her off guard. "Did we... not do right with Peter and Jessica?"

"Now that you mention it, I've been thinking a lot about that."

"What did you conclude?" he asked, kicking his feet again. She tightened her grip.

"I've decided we did the best we could... and better than most parents in our situation. You had a job that required you to work long days, and every time the phone rang, whether it was Saturday morning or 2 A.M. on a Thursday, you had to go. Whenever we planned a vacation someone was bound to get murdered before we had rolled down the driveway. Birthdays, holidays, anniversaries, no day – or night – was sacrosanct. We knew that before we started a family and we made the decision, anyway."

"It wasn't as though we had a choice," he teased and she felt her skin turning red. She didn't reply, however, prompting him to ask, "Did I spend too much time at work? Is that what happened?"

That finally stiffened her and she removed her arm.

"I don't know what you mean by that."

"Yes, you do. We've been estranged from them since they left our house. Maybe... even before that. I'm not sure how close we ever were to them; especially me. I was... never here when they were growing up. I missed the baseball games and the dance lessons. And when I came home from work, I was too dogged-tired to help them with their homework or – share my day with them. Or, you, either."

"I know why, but tell me, anyway."

"Because the job of a homicide cop is brutal. What I saw I never wanted to share. It... shatters illusions about –" He sighed and then concluded, "the world we live in."

"Do you regret it?"

"I regret people are violent; I wish it was otherwise, but it isn't. Greed, anger, lust – a total and complete disregard for human life. Brutality and a contempt for the law exists and it's my job to see that these... monsters pay for what they did. Oh," he dismissed, "they're not all monsters but there is that element in all of us. Those who can't control it have to be punished. Not only because what they did was wrong, but to prevent them from committing other crimes. I don't regret my decision to become a cop – I was born for it." He turned and shoved the pillow behind his back to soften the pressure from the back-board. "And it would be – disingenuous – how's that for a Hugh Kerr ten dollar word? – to say I regret spending so little time with you and the kids because that was part of what I accepted when the badge was pinned on my uniform."

"That's a fair and honest judgment, Mr. Wade."

"What about you?"

"Ask me that at two o'clock in the morning when I haven't heard from you in eighteen hours and you'll get one answer. Ask me that on a beautiful Sunday morning after we've been to church and plan to grill in the backyard and I'll give you another."

"Did you ever think of leaving me?"

If he thought she would take the question as having come out of left field, he was mistaken.

"I wouldn't be the first cop wife to consider that, would I?"

"No. You wouldn't."

"Of course I did. At times when the pain of worry or the anger of despair was nearly overwhelming I thought of packing up the children and moving into an apartment. Or, more sensibly, of packing your suitcase and leaving it on the doorstep for when you eventually came home. But I never did. I had my duty, too, you see. I loved you and I expected you to love me but I also knew that deep inside – that which made you what you are – there was a *need* for you to do what you did. A need greater than being a husband and a father. I wasn't blind to it when I married you. Did I think I could change you? Everyone does," she dismissed, turning slightly away from him. "We both wanted what we wanted and the job won."

"Even now?" he asked in so low a voice she almost missed it.

"Always."

"And when I retire? Eventually, I'll have to."

"You answered your own question. 'Eventually, I'll have to.' Not, 'Eventually, I'll want to.' You'll always be a cop, Hank. In the night when the nightmares wake you up; when you can't sleep and get up to sit in the living room revisiting all those dead bodies you've seen and all the lies you've heard. On a beautiful Sunday morning after church when you hear the wail of a police siren and your thoughts shift into a detective's frame of mind."

"Was it – is it worth it?" he corrected.

"Of course it is. Is there a price to pay? Yes. Did Peter and Jessica pay it? Life is a series of trade-offs. We gave them what we could and they made the best of it. They're well-adjusted, successful people with their own lives to lead. Do they regret never having you around? I can't say. They've never spoken of it. Do they make their own decisions of work over family? Of course they do. Could we have done better? That's one thing I don't ask myself. We gave them our love. In the final analysis, that's what counts."

Turning to stare out the bedroom window, Hank sighed.

"I'm glad you never left me."

She sighed.

"You'd have gone on."

"Can you think of something slightly less depressing to say?"

"I'm glad I never left you. How's that?"

Taking back his pillow, Hank repositioned it under his head.

"Better." But, it was not yet time to sleep. "What did you do, today?"

"Spent hours going over Hugh's correspondence, trying to decide what was important from what could wait."

"What," he demanded in curiosity, "could wait?"

"Invitations to speak at legal gatherings; letters from graduate law students asking for an internship with him. Solicitations for donations to this charity or that school."

"Which went into the round file?"

"I didn't throw anything away," she replied in shock. "That's for Ellen to decide when she finally gets around to looking at them."

"What was important? Or, shouldn't I ask?"

He felt her shoulders shake in amusement.

"You probably shouldn't, but I didn't find any State secrets transmitted in code."

"Would you tell me if you had?"

"Probably," she decided which satisfied him. "You know what I did find?"

"No. What?"

"Checks. There were five written out for $5,000 each. From different clients for 'legal services rendered,' and a dozen more for lesser amounts, but all four figures."

He whistled in awe.

"We knew he made a good living...."

"If someone had sent us even one of them, we'd have called an armored van to transport it to the bank. Hugh brought the mail home in a waste basket. A king's ransom. And just several weeks' worth of mail. And neither were in a hurry to open it, obviously. Can you imagine?"

"No."

"I was afraid to touch the first one I found. After that," he felt her smile, "it got easier until I was actually bored by the smaller ones."

"I guess they're not embarrassed by it, either, or they wouldn't have you opening the letters."

"It does make me feel better about taking a salary."

Hank answered quickly, so she knew he had given the matter previous consideration.

"Some of it has to go to paying rent on his office. That must cost a pretty penny. And he pays Merrick out the ass."

"Which you could have had a piece of," Mary gently reminded him. He made a crude noise in return.

"What would we do with all that money?"

She had set him up for that one.

"You could retire from the police force."

He laughed on cue.

"We're been all over that."

And so they had. And concluded it with, "No regrets."

Jack promised he would give the case two days. Depending on the client and how much he thought of the assignment, that meant a strict interpretation of two calendar days regardless of time spent, or forty-eight hours. In Dana Dwight's favor, he had unofficially decided on the latter. Counting commute time to and from the racetrack and the expense of putting a man on the Second Cup Café, the clock was ticking. Fast.

He didn't work for nothing. He had bills to pay. Being sentimental was not listed on the job application for "private eye." That's what he told himself and that's what he believed.

Hard boiled.

Another movie expression.

Judy would have come up with that. He had been surprised to see her at the baby's blessing although he shouldn't have been. She was Ellen's best friend. He wondered if Ellen had asked her to be Jackie's godmother and supposed she had. That meant Judy turned her down. He knew nothing about her religious beliefs but no one could have refused to take a vow to protect the little sucker. Whether or not you believed in God, standing in as a surrogate parent was sort of like being an understudy: something she ought to have related to.

But maybe she didn't fancy herself that way. It was just possible Judy Viele imagined herself a leading lady. Being cast under the title was an insult, just as receiving a nomination for Best Supporting Actress when you were expecting the statue for Best Actress was a let-down.

Just like Anne Baxter, he chuckled. *The studio wanted to nominate her for Best Supporting in* All About Eve, *so she wouldn't cancel out Bette Davis, and give her a better shot at winning. She refused, saying, 'It's called* All About EVE,' *isn't it? If anyone ought to be nominated for 'Best,' it's me.' She was right, too. And so was the studio. Judy Holliday split the ticket and walked away with it for* Born Yesterday."

The analogy pleased him and he didn't pursue the fact Judy couldn't have children and perhaps didn't have the emotional stability to raise an adopted one. Or, for that matter, couldn't face the idea of Hugh and Ellen dying prematurely. Or, at all. A category in which he might have cast himself.

The parking lot was nearly devoid of cars. Parking by a cluster of expensive vehicles near one end, supposing their position indicated the shortest walk to the claiming auction, he got up and sauntered toward the track. The time and place had been listed in the sporting paper, buried below the results from the previous day. Going against his own promise, his eyes had shifted upward. Brass Buttons had come in second.

Too bad.

He softened the edge by remarking out loud, "B.B. always does."

A group of men were gathered around the track. All were smoking cigars; most had the racing forum in their pockets. It was all part of the costuming, he decided. Playing the role. They were looking for bargains; a diamond in the rough. Once in a blue moon one of them came up with a winner. That's what kept them coming back.

The wealthier a man was, the more he appreciated a good investment.

Before he reached the gathering of men and horses, a security guard dressed in a suit and tie blocked his way.

"Buying or looking?" he inquired, having already made the determination for himself.

Jack gave him an affable smile.

"I'm a friend of Bill Boerner's. He asked me to drop by this morning."

Flashing an inquiring look at the trainer, Bill caught his eye and nodded. The man stepped aside and Jack passed him with smug superiority. Hand out, the two acquaintances shook. Although the morning was fine, Jack glanced skyward.

"Lousy day for an auction."

Appreciating the sentiment, Bill nodded.

"You lost your two dollars."

"In a good cause."

Lowering his voice, Bill turned to his side.

"That's your man over there. In the cheering section."

"Yeah. I spotted the rat as soon as I came in. I'll keep one eye on him." Having dismissed that business for the moment, he indicated a preference for appraising the horseflesh and Bill obliged. Crossing by Brass Buttons, Jack affectionately petted its forelock. "What's he gonna go for?"

"Five hundred."

"Ever thought of buying him, yourself? Racing your own horse?"

"Everyone does. It's a godawful expensive proposition."

"Is this one worth taking a chance on?"

"I'd like to say yes, but I can't." Jack hitched a shoulder and they walked past several other finely chiseled animals, ears alert, eyes roaming as if they were looking for someone special to take a chance on their racing future. "Nothing much here. 'Buttons' is the best and he'll go for a song. You'll see his name on a few cards here and there, mostly to make the better horses look good. He'll pick up enough small prizes to pay for his upkeep and then he'll disappear and you'll never hear from him, again," he sighed. "He's a perpetual second or third-place finisher. With the right jockey he might win a few," he added as an afterthought. "I thought he ran well yesterday. It won't help him much."

"Tough to be a horse with no future."

Staring off in the distance, Bill appeared lost in thought. When he looked back, his eyes sparkled.

"There is one I'd buy in a minute."

"Yeah?"

"A filly. Jesus, she's fast as the wind."

"But –?" No answer. "Too expensive?"

"She'd be well out of my reach, but…" He hesitated then shook his head. "She can't race."

"Afraid of the gate?" he guessed? "Tried blinders?"

"Not that."

"Legs too thin? Temperamental? Gimme."

Bill brushed him off and wandered away. Having nothing better to do, Jack took a seat and watched the auction, keeping one eye on Jim Ewell and the other on the auction. Short and sweet, the group of seven horses was sold, some going for as high as $1,500. As predicted, Brass Buttons was sold for the bottom bid of $500.

Jack was on the verge of seeing to his own business when Bill Boerner rejoined him.

"Want to see her?"

He did not have to ask for further elucidation.

"You bet."

"You'll lose your man –"

"Now that I've pegged him he'll be easy to spot. He's not going far."

"Come on, then."

Leading Jack toward the barn, Bill received a number of acknowledgments from the grooms and stable hands hanging around. Nodding to each as though they were family, which, Jack decided, they were in an extended sort of way, he followed him to the stalls. Taking a keen interest in the animals there, it was a matter of no consequence to identify the filly that had caught the trainer's eye.

"Geez, she's a honey!" Offering his hand, the horse sniffed it curiously. Jack started to respond then immediately identified the problem. One word expressed a furlough of thought. "Oh."

A wide line ran across the forelock where hair had been rubbed off. Worse, the skin beneath had been worn raw, leaving a seeping wound.

"From the bridle," he diagnosed.

"You can't race a horse with an open sore."

"What did the vet say? Surely –"

"Not surely. And yes, we've all seen such sores. Most respond to treatment. Some medicine, a padded bridle, a week or two to recover and no one thinks any more about it. But nothing works with this filly. Believe me, I've called in the top men. They've tried everything. Their treatments either don't work or they make it worse."

"Tough."

"Tragedy is more like it. The owner can't even seller her the way she is. Not as a race horse. She's worthless. No point breeding her without an established track record. Eventually, she'll have to be...." He left off the end of the sentence out of delicacy to his companion. Appreciating the gesture, Jack nevertheless understood its import.

"Shit."

As if in sad commiseration, the filly lifted her tail.

Averting his head, not from the sight but what it represented, he had almost decided to go out and check on what James Ewell was up to when an idea occurred and he turned back.

"What if her wound got cured?"

"It would be a miracle. I tell you, I've tried everything. The owner's consulted the top vets in the industry." Hands in his pockets, Bill, too, moved away as though he didn't want to speak any longer in front of the horse. As a horseman, he understood the animal had a better grasp of the spoken word than most men of his acquaintance.

"He's spent a fortune on her, too. On my recommendation," he morosely spat. "That horse has a bright future. But, not the way she is. It's a common problem, actually: bridle sores. With most horses you can usually come up with a solution but there are some that just don't respond." Blinking as they emerged into the sunshine, the trainer stooped to pluck a dandelion from the ground. For a moment, Jack had the queasy feeling he was going to put it in his mouth.

"I suppose I should say, a solution that's usually expensive, takes its sweet time working and usually reoccurs. Just when you want to see it the least," he unnecessarily added, tossing the weed aside.

"What if, maybe, I had something that could help?"

"I'd think I wasted my two bucks on you because you're either a garage inventor who's likely to poison himself by mixing chemicals he shouldn't, or worse you're a scam artist more despicable than the guy you're supposedly chasing and you're trying to set me up for a big lay-out. Which is it and who put you onto me?"

"Not supposedly," Jack protested, getting the more important of the charges dispensed with first. "I'm not someone pitching a magic potion and I never heard of you before yesterday. And there's nothing in it for me. Just so we get that straight."

They turned the corner of the barn, continuing their walk by crossing the short-grass field behind it.

"Everyone wants something, Mr. Merrick."

"I'd like to walk up tomorrow morning with my nose in one piece and my hide intact. I don't ask for much and I don't demand more than my do. I'm just putting my idea to you because I like horses. And maybe get a little something out of it for someone else."

Nearly, but not completely convinced of the detective's sincerity, Boerner stopped, looked around, then abruptly changed direction.

"Who's your partner in crime?"

This time, Jack ignored the sarcasm.

"A friend of mine has a dog. An old, three-legged mutt he and his wife adopted... Well, you don't need to know the sob story. Anyway, the dog developed some sort of a skin condition and the poor beast was scratching itself to death. Was in a miserable state. Scratched huge patches of hair off and then kept scratching until the skin turned into open sores. The vet gave them all sorts of stuff to try and nothing worked. The dog kelp scratching and the sores went from bad to worse. A neighbor of theirs saw Mom out walking the dog –"

"Mom?"

Jack stumbled and caught himself.

"A habit. That's what I call them – Mom and Dad. They're not really... only sorta. Adopted, like. It doesn't matter."

The explanation is not germane to the subject at hand.

Even when Hugh wasn't there, Jack always suspected he was looking over his shoulder.

As adopted brothers, they shared a telepathic link.

"Anyway," he continued, "She came out and checked on the dog. She's some sort of research scientist, Mom – I mean, that what Mrs. Wade said."

"You can call her Mom. I like it. Keep going, you've got me hooked."

"A week or so later she offered – Mom – this spray bottle with some liquid in it she made up out of her own formula. Since Mom figured it couldn't do any harm, she used it on Rover." He snapped his fingers. "Just like that, she said, the mutt sorta sighed, like it felt good. And before you can say Jack Spratt, the sores were healed and the hair grew back."

"Lickety-split?" Bill grinned.

"Right on. If they use it regular, the dog doesn't scratch and the hair stays nice and healthy. A miracle – your word."

"The horse's problem isn't itching."

"I get that. It's not the cause, it's the healing property in the lotion, I guess you might call it. I asked Mom and she said the neighbor said 'skin is skin.' Or, words to that affect. Works on people, too. I asked."

Hands in his pockets, Bill scrutinized his companion's face.

"Nothing in this spray officials would object to?"

"I have no idea."

"I'm willing to try it – desperate, in fact. But, I'd have to pay for it outta my own pocket. I wouldn't feel comfortable asking the owner to pay for some – neighbor's spray."

"She gave it to Mom for free."

"People think horse racing, they think big bucks."

"OK, I'll borrow the bottle Mom has. Or, ask her to get another one. We'll try it and if it works –"

"If it works, I'll send a helicopter for your research scientist. Bring her here in style."

Jack shivered and made a face.

"I wouldn't fly in one of those babies if you paid me." He made a whirling gesture with his finger. "They look like an egg-beater. About as safe, too."

"They're safe," Bill grinned. "The Bell Corporation makes 'em. Now, there's something probably worth investing in."

"Maybe, but can they stare at you with big, brown eyes and raise their tail and shit when they hear something they don't like?"

"No."

"Then, I'm safer putting my two bucks on Brass Buttons."

"Safer, but not wealthier. I'll try that spray. Nothing ventured, nothing gained. And if it works, I'm gonna —"

"Don't say it."

"Shit."

He said it and they laughed. Because hope was always a wondrous thing.

CHAPTER 6

"Why does she need a hat?"

Ellen looked up from her not-as-easy-as-it-looks task of making a bow out of two pieces of ribbon invested with a life of their own, courtesy of a perpetual-motion baby, debated how to answer and then inquired, "Why do you wear a hat?"

"She wants to look like her father?"

Ellen scowled as her latest attempt failed and she tried again.

"You wear a hat to look like your father?"

Hugh's expression turned to one of horror.

"Certainly not. Why would you ask such a thing?"

"Because I asked why you wore a hat. Or, were you answering your own expectation? In which case, that's called leading the witness."

Grasping Jacqueline's arms, she debated how to manage the bow with her teeth. Not completely certain she could manage it, yet not completely discounting the idea, the twin ribbons began moving of their own accord. Her head snapped back, suspecting Hugh of some nefarious mischief but surprisingly found him standing too far away to be guilty. Her eyes snaked downward and observed Law Book alternately batting one side, then the other. She shooed the cat away. It retreated precisely three catsteps, testimony to her lack of fear.

"I wear a hat because it's socially required; part of a respectable man's wardrobe."

Ellen returned to the task at hand.

"You wear a useless piece of cloth around your neck, commonly called a tie, for that reason. You wear a hat to protect your head." Receiving no acknowledgment, she pursued the topic. "From the weather; so your hair doesn't get wet when it rains; to use the brim as a sun-shield." Still nothing. "So you don't have to comb your hair in the morning. To hold down your toupee."

Vanity finally won out.

"I don't have to wear a toupee. I have my own hair."

"I was beginning to think you couldn't speak. So: why do you wear a hat, Mr. Kerr?"

"You have explained it to me nicely."

"Using your newly obtained knowledge, why am I putting a hat, otherwise known as a *bonnet,* sir, on your daughter's head?"

"No other babies were bonnets."

The ensuing exasperation was enough to unerringly guide Ellen's hands into the proper formation to grasp the ribbons and twist them into a perfect bow, proving the conversation had some, albeit limited merit.

"There! And don't you even think of untying it, you little rascal," she warned the infant, knowing beforehand that bows, whether attached to bonnets or baby shoes, invariably came undone for no better reason than they could.

Or, to be annoying to mothers as yet another cross they bore.

Grasping the wiggling baby in her arms, she clandestinely checked to be sure the diaper was dry, then returned her attention to her husband.

"We do not base our actions – or reactions – on what other people do or do not do. A baby's head is very delicate; the skull hasn't knit, yet –"

He paled at the image.

"What do you mean, the skull hasn't knit? Has she a hole in her head?"

"Just so," Ellen replied with what some might have construed as a mocking tone.

"I didn't see one," he mumbled, standing on tiptoe in an attempt to view the top of Jackie's head. Ellen held her back.

"You missed it, then."

"Is it... supposed to be there?"

"Certainly. How do you suppose an infant learns as quickly as it does?" Ellen supplied the answer. "So her mother can pour a can of liquid brain through the opening. Sort of the opposite of Drain-O. Instead of clearing her head out, I fill it up."

"With what?"

"Knowledge."

He rocked back on his heels. She waited for him to ask where she purchased such a can and was only slightly disappointed when he didn't.

"You're making that up."

Checking the clock and realizing she had taken the discussion far enough, Ellen shifted the baby from one shoulder to the other.

"Hugh, I won't ask whether you ever took a biology class in college because obviously you were absent that day, so I'll give it to you short and sweet. When a baby is born, the skull hasn't completely sealed. The two halves haven't come together; I suppose," she added, thus deflecting another question, "to make it easier for this Very Large person with a head the size of a Basketball to get through the birth canal and Out without ripping its mother asunder. You can't see it because the opening is covered by flesh and sometimes, but not always," she sighed, "by hair. Step closer."

He complied but only reluctantly.

"Bend your head."

He did so with trepidation. She felt for the spot and pressed her finger down to indicate where it was.

"Right here. It's called – well, I've heard it called, I'm not sure what the medical name is – the soft spot. If you knew anything about baseball, you'd know another way the expression is used. Ask Forshee; he'll explain it to you."

"I'll be sure and do that."

She ignored the sarcasm.

"As the baby grows, the two sides merge and the spot seals. But until that time, it's always best to protect the head. And, as I said, to deflect the hot rays of the sun away from the skull. The bone is thin and heat can do damage to the developing brain. Does that make it clear?"

"You're better than any biology teacher I ever had." Appreciating how fast sarcasm turned to reverence, she kissed him lightly on the lips. "How do you know all this?"

Without intentionally setting him up, she took advantage of the opportunity to have the last word.

"My mother used the extra-large can of brains to pour into my head."

She erred in her supposition as his lower lip protruded.

"I doubt my mother used anything to pour into mine."

Too many rejoinders passed through her consciousness before she grabbed the one almost too small to comprehend.

"The elves did it for you."

"Ah."

He beamed in pleasure.

"Shall we go? I wouldn't want to miss Dad in his Uncle Sam costume."

Offering her his arm, they headed for the door, all three humans plus a very large contingent of invisible but ever-present wee folk well-satisfied with the outcome.

Being an hour early for the start of the 4th of July parade, the Kerrs were able to claim a spot on the sidewalk running parallel to the street, meaning they wouldn't have to peer over other partygoers heads to catch the action. Before they had settled in, however, a madly waving arm from the other side caught their attention. Hugh nudged Ellen.

"There's Mom."

Ellen looked both ways to be certain there was no oncoming traffic, then started ahead, remarking to the baby she carried, "Always remember to look both ways before crossing, Jackie. Your parents expect you to be ever vigilant."

Hugh stopped dead in his tracks.

"I appreciate that training starts early, but do you expect her to understand the word 'vigilant'? I doubt I knew the meaning before I was... two."

"You do realize, of course, there's a good reason people call you 'smart ass.'" She plunged forward. "I don't believe in using baby talk. Goo goo; ga-ga. Cutsie-wootsie. I appreciate the alliteration and the rhyming but I always found it... demeaning. We have a beautiful language; why not use it the way it was intended?"

"That's what I love about you," he stated with unequivocal sincerity. "You understand pride. A sense of worth, which is absolutely necessary for a healthy mind, begins early. And beauty. An appreciation of beauty does not have to be complex; something is beautiful because of its simplicity. The vista of mountains, the stretch of waving grass along the plains; the magnitude of a starry night. Are they complex, each in their own way? Of course they are, but to understand the intricate you must first have a sense of wonder. Therein lies the beauty."

The driver of a car coming down the street, honked the horn. Both parents responded with startled looks in his direction.

"And then, there's hard-won street smarts," Ellen grinned. "Having a profound discussion in the middle of the street is not wise." She expected him to smile, but instead, he charged off toward the car. "Please, Hugh, don't make a scene. We were in the wrong."

"The hell we were." Marching up the driver's side window, he waved his hand in the opposite direction. "This road is closed. It's been blocked off since 6 A.M. What are you doing on it?"

The driver, wearing a police uniform, scowled.

"Don't tell me my business. I'm doing crowd control. You were standing in the middle of the street. Don't you know that's dangerous?"

"You do crowd control on foot, not in a vehicle doing twenty down a barricaded street. Who's your commanding officer?"

"I don't have to tell you that."

"All right, what's your badge number?"

Before the driver could refuse, Mary Wade came hurrying over.

"Officer, I'm Mary Wade, Lieutenant Hank Wade's wife. He's the chief homicide detective for the L.A. Police Department, who happens to be representing Uncle Sam in today's parade. What's the trouble here?"

The man politely touched a hand to his forehead in acknowledgment of her worth.

"This man, a woman and a baby were standing in the middle of the road, ma'am. I honked them on their way and he didn't like it. I'm doing crowd control and if he doesn't like it, I'm going to arrest him –"

"I'll handle this. Hugh, go over there with Ellen."

Nothing could have surprised the officer more than to see her command obeyed with alacrity. Rejoining his family, the Kerrs watched as the conversation in the street finished and Mary rejoined them. Expecting an angry tirade from Hugh, she was therefore caught flatfooted by his huge welcoming grin.

"You were wonderful!"

"I   was?"

"You took charge just like a... triumphant defense attorney."

"You might have said just like an authoritative police lieutenant but I excuse your perspective. I didn't do anything."

"You defused a potentially volatile situation without violence. I was mad," he added. "And right."

"You were mad," she agreed. "And wrong to be standing out in the middle of the street. Whether or not it was blocked to civilian traffic, you had no idea what the officer's orders were. You made an uninformed assumption –" He started to protest but she spoke over him. "Because you knew you were wrong and didn't want to admit it." Hands akimbo, she demanded, "In light of cooler heads prevailing, how do you plead?"

"Guilty."

"That will be a... five dollar donation to the Police Retirement Fund."

"I'll send a check."

"See that you do. I know every woman on the Board and I'll ask if you sent in a donation."

"Word of honor, ma'am." Motioning to Ellen, he took the baby and draped her over his shoulder. "A year ago, you wouldn't have done that."

Mary reflected, then agreed.

"You're right. You've given me a new sense of worth, Mr. Kerr."

"Ellen and I were just discussing that."

"He just never thought to have it turned on him," Ellen seconded.

They laughed and Mary indicated down the street.

"Good thing I spotted you two – three," she grinned. "As wife of the honorary Uncle Sam, I'm invited to watch the proceedings from the grandstand. You're my invited guests. I would have let you know earlier, but I was just informed this morning." She quivered in excitement. "I've never been up there, before."

"It's quite an honor, Mom," Ellen replied for all three. "You lead, we follow."

Marching at the head of the procession, they walked against the foot traffic rapidly filling up the good spots along the route, finally reaching an elevated wooden structure recently constructed at the mid-way point of the parade route. Showing her pass to the guard proved unnecessary as she was immediately recognized.

"Good morning, Mrs. Wade," he replied, tipping his cap. Revealing that he also recognized at least one of her companions, his smile dipped. "Bringing up the enemy, too, ma'am?"

"We have no enemies today, Sam. Besides, he's promised to make a generous contribution to the Cause."

His lips reversed themselves and he bowed to the Kerrs.

"Right this way gentleman, lady and baby." As Hugh passed, he loudly whispered, "That was a great cigar you passed out. And my car could use another washing."

"Bring it by my office Monday morning and I'll see what I can do for you during my lunch hour."

"Touché, Hugh!" Mary exclaimed as they climbed the steps and settled into the front-row chairs. "You're learning. A fine, gentlemanly reply."

"The fact I won't be there Monday doesn't bother you?" he teased.

"No more than Sam, who wouldn't think of bringing his car by. My turn to hold Jackie."

She accepted the baby, deftly re-tied the ribbons which had mysteriously come undone from under her chin, then her eyes grew wide as she saw another early arrival.

"Oh, dear. Here comes..." Biting off the word "trouble," she politely amended her thought to, "another of the dignitaries."

And fooled no one.

Waiting for Christine Bond to make her way up the stairs, the Gang accepted her cold smile as she appraised the situation of discovering the entire first row of three chairs had already been taken.

"Good morning. I see you're here early, Mrs. Wade. With guests. Good morning, Hugh, Ellen."

Jacqueline, apparently, did not require a specific greeting, being too young to recognize the oversight.

"Good morning," the Kerrs replied in practiced unison.

"We assumed," he suavely lied, "you'd be at the start of the parade. To see B.B. kick it off."

"I would have, but they haven't set up any chairs there and I don't intend to stand the entire time."

He obligingly stood and offered her his seat.

"Please, take mine. I wouldn't think of depriving you of a front row view."

She hesitated, giving the women the opportunity of standing and allowing her the royal position Mary occupied. When they gave no indication of obliging her tacit request, she assumed Hugh's place. Rather than take a chair behind them, he complacently stood by the side of the narrow platform, hands folded demurely in front of him. Ellen turned her head away and rolled her eyes. Not at his behavior but that of their newly arrived companion.

After ten minutes of awkward silence, Christine remarked, "The baby looks hot. It's that hat, I expect."

Hugh quietly snickered. Ellen's shoulders shook. While he had scored points with his magnanimous behavior, she was not so predisposed.

"Yes, don't you like it? I picked it up at the flea market the other day. There were so many baby items, I didn't know which to buy. But that bonnet caught my eye and I just had to have it."

A sudden stillness settled over the grandstand. Those coming in behind them might have thought a silent war was being fought.

"Flea market?" Christine managed to reply without choking.

"Yes; down on Lankershim. They hold it every weekend. I'll give you address if you'd like. You can't imagine the bargains. What other people think as junk you can buy for a song."

"Literally or figuratively?"

"Probably both," Ellen gushed, keeping up the farce. "Just the other week – or perhaps it was longer ago than that," she sighed, trying to "remember," "I picked up a secondhand eggbeater. In the original box, too. Hardly used at all. Guess how much I paid for it?"

"I-can't."

"Twenty-five cents! Want not, waste not, I always say."

"I've never heard you use that expression, dear," Hugh tried with a shudder.

"That's because you don't listen to me, dear." Turning to Christine, she added, "You'll have to go with me, sometime."

"I'm busy on weekends."

"Well, give me a list of things you'd like and I'll see what I can do for you. In fact, with two growing children, I expect you have to replace their wardrobes frequently. There's a secondhand clothing store just down the street from here on Hollywood. Neat the Cherokee bookstore. Do you like to read? Why spend money on new books when you can pick up a used copy for –"

Hugh figuratively covered his ears so as not to hear the repeated, "for a song."

"What do you like to read?"

"I'm afraid I don't have time for such leisure pursuits."

"Come, now. Children's books, certainly. When you read to Bart, Jr. and Ann Marie at night. Knights of the Round Table for him and Cinderella stories for her," she darkly added.

Hugh flinched.

"Oh, look!" Mary cried, interrupting the conversation by pointing downward. "There's Jack!" Standing up, she waved at him to catch his attention. "Jack!"

Hearing his name, he looked around before finally realizing the salutation had come from above. Shielding his eyes from the sun, he identified the speaker and eagerly waved back.

"Hi ya, Mary! Hello, Ellen. Where's Hugh? Oh, I see him. Hiding!"

"You're not going to invite him up, are you?" Christine hissed. "The grandstand is for dignitaries. I expect the mayor will be here shortly. And the police commissioner."

"And he's got a girl with him," Ellen interjected, thus ignoring the tacit order. "Who is she, Hugh?"

Making a rapid appraisal, he shook his head.

"I don't know. Jack has a lot of friends."

"I'll just bet he does," Christine disapproved, as if "friends" were a dirty word. She fooled no one as they perfectly well comprehended she meant "women friends."

In contrast to the warning, Mary indicated he step forward. Reading the situation, he grinned and pantomimed eating by putting his hand to his mouth, before indicating a seller hawking grease-stained bags of popcorn. Waving good-bye, he escorted his lady friend in that direction.

"I hope that vendor has a permit to sell food," Mrs. Bond snapped, repelled by the entire scene.

"That's Bill Blaise," Mary explained in an offhanded manner. "He had a night beat in the district. The boys were awarded permission to sell popcorn, Cracker Jack and candy bars for today. Soda, too, I think. All for the greater good. The mayor likes to stay in the good graces of the police department. It's always... politic to have our vote at election time."

"Our?" Christine asked.

She should not have. Mary's face darkened.

"No one shoots at your husband, Mrs. Bond. They shoot at mine. When I send him out at all hours of the day and night I never know if he's coming back. Dreading a knock on the door and seeing an officer standing there with his cap in his hand makes me one of them."

Gritting her teeth in consternation, Mrs. Bond tried to obfuscate her comment.

"I was merely asking if you and... Hank voted in tandem."

Before Mary could answer, Christine pretended she saw someone in the crowd and stood.

"There's Mrs. Poulson, the mayor's wife. She's being escorted to the start of the parade. Perhaps I should go with her. Excuse me, won't you?"

Without bothering to hear whether or not they excused her, Christine gathered in her pocketbook and made a hasty retreat. Hugh promptly took her seat.

"Slick," he approved, before grinning at Ellen. "Is there really a flea market on Lankershim?"

"Yes," she deadpanned.

"But, you didn't buy the baby's bonnet there. I recognize it. It came in a set."

"So you say. I like a bargain."

"And a used clothing store on Hollywood?"

"I made that up."

He settled for one confession out of two. Marring Ellen Thorne was proving to be an experience by itself. One he hardly expected. But greatly appreciated.

The parade, advertised as beginning at 10:00 sharp, gave no indicating of starting, and by 10:30 the crowd started to get restless. Several times some of the local bands began to warn up, leading to expectations of the Grand Shout to begin but as the notes faded away, no forward progression was noticed. Nervously clutching her handbag, Mary's outward expression betrayed no distress when Hugh innocently inquired, "Why do you think it's taking so long to get started?"

"The only thing I care about is whether the delay is over Hank's costume. If it isn't, I can live with it. At least," she added as an afterthought, "I can until he gets home and starts yapping. You know how he hates delays of any sort."

Hugh rubbed his chin in contemplation.

"Yes, I think I can agree with that." Peering down into the swelling crowd, it took him a moment to find who he was looking for. Getting to his feet, he waved frantically while calling, "Jack! Jack Merrick!" When the object of his attention finally looked up, he summoned him over.

"What's up?"

"Can you worm your way upfront and find out why the parade is being held up?"

It appeared Jack answered in the affirmative but as the noise below swelled, his words were lost to posterity. They did observe him working his way against the swelling foot traffic and soon lost sight of him.

"Keep your fingers crossed," Mary whispered.

Ten minutes later Ellen spotted Jack's blond hair bobbing and weaving through a mass of humanity.

"There he is! And he's carrying a paper sack."

Finally reaching the wooden ladder, he scampered up one-handed, a wide grin illuminated by sparkling blue eyes.

"Guess what I got?" he asked, pushing down to the front row. Without waiting for an answer, he shoved his hand in the bag. "Ice cream on a stick! Business is so good, the vendor hasn't made his way this far back." Dispensing the treat to Mary, Ellen and Hugh, he paused a moment to catch his breath from the excitement.

Although appreciating the ice cream, Hugh frowned. Catching and mistaking the sentiment, Jack shrugged.

"I would have gotten you all a bag of peanuts but the line was too long."

"I thought I sent you to find out why the parade hadn't started."

"Oh, that." Jack laughed good-humoredly. "It's your fault."

Hugh's frown turned into a scowl.

"Whenever anything goes wrong in this town it's my fault. What, exactly, am I supposed to have done this time?"

"It isn't Hank's costume, is it?" Mary interrupted.

"Nope. He's the Grand Old Man and hoppin' mad he is, too."

"Oh, dear."

"What's-going-on?"

"Are you sure you really want to hear this?"

"Yes!" Ellen screamed, ostensibly to be heard over the crowd noise.

"It seems Mrs. B – one half of the Mr. and Mrs. B.B. team – was highly indignant she had to share the grandstand with the likes of... well, I won't name names. So she and Mrs. Bigwig Mayor found B.B. and demanded they erect another platform for them at the head of the parade. Mr. Bigwig

Mayor concurred – I guess you're not known as a big donor, Hugh – and so they had to scramble to find the carpenters and enough wood to make another viewing stand."

The three exchanged sour glances before Hugh apologized to Mary.

"I'm sorry. We shouldn't have come up here."

She waved them off with an imperial gesture.

"I have the right to invite anyone I want. And besides, I seriously doubt it was you and Ellen 'Mrs. B' objected to. It was me. Even though my husband was grievously wounded in the line of duty and he was voted by his peers to play Uncle Sam, we're hardly a family of 'quality.' I'm sure the old witch expected me to stand below in the crowd."

Momentarily stunned, Hugh shook with indignation. "That's it." Getting to his feet, he attempted to push Jack into his seat. "You sit here and –"

"Oh, no. I'm going with you. I don't want to miss any of the fun. Besides, you might need a bodyguard."

"Against what? Pocketbooks and hat pins?"

"Sit down, Hugh. Please don't make a scene," Ellen tried, knowing it was too late. "We're supposed to be having a good time."

"There's nothing I like better than a good fight. All right, Jack. You come with me; we'll ask your guest to come up here and hold the seat for us."

"Hey, she'd like that."

The boys disappeared, leaving two women and a baby to hold the fort until reinforcements arrived. Finding his date and giving her instructions to join the ladies on the grandstand, they worked their way to the head of the parade where they discovered several men vainly attempting to hoist up a wooden frame. Watching them in some consternation was the district attorney and Mayor Poulson. The police commissioner was several yards away making useless overtures to "Uncle Sam" to "Calm down and don't make a scene."

Rapidly appraising the situation, Hugh directed Jack to stay back as he pasted a smile on his face and approached the police commissioner.

"Good morning, Troy."

Turning at the unexpectedly friendly voice, he identified the speaker. His expression did not match that of the interloper.

"Good morning, Hugh. I'm a bit busy at the moment –"

Hugh ignored the warning.

"Troy, I'm in a bit of a quandary. Ellen's brought the baby with us to watch the parade and I'm afraid she's getting a bit cranky."

"I'm sorry but we're having a bit of a delay –"

"Whatever it is, I'm sure it can be... ignored, shall we say, by a generous donation to the Retirement Fund? Say, one thousand dollars if you get things started within –" He checked his watch. "A minute or two?"

"You're not serious?"

"I am, absolutely."

Troy Beckman's hands flew into the air.

"Attention, everyone! The parade is going to start in two minutes. Never mind that viewing stand," he dismissed the carpenters. "The dignitaries can watch from the street. Hank – get on the wagon. Bart – where are you?"

"Right here," the D.A. responded, stepping forward. Having missed the conversation between Hugh and the commissioner, the sudden turn of events caught him by surprise.

"You and I are in the lead convertible. Let's go. We've held things up long enough."

"I thought –"

"People are restless, Bart. They came to see a 4th of July parade. We're already 45 minutes late getting started." Glancing across at the two women, he offered them a tight smile. "I'm sure everyone understands. Now: one-two-three-four, march!"

Racing for the open convertible, he and Bond got it, positioned themselves so they wouldn't fall when the vehicle started up, then on the mayor's somewhat disjointed signal, the bands took up the strains of patriotic music. A score of helium balloons were set free, and a cheer rent the air as the parade got underway.

The only one who appeared disappointed was Jack. As Hugh rejoined him and they made their way back toward the grandstand, he mumbled, "I thought we were gonna pummel 'em."

Reaching the grandstand in relative safety, they climbed the stairs and rejoined the girls.

"What did you do?" Ellen asked, not entirely certain she wanted to know the answer.

"Nothing any good ol' red-blooded *American* boy wouldn't have done in similar circumstances." Turning to Jack's friend, he politely tipped his hat.

"I'm Hugh."

"Oh, excuse me," Jack mumbled. "This is Flo. We've known each other like forever. Judy said parades always give her a headache and I didn't want to go stag. She's swell," he proudly added. "You'll like her."

"We already do," Ellen announced. "She brought popcorn."

Flo tried to shake off the compliment and started to get up so he could have her seat, but Hugh shook his head.

"Ladies sit; gentlemen stand."

"But I didn't mean to get in the way –"

"No friend of Jack's ever gets in the way, Miss Flo. You're as welcome here – more welcome – than other women of our acquaintance. In fact, we're honored you have joined us and you're invited to our picnic later this afternoon. We're all going down to Malibu and romp on the beach. Drink a lot of beer, make a fire for steaks and roast corn and potatoes and sing songs until we're hoarse."

"It sounds wonderful, thank you," she replied in awe, first glancing at Jack for his approval. Getting the thumbs-up she happily settled in.

"Look, there's Bond!" Ellen identified as the lead car came into view. "Leading the parade; wouldn't you know?"

Jackie began to cry which only highlighted the event.

Nevertheless, the Gang waved in acknowledgment as the car passed. Not insensitive to the delay his wife had occasioned, Bond looked up, saw the reception from the grandstand and waved back, relieved and pacified.

Once the car was upon them, Mary whispered in Ellen's ear.

"If only he had been dressed in an outfit, I'd have been more pleased."

"Have anything in mind?"

"A clown."

Her comment was meant to be overheard and elicited an even louder round of applause. B.B. Bond waved harder in response.

What he didn't know, the private group on the grandstand decided, wouldn't hurt him.

Behind the lead car came several marching high school bands with baton-twirling girls and serious-looking band leaders, then a group of horseback riders bedecked in white-fringed outfits and white, ten-gallon hats. The silver on their saddles glistened in the mid-morning sunlight while the well-matched white steeds pranced along Hollywood Boulevard. Next followed several troops of World War II veterans dressed in parade uniforms, the lead men carrying the battle flags of their units; a children's chorus dressed in cheerful pastel skirts, or white shirts and black trousers tossing handfuls of candy to the onlookers; more horsemen waving lassos over their heads; and finally, in the middle came a regiment of police officers clad in their natty blue uniforms.

The crowd cheered and waved their hands in appreciation. The roar swelled to gigantic acknowledgment as a line of three open cars passed, carrying those soldiers of the civilian wars injured in the line of duty and too infirm to march. And finally, the horse-drawn wagon festooned with red, white and blue streamers atop which stood Uncle Sam.

Eyes tearing at the honor bestowed her husband, Mary stood and waved. Those with her stood, hands raised in salute at the bravery and the patriotic duty performed by one of their own. Eyes trained upward, hand shot high in love and respect, Hank Wade blessed his family before turning to salute those on the other side of the street.

"Here, Hugh," Ellen remarked, passing Jackie over to him. Reaching under her seat, she removed her camera from the diaper bag, drew Uncle Sam into sharp focus and snapped picture after picture. When he was finally out of sight, she winked at Mary.

"I wanted all of us to have a permanent reminder of this day."

Proving she was a policeman's wife, Mary noted, "You didn't take any of the commissioner; or the D.A."

"Pity. I ran out of film."

Considering those illustrious men had passed prior to the arrival of Uncle Sam, the joke was enjoyed by all.

By noon the parade had finished its long trek down the street and the parade-goers slowly dispersed. Waiting until the crowd below them cleared, the Kerr Gang made their way down the wooden steps.

"A perfect day," Hugh approved. "Dad was magnificent. What do you say we gather at our place and then drive down together to the beach?"

"All right," Mary agreed. "I'll go get Hank. He usually goes to the Policeman's Picnic but he agreed they'll have boys in blue tripping over one another, so he agreed to your plans. We'll see you there in about an hour."

"Right," Jack agreed. "I've got a van; want me to bring it over? That way, we'll all fit into one car. Parking may be a bitch – may be hard to come by," he quickly amended.

"Good. Then, you can help me load it before Mom and Dad arrive."

They parted company, Ellen slipping her arm under Hugh's.

"What did you really do to get the parade started?"

"Offered the commissioner cash money."

"How much?"

"One thousand dollars."

"That was a bit generous, wasn't it?"

"All for a good cause. I was planning on sending in two thousand."

Which unknowingly put him in the same boat as B.B. Bond, who had saved himself from giving Baby Kerr a $100 savings bond by buying helium balloons for her blessing celebration.

Leaving it to Ellen to make it right.

"Send that much, anyway. All for a good cause."

Which, unknowingly, put her head and shoulders over Christine Bond.

CHAPTER 7

If Hugh had poled the "jury" as to which of the eight gang members had gotten the wettest, there would have been a unanimous consensus. They had all taken "the plunge," even Jacqueline, securely wrapped in her mother's arms, but only one of them had rolled in the sand.

"That," he declared, shaking his head while pointing at Irish Rover, "is the most... disgusting sight I've ever seen."

Hank rubbed his chin in faux contemplation, using his smug police voice to sharpen the image.

"Now, I don't know, Kerr. I've... caught you at the scene of many a grizzly crime – which I suspected you of having a hand in, by the way – and none of them were too pretty. You're going to compare any of those murders to a happy dog enjoying the beach?"

"I stand corrected, Your Honor," he grinned, then pointed upward. "I have only two remaining questions for the witness." Who the witness might be, he didn't specify. "First, who's going to wash the sand off that tangle of fur, and second, I'm very glad we didn't drive down here in the Continental or I'd have to take it to the police station for a good wash and vacuum."

Kneeling on the sand changing the baby's diaper, Ellen clucked her tongue.

"Oh, dear, where to start? I can see the consumption of a steak and half a dozen roasted ears of corn – to say nothing about the baked potatoes – has sharpened your intellect."

"How's that?"

"I'll begin by reminding you dogs have hair; cats have fur."

He pouted.

"A point in your favor."

"You didn't ask two questions, you asked one and then stated an observation."

"Lastly," Hank added with a grin as wide as the ocean, "It's *you* who does the car washing at the station, not my boys. But, I'm sure they'd be glad to supply you with the rags and a bucket –"

"And their own cars, too," Jack happily agreed. "And since the van we came in is *mine*, I'm all too happy to drop you and it off there tomorrow morning."

As Ellen snapped the last safety pin into place at the corner of the diaper, Jackie gave a satisfied grunt and kicked her legs, making moot the diaper change. Her mother withdrew and stared pointedly at her father.

"Your turn."

"You had the easy one," he deferred, stepping back.

"We never agreed to quantify easy from hard."

He woefully looked across at Mary, who was suddenly busy untangling snarls from Rover's hair.

"When," he sadly tried, "is she going to be able to do this on her own?"

"Every parent's lament. Welcome to fatherhood," Hank chuckled.

Hands akimbo, Hugh demanded, "How many diapers did you change in your day?"

"None. I never saw either one of them until they were sixteen and only then because they called me at the office asking to borrow money. And don't ever let anyone kid you: there's no such thing as 'sweet sixteen' – at least not from a parent's perspective."

"Then, why is there such an expression?"

"To instill false hope in your heart that there's an end in sight to dirty diapers, dripping noses, broken tricycle wheels that need instant repairing, trips to the Emergency Room for broken arms and stitches for a gash in the head, monitoring field trips for two dozen screaming, out-of-control banshees and staying up until three in the morning working on an arithmetic problem trying to determine how long it takes a train to get to St. Louis when the track outside Chicago is broken and they have to detour through Stafford, Indiana."

"Where is Stafford?"

"No one knows," he deadpanned.

"And why is there no 'sweet sixteen'?"

"Oh, there's a sixteen, but it isn't sweet."

"Why not?"

"Please don't answer him," Mary pleaded. To deaf ears.

Hank went after Hugh with far more zest than he ever displayed on the witness stand.

"At sweet sixteen every teenager ever born – with rare exceptions," he scowled, "think his – or her – parents either print money in the basement or grow it on a tree in the backyard. They need driving lessons – God help mankind – which also means your insurance premiums will skyrocket and you learn to live with dent fenders because after the third accident you give up on body-shop repairs. Their faces are all broken out and they look as though they're in a constant state of measles, which they are in a continual and loud state of bemoaning because their life is 'ruined.' Boys no longer think girls have cooties and girls park in the sole-bathroom-in-the-house and never come out until your bladder has burst. There are games to transport them to and from, tuxedos to rent –"

"Or prom dresses to buy," Mary added.

"Colleges to consider, strange young people being brought into the house that I'm more familiar seeing down at the railroad yard –" He paused for breath before giving Hugh the evil eye. "And then there's the money they need to borrow – 'borrow' being a euphemism for 'I need right now, it's an emergency and I'll pay you back when that summer job comes through,' which, of course, when it does, they've long forgotten. Did I mention the fact they go through money like water through a sieve?"

Hugh stated at the Wades in blank amazement.

"I missed that stage."

"Perhaps you skipped childhood, but your daughter won't. And neither will the rest of the little Kerrs."

"Let's worry about one at a time."

The Wades laughed. Hugh stamped his foot, leaving a deep impression in the sand. One destined to be washed away during the next tide.

"What about you, Ellen? Did you ever go through that horror?"

"More or less," she confessed.

"And you, Jack?"

"Well," he debated, tugging on an earlobe, "My sweet sixteen had more to do with learning how to pick locks, avoid the cops, survive on my own cooking and lie about my age to get into the Navy."

"I think I'm going to be sick."

"It's the corn, dear. You boys go down to the water and swim it off so you'll be ready for dessert."

"I'm good," Jack protested, patting his rotund stomach. "To me, picnics are a gourmet meal."

Hugh, however, was only too glad to take Ellen up on the offer.

"I'll be back in half an hour."

He trotted off. They watched him go and when he finally convinced them he actually was going to swim, Mary sighed.

"You let him get away with leaving the diaper to you."

"I think you shocked him enough for one night." As Jack dropped into a reclining position where Rover was digging in the sand, Ellen experienced a moment of dread. Puzzled by the sudden change in mood, she searched her memory for an explanation and just when she thought it would elude her, the image came back, making her almost sorry to have pursued it.

The corpse of a headless man lying on a morgue slab.

And she, leaning over trying to identify it.

Her throat constricted and she fought back tears before gathering in her courage. Looking across at the detective, she studied his body in the firelight. Tall, lean, muscled, tanned. No Navy anchor tattooed on his arm, no obvious scars.

"Come over here," she called and he unquestioningly complied. Running her hand around the back of his neck, she felt the small raised line and shuddered. Where the chain from his St. Christopher's medal had burned him from the scorching Philippine sun.

She had remembered then and she remembered now. Leaning over, she kissed him on the cheek.

He didn't ask why. He knew without knowing.

"I'm alive," he whispered.

"I love you, Jack. Please be careful. I don't know what Hugh and I would do without you."

"Came close to finding out, didn't you?" As a jest, it fell flat.

"No," she tonelessly responded before pinching his arm. "You're not wearing your medal. They recovered it. Didn't you get it back?"

Turning his head away, she felt him nod in the growing darkness.

"I did. I tried to convince myself it had saved me, but I couldn't. Somehow, it seemed to belong to that other guy – the one they tried to pass off as me. That... tainted it." His voice raised. "Besides, it was you and Hugh who saved me, so I decided to keep you two around, instead."

Since she couldn't promise to always be there when he was in trouble, she answered the only way she could.

"Silly boy." Wiping a tear from her eye, she pursued, "And why didn't you say you were going to school studying engineering and working a fulltime job, instead of giving that glib reply about avoiding the cops?"

"That was another Jack."

"No, it wasn't."

"Yes, Starlet, it was. Besides, that's a secret I don't blab to just anyone."

Without being privy to the private conversation, Mary intuitively felt it had grown too serious and required a mother's touch to relieve the tension.

"Help me get the tangles out of Rover's hair, Mr. Merrick."

Grinning in appreciation at the reprieve, he crawled across the sand and ran his fingers over the dog's ears.

"Pretty good time, wasn't it, boy? And I bet you're the only three-legged pooch on the beach tonight. Those tracks you left will puzzle a dozen amateur sleuths. That's an added plus." The dog wagged his tail at the compliment, sensing no one could turn a disability into an advantage better than Jack. It was the luckiest break in the world, having been adopted by a family who understood him. It didn't make losing his Mom any easier – the beloved old lady who had stood with him through thick and thin and who he still remembered in the recesses of his canine memory – but it helped.

Dogs did not question if they would ever be reunited with their family in heaven. That was part of their make-up; one their human counterparts often sorely lacked. It was a gift from God all animals shared in common. "An edge," Mr. Jack might have said.

"Wow," Mr. Jack observed, unfortunately being unable to read Rover's mind. "Your hair is coming back great."

"It is, isn't it? I told you. And the itch is gone, too. He looks so much better – and he feels better. It's that spray I told you about. Which reminds me, I brought you a bottle of it like you asked."

"Great! I have this idea – I'll let you in on it, if it works."

She reached into her pocketbook and handed him the bottle. Peering at the clear-colored substance through the plastic, he whistled.

"Doesn't look like much, does it? I guess miracles come in all sizes and shapes."

Reaching over to where he had dumped his street clothes, he tucked the jar away in the pocket of his jacket, then retrieved a comb from another pocket. Using the wider-side where the points were more widely separated, he began working on the coat. Rover puffed air into his cheeks and settled down for a not entirely appreciated grooming. Sometimes, he decided, a dog lived a dog's life.

"I got it," Jack exclaimed, patting his pocket.

Bill Boerner came out of a stall where he had been examining the leg of another thoroughbred horse, wiped his hands on a towel hung over the gate, smiled, then shook his head.

"It's too early to be so happy."

"Early in the morning, or early as in, 'wait to see what happens'?"

"You got it."

Bill nodded and they walked through the barn, both men with their hands in their pockets but for different reasons.

"I had orders to ship her back to the ranch, but I put it off. I don't know why. I must be crazy."

"I saw the dog last night – the one I told you about. His hair – dogs have hair and cats have fur," Jack suddenly explained. "Did you know that?"

"Just maybe."

"What does a horse have?"

"Hair. Like you and me. Only, you got more'n me and I'm jealous. Will this spray of yours work on people's heads?"

"No, no, you got it all wrong. I told you: it's not a hair restorer, it heals the skin so the hair can grow back. In the case of Irish Rover, he has some sort of condition that caused a terrible itch. He kept scratching and rubbed all the hair off so he looked like he had the mange."

Bill stopped in mid-stride and shook his head.

"Irish Rover? Good name. I like his owner, already."

Jack's lips formed into an "O."

"I'd be careful about that. He's a cop."

"Oh, hell. A cop?"

"The worst kind: a homicide detective. And a good one."

"How come you know a – good cop? In your line of business I'd think you were on opposite sides."

"We used to be," he grinned. "One hardnosed cop against one hardnosed gumshoe. But, then I found out he was human. Imagine that."

"I can't."

They continued walking until reaching a stall at the end of the row. Hearing them come, the filly stuck her nose out. Bill gently rubbed it.

"She's desperate for company. A horse knows; maybe not the cause, but they understand when something's wrong. She wants attention. More than that, she wants to run. It's in her blood. Horses like this, when they can't race just sorta pine away. They don't get it."

"Hey, girl," Jack soothed. "Maybe we can help you. Whatta ya say about that?"

The horse stomped her hoof.

"She likes it just fine," Bill interpreted. "But, don't get her hopes up. They speak 'human' you know."

Jack took the bottle from his pocket and handed it over.

"Here it is. Let's give it a try."

Unscrewing the top, Bill stared at the unimpressive-looking nearly translucent liquid compound.

"Is it safe to touch? Do I need gloves, I mean?"

"Mom didn't say anything about that. I don't think so. Want me to put it on?"

"Better not. You don't have a license and like I said, she's not my horse. I'm doing this on the sly. I could get in big trouble. And if it works," he stated with more expectation in his voice than he realized, "it'll have to be cleared with the racing commission. At least to be sure it doesn't contain any dope or something like that."

"Sure. I get it."

"So, what do I do?"

"Just spray it on the open wound. Maybe all around it, too, to make sure we get all the affected area."

Bill ran his finger along the edge of the trigger, hesitated, then depressed it, squirting some into his palm. Bringing it to his nose, he sniffed.

"Doesn't have any odor. You'd think to work, it ought to smell bad."

"Ain't that the way of it?" Jack considered, then added, "Maybe miracles don't stink."

"Makes sense."

Bill hesitated, then met Jack's eyes.

"Just so you know…. I called your office – the number on the card you gave me. Just to make sure you were who you said you were. In case… you turned out to be a kook, pretending to be someone you're not. In this game, you never know. You hang out around the track. Looking for an edge; what do I know? Selling me some story so you can get into the barn. Hear some of the guys talking. Whatever."

"I know." Bill raised a questioning eyebrow. "I keep a phone log at the office. Every call that comes in, whether it's business or not, my secretary writes it down. I check it when I come in every morning. I saw the entry: man called, wanting to know what Jack Merrick looked like. I figured it was you."

"You're not sore?"

"Why should I be? I coulda been a kook. You got a lot to lose."

"Thanks. Thought I'd confess up front."

Grabbing the horse, the trainer cautiously sprayed the compound over the wound stretching across the animal's muzzle. Going on clear, it disappeared almost immediately.

"Well, will you look at that! It vanished."

"Sunk in, I guess."

"How much do I use?"

"It was free. Try a lot."

He applied more, with the same effect. The horse didn't react.

"Doesn't seem to bother her. Some stuff the vet uses stings." He wrinkled his nose. "Smells, too."

"We're two-for-two. If it works, we've got a trifecta."

"If it works… well, never mind." Bill wiped his hands on his handkerchief. "How long does it take? Before we see results?"

"I forgot to ask. I think Mom said it started working in a few days." He backed away, suddenly nervous. "Call me, will ya? Tell me if anything's happened? Either way?"

"I will. And I'll keep an eye on that fellow you're following."

"Thanks."

"Small payback. And if it heals the sore, Irish Rover and I will be dancing a jig."

"That would be something to see." Jack took a step back, then turned. "What's her name, by the way? You never said."

"Barrister's Baby."

Jack put a hand on the gate to an empty stall separating the horse from those racing.

"You're kidding, right?"

"No. Why? Does it mean something to you?" Jack's expression conveyed the fact that it did. Two things, by-the-by: another "B. B." and Jacqueline Thorne Kerr, his goddaughter. He hoped they cancelled one another out. With a slight edge to Jackie.

And he had promised to buy her a pony. He wondered if a racing thoroughbred would serve just as well.

Without answering the question, he waved and trotted away.

"Mr. Kerr! What are you doing?" Geraldine gasped. Standing in the doorway of the lawyer's office, her eyes took in the ghastly sight with trepidation. "You shouldn't be doing that, sir." Taking a step back, she began to shake. "Maybe I ought to call Mrs. Kerr."

Glancing up from his task, Hugh frowned.

"Shouldn't be doing what?"

Although the answer should have been self-evident, she bravely stated the obvious.

"Dumping everything from your In-basket into that U.S. Postal bag."

He chuckled, stooping down to retrieve several letters that had fluttered away from the yawning mouth of the receptacle.

"Do you suppose Mrs. Kerr would be annoyed?"

"I think, sir, she would be shocked."

"Then, let's don't tell her. How would that be?"

"It's your mail, Mr. Kerr, but... I think it advisable she be informed."

"You'd rat on me?"

"No.... Maybe." Wringing her hands, she dared take a step inward, as though any closer proximity might put her in danger of catching his contagion.

Briefly scanning the envelopes he saved from the floor, Hugh clucked his tongue.

"I recognize the return addresses. Probably checks inside. Oh, well. Into the proverbial dust bin, as we say in Montreal."

Almost more horrified at his reference to Canada than the fact he was tossing away money, Geraldine's trembling increased to the level of ague.

"Are you ill? Shall I call a doctor?" As inspiration hit, she stiffened her back. "You've had a fight with Mrs. Kerr. She's accused you of... malingering. Letting your correspondence build up. So, rather than admit to her she's right, you're getting rid of it so you can tell her you're all caught up."

"You suppose my conscience would bother me that much? You may be right, at that." Tossing the letters he held in his hand back into his In-basket, Hugh pantomimed speaking on the telephone. "Hello, dear. Guess what? There were only two letters in the In-box. I assigned them to Geraldine and she promised to take care of them. See you soon. Bye."

Reacting as though he really were speaking to Ellen, the receptionist brought hands to her mouth, stiff posture swaying at the horror of his statement.

"Don't mention my name!"

"Why not?" he tried, widening his blue eyes in an exaggerated look of surprise. "Because I've implicated you for my crime?"

"Yes." He guessed right but for the wrong reason. "I know what you're really doing." He motioned her to continue as her eyes hardened at his duplicity. "You brought the last batch of mail home for Ellen to answer and she didn't appreciate it. Rather than face her wrath a second time – because you failed to hire a secretary and save her the trouble of working when she has a newborn to take care of – you stole a mail sack from downstairs. You're putting everything inside and when no one is looking, you're going to dump it back in the mail box. That way, it has to be taken to the post office, sorted and delivered all over again. That tactic, Mr. Kerr, won't save you forever, but it'll put it off for several days. Giving you an immediate reprieve."

His jaw slackened in astonishment.

"That, Miss Sterrett, is diabolical! Brilliant, in fact! I like it. You're a genius!"

Failing to be coerced by his flattery, she held her ground.

"It's illegal. No civilian is permitted to misuse postal property."

He waved away her objection.

"Now, you've embarrassed me. Instead of coming up with that scheme myself, I merely dropped in at the mail distribution center downstairs – as you suggested – to get a sack to stuff all this correspondence inside." His head drooped. "I didn't want you laughing at me, again, like you did the last time when I put it in the waste can to take home. I thought I'd be more clever, but you've out-clever-ed me. I'm impressed." He laughed out loud. "Wait until I tell Jack. And no, he can't hire you away from me."

"No chance of that, sir."

He brightened.

"Good girl. You're loyal."

"You pay better."

She might have added, "Much better," but didn't care to return the compliment.

"Oh. That, too."

"Take it out of that mail sack immediately. And don't bother using the trash can. I had to lie to the janitor about what happened to the last one." On his look, she added, "You neglected to return it. Since it belonged to the Conner Building, the loss is considered theft. I had to fill out a report before we were issued a new one."

"You didn't say what happened to the old one, did you?"

"No. But I was tempted."

"What prompted you to hold your tongue?"

He expected her to say, "Loyalty."

"My pay check. Petty theft isn't a crime worthy of a jail sentence – except when it involves Los Angeles' most irritating defense counselor. I'm certain the misdemeanor would be brought to the attention of the D.A. and Mr. Bond would be compelled to inform his wife. Mrs. Bond would tell him to throw the book at you and he would. I suspect by the time 'they' were through, you'd be sentenced to six months behind bars. I can't wait that long to get paid."

Crestfallen, he offered her a shrug.

"Don't you think I could plead 'no priors' and get off with a fine and restitution?"

"I wouldn't go there if I were you. Sir."

He took her point.

"I think I had better send you to school. You're due for an upgrade. Wouldn't you like to be a secretary?"

"You couldn't afford me," she deadpanned.

"I see. Was there something you wanted? Or, did you just come in here to read me the Riot Act?"

The sudden jar to her memory caused Geraldine to start.

"Oh, yes, sir. There's a call for you on line one. I wouldn't have put him on hold but he said he was a Father and I thought it might have something to do with Jacqueline."

He swallowed, Adam's apple sliding up and down.

"A father? You mean, someone else is claiming to be her father?"

She scowled at the impropriety of the suggestion.

"A Brother: as in priest."

"Oh. Brother Manolo?"

"Yes. That's it."

He sighed in relief.

"Thank you. I'll take it."

Pausing a second for his hand to steady from the unexpected, albeit misconstrued idea, Hugh picked up the reliever, assuming a cheerful tone.

"Como esta, Padre?"

"I am perfectly well, Mr. Kerr," Brother Manolo replied in perfect English. "I wanted to call and congratulate you on the birth of an heir."

The expression caught him off guard and for a moment his eyebrows pointed downward.

"We have welcomed a daughter into our home, *Father*."

"Ah: so we are to play word games together, *my son*. Pray, tell me her name."

"Jacqueline-Thorne-Kerr," he carefully pronounced.

More astute about his peculiarities than the lawyer gave him credit, the man of the robe, if not the cloth, chuckled.

"As I said, you have received a gift from God by the arrival of a girl child. An 'heir,' Mr. Kerr, is generally acknowledged to be an offspring who carries your name. Not only have you pronounced her a 'Kerr,' you have bestowed upon her the surname of your wife. Jacqueline Thorne Kerr. Therefore, I am only mistaken by not calling her a *double heir*."

Hugh heaved a sigh of relief before ruefully acknowledging the point.

"I might have known you, of all people, would understand. It's only that I've been so –" He hesitated, debating how to finish the sentence. His friend was only too glad to complete it.

"– put out, by well-wishers regretting the fact your first born was not a son. Alas, they overlook the fact modern civilization no longer requires males to put on their armor to defend the castle. However, should such regrettably become the case, you may remind them St. Joan proved herself braver and more adept at martial skills than her brothers-in-arms."

"I wish I had your silver tongue," he replied with sincerity. "I will remember that in future."

"Let no one diminish your joy, for your ability to see God's world as He would wish is not shared by all. Life is a learning experience."

"I'll accept two of your statements of wisdom, Father, and admit I'm... a bit shaky on the third."

"To doubt is the beginning of understanding."

"Now, you sound like Confucius."

"Sentient beings share like beliefs. Now: to the purpose of my call. When am I to see your beautiful baby?"

"As soon as you like. Ellen would love to show her off." Checking his watch, Hugh made a rapid calculation. "I'm just finishing my work here at the office. Would this afternoon be too soon?"

"Splendid! Your extended family looks forward to seeing you."

"More so, I fear, than her immediate family. Check that," he corrected. "More so than her family by blood."

He sensed, if not saw, the padre scowl.

"No bitterness at this period of your happiness. Shall I wag my finger at you and make you stand in the corner?"

"Worse, you may assign me your books to correct."

"It is agreed, then. And we may both rejoice in the grace of heaven."

"You, sir, are incorrigible."

"I have been told that."

"By men of higher station than me?"

"I was going to say 'lower,' but we will not discuss that now. Good-bye for the present."

"Good-bye. See you soon."

Dropping the handset onto the receiver, Hugh turned and grinned at Geraldine.

"Want to go with us to Brother Manolo's mission?"

"Across the border?"

"Yes. From the wealthy section of Los Angeles to the poorer."

Shifting her weight from one leg to the other, nervously clutching her hands, she softly inquired, "Is he going to baptize the baby? Take back what... we've done? I understand Mr. Merrick and I aren't really official godparents in the eyes of the Church –"

Crossing to her, Hugh wrapped his arms around the slim, frightened figure.

"You must never say that to me, again. Nor, do I want you to question your place in Jacqueline's life. You and Jack are as 'official' in the eyes of

God as any who have ever stood as guardians to a blessed child. And," he added in a slightly different tone, "if it will make you feel any better, Ellen has already 'baptized' her into the fellowship of the Almighty. The blessing was for my sake."

Straightening her shoulders, she jutted her chin.

"No, sir. The blessing was for God's sake."

Tightening his grip, he offered her an expression of puzzlement.

"Speak clearly."

"So He could get a snapshot of Jackie and her family gathered together. For His celestial scrapbook."

Before he could drop his arms, she felt them shake. As she left, she heard him laughing.

"I feel terrible, Hugh."

"How so?" Glancing over his shoulder, he stared at Ellen sitting beside him in the car. "Aren't you feeling well?"

"I haven't sent out birth announcements. I've had all this time and yet it seems the days have just flown by." Relieved, he returned his attention to driving. "How do you suppose he heard?"

"He read it in the paper. There was a very nice birth announcement in the Sunday supplement." He quoted from improvised memory. "World Famous attorney Hugh Kerr and his wife, the beautiful and artistically gifted Ellen Kerr *nee* Thorne, also known around town as Mr. Kerr's legal associate, welcomed the arrival of their first child, a bouncing baby girl on May 7, 1957. Weighing in at 7 pounds, 6 ounces, the baby elephant extended a humongous 21 and a half inches long. The proud parents have named her Jacqueline and she is expected to join the firm of Kerr & Kerr after graduation from Harvard Law School.

"Expressions of welcome and presents of bribery may be sent to the Conner Building, in care of the overworked and reputedly underpaid receptionist, Miss Geraldine Sterrett. While extending well-wishes for the new arrival, those seeking appointments may be reassured that Hugh Kerr, Esquire, and Miss Thorne will presently resume their professional occupations, as it well known they have a waiting list longer than 21½ inches. Bartholomew Bond, the district attorney, has let it be known he and his wife are taking an extended holiday in the Bahamas and do not plan on returning to our fair city until Mr. Kerr's caseload has been whittled down to misdemeanors and traffic tickets."

Grinning at his exaggeration, she lightly inquired, "Bahamas?"

"Did I remember it wrong?"

"The fact you remembered her birth weight and length is even more astonishing."

"I keep it with me." Reaching into his pocket, he withdrew a piece of paper and showed her. The pertinent data was clearly printed in his bold handwriting. She groaned.

"I see. And you referenced it before we left?"

"I wasn't expecting to be grilled in the car. I checked it in case Brother Manolo asked and you left it up to me to supply the pertinent details."

"It was, however, a very nice write-up. Did you clip it out for baby's scrapbook?"

"No. I left that for God to do."

Not failing to detect his sarcasm, Ellen let it go.

"Why is Geraldine underpaid?" she asked, instead, going back to his make-believe birth announcement.

"I asked if she wanted to be a secretary and she said I couldn't afford her."

"Wise woman."

"Do you want a raise?"

"If I do, I'll give myself one."

"Nice perk, if only you'd take advantage of it."

She cuddled the baby before re-tying the ribbon under Jackie's chin.

"Marrying the boss was the best perk I'll ever get."

"What about the baby?"

"She comes under the subheading, 'Marrying the Boss.'"

"Here we are. Oh, will you look at that?"

Across the doorway of the mission a large, hand-written banner proclaimed, "Welcome Jacqueline Thorne Kerr!"

"Our heir," he explained with a grin.

"Of course she is –. Oh." Suddenly getting the point, she brought the baby's hand to her lips and kissed it. "Brother Manolo must have said something that –"

"– pleased me," he finished before she could draw the opposite conclusion.

"I'm so glad." And then, as he cleared his throat into his hand, she added, "He also said there was a sink full of dirty dishes and seven months of his ledger that needed review: have your pick."

"He didn't mention dirty dishes, but I fear the other is true. If I do the ledger, what are you going to do?"

"Show off the baby, of course."

"And brag about all the hard work you did, carrying her for nine months, then giving birth –"

"Are you questioning my participation in our child's birth?"

"I did take a class," he gainfully tried.

"Try using that lame excuse on the mothers here and see how far it gets you." Snapping her fingers, Ellen waited until he parked in their reserved space in front of the mission, then shoved baby Kerr into his arms. "I'll audit the books while you give lessons in baby care – including how to change a dirty diaper – and the techniques of wiping vomit off your shoulder."

"Using Jackie as a model?" he gasped in horror.

"Hardly. Knowing Brother Manolo's open door policy, I'm sure there are any number of small children housed inside. Use them."

Rolling his eyes, Hugh began a quip.

"I think I hear my –" Catching himself, before it was too late, he turned away, hoping to deceive.

And failed.

"The full sentence of that lame excuse is, 'I think I hear my mother calling.' You are getting better at idiomatic phrases, but not so good at when to use them. Or, which ones to choose."

"Damn."

"That is not a phrase, it's a single word. And we do not cuss in front of Jacqueline."

"Yes, ma'am. I'm sorry, baby."

He was saved the bother of attempting an exit from the car by simultaneously manipulating Jackie and jabbing at the door handle as Brother Manolo bounded out, assessed the problem and opened it for him.

"Welcome, most honored guests!" Taking the baby from him, he kissed her forehead before making the sign of the cross over her. Then, fearing he had gone too far, his eyes sought those of Hugh. "You do not mind?"

"Ellen and I always welcome displays of love and faith, my friend. As I am learning, they come in all demonstrations and denominations."

"It is well, friend Hugh. You are now able to express in language what your heart has always told you." Scooting around the other side of the car, he graciously opened the door for Ellen while making her a happy bow. "Blessed be she who has taught others to see the light."

"As you so eloquently said, Brother, he saw the light: he just didn't know how to absorb it."

Kissing the baby a second time, he offered her to Ellen, who indicated he keep her. With a radiant smile, he led them inside the mission where he was immediately surrounded by those who dwelt within. Their cries of joy were enough to fill any parents' hearts.

Reluctant to share his bundle of joy, Brother Manolo found himself the victim of too many eager hands and soon Miss Jackie was grabbed away and fussed over by the women. In a moment, a throng of gifts appeared out of nowhere. Her bonnet was soon replaced by a knit cap, new socks sprouted on her feet, and half a dozen hand-crafted toys appeared in her arms. Shaking her head in awe, Ellen turned to Hugh.

"I'm not sure we're going to be able to find her amid all these lovely gifts."

"A doll among dolls," he agreed.

"And over here," Brother Manolo indicated, motioning the Kerrs toward a long card table more traditionally used for dining. "Presents for the parents, as well."

"They shouldn't have," Ellen protested, but as she saw the brightly woven blanket, infused with patterns of reds, yellows and blues, her eagerness overcame reluctance. "How beautiful!"

"For you, Señora," an elderly Mexican woman offered.

"I am so honored." Rapidly inspecting the other gifts on the table that included shawls, small silver jewelry and a number of ankle-length dresses, she cried, "This is too much!"

"Please," Brother Manolo interrupted. "You have done so much for us; my people are grateful. They wish to show their appreciation – and their happiness for your new joy. Accept the presents with the grace in which they are given."

"Hugh –"

But Hugh had found his own pile of presents and was hardly in the mood to refuse. Holding out one item in particular, he grinned in delight.

"A pipe!"

"A corncob pipe, Señor," a middle-aged man identified in heavily-accented English. "I made it, myself. The Brother has told us you like a pipe. Not so fine as what you are used to, but you will find it of use, perhaps?"

"I have never smoked a corncob pipe. Of course I will find it of use. You made it, yourself?"

"Sé, Señor. I was taught the trade many years ago. When I worked in Missouri: that is a state in your country." Hugh nodded agreement. "Very good people. I was very happy there. The factory was on the Missouri River. I was working one of the boats, but I was injured and put ashore at a place called Washington. Named for your very great President. You know it?"

"No. But I will." His eyes twinkled. "What is the official name of this pipe?"

The man responded with pride.

"It is called a Meerschaum."

"Excellent. And what is that meaning?"

"A corncob pipe."

"Let me explain. There are several meanings. 'Meerschaum' is a Turkish stone used in producing a high quality smoking pipe. In German, the word means 'sea foam,' because of its appearance." Turning the pipe over in his hands, he admired the quality workmanship.

"You have great knowledge, Señor Kerr."

"And so have you. I didn't know Meerschaum pipes were made in Missouri. So, we have both learned something. You crafted this here? Or, when you worked in Missouri?"

"Here. It is not as fine as those made in that great state, but I have tried my best. The cobs I find here are smaller, so the bowl is not as wide. They must be dried two years before a pipe can be made from them."

"Two years? Really? I'm impressed."

"It requires time for the cob to dry. Once they are cut to size, a clay – a plaster – is smeared on them, they are dried again and then the clay is sanded off. A hole is then bored for the tobacco and the stem."

Fitting the stem between his teeth, Hugh tested the draw before nodding in satisfaction.

"I wouldn't have thought it possible. But, how long does a corncob pipe last? A week? A month?"

The artist vigorously shook his head.

"Years, if you treat it with respect."

"I will do that. And let you know," he winked. "But, with such a skill, why did you leave Missouri?"

A sadness came over the man.

"I went back for my family. But… it is hard to return…. So many factors."

"Because you are an immigrant? I see. I may be able to help you."

Tears came to the man's eyes and he looked away in embarrassment. Hugh did the same, twitching his nose toward Brother Manolo. "Is that food I smell?"

"A feast has been prepared in honor of Señorita Jacqueline."

"I was hoping you'd say that. I'm starving. And we'll see her mother gets plenty to eat so she may feed the Baby of Honor." Bowls of steaming food were brought out from the kitchen and set on the other dining tables, along with utensils and drinking ware. Seeing the celebratory offerings, Hugh nudged Ellen with his elbow. "Sure you don't want to revert back to my original proposition? Dishes or ledger?"

"I believe you were right, at that. I'll do the ledger and you do the dishes."

His face fell.

"I expected you to choose the opposite."

"I know. Eat hearty, my man. You'll need your energy for the kitchen. And if you do a good job, I'll reward you by allowing you to change Jackie's diaper."

"That's a reward?"

"Most fathers apparently think so when they leave it for their wives."

Rounding his lips into an "O" shape, he sidled away. It was as much to say, "You win."

CHAPTER 8

Jack's intercom buzzed. Feet propped up on the desk, hands up, a rubber band suspended between two outstretched thumbs, he glanced at the annoyance, then ignored it. Aiming his missile at miniscule "X" inscribed on the door, he squinted one eye, took aim and let go. The projectile hit dead center.

"Hot dog!" he exclaimed in delight. "If I get any better at this, I'm heading for the World Championships."

While there were no international games in rubber band proficiency, just the thought of participating was enough to bring a smile to the private investigator's face. Slapping his hand on his thigh, he reached for the institutional-sized box of said articles within easy reach on the desk when the door was unceremoniously shoved in. Appraising the situation, Marie Sanchez did not bother informing her boss she had attempted to get his attention three times before invading his inner sanctum.

"There's a call for you on line one."

"I'm busy." As though suspecting she thought otherwise, he added, "I'm preparing for competition."

"I should think otherwise."

"Why?" He sounded hurt. "I've hit the bull's eye ten times in a row."

"Because rubber band shooting is generally considered the occupation of the five-to-ten-year-old set. They usually play it in school and spend the afternoon in the principal's office before being assigned to write, 'I will pay attention in class' five hundred times on the blackboard." He started to object, but she waved it away. "Furthermore, when grown men fill in their empty hours thus occupied, it cries to the paying customers that they have nothing what-so-ever to do."

"I don't."

"It never occurred to you I was attempting to get your attention to answer the phone because there was a man seeking your professional services?"

"No. Now, if it was a woman, I might be more interested."

"A hysterical man?"

He fitted another rubber band between his thumbs.

"Men don't get hysterical. Only women do."

Reaching over him, Marie took a rubber band from the box, fitted it in place and let it fly. She struck his groin with marksman's accuracy. His legs dropped like leaded weights and his hands went to the point of contact.

"What was that you said, Mr. Merrick? I didn't quite catch it. Your words were obscured by hysteria."

Face red, he gasped for air. Knowing perfectly well he was play-acting, she grinned at his performance. "I realize things have been a little slow around here since Mr. Kerr has taken his sabbatical, but there is a man on the phone and he did sound urgent."

"Urgent to spend money, or urgent for me to locate a lost dog?"

"I should think with your talents you ought to be able to combine the two. But, I'd hazard a guess his hysteria had something to do with money. Lots of it."

"Why didn't you say so in the first place?" Grabbing the handset, he brought it to his ear. Marie bent over and depressed the switch, opening the connection.

"Hello? This is Jack Merrick, president and chief of the —" He was apparently cut off by the man on the other end. "Oh, yeah, hi —" More conversation ensued. His eyes grew wide. "Jiminy Cricket! You don't say!" He looked at his watch although the action was superfluous. "No, I can't make it down there in ten minutes. Not even twenty —" His head bobbed. "All right; thirty. But I'll have to fly. You know traffic at this time of day." Slamming down the phone, he leapt to his feet. "Gotta go."

"There's a men's room down the hall."

He stared at her in blank incomprehension before grinning.

"Yeah, that, too, but no time. I have to get down to Santa Anita in thirty."

"Don't expect Lieutenant Wade to fix your ticket."

"Nah. He never does, the old skinflint. I'll give it to Hugh. He's a whiz in traffic court."

Grabbing his hat, he brushed past her.

"Put two dollars for me on whatever the horse is to win," she called after him.

"Oh, honey, this is worth a sawbuck. See ya."

She waved at his back, ruefully wondering how she was going to cover the loss of $10 from her weekly budget.

He did not make it to the racetrack in half an hour but seeing Bill Boerner's smiling face near the finish line, he matched the expression with one of his own.

"Good news?"

Putting a finger to his lips, the trainer enthusiastically nodded while motioning him over.

"She flew like the wind."

"You ran her? How? I thought –"

"The wound completely closed. Honest-to-God, it was like the skin healed while I was looking at it. Never saw anything like it." He shrugged to tone down his racing heart, then snapped his fingers. "Whammo! Three days. Gone. In another week, I bet the hair will be back. I know I shouldn't have, but I had to put the bridle on and test her. Come on."

Leading him toward the stables at a quick-step, the two men found Barrister's Baby out back, fresh from being washed down, coat still glistening with water molecules catching the early morning rays. Slowing his approach, Bill put a hand out for the horse to sniff, before taking her head.

"Take a look for yourself."

Stepping beside him, Jack whistled.

"If I didn't know any better, I'd say she never had a sore there."

"And this is after her run, don't forget. The wound isn't just closed on the surface, it's sealed all the way down."

"I told you, didn't I?"

"Yeah, but who can believe it? I mean, this filly has delicate skin. Once it breaks open, you've got a crater. No vet has been able to help her. The owner's put real dough into trying to save her, but no go. And some – excuse the expression – but, some private dick hanging around the track looking for a bum who fleeced a dame, comes up with a magic potion. It defies reality."

"Don't it, now? But," Jack seriously added, "I told you. It's not my spray. I have nothing to do with it. It belongs to the neighbor of my Mom. I just suggested you give it a try because it worked on a dog."

"Sure. Sure. Before I take this any further, I wanted you to see for yourself."

"OK, I see it. What do you do, next?"

Bill probed the horse's muzzle with his finger.

"She doesn't even bat an eye. That means it don't hurt. It's cured. But, before I go head-over-heels crazy, I have to give it time. Put her through her paces again and again. To make sure that after a number of strenuous workouts the skin doesn't break down. If it doesn't, then we're sitting on a powder keg."

"One that explodes on us?"

"One that explodes on the racing world. Do you know what this means?"

"Barrister's Baby makes a lot of moola on the track?"

"That's number one. But number two is even bigger. Come on: you're a bright boy."

"There are other thoroughbreds who have the same problem?"

"Not just racing horses; all horses. Riding horses; draft animals. Any type of horse that wears tack. It's a common problem. Most horses heal with rest, but some don't. The skin keeps breaking open. That means they're pretty much useless for anything. You can't even sell them. Not fairly. They're a total loss."

"Geez Louise."

"See what I mean? That spray of yours could make us a mint."

"Not us, pal. We don't own it."

"OK, we buy the formula. We don't have to tell this neighbor —"

Jack held up his hand for Bill to stop.

"Yeah. We do. For damn sure."

"OK, OK, I was going too fast. A partnership, then. But first," he added, tenderly rubbing behind the horse's ears, "I'm gonna buy B.B. She's gonna be our poster boy."

"You're not going to tell the owner about the spray?"

Bill withdrew into himself a moment before speaking.

"I got carried away and I apologize. Fair is fair. Yeah, I'm going to tell him. But, he won't believe me. I'll give him a chance and he doesn't take it I can buy the horse for next to nothing."

"Doesn't   the   owner   have   eyes?"

"Jack, he's been in the racing game all his life. So has his father and his grandfather. No one has ever cured a horse like this. He'll sell her because he can afford to move on. Men like him don't believe in pie-in-the-sky. They believe in stopwatches and bloodlines. When they pay vets who can't help them, they cut their losses and stake their hopes on another horse." He sighed and looked into the distance. "And if it happens he does believe me, we still have the spray and I find myself another horse."

Jack slowly shook his head.

"No. This has gotta work out. The stars are aligned. A horse nicknamed B.B., the baby of a barrister and a magic potion. It's symmetrical."

Catching the implication, Bill hitched an eyebrow.

"Who's the lawyer?"

"The father of my goddaughter."

"The 'dad' to go with your 'mom'?"

He shook his head to indicate someone else.

"My best friend."

"You have a shyster as a best friend?"

"Considering my 'dad' is a cop, anything can happen."

"You're right. The stars are aligned. When can I meet this neighbor of yours?"

"I don't know. I've never met her, myself."

Bill Boerner took a step back, started to say something, then made a motion with his hand and led Jack around the barn. When they were safely away from all prying ears, he stopped and stared at the detective.

"What gives with you, anyway?"

Having already determined the trainer's line of thought, Jack was ready for him.

"It's a dog-eat-dog world, right? You know that and I know that. So, you figured the first thing I'd do once you told me the spray worked was to meet the scientist and have my 'shyster' friend write up an exclusive contract, none too favorable to her. Then, I'd come back to you – or, maybe not," he added to underscore the fact he knew the terrain, "get myself a partner in the horse business and be off to the races. That right?"

"You nailed it. So, why didn't you? That is, if I believe you haven't already done that. Don't you like money? I told you: this could be big."

"I like money and I'm not a dope. So, sure, I thought along those lines. Who wouldn't? Early retirement; a beach house in Malibu. Fancy car with a flying lady on the hood. Beautiful women running their hands through my hair. A gourmet chef preparing me steak for breakfast every morning. The good life. Everyone dreams like that. It's OK to fantasize about but it's not for me."

Bill grunted and stooped down to pick up a food wrapper that was blowing across the grass. Crumpling it in his hand, he shoved it in his pocket.

"You're a fool."

"Why? I have a job that gives me a lot of satisfaction. Is it down and dirty? Can be. That's what I like best. I got no worries: no accountants fussing about the stock market going down; no tax man ringing my doorbell with a briefcase full of exemptions he's not gonna allow and threatening jail time. No indigestion from a third helping of coconut cream pie. No auto mechanic sending me a bill charging two-hundred smackos for fixing a dent in the fender of the Rolls." He finally grinned. "Paying a lawyer instead of getting paid by him."

"Sounds all right to me."

Jack turned back to stare at the race track.

"Does it? You wanna buy your own nag: That, I understand. Right now, Barrister's Baby means a whole lot to you. You're a horseman and she's the apple of your eye. Let's say you race her and she runs like the wind. You earn enough to prove you're at the top of your game. That's legit. But it goes beyond that. The spray sells like hotcakes. You make millions. You don't have time to train the horses you've stocked at the ol' Kentucky farm you purchased. You're too busy entertaining other new-wealth bluebloods. Or, traveling around the world. So, you get a telegram while you're in Paris – Barrister's Baby broke her leg. Oh, well. Put her down. You've got plenty of other fillies. Move on. Two new colts born in the spring. Real potential. One's temperamental, needs a cracker jack trainer. Not me, you say. I'm busy. I got money to look after. Someone else takes charge, the horse wins the Triple Crown. You stand in the winner's circle smiling like a chimp. And what have you done for it? You didn't train it; you've hardly ever seen it. Only recognize it from the painting you hired some equine artist to make after it won the Derby. How do you feel? Are you happy to be the dressmaker's dummy wearing the $500 suit, or do you wish you were the guy who nursed that horse through the colic and walked him around after a workout to make sure he cooled down all right?"

"Jesus, you're a talker."

"I have a lot of time to think when I'm hiding in the bushes waiting for some joker to slip out of his mistress' bungalow."

To break the sudden tension, Bill asked, "I thought they only do that in the movies"

"Movies imitate life, pal." He winked. "With a lot more romance thrown in to satisfy the paying public."

"You got a woman?"

"Dozens."

Giving credence to the idea which Boerner thought might be true in any case, Bill grinned.

"So, you're a private dick and I'm a trainer. We both got fantasies and we're better off where we are. But better would be good, too. When do we meet the neighbor?"

"I'll see if I can arrange it. I'll call you."

"You do that. Which reminds me: your boy has another pigeon. I saw him with her the other day. They were out at morning workout. He was waving his arm around like he owned the joint."

"He owns an ol' Kentucky farm, too."

"Does he drive a Rolls?"

"No. I imagine he told her he's going incognito." He chuckled. "That's another movie word."

Bill looked crestfallen.

"You mean, you boys don't really use it?"

"I doubt any of my 'operatives' even know what it means. We call it playing dress-up."

"I like the movies, better."

"And I'd rather collect at the two-dollar window on a hunch I got from my barber, than have a horse with a runny nose sneeze on me. And I bet you always say, 'gesundheit," he added.

"Never," his partner avowed, making them even.

"Be seeing you. I got work to do."

"Out saving the world?"

"One sucker at a time," Jack agreed.

Bill Boerner waved, whispering, "God bless," translating the Greek into American.

Jack hung around the track another hour. They were easy to spot. A man in a sport coat broadcasting a smug air of superiority to a wide-eyed woman wearing a spring coat and following him around as though he held the keys to the kingdom. Which, in her eyes, Jack determined, he probably did. Unfortunately for the "mark," the royal house was seeking to take, rather than give.

The woman was not his client and he had no right to interfere. His business was to shake $2,000 out of James Ewell. And then turn him over to the cops, if circumstances warranted. The latter being far more likely than the former.

Unless he could out-scheme the schemer.

That was what made being a "private dick" more fun than sunning himself on the beach at Malibu.

The ostensible business partners watched the last of the workouts, then Ewell guided her away, leaving Jack to conclude the woman had already been taken on the Grand Tour around the track and betting booths. It was now time for the operator's own "morning workout," where his golden tongue would practice alchemy. In this case, it wasn't lead he would turn into gold, but racing tickets.

Trailing them at a respectable distance, Jack wondered how much he had set her up for. Two-thousand like Dana Dwight? More? Less? Less would hardly make her worthwhile, yet if Ewell were short of cash he'd have to take what he could get.

"Five-hundred, rock bottom," he muttered as he slipped through the gate and made his way to the parking lot. That would be enough to stave off the bill collectors – bookies in Ewell's case, rather than landlords – and leave enough to put his scheme into operation. "Scheme" being a double-edged sword, where one side of the blade severed his personal ribbon, allowing him to cross the finish line a winner, while the other cut the connection between him and his marks.

Jack didn't have the slightest doubt in the world James Ewell actually did have a sure-fire-can't-miss plan. One he absolutely believed in. What he needed was enough capital to make it work. When he won – as assuredly he believed he would – he would conveniently forget about his partners and abscond with the purse.

"What I have here," he continued talking to himself as he slipped behind the wheel of an Agency car, "is two fools. Three, if you count Dana Dwight. Four, if you add me into the mix."

The last he announced for whatever ears were listening. He didn't consider himself a fool. Far from it, despite the fact his time on the case promised to far exceed the timeline he had given his client. It was all part of a greater scheme. One where he would play the hero, even if it cost him more than the effort was worth.

"We all wanta be like the guy in the movies," he chuckled. "The hard-hearted SOB who turns out to have a tender side after all. Even after he turns his back on his good deed and disappears into the sunset, he leaves everyone with the hope that maybe he'd look up, at some distant time, that dame he left daubing her eyes at the train station."

Wondering what Judy was up to and reminding himself to give her a jingle, he snapped on the turn-signal and followed the Chevy with the dent in the rear fender out of the parking lot. Passing the car on the freeway back to Los Angeles, he changed lanes, dropped behind so Ewell could pass, then fell in behind.

"Like taking candy from a baby."

The driver of the Chevy never once glanced in his rearview mirror, and when he pulled off, Jack was right behind him. Five minutes later, Ewell stopped at an apartment building and Miss Fool got out. Speaking through the open window, Jack presumed they were making an arrangement for Mr. Scheme to meet her later and collect the "investment." Noting the address for future reference, Jack drove past, turned at the next corner and picked Ewell up as he drove past. Hoping he'd lead him to his own pad, he was disappointed to see the man make a beeline to the coffee shop. Not yet ready to confront him, and having no immediate need to warn off Miss Fool, he make a left at the next stop sign and headed back to The Place.

Too many good deeds in one day made him nervous. He wasn't, after all, in the movies, and the ninety-minute time constraint didn't apply to him.

Nor, did he have a good heart. That's what Jack told himself, and he never lied.

"This is hardly what I'd call domestic bliss."

Looking up in annoyance, Ellen shot Hugh a look that would have withered an oak tree.

"What would you call it?"

Ruling out the word, "hell," for even he wasn't fool enough to state that assessment aloud, he tried a smile to mitigate his previous statement.

"Unpleasant."

"I don't know why you say that," she retorted, looking around the room. "Just because your baby is screaming her head off, your cat has knocked the coffeemaker off the counter, your bird has crapped on the carpet for the tenth time today and your fish are gasping for air because you haven't cleaned their bowl – and your wife looks like a train wreck – everything seems perfectly normal to me."

"Somehow, I seem to have walked into the wrong house."

"That's because you're used to coming home and finding everything in perfect order. An order, I have overseen. But, my dear, I'm afraid your life has irrevocably changed. I regret to inform you, but the introduction of a newborn into your domicile has taken my attention away from housekeeping. I no longer have time to keep an eye on Law Book, clean up after One-Eyed Jack, change the guppies' water, vacuum the floor, or make your lunch. Nor," she hastily added before he could offer, "do I have the slightest desire to go out to eat because I look a mess. Also, we have no babysitter for Jacqueline."

"Where's Mom?"

"I expect her back this evening."

"Good!" he exclaimed, flopping down on the couch.

Her eyes narrowed.

"You're supposed to be enjoying this."

Hands outstretched, palms upward, he piteously inquired, "How?"

"Because this, as you so sarcastically missed the point, is domestic bliss."

"I must have erred in the translation."

"Your English is perfectly fine. What you missed, is how life is going to be for the next twenty-one years. With only slight amendments along the way."

"Such as?"

"Teething. The joy of potty training. The first day of school when you have a court date and I threaten homicide if you aren't with me at the bus stop. Correcting homework on a topic you haven't studied for twenty years; trips to the emergency room when your daughter breaks her arm falling off a pony. Buying a new wardrobe and shoes every six months. Another blessed event and the cycle begins anew. Your wife in a bad mood because she's working full time for you and you're upset she doesn't have time to rub your feet because they're tired from sitting all day."

"I'm not sure we thought this proposition out thoroughly enough."

"Yes. You should have presented me with a legal brief, outlining all the drawbacks against the positives."

"So far, I haven't heard you enumerate any."

She was waiting for that.

"My mother wants us to come to San Francisco. She's invited my brothers. They want to see the baby."

"That was a positive?" She didn't bother answering. "We'll send pictures."

"You're the one who's always placating her. You handle it. That will give you something to do while I tidy up your domestic bliss."

"I thought you were getting along better with her."

"A passing phase."

"I have a headache."

"Take two aspirin and call me in the morning."

She moved quickly across the room.

"Where are you going?"

"To the hairdresser," she decided on the spur of the moment. "For my benefit, not yours. And kindly have a meal prepared by the time I get home. You know how to cook. You fed yourself for God-knows-how-many-years while I was waiting for you to propose."

"There is one upside to that." She arched an eyebrow. "If we had married sooner, we'd have had that much longer to enjoy hell."

That did it. Shoving the purple-faced baby into his arms, Ellen stormed into the bedroom, returned with her purse and marched to the door.

"I also expect you to have the coffeemaker up-righted, the rug cleaned and the baby changed. Don't forget the rubber pants this time. And put her in a new outfit. The one she's wearing needs to be washed. And socks," she added, going out the door. "The last pair you put on her were mismatched."

"That's because I folded the laundry in the dark. You're the one who wanted your own washer," he dared remind her.

"Did you ever think of turning on the light?"

"I did. The room was still dim."

"Then, put a higher watt bulb in the socket."

Averting his ear from the high-pitched wail, Hugh grimaced.

"What do you want me to do first?"

"Everything. I should think that would be clear. Have you put gas in my car?"

He rolled his eyes.

"I forgot."

"Then, I'm taking your car. I suppose that has gas?"

"Yes. But, you can put gas in your own car, you know. You did it for years."

"Hugh, there are certain lines no self-respecting *married* woman will ever cross. Putting gas in her own car, taking out the trash and mowing the lawn are three of them. You get a pass on the last two because we have no heavy barrels to roll to the curb and we don't have a lawn. I would think you could at least perform one chore without complaining. And with competency."

"I can do it for you, now," he hopefully offered.

"Too late. There's a bottle of breast milk in the refrigerator. Don't forget to warm it up before you feed her."

"You didn't mention that."

"Even neophytes know better than to give a baby a cold bottle."

"I meant, feeding her."

"I thought you took a class."

"I'm coming to regret my good intentions."

She laughed and made good her escape.

Sensing she had been left in control of the battlefield, Jackie immediately took charge. Clenching her fists, she kicked her feet, dropped her head back and howled. Startled by the onslaught, Baby Jack lifted his tail, pooped and fled the room. Law Book, equally disturbed, jumped down from Hugh's desk where she had been pursuing papers in order to determine their relative value before using them for a scratching post, while the unnamed guppies carried on as though everything was normal. It being supposed that in their group consciousness, their universe in a bowl, however untidy, was better than an ocean full of whales.

Finding his own world fraught with danger, Hugh clutched the baby and began walking.

"Hush, little one, hush. Daddy's here and everything is all right." The crying increased. He would have bet his last dollar on the impossibility of that happening. "Shhh, Jackie. Let's go to the window and see what's outside." Carefully maneuvering around furniture that had never before presented dangerous obstacles to be avoided, he managed to reach the picture window. The drapes were closed. He groaned. The baby wailed, possibly in disappointment. Lacking a free hand, he attempted to grasp the cord with his teeth and pull it down. Discovering the drapes had a life of their own and were determined to thwart him, and all too cognizant he risked losing his choppers, Hugh abandoned the effort as a lost cause.

More dubiously, he tried, "Let's sit in the rocker. You like that."

Listing forward, as the newborn had miraculously gained the equivalent weight of a wet elephant, dry ones, apparently tipping the scale at considerably less tonnage, he re-crossed the obstacle course, known before parenthood, as the living room, and reached his recliner. Positioning himself with his back to the seat, he attempted a slow retrograde movement. His knees buckled, dropping him like a tree. Jostling the baby, she grew incensed, making him glad she couldn't talk for what was spewing forth was surely of greater magnitude than any vulgar expression which readily came to mind.

Rocking might just have done the trick, but for the near fatal cramp that developed in the calf of his right leg. Feeling the Charlie-horse knot into the size of a grapefruit, Hugh groaned. Had he been alone he might have doubled over, but with Jackie in his lap he was prevented that action. Unable to sit, he gathered what waning strength remained to him and stood. The effort almost proved his undoing as it required an almost superhuman effort to regain his feet, prompting him to make an errant promise to visit the gym.

"Fatherhood has made me soft."

For a lawyer, such a confession was tantamount to treason and he bit his lip in annoyance.

"I need to get back on the track and run. That will toughen me up."

He thought he ought to go immediately. If only Ellen were home and the twisted muscle in his leg wasn't going to cripple him. Possibly for life.

Sniffing back the mucus that suddenly poured from his nose, he wondered if he wasn't becoming allergic to children. The idea bolstered his courage.

"Come on, sweetheart. You're breaking Daddy's eardrums. May we have a truce? Five minutes of silence and I buy you a –?" Buy her a what? He faltered. He could think of nothing a newborn needed. A steak and mushroom dinner was out of the question before her teeth came in. A trip to Hawaii? She was too young to appreciate its charms. A teddy bear? She had twenty of those oft-described but patently untrue, sweet-natured cuddle toys. Besides, he never had one as a child and saw no good reason his daughter should, either.

Children required discipline.

"Stop this crying, immediately!"

Jacqueline did not hold the same opinion. The decibels reached humungous levels. He feared for their Scottish crystal.

He felt the beginnings of a headache. An entire bottle of aspirin was not going to silence the throbbing.

"It's this house," he suddenly decided in a flash of inspiration. "She's bored. Who wouldn't be? We need to go out; see the sights. Where would you like to go?" A vision struck like lightning. "We'll go to the courthouse! Sit in on a trial. You'll like that. Listen to the testimony. I'll explain what's going on." A warmth spread over his body. "I'll whisper in your ear what the attorneys are doing wrong. Explain their tricks – what works and what doesn't. And why. You'll need to know that. And the witnesses – who's lying and who's telling the truth. Another important thing to learn. Well, not learn, exactly; divine. By their body language; the tone of their voice. Whether they look at the lawyer or stare away. How they hold their hands. Even by what they're wearing. And then, we can come home and practice." An evil sensation clutched his insides. "We'll put Mommy on the stand and make her the liar. I'll show you how to extract the truth. It'll be fun."

He was nearly over the top in excitement when bitter truth struck. Not only would he be barred from trial with an infant in his arms, he couldn't hold a baby and drive downtown at the same time. The objections were insurmountable.

The wailing continued, uninterrupted.

He required assistance. There was only one sensible thing to do. Carefully, but with great determination not to fail, Hugh extracted one arm from around the baby, whose weight now more closely approximated a ten-ton eight-wheeler, and used his free hand to dial the phone. When it was picked up on the third ring, he eagerly gasped, "Hello, Mom, I need you! Ellen's left me and the baby is purple."

The voice on the other end was decidedly masculine.

"If your wife's left you, buy her flowers and chocolate. If the kid ain't breathing, drop it upside down and swat its bee-hind."

When his heart resumed beating after what he supposed to be an episode of cardiac arrest, he muttered an expletive, more clearly apologized by articulating, "Wrong number" and hung up, having brightened one day while darkening his own.

"That – that – son of a –"

Unable to finish the sentence for fear of being reported by Her Highness, whom he suspected of complicity with the Queen Bee – a thought likely to get him horse-whipped if ever verbally expressed – Hugh decided the only way to face defeat was to instill into his mind the hope, "Tomorrow is another day," while secretly replaying the equally famous retort, "Frankly, my dear, I don't give a damn."

Briefly considering re-dialing the Wade house, he dismissed it as too risky, considering he was certain he had not misdialed. If true, what that portended was beyond even his ken, so he let it pass. He might call Jack, but it was a work day, meaning he would have to go through Marie Sanchez. Being a female, she would instantly read panic in his voice, put her own interpretation to it, and come up with what might be an even more disastrous conclusion. One, his image might never recover from. Geraldine was his best bet, but he dismissed her for like reasons.

In his limited circle of immediate family and friends, that left Dad Wade, Bartholomew and Christine Bond. The latter was a woman who had two children of her own. She could certainly help him. But the jury was out on whether she would. Uncertain how she ever got on one of his juries – even a hypothetical one – he retroactively dismissed her for cause.

That left Dad and B.B.

He dialed the police station.

"Lieutenant Wade," he stated, praying his voice didn't shake.

"He's out of the office. What is your problem and I'll try and assist you."

"My baby is torturing me."

He hadn't meant to say that. He hung up before the call could be traced.

Only B.B. Bond remained on his diminished list of possible saviors.

Helen Stacy answered the phone on the first ring.

"District Attorney Bartholomew Bond's office. How may I help you?"

"Helen, it's Hugh Kerr. Is he in?"

"Certainly, sir. One moment."

The transfer was immediate. He suspected Helen heard the baby screeching in the background.

"Hello, Hugh," came the pleasant voice on the other end. She had surely warned him and he was savoring his triumph. "What's up? How's vacation treating you? Nice and relaxing? Don't miss the fray, you say?" Hugh envisioned him smiling at the unintended rhyme. He decided he hated him.

"I need your expertise." "Help" sounded too weak.

"Where are you? At the fun house? Speak up, I can hardly hear you."

"The baby is crying and I don't know how to make her stop."

"What? Say again."

"The-baby-is-screaming-and-I-don't-know-how-to-make-her-shut-up."

"Where's Ellen?"

"If she was here I wouldn't be calling you."

"Babysitting, ugh? That's rough. Where did she go?"

What does it matter!?

"To the hairdresser," he answered because to lie would only prolong the cross-examination.

"Bet I'll be seeing you back in court sooner than expected."

I wouldn't touch that bet with a ten foot pole.

"What-do-I-do?"

He envisioned the D.A. counting off on his fingers.

"Change the diaper. That's always the first order of business. You don't have to do a good job; almost anything will do. If you can't get the pins in, hold it up with the rubber pants. But, after that, be careful! If that doesn't quiet her, put the baby over your shoulder and walk with her. Or, sit in a rocker. No luck? Did Ellen leave you a bottle? Try feeding her. Don't forget to heat it up, first. Not too hot," he added with the seriousness of one instructing the jury on sentencing. "And then burp her. That's critical. Put a towel over your shoulder first, because she'll spit up on your shirt. If none of that works, turn on the TV set. Put the volume on loud. That will at least partially block her out. Two minutes after her mother gets home she'll fall into a deep coma. At least you have that to look forward to. But Hugh, here's the critical piece of advice. Do you know the hairdresser she uses?"

"Yes," he gulped.

"Whatever you do, don't call there. Trust me on this. No matter how desperate you get, never admit defeat. It will be held against you for the rest of your life. Never give your wife an edge. That's a secret among men. Got it?"

"Got it," he sniffed in terror. "I never thought I'd be afraid of Ellen."

"You can throw everything you know about women and marriage out the window. Your first child changes everything. You're going to have to get to know her all over again."

"No one ever told me that."

"If we knew it beforehand, we'd all be childless."

"Will it ever work out?"

"If you're lucky. If not, we keep the divorce lawyers in business."

The contents in Hugh's stomach churned.

"You're still married." It was almost an accusation.

"I wasn't fool enough to take three months off after the first or the second was born."

"All right. I've tried everything but the bottle. I owe you a box of cigars."

"Make them Cuban this time."

Hanging up the phone, Hugh had the sinking feeling he had made a mistake. He did not clarify which one.

CHAPTER 9

"All right, Jackie. We're going into the kitchen. Daddy is going to make you some lunch." He had promised himself he would never speak "baby talk" to his children. It was demeaning. "Daddy" fell into that category. Listening to other people use such terms had always irritated him. If a child were going to learn proper speech, beginning with corrupted language was a poor way to start. Once ingrained, they would be passed on for generations. Even into the sanctity of the courtroom.

Your Honor, I have an itsy-bitsy objection to make.

What is it, Hughie?

This big, fat bouncy ball found at the scene of the boo-boo that the 'D' for dumb and 'A' for ass says is the murder toy has no grimy marks on it. Nor, is there any sticky red stuff on it. How can it be supposed to have inflicted a bad cutsy-wutsie on the dead guy's noggin without those stains that won't come out in the wash?

Half silliness, half advertising brainwashing, Hugh shuddered. He repeated his question in Latin. It had no effect on Jackie. He tried French. Same non-result with the sole exception being that her face got darker as rage replaced mere anger. The wailing was ratcheted up two notches. He remembered a joke Geraldine had once told him.

What does the purple grape say to the green grape?

For goodness sake, breathe!

In fairness, he had also translated that conversation, substituting "goodness" for "God," and "sake for "sakes." The rewording did not assuage him, either.

Using one aching arm to hold the perpetual crying machine and his opposite hand to open the ice box, he grabbed the baby bottle. Relief swelled his being until closer inspection revealed it had no nipple. His astonishment was so great he silently cursed, then rescinded the otherworldly threat and retraced his thought pattern.

The only logical interpretation could be that Jackie had already advanced from nipple to drinking from a glass.

"Pretty advanced," he announced. "I knew you would be."

Taking the bottle, he paused to admire it. The door closed on his hand. He did not have to look to know his wrist was already swelling to gigantic proportions. If it was broken, he would have to go to court wearing a cast. Since it was unlikely the judge would assess blame on an infant, he would draw the conclusion Ellen had beaten him. He errantly hoped the jury would look upon him, if not his client, with sympathy.

That meant he would have to dismiss all potential female jurors for cause.

Placing the bottle on the counter, he rummaged through the cabinet for an appropriate pot in which to boil water. Measuring them by eye, he astutely determined none were tall enough to cover the bottle. Annoyed and befuddled by the fact the Kerr household had no appropriate tools of the baby-trade, he selected the double boiler. Discarding the inside liner, he dropped the enormous pot into the sink, turned on the faucet labeled "H" and filled it to the brim. When completed five minutes later, he grabbed it by the handle, belatedly discovering it was too heavy to lift with only one crippled hand. The aborted effort caused very hot water to splash over the top and down onto his feet. Hopping in sudden pain, the unexpected movement had an entirely unanticipated result. Jackie stopped crying.

For a moment Hugh suspected her to be laughing at him.

He had almost decided the trade-off was worth it, when she threw back her head and resumed her tirade. Like any normal human discovering even a temporary reprieve, he repeated the action, hoping for like result. No luck. He hopped harder. She cried louder. Adding several swear words into the mix did not appreciatively better his situation.

Would you mind turning your face to me, Your Honor? Fatherhood has rendered me deaf and I'm compelled to try and read your lips.

There were no two ways about it. He would have to put the baby down in order to use both hands to lift up the double boiler and place it on the stove. Searching the kitchen for a likely place to deposit her, his choices were grim. The eat-in table was the obvious choice, but one good twist and she'd end up on the floor. The chairs were lower, making for a shorter trip but still too dangerous. He could bring her into the bedroom and deposit her into the cradle, but the journey seemed a long one and his strength was fading. It was then his eye caught the counter. Thankfully, there was a double sink. The sides were just high enough to hold her for the twenty seconds it would take to move the pot. Carefully cradling her head so it wouldn't strike the metal, he placed her inside, then stood back to admire his clever handiwork. Seeing his child in such an unlikely place suddenly struck him as immeasurably amusing and he started laughing. The more he laughed, the funnier it became until his sides hurt.

Failing to diagnosis the symptoms of hysteria, he was still chuckling as he managed to lift the pot from the opposing sink and set it on the burner. Disregarding the water which splashed on the stove from the clumsy effort, he turned the knob. In spite of the clicking, the gas failed to ignite. It was only after detecting the ring around the burner filled with water that he realized he had soaked the gas jet. Shoving the pot to the adjacent burner, he sloshed more water onto the floor. He decided the mess was inconsequential as it needed cleaning, anyway.

"Now," he declared aloud in his best courtroom voice, "we wait for it to boil."

A watched pot never boils.

He should have learned that in grade school.

Twenty minutes later without seeing the faintest bubble that would indicate the water was coming to a boil, he gave up and placed the bottle inside. Water, that he would have sworn on a stack of Bibles was, in actually, well past the boiling stage, swirled over his fingers. Worse, the bottle tipped sideways. Miserably shaking his scalded fingers, he searched the junk drawer, came up with an oversized clamp used for extracting corn from searing water, and used it to straighten the bottle. The test worked until he withdrew the instrument, after which it listed to the other side. Thereafter, he held it in place, enduring the deadly steam that barreled up over his exposed flesh.

Jackie encouraged him by continuing to cry.

"Three minutes," he promised her.

Unfortunately for Hugh, the clock on the kitchen wall was malfunctioning. The second hand moved too slowly and the minute hand refused to move at all. He damned modern conveniences.

Timing the three minutes in his head, he lost count somewhere between seven and nine and removed the bottle. Grasping it in his eagerness, he found it had reached the temperature of molten lead. Nearly, but thank *God* not dropping it, he juggled the "hot potato" in his hand before smothering it in a dish rag. Certain it would leave scorch marks, he mentally assigned the poor rag to the dust bin before uncovering the bottle and blowing on it. That action, he ruefully determined, would be effective sometime in the lifetime of his grandchildren. If Jackie did not starve to death before reaching the happy state of motherhood.

With tears in his eyes that had nothing to do with the blessed event of becoming a grandfather, Hugh brought his orbs back to the infant in the sink. Infinitesimally tiny, squirmy and purple, he came to the unhappy conclusion there really should be a nipple to go on the contraption he had just heated. With attention divided between the baby and the baby bottle, he groped through the junk drawer, hoping lightning would strike twice. It did not. No nipple.

"Where the devil does Ellen keep those things?" he demanded of the walls. The obvious answer made him blush. "Yes. I know. On her breasts. Thank you. Why hasn't she left out the fake ones?"

That sounded obscene and his blush deepened.

Abandoning the junk drawer as hopeless, being overfilled with Items of No Obvious Purpose, several variety of corkscrew depending on the difficulty of extracting a cork, can openers, most of which had broad, colored advertisements printed across the flat of the metal, courtesy of Jack, a cheese grater, garlic press, any number of mismatched measuring spoons broken from once deluxe sets, match books, a nail file he had once tried using to smooth the edge of a glass, thus ruining both; assorted safety pins, most of which he had stuck his finger on while rummaging for something else, several variety of Canadian coins he had shoved there out of the way so he wouldn't roll them with his *American* change, and rubber bands that had rigor-mortised into brittle, useless dust collectors.

There were no nipples.

And then inspiration struck. Not exactly like lightning but close enough to be useful. They had received twenty or thirty boxes of packaged nipples from many of Ellen's friends. He would open one of them. Problem solved.

Abandoning Jackie with the admonition to "Stay put, I'll be right back," Hugh crossed into the formal dining room where they had stacked the gifts, either those which were duplicates, too large or too small, bulky or as of yet unopened, and began a search. Highly annoyed Ellen had not thought to prepare an inventory of what might have been called the "Kerr Baby Department Store," grouping like items together in order of necessity, he had almost reached the startling conclusion they had not received nearly enough nipples to last a mere several months into Jackie's life, and severely chastising Ellen's friends for their oversight, when he finally spotted that which he sought.

Gasping in delight, he grabbed the small cardboard box with the cellophane window and returned to the kitchen. Popping up the flaps, he removed one of the soft, pliable nipples from a nesting stack of six. Never having actually handled one up front and personal, Hugh paused to study the item. Marveling at the shape which did not appear to have any sort of opening, he squished it with his fingers. A small hole opened at the tip.

"Well, I'll be."

The Canadian version of, "Will wonders never cease?"

Or some other likely translation.

Saved the effort of cutting a slice in the tip with a scissors or the edge of a blade, he smiled in satisfaction.

"Lunch, coming right up."

Finding the bottle still too hot to touch, he wrapped a potholder around the side and placed the nipple atop the opening. Not aligning it quite correct, the nipple toppled off. He frowned and replaced it.

"OK, baby. Dinner is served."

Since it would have been unfair to describe Baby Kerr as being dubious, that being a grade above her present level of education, he dismissed the wide-open blue eyes and brought the bottle forth for critical analysis.

"See what Daddy has here."

Ignoring the fact his own vocabulary had deteriorated, Hugh used one hand to life Jackie's head up and the other to bring the nipple into easy reach. Before the famished, possibly starving infant had a chance to sip the life-sustaining mother's milk, the nipple fell off. A stream of lava-like liquid spilled over his hand.

"Son of a –!" And then, louder, "Hell's bells!"

The first covered the accident; the second the excruciating pain he felt radiating throughout his manly body.

"How the devil is this thing supposed to stay on?"

Clearly, he was missing a step. Wrapping his throbbing fingers around the flat base of the nipple, he pressed it tight and repeated the effort. Scalding liquid dribbled down the sides of the bottle.

Blowing on his fingers rather than the bottle to cool them, and finding scant release, he jammed them into his mouth in an effort to assuage the pain. Anticipating a hot, yet pleasing flavor, the moment his taste buds registered the distinctive taste of mother's milk his stomach rebelled and he spit it out, covering the baby with a shower of saliva.

"It's gone off!" Having no better definition than, "sour," he shuffled to the sink and poured the contents down the drain. Having rid the world of that very-nearly poisonous substance, he hesitated before opening the ice box and removing a second bottle. Proving the axiom, being forewarned was to be forearmed, he sniffed the contents. It did not smell any better than the first, and followed its fate.

Grimly satisfied he had averted a disaster and an immediate trip by taxi to the pediatrician, his self-congratulations were short-lived. The milk had been bad, but that left him with nothing to feed the baby. Sidling back to the sink, he woefully shook his head.

"How long can you survive without eating?"

Had she answered him in ancient Greek he would not have been surprised. The fact she did not answer him at all proved more troubling.

"When I ask a witness a question, I expect to have it answered, Miss Kerr." His courtroom speech failed to elicit an explanation. Clearly, she required more training. He would repeat it, more forcefully. "When I ask a witness a question, I expect to have it answered, Miss Kerr."

That proved the charm. Taking in a deep breath, the better to be heard, she screamed.

Proving, to his well-attuned ear, he was dealing with a hostile witness. Unfortunately, there was no judge to order, "Quite in the court," much less call for decorum.

"Life," he ruefully announced, "should be more like a courtroom."

The wailing continued, unabated.

Abandoning the prospect of feeding her as hopeless, Hugh reached for her, realized his fingers were sticky and turned on the tap of the twin sink. Running his hands under cold water to wash away what was possibly more deadly than puffer fish poison, he air-dried them with a less-than vigorous shake for fear of contaminating the dish towel, then redirected his attention to the Noise Box.

"This will not do, young lady."

Awkwardly extracting her from the sink, no easy task as she had swelled to over-fit the container, he tenderly brushed down her displaced strands of baby hair, then draped her over his shoulder. She promptly burped and spit up over his shirt.

"What are you doing that for? I haven't even fed you!"

The thought elicited the idea she might have been over-fed, thus explaining her crying. Ellen was a new mother, after all. She might have gotten carried away. Which broached an even more dreadful scenario. If the milk in the bottles was off, what might she be carrying around in her breasts? Was there an expiration date on that? Use it or lose it? Without bothering to look, Hugh knew there was absolutely nothing in the weighty tomes of his law library to address that question.

Death by mother's milk.

If ever called upon to defend a client on such a charge, he would be ready.

Or not, since he had no solution.

His afternoon was turning sour-er by the minute.

Not only had he failed to coerce his own child from screaming like a banshee, he had lost a figurative court case.

It was problematic which scenario tipped Themis' scales the lowest.

"This is my mom, Mrs. Henry Wade," Jack introduced, indicating the older of the two women to Bill Boerner.

"Pleased to meet you."

The trainer had been introduced to many blue-blooded women in his career and knew better than to offer his hand. The help, no matter how vital to the success of the endeavor, was never on an equal footing with the monied and the gentry.

"And this is Mrs. Amy Pazel. Our scientist."

Amy, on the other hand, with a vivacious aura about her head augmenting her bright blue-green-hazel eyes, shoulder-length straight brown hair and well-built frame, assumed the initiative, holding out her hand.

"How do you do, Mr. Boerner?"

Meeting her half way, he was surprised to feel the powerful grip and responded in kind.

"Honored," he mumbled, feeling strangely intimidated. A cop's wife was fearful enough, but a woman scientist another, entirely. "I've never met a –"

He faltered and she filled in the blank.

"I know. Everyone thinks researchers are men with thick glasses and wild hair. Even my staff was skeptical at first. They assumed I'd be assigned bench work: which means testing the Big Boy's formulas rather than creating them. And, in fact, one of my first jobs at the laboratory was to study the durability of fingernail polish."

Nearly as frightened as Bill, although he had met Amy earlier in the day and succumbed to her instantly likeable personality, Jack blurted, "Yeah. Who cares about that?"

"Women who spend their hard-earned money," she explained, a grin forming at the corners of her mouth. "No one wants to pay fifty cents for a bottle of red polish, only to have it fade or chip off the next day. You may not realize it, but there are numerous factors involved. Some colors retain their original tint longer than others. The viscosity of a polish also determines how long it takes to dry. Those that are too thick take longer." By way of example, she waved her hands in the air. "The average woman doesn't have time to sit around shaking her fingers or blowing on them."

Jack stared at his hands while Bill nibbled at a hangnail.

"More to the point of the formulator," she continued, amused by their reaction, "the chemicals used in the product have to be taken into consideration. How they penetrate the keratin – the fingernail," she clarified. "Some chemicals may work beautifully in the lab but when tested on women, we may find they are too harsh and are irritating or actually dangerous. That's far worse."

"I can see that," Jack agreed in wonder, appraising his unvarnished nails with new appreciation.

"Naturally, the company wouldn't ask a man to field test the nail polish so it fell to me. To expedite matters, I wore ten different colors and consistencies: one for every finger."

"And you wondered why so many people were staring oddly at you," Mary deduced, delighted by the explanation.

"It never occurred to me. It took my secretary to point out my... fashion mistake. She thought, perhaps, I was colorblind."

"And you explained –"

"I did not. While I appreciated her courage in speaking out, I rather liked the idea of being thought of as peculiar. I am," she decided. "I kept that reputation the entire time I worked at that company."

"Did people keep their distance?"

"Only until they had a formula that needed tweaking. Or, required the creation of a new one. Then, they came knocking at my door."

"Who ever thought nail polish had a formula," Jack mused.

"Yes," Amy agreed. "It just appears on the department shelves by magic."

"You create formulas," Bill repeated in awe.

"The entire line of 'Beauty-Plus' cosmetics is mine. As well as numerous others, but you know those products, Mary?"

"I use them every day. They're wonderful."

"Thank you. I have seventeen patents in my name. Of course, that doesn't mean I own the formulas I design. By law, the company has to give me credit for the formulations, but they actually own them, as well as the products created by them."

"That doesn't seem fair."

"I wouldn't disagree but that's the stipulation every scientist enters into before they go to work for a cosmetics company. I'm... well paid for my work. That's the compensation I receive." Looking aside, she added, "Not as much as the male scientists and I'm not nearly as likely to be promoted, but those are the rules of the game. You either work by them or you don't work."

"Judy says the same thing about actresses," Jack readily supplied. "Judy Viele: my girlfriend. She works at all the major studios. Not as an actress," he hastened to explain, "although she could be. She's a... jack-of-all-trades.

Indispensable. But, you never see her name in the credits. And, I suppose her paycheck is half what the other fellows make."

They paused in their walk around the outside of the race track as Bill curiously inquired, "It seems a long leap from cosmetics to healing creams, Mrs. Pazel."

"Amy, please. Not really. Just as I mentioned with the nail polish: a major component of my work is to ensure the products cause no harm to the body. Many of the chemicals we use are harsh, requiring them to be titrated or mixed with others – or, in many cases, abandoned altogether – to ensure safety. That has to be the first concern."

"Really?"

Catching his drift, Amy nodded.

"It is with me. And to the company, if it practices sound principals." She winked at Mary. "If it wants to avoid lawsuits. No one wants to keep lawyers like your son, Mr. Kerr, in business."

"I do," Jack blurted before realizing his mistake. "That is, I mean, in business with cases other than those brought against you."

"I've never had any charges brought against me," she grinned. "And I expect never to. If I think a formula isn't safe, you can be sure I'll let everyone know." Turning back to Bill, she continued. "I'm an expert in dermatology; skin. Preserving it and taking care of it." Stopping by the railing, she leaned over it and studied the sweeping view of track, grasses and horses. "In the early days of facial make-up, either in society or the theatre, people used egg whites to make their complexion appear stark white, which was the fashion of the times. By itself, whipped egg whites don't hold together and you didn't want it to start dripping, making you appear like an undercooked meringue. Formulators tried various chemicals to stabilize the compound and came up with arsenic. They didn't realize the long-tern effects, but with repeated use the arsenic eventually ate through the skin. That caused horrific, long-term damage which no one knew how to treat, much less repair. Part of my studies has to do with precisely that. So, when Mary came to me with Irish Rover's problem, I developed a formula that would help." Turning back, she met Bill's inquisitive eyes. "Not just cure the wound – but to repair the skin. If I understand your problem correctly, that's what worked for your horse."

"Like magic," he agreed. "Better than having nail polish appear on store shelves out of thin air. Would you like to see my filly?"

"Very much."

He pointed across her right shoulder."

"Look over there. I've got her out this morning."

As Amy turned to take in the grand spectacle of an early morning workout, Bill gave a signal and the rider moved Barrister's Baby into place, gave the filly a moment to settle down, then like the flash of a camera bulb they were off. The horse, eager to be put through her paces, flew around the track, stretching out her neck at the end of the circuit as though to win by a photo finish. Greatly impressed, Jack bounced on his toes.

"That was some ride." Seeing Bill's empty hand, he went from asking the time to inquiring, "Why weren't you timing her?"

"My eyes tell me she's fast. But, that's not my immediate concern. She could be a Triple Crown contender and I wouldn't have had out my watch. Right now, her value to me is as a test case: whether or not the spray actually heals, and if so, does it have lasting power? In other words, is it a cure or a quick fix?"

"Oh. Got it. Sure," Jack agreed.

"We'll let Barrister's Baby cool down and then take her off the track. Would you mind inspecting her after that, Miss – Amy?"

"I'd love to."

They went for a cup of coffee and after they had settled in around a small round table away from others, Bill leaned forward, chin resting on one hand.

"What I've already seen is enough to convince me you're onto something big. Nothing the equine specialists have tried worked nearly so well – or so fast." He shrugged. "Some didn't work at all, but it didn't stop the vet from charging the owner an arm and a leg. So, I won't disguise my interest. If your medicine has staying power, it's a gold mine to the industry. So, you see," he continued, glancing at Jack, "I'm putting my cards on the table. I'm not trying to schmooze you."

"I appreciate that."

"You've got the brains and I've got the contacts. That's a partnership, as I see it. How do you see it?" When she hesitated, he added, "Jack brought us together. I'm willing to cut him in for a share of our enterprise."

"Oh, no," Jack demurred, holding up his hands and pulling back. "I like money as well as the next guy, but I fell into this by accident. I hate to be called a good Samaritan, but whatever success this venture makes is between you two."

"We'll settle, don't worry. So, then we have the big question. One I wouldn't even know to ask if you hadn't brought it up. The patent. You said whatever you develop belongs to your employer. Does that mean you don't own the formula" And, we'd have to dicker with some big organization that'd cancel us out of the deal in a flash if they knew the potential of what you'd   created?"

"I've thought about that," she readily conceded. "The formula has been patented: in my name, but as I told you, it belonging to Mega Enterprises."

"Can we buy it from them? Or, will they hold on because it's a gold mine?"

"The spray is actually of no value to them. It doesn't fit into their product lines and I doubt very much they'd ever consider bringing a treatment such as I've developed to market. I don't know whether they'd sell it, but I have a better idea."

"Tell us," Mary encouraged, greatly excited by the prospect.

"I originally developed the treatment, as you call it, as an aerosol spray."

"What's that?"

She turned to Jack.

"You must know." He started to shake his head, prompting her to speak over his denial. "Simply stated, the idea is to propel an aerosol mist – a spray – from a container by use of a propellant under pressure. The idea has actually been around since the 1790s. One of the earliest suggested benefits was to use the pressure to mix ingredients as a simple and effective way to make whipped cream."

Her listeners reacted in surprise.

"I like that idea," Mary announced. "What happened to it?"

"The idea was eventually abandoned, but you'll see it again because it's commercially viable. More work was done on the concept and in 1941 two Americans – Lyle Goodhue and William Sullivan, of the United States Bureau of Entomology and Plant Quarantine – created a product familiarly called by a name you might recognize, Jack: a bug bomb."

Slapping his hand on the table with such enthusiasm, coffee spilled from their cups. No one noticed.

"Oh, Jeez, you're right! They were issued to GIs in the Big One. Small cans of stuff we sprayed in tents to kill the malaria mosquitoes!"

"Exactly right. So, you understand how it works."

"Yeah. You press the button on top and spray comes out. It was neat. And effective. We used to 'shoot' it at one another."

"Yes, Jack, we get the picture. Like small boys playing with a new toy," Mary elucidated for the rest.

"It's a little more complex than you suggest," Amy grinned, "but you have the idea. When Mary asked me for help with Rover, I re-formulated my work so it was dispensed as a spray. The propellant in this case being nothing more complex than a hand pump."

"Why?"

"Contents expelled by pressurized gas make noise. It may not frighten us, but to an animal it's terrifying. I didn't want to do more harm than good. If Rover came to dread the application, he might suffer from anxiety and become so nervous or downright violent it would be a disaster for everyone involved. But the gentle spray from a pump isn't frightening."

"Wow, you think of everything," Jack gushed. "You shoulda been a people doctor."

"I'm not a doctor, at all. I'm a researcher. I love to work at my bench in the lab. It's an entire field of mystery and suspense for me. Mixing chemicals; finding out what works and what doesn't. Solving complex problems. Developing longer shelf-lives; testing various viscosities; mixing techniques. A better night cream. A cure for skin problems."

Bill leaned forward, eyes sparkling.

"You're spot on about the noise. And as a trainer, I can tell you I appreciate the consideration. There's no way you're gonna get an 'aerosol' spray on a spooked horse. But, how does this help us get around the patent?"

"I'll re-formulate it again. There's nothing illegal about that. It's done all the time. You have to understand: patents are very specific. They cover exactly what is presented and nothing else. I'll alter the ratio of some chemicals and change the medium to a cream. But, of course," she hesitated, "to patent it in my name I'd have to leave Mega Enterprises."

"Give up your job, you mean?"

"Yes."

"That's a problem."

"It's how I earn my living."

"Bummer," Jack agreed.

"Then, how can you be using it, now?"

"Because I'm not selling it. I'm giving it away for free. On a very small scale. I don't think Mary is going to report me to the head boss at Mega. Nor you, either, Mr. Boerner. I helped a dog and now a horse. I suppose you could say I'm doing field testing. That's part of my job as a research scientist. You can't market a product without proven statistics."

"What kind of statistics would we need?"

"If we were using it on humans, there's no way we could bring it to market for years because the government would have to approve it and that's a complicated process. But the regulations concerning non-humans – animals – are much looser."

"You mean, with animals, the proof is in the pudding."

"You could put it that way."

"All right," Bill sighed. "Now, we know where we stand. It doesn't have to be insurmountable. Let's go see B. B. If the filly's come through the workout without new sores, we'll put our heads together and see what we come up with."

"B.B.?" Mary cried in dismay. "Why are we going to see him?"

"Not him, as in Bartholomew Bond," Jack chuckled. "He's the district attorney," he explained to the uninitiated. "'B.B.' as in Barrister's Baby."

"Oh, what a relief. You had me going there for a minute."

On that happy interlude the four got up and went to see the providentially nicknamed horse.

CHAPTER 10

Standing in the open doorway, Ellen stared into the living room. Hugh was lying on the couch, presenting a picture of woe. Having kicked off his shoes, his stockinged feet were propped on the armrest nearest her, while his shoes were nowhere to be seen. His white shirt bore witness to dueling stains: those under his armpits and that on his shoulder. A wet washcloth was placed over his eyes. One arm draped listlessly to the rug. The other lay across his stomach as though attempting and failing to hold in a ruptured appendix. Had a photographer from *National Geographic* been there to snap his picture, it might have been used to illustrate an article about the aftermath of battle.

Unfortunately for the combatant, his superior officer had no sympathy.

"Why does Mr. Forsch have my baby?" she demanded in a shrill tone meant to awaken the dead.

Hugh groaned, twitched, then finally stirred. The towel slipped from his head to the floor as his feet reluctantly left their not-so-final resting place for the carpet.

"Oh, God. Have I had a day."

His piety, however sincerely uttered, went unappreciated.

"When I drove up just now, Mr. Forsch came out to take the car. Imagine my surprise to see him holding Jacqueline."

Opening one eye, Hugh whispered, "Had she stopped crying?"

"You cannot answer a question with a question, Mr. Kerr. Get up off your derriere and give me some answers."

Reluctantly opening the other eye, he beheld the image of Aphrodite. His heart skipped a beat, proving it was still functioning.

"My God, you look stunning."

Evoking the name of the Lord a second time failed to elicit the proper response.

"What is the matter with you?"

Confused by the response to his compliment, Hugh wearily brought himself into a sitting position.

"My God, I have a headache."

"If you say that one more time, I'm going to throttle you." His bleary eyes tried to focus. "Have you been drinking?"

"No. Yes." Confusion made it hard to articulate. "I mean, not alcohol. Never. Not when I'm in charge of the baby."

"You are not 'in charge' of the baby. Forsch is."

"Oh. I remember, now. He came up to help me."

"Help you what?"

"She wouldn't stop crying. I was losing my mind."

"You're in danger of losing more than that."

The threat went over his head.

"The milk in the ice box was bad."

"No it wasn't." Stepping into the room, Ellen slammed the door behind her. Making a piteous mewing sound, Hugh paused to put his hands over his ears. It did not block out her follow-up. "I just put it in there this morning."

"Trust me. It was sour."

It was her turn to see stars.

"How-would-you-know?"

"I tasted it."

She could barely articulate her one-word response.

"Why?"

"Because I spilled some on my hand and licked it off. It didn't taste right."

"What were you expecting? To taste like it came out of a bottle of Borden's milk?"

"Yes."

"I-am-not-Elsie-the-cow."

"No one ever told me that."

The insult went over one head but not the other.

"Get up. Go in and take a shower. Then I want you dressed and out of here."

"Where am I going?"

"Back to work."

"Today? Now?"

"This instant."

"But, I thought I was taking three months off."

"Consider it a failed experiment." Had she not been so angry, she would have cried. "You disappoint me beyond words, Hugh."

Suddenly realizing the dire predicament in which he found himself floundering, his mind cleared and his eyes resumed their normal blue.

"Ellen, I'm so sorry. I tried. I really did. Call me anything you want: a jackass, a blithering idiot, a no-good, useless father; a failure, but please don't say you're disappointed in me. That hurts more than anything." Rising on unsteady legs, he approached his wife, stopping short of spitting distance. "I thought I had all the answers. All right, I confess. I was smug. Taking care of a baby seemed so… easy. I was in grave error. She scored a knockdown within thirty seconds of your leaving. Nothing I did appeased her. And," he added, vainly attempting to save face, "when I tried to feed her, it took me at least an hour to find a nipple for the bottle." His lower lip protruded. "And when I did, the damned thing wouldn't stay on."

Realizing she shouldn't give him any latitude by answering, Ellen gave in to her curiosity by asking, "What do you mean, it wouldn't stay on? Of course it does."

Wobbling into the kitchen, briefly casting a glance over his shoulder to make sure she was following, he indicated the bottle and the nipple. Picking up the instruments of torture, he placed the nipple over the top then used his thumb and pointer finger to knock it off.

"Where is the rest of it?"

"The rest of what?"

Striding to the counter, she grabbed the box he had opened, removed the remaining nipples, then poured the rest of the contents onto the counter.

"These."

Deftly pushing the nipple through the screw-top holder, she affixed it to the bottle then copied his gesture by hitting it with her fingers. It remained in place.

"Safe. Secure. In proper alignment."

"I didn't see them."

"Were you looking?"

"No."

"Could that be why you didn't see them?"

"Yes."

Opening the cabinet, she pointed to a well-arranged set of baby bottles, nipples, screw tops, bibs, and whatnots.

"Why didn't you use some of these? There was no need to open a new box."

"I looked there. I didn't see them."

"You didn't look."

"Yes. I did. They weren't there. I swear."

"I'm the only one in this family entitled to swear." He nodded. She was not pacified. "You do live here, don't you? They did have cabinets in Canada when you were growing up? You have seen me open one, take out what I needed and prepare a bottle, haven't you?" His mouth went dry. "You do possess a modicum of intelligence, don't you? Why didn't you use it?"

"I called for help," he whined.

That was nearly the last straw.

"Who did you call? The fire department?"

"Mom. Some man answered the phone."

"Would that have been Dad?"

Even in his disoriented state he recognized sarcasm when he heard it.

"No. It was a voice I didn't recognize. He told me to hold the baby upside-down and swat it."

Ellen's face went from red to white.

"You didn't, did you?"

"No. I hung up. I tried Dad next, but he was out."

"Why didn't you call me? You have the number to the hairdresser."

"B.B. told me not to."

Her already pale complexion blanched.

"What the hell has he got to do with it?"

"I called him next."

"I rescind my supposition you possess a modicum of intelligence."

"I thought... being a father himself, he'd know how to make Jackie stop crying."

"What did he say?"

"Whatever I do, don't call Ellen."

"Why-not?"

He faltered.

"I don't remember, now. Some... man thing."

"I'm going to kill you."

"I wish you would."

Her shoulders sagged. It was either that or throttle him. And that would ruin her new manicure. Without his income she would have to economize. Which prompted her to ask, "Do you carry life insurance?"

"Substantial."

"Who is it made out to?"

He looked surprised.

"You. Who else would I leave my money to?"

"I thought, perhaps, you'd leave it to 'B.B.' Considering how close you two are. Both being men."

This time, he missed the sarcasm. If, in fact, she was being sarcastic.

"Never."

"I give up. You have your marching orders. Take a shower, dress and go to the office. Tell Geraldine you're back for good. Gather your wits together and do whatever it is you have to do. See a dozen clients. Set court dates. Open some mail. By the time you get home, I may have forgiven you."

He started to move, then froze in his tracks.

"You are going to get the baby back, aren't you?"

Her eyes rolled under closed lids.

"That was my intention. You do want me to, don't you?"

Without knowing, Hugh was confronted with the ultimate test.

"God, yes!"

Being a Canadian and thus, by birth, a hockey fan of sorts, he would have understood the expression, "Golden Sombrero." Four times he had uttered the word "God" in reverence.

That thought did cross Ellen's mind before dismissing it. He would only have comprehended the reference if it had been uttered in French. The fact did nothing to raise his status.

"I'm back!"

Geraldine's head shot up. Her pupils dilated. Her mouth gaped. Her unintended performance of a hat trick.

"Thank God!"

The Kerr Gang was becoming more pious by the minute.

Babies, it might be supposed, had a way of instilling religion in the heathen.

"What have you got for me?"

"Nothing. You're still a month out."

"Start calling. I want to be so busy my head will swim."

He received no credit for the "Americanism."

"Ellen kicked you out of the house."

Not a question but a statement.

"How'd you guess?"

He tried to sound amused.

"It was a good try, sir. You lasted longer than expected. The office pool had you back within two weeks."

"Did you win?"

"No." She pouted. "I bet on three days."

"You didn't have any faith in me?"

"Every faith you'd be back in three days."

"How do you women do it? Raise a child, I mean."

"We're quick learners."

"And I'm not?"

"Your presence here answers that, sir."

He made a low, deprecating noise and twirled his hat around his finger.

"Get cracking."

Geraldine decided she liked him better when he was not using slang.

"Mr. Merrick was looking for you. Shall I call him?"

"Please do."

Attempting a nonchalant whistle, he walked down the corridor to his office. Opening the door with a flourish, he beheld a mountain of paperwork spilled over the floor. He suddenly didn't mind.

When Jack arrived, he found Hugh sitting behind a perfectly manicured desk, every pen, paper and letter neatly in place. For the first time in months he was able to find and identify the blotter.

"Ellen back?" he asked with a knowing assertion.

Hugh innocently clucked his tongue.

"No. She's out for three months. Why do you ask?"

"You hired a private secretary?"

"If you're playing Thirty Questions, it's going to take you a considerable amount of time to get around to the point of your visit. And since I'm not presently working on a case, that means you're not working for me and thus have personal business to pursue. Considering our professional relationship, I think it fair to establish a fee of $50 an hour to begin. Adjusted upward as circumstances warrant, naturally."

"Who are you?"

"Hugh Kerr." He stood and offered his hand. "I beg the familiarity in not introducing myself sooner, but I presumed – erroneously – that we were beyond the formal stages of lawyer-client association."

Jack snapped his fingers.

"I get it. You and Ellen had a whopper of a fight and you're pretending to be someone else so she'll let you back in the house."

Hugh stared at him under hooded lids.

"The party of the first part, hereby identified as Miss Jacqueline T. Kerr – with or without malice aforethought – which has yet to be determined by a court of law – has shattered the self-reliant image of the party of the second part, one Hugh D. Kerr. A preliminary injunction has been placed on the latter, whereby he had been bound by a temporary restraining order to vacate the premises, heretofore referred to as the Executive Residential Hotel."

"That's what I said – in real people-speak."

"Sit down," Hugh sighed, waiting until Jack had pulled up his bar stool and settled down before resuming his seat. "What can I do for you while I'm waiting for an avalanche of clients to come knocking on my door and hopefully take my mind off the events of the day?"

Remembering the former warning and not quite reassured Hugh had resumed his normal persona, Jack began, "I'm not asking for free legal work. I'm not even asking for myself. I have two friends who need a contract drawn up."

"Then, why aren't they here instead of you?"

"They're afraid of you."

He gave a deprecating snort.

"They wouldn't be if they had seen me this morning. Is one of them a woman?"

"Yes. A chemist."

"Does she do consulting work?"

"I don't know. I could ask. Why?"

"I require the back-up services of an expert. I'm willing to pay."

"An expert in what?" he asked, becoming more confused.

"Babies."

Hugh pronounced the word as if it were dirty. The lightbulb went on over Jack's head.

"Oh. Now, I get it. You were left alone with the kid and she beat you, hands down."

"I called the police and told them she was murdering me."

Spoken straight, without the least inflection. Jack's eyes widened in response.

"Gulp."

"Precisely."

"And that's why you're here. Banished."

"My sabbatical is over. Finis. Kaput."

"Out the door, along with fatherhood."

"You needn't put it that way. I'm not abandoning fatherhood, just the 'know it all' attitude. And, you needn't smile. It wasn't funny."

"Just keep saying to yourself, 'practice makes perfect.'"

Hugh drummed his fingers on the very neat desk.

"I'm about ready to throw you out."

"Yeah. Being the party of the fourth part, I'm on Ellen and Jackie's side."

"You don't even know the details."

"Don't have to, bub. I'm the godfather, remember?"

"What-do-you-want? And I'm charging you for this preliminary consultation."

"It's about a magic cream."

"Jack and the cream-stalk?" he jested without humor.

Never having climbed a beanstalk, the re-worded expression went over Jack's head.

"The lady scientist created a cream that started out life as an aerosol and then changed to a spray before turning into a goo."

"It's alive?"

Wondering at Hugh's damaged mind, Jack bypassed the question as irrelevant.

"It's some kind of wonder medicine. It cures a lot of stuff like itching, I think, but its real value is in repairing skin. She used it on Mom's dog and then I met this guy down at the racetrack and he had a horse with an open sore on its muzzle from the bridle. Other stuff healed it but it kept breaking open, so we put the spray on the wound and bingo, it worked. No more breaking open. Bill – that's the trainer – said it was a miracle and worth a ton of money. They want to form a partnership and market it."

Said all in one sentence, Jack huffed after completing the narrative.

Hands folded, Hugh leaned across the desk. "Somewhere through that, you've caught my attention."

"Thought I would. They need a contract."

"Yes, they do."

"Can you write one up?"

"I'll have to speak with them, first. You were a tad short on details."

"Sure. They were going to wait until you came back to work, but since you're here, that's swell."

"Considering my calendar is slightly anemic at the moment, my afternoon is free. Why don't you see if you can get them in here by 2:00?"

Slipping off the barstool, Jack grinned.

"Thanks, buddy."

Before he reached the rear exit, Hugh asked, "What's your angle?"

"I'm the Good Samaritan."

"Now, that makes me nervous."

"Me, too. When pigs fly and all that."

He laughed and slipped out, Hugh silently wishing he could follow him.

Having nothing better to do, he opened the lower desk drawer and reached for one of ten-thousand letters stored there. Slicing across the top with a sharpened blade, he removed the contents and began reading. An hour later a soft tapping on the main door caught his attention. Looking up he saw Geraldine and smiled.

"I thought, if it was safe, you being here, sir, I'd run out and grab something from the deli. I didn't bother brown-bagging it because I never have time to eat when I'm alone in the office."

Glancing at his watch, he made a quick determination.

"Let's put a 'Closed for the Holidays' sign on the front and go out together. It would be my pleasure to buy you lunch, Miss Sterrett."

Not for the first time that day someone questioned his wisdom, if not his sanity.

"It isn't a holiday, Mr. Kerr. The 4th of July is over and there isn't another until –"

"Yes, it is: a holiday in reverse. We're celebrating 'Hugh Kerr is back to work day.' Lock up shop and forget the deli. I'm taking you out for a real meal."

Disconcerted, she glanced down at her dress.

"But, I'm not presentable."

"Second to my wife, you're the most beautiful woman in the world and no one will care what you're wearing. They'll all be staring at your face."

Flattered by the compliment, she put a hand to her cheek, considered, then back-stepped.

"Just let me freshen up, then… Are you sure? What would Mrs. Kerr say?"

"Ellen would say anything that keeps me out of the house right now is a good thing. And," he added with a wink, "she'd say, have a martini on me."

"I don't drink."

"All right. Make it a milkshake."

Nearly faint from excitement, she skipped away. Happily returning the unopened correspondence back in the drawer, he prepared to follow. All things considered, escaping with Geraldine presented more fun than trailing a detective.

"Pleased to meet you." Hugh stood and held out his hand as Amy Pazel, Jack and Bill Boerner entered his office. Striding ahead of the others, Amy's smile was infectious and the lawyer was grinning as the two shook. "Mr. Merrick told me a little about you and I had trouble believing his glowing report. You've sold me on first impressions."

"Pleased to meet you, sir. Mr. Merrick has informed me you were the only one in the whole wide world good enough to be our lawyer, and I believed him implicitly."

"Then, you're one ahead of me." Shaking his head at Jack for the compliment, he turned to the man accompanying him. "I'm Hugh Kerr, at your service."

"Bill Boerner. Thanks for meeting us on short notice. Jack said you're just back from vacation and I imagine you have a lot of catching up to do."

"I'd hardly call it a vacation. My wife has just given birth to our first child and I spent some time with them. Not entirely successfully. That's why I'm back in the office ready to go back to work. Even technical legal matters seem easy compared to the complexities of fatherhood. Do you have children, Mrs. Pazel?"

"Three. Little hellers, all, so I can sympathize with your plight."

"Good. Then, I may turn the tables and call you seeking advice."

"Children don't come with instruction manuals."

"So I've been told and confirmed to my cost. What's your secret?"

"Trial and error. The same as I practice in my lab. I love to mix chemicals; you never know what you may come up with. It takes curiosity, imagination, and occasionally courage. Some formulas turn out to be spectacular successes, while others flop."

"Where does the courage come in?"

"I once tried to improve the shelf life of a lotion by changing the preservative. It looked solid on paper, but unfortunately it had an adverse reaction to the lilac scent. Once the smell got into the air ducts, we had to close the building down until the ducts were flushed."

"Didn't make you very popular around the office," he chuckled.

Her smile flashed brighter.

"On the contrary, I was everyone's best friend. They all got the afternoon off. The next morning I had three bouquets of flowers on my desk."

"Lilacs?"

"You guessed it."

"Nice. Now, tell me about this spray you want to market and what sort of contract you need."

"When we market it, the product will be a cream. That's because I originally developed and patented it as an aerosol. For my private use, I reformulated it as a spray."

"Why was that?"

"Several reasons, one of them being packaging. Aerosol cans are just being developed for mass production. Because they're something the public isn't familiar with, consumers tend to shy away from innovative products. Especially women."

"Explain, please."

"The average woman doesn't have the money to spend on something that may not work. She tends to favor the tried and true because she knows she can count on it. A mass media campaign may tempt them to try the product, but most companies would rather use their advertising dollars on product rather than packaging. And then, there's costs to consider. An aerosol can is far more expensive to manufacture. Cosmetic companies are very good at using jars and tubes, but they would have to purchase these cans from an outside vendor. More problematic, they'd be required to train their employees in the new technique."

"How to get the product into the can," he guessed.

"Exactly. Mega Enterprises has manufacturing plants in several states as well as Mexico. While specific rules and regulations go out to all of them, that doesn't prevent individual processors from tinkering with the product. I once received a report that one of my lotions wasn't holding viscosity more than three months and customers were returning it in droves. I traced the problem to a specific part of the country and made a spot inspection. I found they had omitted one seemingly unnecessary chemical from the process because the resident chemist felt it was too expensive. By removing it, he saved a great deal of money and earned himself a bonus."

"That was a mistake?" She nodded. "How could tampering with a formula be permitted?"

"It isn't, but it happens all the time. No company's quality assurance program is foolproof, Mr. Kerr."

"That's a depressing thought."

"You wouldn't want to know what I know. And not just about the cosmetics industry."

"As a lawyer, I probably would, but as a consumer, you're right."

She stared at him a beat, then shook her head.

"Actually, your answer should be the other way around."

He reconsidered as his eyes opened in wonder.

"I see your point." Jack snickered, causing Hugh to glower at him. "What would your answer have been?"

"I don't consume anything," Jack huffed.

Slightly put off, Hugh demanded, "You eat, don't you?"

"Sure. But I trust to the agricultural department of the good ol' U.S. of A. to protect me."

Holding up a hand, Amy took control of the discussion.

"My father was a district inspector for the railroad. As part of his duties he was required to check fresh produce shipped in refrigerated cars to ensure they were delivered to the purchaser in good condition. If, for example, the cooling system failed or the crates had been stowed without enough space between them and the vegetables had spoiled, the railroad would be liable. He was occasionally called to inspect produce at a plant which had its own side track, making it easier to unload the large quantity of fruits and vegetables they manufactured into baby food. He never liked going there. Ask me why, Mr. Merrick."

Jack swallowed hard.

"Is this something I don't want to hear?"

"Not if you don't have young children."

He stole a look at Hugh and blanched.

"Why didn't he like going there?"

"Because, as he put it, they purchased huge lots of 'horse' food; by that, he meant such things as carrots as large as your thigh. Of no commercial value to a grocery store, but quite adequate if cooked down to puree. Nutritionally deficient but who was to know? Furthermore, inside the plant were huge cooking vats, while overhead, as you would find in any food processing facility, rats scurried across the beams. If one lost its balance, which they seemed to with some regularity, it fell directly into one of the open-topped caldrons. And became –?"

"Baby food," Hugh grimly supplied.

Jack gagged.

"That's illegal, isn't it?"

"I can assure you the company passed all state and federal regulatory inspections."

"Now, I'm gonna be sick. Hugh, I don't want my godchild eating any of that crap."

"Neither do I. What's the name of the company?"

"I'm just giving you one example of how a product may be... altered along the production line. You did ask."

"Me and my big mouth," Jack gulped.

"Yes," Hugh sighed, seeing she would not be more specific. "Let's get back to the contract. You developed your formula as an aerosol and then made a spray. The original patent is in your name but belong to Mega Enterprises, your employer?"

"Yes. What I intend to do is reformulate it as a cream and patent it again so it belongs to me. That way, we can sell it. For use on animals, only."

"But it can be used on people? Because if it works on a dog or a horse as Jack has already explained to me, people are going to want to try it on their own problems. Forgive my ignorance, or is human skin different than animal skin?"

"All skin types have differences, even between the men and women. One of the research projects I designed concerned the study and development of cosmetic lines specifically formulated for men. Which is not to say one product doesn't cover all: most do, but those designed specifically for thicker or thinner skins, or thinner or lighter consistency are superior for those groups. But, as I explained to Mr. Merrick and Mr. Boerner, marketing it as an animal product eliminates years of federally mandated testing."

Hugh turned to Boerner.

"I understand this spray was tested on one of your horses. And was proven satisfactory?"

"Better than that – it was a miracle cure. Only, to be perfectly up-front, it wasn't one of my horses. I don't own the filly. I'm a trainer. The horse had great potential but she was useless as a racer because of the skin problem. You can't race a horse with an open wound."

"I see. Did you ask permission of the owner before you used an untried remedy on a valuable race horse?"

"No. But, I was at my whit's end. It's my job to get these animals fit to race. She wasn't. In fact, we were in discussion to send her back to farm. That's... never good."

"Next step, dog food," Jack less than helpfully supplied, but Hugh picked up the point and pursued it.

"Is that true?"

"A thoroughbred that can't race and has no track record isn't worth anything. She can't be ridden and there's no point breeding her. Aside from the fact she doesn't have any proven success as a racer, there's the probability she'll pass along her – thin skin – or whatever it is she suffers from."

"Is that still the plan?"

"Actually, I was thinking of buying her."

"With or without telling the owner about this 'miracle' cream that seems to have alleviated the health concern preventing her from racing."

"I plan to tell him."

"That would not only be wise, it will prevent legal complications down the line."

"How do you mean?"

"Best case scenario the cream works and you race her under your own colors. She wins. Not just one race but a dozen. She garners national attention: you place her in some of the major races and she takes those, too. Her purse grows and so does her value. At that point you can either sell her for fifty times what you paid, or she becomes invaluable as a breeding mare. How do you think the former owner feels about that? A little investigation on his part points to the fact you knew you could get her in condition to race but purchased her on the supposition she had little, if any value. That's not only a breach of your professional standards, it's a deception he can take to court and win."

"Yes, I've thought about that. I will tell him."

"How, then, is it likely he'll sell?"

"I don't think it will matter. I've talked this over with Jack. Every pitchman has a miracle cure. None of them work. He won't believe me. And even if he does and won't sell, buying the filly is only a dream of mine. It has nothing to do with the company we want to form."

Hugh let a faint smile cross his otherwise stern countenance.

"Because you're a pitchman who actually does have a miracle cure?"

"That's right. I know everybody in the business. If Barrister's Baby isn't my proof, there are lots of others that can be."

"Barrister's Baby?"

"That's the name of the filly," Jack eagerly supplied. "Thought you'd like it."

"As a gambler, Jack, you're better off developing a system than playing hunches."

"Ha. I'm hot on the trail of just such a scumbag. That's how I met Bill in the first place. All the pieces just fell into place like... magic."

"Betting the farm on it is always a dangerous petition."

"Yeah, but when the big one comes in there's nothing like it in the world."

Hugh let is ride and returned attention to Amy.

"Are you still employed by Mega Enterprises?"

"Yes."

"Then, that's a problem."

"I know. I'd have to resign."

"Can you afford to do that? I'd have to review your employment contract, but there may be a waiting period, typically a year, before you can attempt to use whatever knowledge you obtained from your job. Because what you developed, even on your own time, is likely to be considered a trade secret."

"I'm aware of that. And no, I can't wait a year without earning a salary."

"Then, you need a financier: someone willing to put up a substantial amount of money not only to cover the cost of your living expenses but to bring the product to market. I can't imagine that would be inconsequential."

"Why don't you come in on this, Hugh?" Jack hopefully inquired.

Hugh didn't drop a beat before answering.

"No. Since you've come to me for legal advice, I see a potential conflict of interest. Everything I invest from this point on could be construed as benefitting myself rather than the partnership."

"We won't sue you."

"I'm afraid I won't budge from my position." He turned to Bill. "It seems to me that as you've already told me you know everyone in the racing business, you might appeal to one of them. After all, they are the ones who are going to receive the biggest benefit from Mrs. Pazel's cream."

"But, the treatment doesn't just cure horses –"

"All right; then appeal to a veterinarian. Or, even, a pharmaceutical company. They're already in the business and have testing facilities, laboratories and established marketing for products like yours."

"Then, they make all the money."

"That would depend on the contract you negotiate with them. I think a fair percentage of the profits could be substantial. That way, you eliminate the risk and the necessity of obtaining up-front investment capital. I'd be glad to review any paperwork before you sign it."

"We'll think it over."

Bill got up and indicated Jack and Amy follow.

"We appreciate your time, Mr. Kerr. I think we'll try it our way, first."

Giving Jack a pointed stare, Hugh stood and addressed Amy.

"It was a pleasure meeting you. Good luck. And if you do work it out, or need any other legal help, please feel free to call on me."

"Thank you."

Hugh watched them go with the disquieting feeling all was not right with the world. Having returned to work to get away from one such a disaster, he had the feeling he had jumped back into the fire.

CHAPTER 11

Jack shook his head, a lock of dirty blond hair falling down his forehead. With a neat sweep of his hand, he pushed the hair back from his eyes.

"I can't go. Don't you see? I'm due for a visit to the barber shop."

"Oh, man, you've got to be kidding." Hands akimbo, Bill Boerner shook his head in frustration. "Your hair looks great just the way it is. You always look good."

Slightly offended, Jack pulled back.

"Wait a minute. I don't want to look too good. Then, clients will think I'm a bean-counter and thugs will mistake me for a pushover."

"OK, then you look like a sharp cookie packing heat."

Jack's blood pressure rose at the unintended insult.

"I'm not supposed to look like I'm carrying a gun. It's the latent threat I represent that's supposed to intimidate." He tapped his head. "Brains and body."

Bill was quick to pick up on the unintended significance.

"So, you're 'B. B.' too, are you?"

Horrified at the idea, Jack's hands flew into a defensive position.

"No way, Jose."

Losing patience, Bill gave up.

"Then, what do you want to look like?"

Although pretending to mull it over, the answer was on the tip of the detective's tongue.

"A beach bum with money."

"That's an oxymoron." On Jack's exasperated expression, he glibly explained, "You can't be a derelict with deep pockets. They're opposites."

"Now, you've got it." Raising a suggestive eyebrow, he completed the idea. "A man of mystery."

"You're a guy in a sport coat who needs a haircut. You could be anyone, or you could be no one. Right now, Mr. Mystery, I need you to play the part of a respectable Joe who's been invited to a meeting with Mr. Wexler."

"But, why me? I told you. I'm not part of the package."

"Mr. Wexler owns Barrister's Baby. I told him I wanted to buy her. Since, as far as he knows she can't be raced, he was naturally curious why I'd want to sink my money into a worthless horse. I told him there were three of us in on it and I'd be happy to explain. So, he wants to meet us. Me, Amy and you."

"I'm not in on it."

"You brought Amy and me together. That's 'in on it,' as far as I'm concerned. And," he added with sincerity, "if we hit it big, you're entitled to a bonus. Call it a finder's fee. Your secret identity as a beach bum can't turn that down."

"A beach bum with money," Jack corrected.

"No one turns money down. And since you're not really a beach bum – notice I qualified the word 'bum' – you're a private eye who's always hoofing for dough – you're one of us. Besides, Amy wants you there."

"You made that up."

He shrugged.

"No accounting for taste. So, come on. We've got an appointment."

Realizing he had been maneuvered into accepting, Jack tugged forlornly at the cuff of his jacket.

"Geez, do I have time to change? There's a ketchup stain on the sleeve. I had an appointment this morning at a Mom and Pop's and put my arms down on the table; didn't realize it hadn't been wiped."

"Beach bums don't worry about stains."

"Beach bums don't wear sport jackets," Jack countered.

Bill quickly appraised the sleeve.

"Looks like blood to me. It augments your aura of mystery. And no, you don't have time to change. I've got my car outside. We have to pick up Amy and get to his office by ten o'clock."

"I bet she's dressed for the occasion," he grumbled, following Bill outside.

"Classy dames are always dressed, whether they are or not, if you catch my meaning."

Which ended the conversation, making it Bill two, Jack zip.

As a part-time gambler, the hairs on the back of his head prickled.

Had he been a full time one, Mr. Merrick might not have gone, the odds being decidedly against him.

An hour later, having rushed through late morning traffic, the three arrived promptly at Mr. Stanley Wexler's prestigious office, tucked carefully into the confines of the Santa Anita racetrack. Holding open the door, Jack stood back allowing Amy and then Bill to enter before him. As the door swished shut, he drew air in through his nostrils then caught Amy's eye. Transmitting to her, *the stink of big bucks,* he shifted his attention to the walls. Black and white photographs of thoroughbreds lined two opposite sides, presenting dozens of images. Several were single shots of stallions standing in expansive fields, but most showed prize animals in winner's circles surrounded by their jockey and smiling men in business suits, beaming with the satisfaction of having won what others achieved. As Bill crossed to the receptionist's desk, Jack and Amy wandered toward the left. A rapid survey made identification simple.

"That must be him," he indicated, pointing to man whose face appeared most frequently.

"Mr. Wexler through the ages," she clarified, noting the earliest depicted him as a young man, while in later pictures signs of graceful age showed on his features.

"Three piece suits, hand tailored," Jack agreed, holding his offending right arm behind his back. "Slick hair style, shoes shined. Those never walked through muck." She grinned as he added, "And a tan to die for. Gotten on the Riviera –"

"Sunlamp," she disapprovingly identified. "Very bad for the skin."

Impressed, he shot her a glance.

"Really?"

"Tanning lamps ought to be outlawed. No one realizes the damage they do until it's too late. The same," she added, eyeing him suspiciously, "could be said for the sun. You see all the bronze beauties on the beach? Men, as well as women? They'll pay for their vanity."

"How so?" he hissed in a tone of suspicious dread.

"Wrinkles. By the time they reach middle age they'll look like they're in their eighties." His eyebrow arched. "What do you think a tan is?"

"Skin browned by the sun?"

"Skin fricasseed by the sun. As in, stewed in its own juices. Or, rather, deep fried. Like chicken."

He groaned and rubbed his stomach.

"I could have lived without that analogy."

"You'll live longer with it. Wrinkles are the least of your worries. Too much sun can also give you skin cancer."

"You're dangerous to be around."

Before she could answer, Bill joined them.

"We're to wait," he whispered.

They amused themselves for twenty minutes by studying the photographs, all of which Bill readily identified, sharing stories of several horses he had trained before they grew weary of the subject and settled down to bide their time. After a third man had come and gone while they waited, Jack shook his foot in annoyance.

"I feel like the janitor hoping to get in to pull the trash between Hot Shots."

"If that were the case," Amy easily explained, "you wouldn't have been invited to sit. You'd be standing in the corner out of sight."

"Yeah. They wouldn't want me transferring cooties to the leather sofa."

"I was referring to your lowly status, but that works, too."

"What kind of leather is this, anyway?" he continued, running his fingernail along the arm of the couch and leaving a line. "Horsehide? You think they sacrifice all the nags that don't win? Half to the glue factory and half to the furniture makers?"

Bill groaned and turned away, leaving his companions to make their own determination.

The little hand rested on the 11 and the big hand had just passed the 4 when the receptionist looked over at them.

"Mr. Boerner, you and your group may go in now." As they stood in unison and filed past, she continued in an undertone, "I'm sorry he kept you waiting, Bill. He's had an unusually busy morning. I fit you in because you said it was urgent but not about a horse issue. You know the boss. If you had said one of his four-legged family members had a sore leg, you'd have gotten in before the bank president."

He laughed and waved her apology off.

"I don't know what he'd do without you."

"He'd find another pretty 'filly.'"

"Then, come work for me."

"Are you leaving?" she whispered in shock.

He grinned and shook his head.

"Never. I'm purple and green through-and-through." Pointing to the racing colors proudly displayed on an escutcheon over the door, he winked. "Royalty and grass."

She chuckled at their private joke and waved them in. Bill went first, followed by Amy, Jack pulling up the rear. The office was decorated with photographs similar to those in the waiting room, augmented by a large trophy case opposite the picture window, situated to catch the rays of the western sun. Stanley Wexler sat behind an impressive desk dominated by a statue of a racing stallion serving as a pen holder. Otherwise, the top was devoid of any other accoutrements or paperwork.

Standing as the group entered, Mr. Wexler nodded familiarly at Bill before turning his attention to Amy. Meeting her eyes as was customary before an introduction, his attitude conveyed the impression he had appraised her in a second's time before speaking.

"You are Mrs. Pazel. Pleased to meet you. I'm Stan Wexler." Ignoring Jack, he indicated she take a seat. "A scientist, he said. I didn't realize they came in such pretty packages."

"They come in all shapes and sizes."

"And as females?" he baited.

"Not so much," she suavely admitted. "But, that's changing."

"I'm glad to hear it; at least from the male scientist's perspective." Turning to Bill, who had remained standing, he motioned him down. Jack remained invisible and took a chair for himself without permission. "How's tricks, Bill? What have you got to tell me that's urgent but not about a horse? Coming from my trainer, that would seem to be an oxymoron."

"Actually, sir, it is about a horse. I just didn't want you to think there was a problem; one you weren't aware of. Actually, it's more about the solution to a problem."

"You've caught my attention." He returned his eyes to Amy. "Normally, I don't offer Bill any refreshments but considering he has brought along a lady scientist, I ask you if there's anything I may get for you? Coffee? Tea? Sherry and biscuits?"

"I'm fine, thank you."

"You don't mind if I order coffee for myself?" Waiting for her to demur, he summoned the receptionist via intercom, placed his request without extending the invitation to the men, then settled back. "I want you to tell me why you're here and what problem you've supposedly solved. About horses."

Bill started to object, having planned his introduction, then thought better of it and remained mute as Amy was perfectly content to provide an answer.

"Let me begin by saying I am a chemist; my specialty is in skin care. I work in research and development for Mega Enterprises, in the cosmetics laboratory."

"You want to put... hoof polish on my fillies?" Wexler teased.

"I want to help heal skin problems caused by the abrasiveness of a bridle. One, which I understand, is not an uncommon problem but one which has proven extremely difficult, and sometimes impossible to heal."

All semblance of levity left the owner's face and he leaned forward with interest.

"Go on. With some background, please."

"Like many good chemists I have a bench at home; a small laboratory," she clarified. "I work there on projects that interest me. Not ones pertaining to my work, but just as... experiments. Or, when someone asks for help with a specific problem and I think I can offer a solution. I appreciate the challenge."

"You have a creative mind, then."

"I like to think so. A neighbor of mine asked for help with her dog. He suffered from a condition that caused extreme itching. By scratching the irritation, the animal rubbed off most of the hair at the site and then broke the skin, causing wounds that wouldn't heal, so he was constantly in distress. The vet prescribed treatments, of course, but they didn't work. They aided in knitting the edges of the skin together, but not in permitting the gaping hole beneath the surface to fill in with appropriate tissue and blood vessels. Does that make sense to you?"

"It does, as you explain it."

"Whenever the dog scratched, the skin was re-broken and the injury below got a little deeper. I formulated a spray that would help the wound to heal from the inside out, rather than merely allowing the skin on the surface to knit. The dog was relieved of his suffering and my neighbor, Mrs. Wade, told Jack – Mr. Merrick, there," she indicated, "about the 'miracle.' Mr. Merrick mentioned it to Mr. Boerner and they asked me for permission to try it on one of the horses suffering from a similar predicament."

"That was Barrister's Baby," Bill interjected. "You and I discussed her condition; the issue with the bridle. Without being able to heal her by conventional methods, you agreed we couldn't race her. Rather than lose a valuable thoroughbred, I thought it was worth taking a chance with Mrs. Pazel's treatment. At that point, sir, we had nothing to lose."

"Did you have this spray tested by the stable veterinarians before you used it?"

"No, sir. Since we had already discussed having the horse sent back to the farm, I realized the urgency of the situation. If it worked, there would be time for that, later."

"And it worked?"

"Like a charm. The wound healed almost overnight. You know I had her back on the track. She flew like the wind."

"And afterwards?"

"No problem at all. No sign the healed skin was broken, or about to break. I've had her on the track several times since then, with the same result."

Wexler waited as the receptionist came in with his coffee before continuing.

"I'm impressed. Very. But, you haven't explained the purpose of this meeting." Turning to the scientist, he asked, "You've come to be compensated for your spray?"

"Actually, sir," Bill spoke for her, "there are a number of issues we'd like to discuss."

"Oh? I'd like to hear them."

"The three of us intend to market the spray. Or, actually, Mrs. Pazel is going to –"

"Reformulate," she supplied.

"Reformulate it into a cream –"

"Why is that?"

"Because it's already been patented as an aerosol," she offered. "In my name, by Mega Enterprises where I'm employed. Because I developed it while working for them, they own everything I create. By slightly adjusting the formula, I can obtain a clean patent."

"Only so long as you no longer work for them. Is that correct?"

"Yes. I would have to resign."

Wexler thought a moment before turning to his trainer.

"And you, Bill?"

He cleared his throat before facing the music.

"I'd like to buy Barrister's Baby from you. Without the spray – or the cream we're going to turn it into – she has no value. You acknowledged as much by taking her out of training."

"Purchase the filly for what purpose?"

"To race her; and to use her as an advertisement of our product."

"You're speaking of a very serious investment. Wouldn't it make more sense for you to sell me the formula and let me market it?"

"It would, but –"

Wexler smiled.

"You want the full profits for yourselves."

"We'd like to give it a try, yes, sir."

Sipping his coffee, Wexler stared out the window a long beat before answering.

"You don't need my permission for that."

"What we need is Barrister's Baby."

"Which, as you pointed out, is of no value to me without Mrs. Pazel's formula."

"Yes."

"Meaning, you'd like me to sell her to you at a bargain basement price."

"Yes."

Toying with the coffee cup, Wexler turned it so the handle faced the opposite way, picked it up with his left hand, changed his mind before taking a drink and replaced it on the desk.

"Why did you tell me all this, Bill? Wouldn't it have been smarter for you to keep quiet about the spray, let the horse be sent away and then made me an offer on her?"

"It would have. But, I wanted to be fair."

"Did you have a lawyer advise you?"

Bill stiffened at the insinuation.

"Yes. But, I had already made the determination. You've been good to me and I didn't want to do anything that would jeopardize our relationship."

"I appreciate that. We've been together a long time." Pushing the coffee cup away from him, Wexler got up, signifying the interview was at an end. "Let me give the matter serious consideration. I'll get back to you as soon as I've made a decision." Turning to Amy, he added, "It was a pleasure meeting you."

"Thank you."

Closest to the door, Jack opened it and let the others pass before following. Taking care to close it behind them, they hurried into the corridor. Having had nothing to say during the meeting, he was the first to speak when they were alone.

"So: how did it go?"

"So far, so good, I think. I didn't expect an immediate answer. I made it clear Barrister's Baby wasn't worth keeping."

"Which he might have taken for a threat," Jack pointed out.

"I know. But, it's the truth. Without the spray, she's worthless. Getting something from me is better than nothing."

"Were you surprised he asked about buying the formula?"

This time, Bill shook his head.

"He didn't mean it. I told you before. He's a horse man first, last and always. He's not interested in formulas more complex than how to make a dry martini. Marketing a cream is the last thing on his mind. I think he just wanted to hear what we'd say."

"You didn't leave any doubt about it."

"I didn't think I had to."

"And, you're a fair guy."

"Sure. And I had a lawyer advise me," he sourly added. "Well, it was an honest question." As the elevator came, he swept his arm out, indicating the lady be the first to enter. "I do believe we have a long but successful track ahead of us."

Grinning at his use of the racing term, Jack punched the "L" button.

"Here's to broken tape at the finish line."

"As long as it's my horse that breaks it," Bill clarified.

Which set their downward course to the lobby.

"Are you going to endorse these checks?"

Hugh looked up from the newspaper he was reading.

"What checks?"

"The ones Mom collected."

"That sounds suspicious; possibly even illegal. Where did she get them?"

"From your mail."

"Oh. I'd forgotten we'd given it to her."

"She also went to the office and took that which you had hidden to make it look as though you'd actually done some work."

"I did work," he protested. Geraldine started calling clients and they fell like raindrops into the waiting room."

Walking into his line of vision from where she had been standing in the kitchen, Ellen sat down opposite him.

"Since you never mentioned a word about that, I presumed you either decided not to take on any new cases... or no one showed up with legal problems."

"I told you about Jack and the horse."

"No," she sourly demurred, "Mary told me about it and when I confronted you, you embellished the story. If it hadn't been for her, I'd still be in the dark."

"It wasn't much."

"When I'm here alone all day with an infant, a little is much. I'm used to sharing your life – every aspect of it. Now that we have Jacqueline, I feel as though you've shut me out. Then, you sit at the breakfast table reading the newspaper and not talking. I'm a little lost here, Hugh."

Reacting to the pain and confusion in her voice, he folded the newspaper and set it aside.

"I'm sorry. You're not the only one who's floundering. I feel like a fifth wheel at home and I'm afraid if I rattle on about work, you'll think I'm not interested in you and the baby. Which I am. But you haven't spoken a word since my failure at babysitting. We go to bed, you lying on one side and me on the other and it's gotten so I'm afraid to touch you. It used to be we'd curl up together, say a few silly things, exchange a dozen kisses and drift off. Since the baby's come, we lie there like wooden soldiers waiting for the other to fall asleep so we can finally relax."

"All right," she sighed, expressing relief. "Now, we're finally having a conversation. Like we used to have – where one of us says something the other was thinking, or we'd finish off each other's sentences. We've always been in tune with one another, until... as you said. The baby came. She shouldn't be a wedge between us, she should be a bond."

"There's that word again," he groaned in mock frustration. "Bond."

"I used it on purpose. To see if you'd react. The way we used to play off one another. It's good to know we still can."

"Of course we can. Can I get you more coffee?"

"Please."

Taking their cups, he went into the kitchen, refilled them and returned.

"How about some toast and a soft-boiled egg?"

"Can you handle it?"

"I'm not as smug around the house as I used to be, but I think it's not beyond my capabilities." Stooping down to kiss her forehead, he returned to the kitchen. "No murders have come our way," he continued, getting out a pot and placing four eggs inside to boil. Not insensitive to the fact he used the plural possessive, Ellen sipped her coffee and watched him work.

"Does that imply when you take time off the good citizens of Los Angeles act like peace-loving people?"

"If that were true, I'd market my powers and we'd be fabulously wealthy."

"And bored."

"That, too. Three minutes?"

"Yes, but turn down the gas so they don't bump into each other and crack."

He complied, then dropped two pieces of bread into the toaster.

"A good case of embezzlement popped up but I passed on it."

"Why?"

"It was the embezzler who wanted my services because he thought I could get him off."

"He told you that?"

"Uh huh."

"Brazen."

"He wanted me to pin the blame on a co-worker. Had the patsy all picked out. He even offered me the key to the man's desk so I could plant incriminating evidence."

"What did you say to him?"

"That wasn't exactly my line but he might try the Merrick Detective Agency."

"You didn't."

"Why not? Knowing Jack, he'll accept the case, charge the joker a fortune, put in a few hours 'casing the joint,' and then make up some story about security being too tight and put an end to the folly."

"Keeping the fee, of course."

"Naturally. That's why he charges up front. The client could hardly complain to the police he was taken, can he?"

"I'd like to see him try."

"Me, too. Because then he really would need a lawyer." The toast popped and he went about buttering it. "Jam?"

"What do we have?"

He checked the ice box.

"Strawberry."

"Which tells me who did the grocery shopping."

"You may resume your duties at any time, Mrs. Kerr."

"And speaking of which, are you going to sign those checks before you run off to work?"

"I thought you always signed them."

"I'm on 'vacation,' remember?"

"Damn!"

"Hugh –"

"I forgot to time the eggs. How long has it been?"

She grinned, knowing he had set her up.

"Better forget about soft. I'd rather not take a chance. Give them another five and we'll have hard boiled."

"By that time the toast will be cold."

"Give me mine, now, and I'll eat it before the eggs are ready."

"With or without jam?"

"With orange juice."

"Orange juice wasn't an option."

Ellen finally laughed.

"This is better, isn't it? We're finally talking."

"And you finally let me kiss you."

"That, sir, was never off the table."

"Lips, too?"

"Unless you think a full frontal smack is going to turn you into a raving maniac."

"There's that consideration."

He returned with a plate of toast spread liberally with strawberry jam, set it in front of her and went for her mouth. After a prolonged kiss, she finally broke away.

"Ding." He raised an eyebrow. "Eggs are done. That was five minutes if it was a second."

"Ha! My plan, exactly. You're better than a timer."

He served the eggs in four brightly colored ceramic holders. Using her knife, Ellen lopped off the top of one of hers, stared at the result, then shrugged.

"We're going to have to work on our kissing. You've achieved something between soft and hard."

"Yes," he agreed with a devilish wink. "I believe you've hit the nail on the head."

"That, Mr. Kerr, would be painful. For you."

He groaned in feigned agony and they consumed their 'tween eggs without further complaint. After finishing, he cleared the table.

"Want me to do the dishes before I go?"

"No, I'll clean the kitchen. Jackie should sleep for another hour."

"Don't say I never offered." Crossing into the living room he slipped on his jacket. "Is my tie straight?"

She fussed with it, then kissed him.

"Perfect."

"Thank you. Tonight when I get home, I'll have a full itinerary of stories to tell you."

"I appreciate that, Hugh. And I'll have the checks endorsed and a deposit slip made out so you can drop by the bank tomorrow on your way to work."

He clucked his tongue.

"I'll have Geraldine do it on her lunch hour."

"Then, give her an extra fifteen minutes."

He pulled back in surprise.

"You always went to the bank on your lunch hour and you were never late getting back."

"That's because I had plans of marrying the boss and I figured whatever I deposited was eventually going to be mine. She doesn't have that option."

"Nope. I'm taken." He kissed her again. "Very," he concluded, smacking his lips. "I never realized breakfast could be so –"

"Stimulating?"

"I was going to say 'elucidative,' but you answer works better."

"Thought it might. And, I'll have a full report for you on Miss Jacqueline."

"As Jack would say, now we're cooking with gas."

"Yes: the ten minute kind. Don't forget your briefcase."

He grabbed it and waved good-bye.

"I love you, Ellen Thorne Kerr."

As innocent as his statement was, it stirred in her memory something the Wades had said when discussing the trials of a police family.

Never forget to say 'I love you' when you leave the house because you might never see one another again.

She therefore answered by blowing him a kiss.

For luck, in a perverse sort of way.

CHAPTER 12

The door blew open, rocked on its hinges then slammed into the opposing wall. Shocked by what could have been taken as an explosion, Marie Sanchez's head shot up as her eyes drilled a hard stare at the intruder. What she saw was a mad man. If he had been frothing at the mouth, she might have called an ambulance for fear he suffered from rabies. As it was, she slid the desk blotter aside and hit the hidden switch beneath. In less time than it would have taken to dial "0" for the police, Jack Merrick was striding down the corridor, ready to face whatever trouble required the business end of a revolver.

Immediately identifying the culprit, he shoved the gun in the waistband of his trousers and put out a warning hand.

"It's all right, Marie."

Keeping the telephone receiver well within reach, her eyes narrowed in anger.

"Whoever he is, he needs a good thrashing. No one comes into an office and acts like he's going to commit violence."

"Let's go, Boerner," he ordered, pointing toward his office.

"Whatever he wants, charge him double and tack on a fee for damaging the wall. I'm going to have to call maintenance to have it patched and that'll be added to the rent."

"Yeah. I'll do that. Move it, Bill."

Muttering an apology mixed with curse words, the trainer followed Jack. When they were safely alone, Bill kicked the chair placed by the detective's desk.

"The son of a bitch!"

"Keep your voice down. I got other clients here. What happened?"

Without asking, Jack poured two shots of scotch and handed one to Bill. He downed it in one swallow.

"Wexler."

"I gathered that. He wouldn't sell you the horse?"

"Hell, no, he wouldn't. But that's only the half of it. I got a letter in the mail this morning. Certified. You know what that means?"

"You had to sign for it as proof of receipt."

Less than mollified by Jack's calm tone, Bill refilled his glass from the bottle Jack left within reach, swallowed another mouthful then wiped his lips with the back of his hand, an uncouth gesture out of character with the man's usual demeanor which Jack attributed to his extreme agitation.

"Do you know what it said?"

Several options ran through Jack's mind. He offered none of them.

"Tell me."

"It was a cease-and-desist."

That not being one of them, Merrick arched an eyebrow.

"Cease and desist what? You mean, he fired you?"

"That, too."

Moving the bottle out of the other man's reach, he indicated Bill sit.

"What else?"

"Guess."

"Don't play games with me. I don't play twenty questions with clients. And, I said sit down."

Bill dropped into the chair, wringing his hands as an excuse not to strangle the arms.

"Stop using the spray."

That being the second unexpected answer, Jack grunted in surprise.

"Why?"

"He's bought the formula."

"From Amy Pazel?" he gasped in shock.

"No! From some asshole named Philip Shaffley."

"Who the hell is that?"

"The chief honcho at Mega Enterprises. I was dead wrong about Wexler. He was a hell of a lot more interested in what we were saying than I thought. Horseman, hell. He saw a golden opportunity and grabbed it. He plans on marketing the spray, himself."

"I warned you –"

"I know. I made a mistake. I thought I knew the man. I should have realized that rich men only care about one thing: getting richer. I tried to be square with him and he turned the knife on me."

Attempting to be reasonable, Jack sat on the corner of his desk to collect his thoughts.

"All right. But, Amy said she could re-work the formula, so we're not out of business."

"Wexler's got all the money in the world behind him. He can bring the spray to market next week if he wants to. He's got Barrister's Baby as proof it works. He's already arranged for her to race next month. If she wins – and she will – he's got an advertising bonanza. We got nothing."

"I'm sorry, man. It was maybe too good to be true."

"Is that all you can say?"

"What is there to say? You laid the cards on the table but he had the winning hand."

Slumping in the chair, Bill dropped his head.

"Jack, I'm out of a job. God knows, my reputation is probably ruined."

"How so?"

Boerner curled his lips in disdain.

"I tried an untested, unapproved 'concoction' on a horse that wasn't mine. Without asking permission. No one in the business is going to trust a trainer with valuable property after hearing that. And who would blame them? I knew I was taking a chance but one I believed was in the best interests of the horse. And the owner. See where it got me." Fighting his rising anger, he pounded the desk. "I had nothing to lose until I did."

"Tough break."

"I'm going to get him for this."

"Whoa. No, you're not. You're going to go home, take a few more stiff drinks, get stinking drunk, sleep it off and restart your life in the morning. There's no percentage in 'getting him,' Bill. The only thing that achieves is a stretch in prison."

"I don't care."

"Yes, you do."

"Then, I know a good lawyer to get me off. What do they call it? Justifiable homicide?"

"No. They call it first degree murder. And not even Hugh Kerr can get you off on that. Even with mitigating circumstances."

"We'll see."

Pushing away from the desk, Bill stood, clenched his fists and walked toward the door.

"I don't even know why I came here. To have someone to scream at, I guess. Forget what I said about getting even. I don't want you to have to testify at trial." Stopping half way through the entranceway, he turned back. "Send me a bill for the damage I caused. Certified. That way, I'll be sure to ignore it. Just like I'm gonna ignore that damn letter Wexler sent. See you around." He shrugged. "But, not at the track, I guess. We'll meet up at a bar someplace and talk about the good old days. You'll have to pay. Give Amy my regards. I don't have the heart to face her."

"Yeah. I'll do that."

Body twisted at an awkward angle, the former trainer slunk away. Marie Sanchez's steely glower as he departed putting a period on his association with the Merrick Detective Agency.

"So, that's it, Hugh."

Jack slumped down on the couch, kicking the coffee table away from his entangled legs.

"I'm sorry, Jack," Ellen tried. "It all sounded so wonderful."

"Didn't it, now. Slobs like us −" Catching himself, he rearranged his thought. "Slobs like me and Bill and Amy were never meant to make it. The deck is stacked against us. Big bucks win every time."

"Need I remind you," Hugh observed, moving the crystal glass on the end table away from danger, "you weren't financially involved. Or, so you led me to believe. You're not out anything."

"OK, you're right. But the dream bubble burst and that hurts almost as much as if I were."

"Has anyone told Mrs. Pazel?"

"I don't know. Not me."

"Someone should."

"I'll tell Mom and she can break the bad news."

"What about Bill?" Hugh asked. "According to what you told us, he didn't leave your office in a very good mood. Should we be worried about him? He did threaten Wexler. Do you think he meant it?"

"How do I know? I tried to talk him out of whatever he had in mind. Guys talk big. I suppose he did as I suggested: went home, got drunk and slept it off."

"I hope that's all there is to it."

"Yeah, well, I told him you couldn't get him off if he killed the rat."

"I'm sure that cheered him up considerably."

Kicking the coffee table a second time, Jack straightened.

"So much for Barrister's Baby. I thought it was a sign. You know − like Jackie and a pony and you being a lawyer and all that. Boy, was I sure wrong. Makes me feel like… I can't trust my gut anymore."

Ellen got up and crossed to Jack, putting a comforting hand on his arm.

"That wasn't the pony you were talking about. And besides, nothing based around the initials 'B. B.' was bound to work out the way you expected."

That seemed to brighten his outlook and he grinned.

"You're right about that. I should have known." Stifling a fake yawn, he got up, stretched and sighed. "It's late and I have to be at the office early."

"That's my line," Hugh teased.

"OK, I gotta get home and feed the cats. They'll have scratched the furniture to shreds if I'm not there for dinner."

"Then, have them −"

"Declawed?" he finished in horror. "No way. You know what that means? I asked around. It's not filing their claws down; they grow back like fingernails. It's an operation. A cat's claws are attached to bone. You gotta actually take what amounts to the first digit of a knuckle off; like an amputation. It's major surgery. It hurts and it disfigures them. They can't defend themselves. It outta be illegal."

"I was going to say, have them trained. I would never suggest declawing. I know what it is."

"Right. What's a cheap couch and a few chairs worth, anyway? Maybe I'll stop on the way home and buy them some toys. They like the stuffed mice filled with catnip. Drives 'em crazy for about five minutes. Then, they get all slobbery and I have to throw them out." He made an exaggerated face. "I bought a poster; put it up in the living room."

Almost afraid to ask, Ellen tried, "What's it about?"

"It's a picture of about five cats spread out in the living room with this pink mouse toy on the floor between them. The caption says, 'The kill went down just fine, but they couldn't decide what to do with the body.'" He laughed in genuine good humor. "Too funny."

"As long as that's the only 'kill' we're talking about," Hugh chuckled, "we're all in on the joke."

"See ya. You going to be in at the office tomorrow, Hugh?"

"Thought I would be."

"Who's making the coffee these days?"

"I am."

"OK, maybe I won't see you. Bye."

He waved and trotted off. The couple exchanged glances.

"Sad, the way it turned out," she tried.

"I don't know about you, but I don't have a good feeling about any of it."

"Well, it's not our business. If you'll wait for me, I'll check the baby and we can go to bed."

"Exactly what I had in mind."

Ellen went to the bedroom while Hugh gathered in the glasses and set them in the sink. In fifteen minutes all three Kerrs were fast asleep.

"Make it go away."

It might have been either one of them who issued the command, but it was Ellen who fumbled for the light and turned it on. Best intentions aside, the action had two immediate and obvious effects: Jacqueline began screaming at the top of her lungs and Hugh grabbed the pillow out from underneath his head and shoved it over his face in a vain attempt to cover his ears.

Grabbing the offending telephone by the neck, Ellen considered throttling it before giving in to her better if not more sincere instincts. The ringing stopped. The baby continued crying. Discovering that one out of two did not ensure even a modicum of peace, she brought the mouthpiece toward her face and yelled, "Whoever this is, you just woke us, the baby and everyone within the vicinity of a mile. If you know what's good for you, you'll hang up now before this line is traced."

The threat, unfortunately, went unheeded.

"Sorry, Starlet, I gotta talk to Hugh."

"Hugh, who?"

It was the first thing she could think of and wouldn't have regretted but for Jack's reaction.

"Oh, Geez, did you two have a fight? Is he sleeping on the couch? Can you go and get him?"

"You have the wrong number. This is Dewey's Pizza Parlor and we're closed for the night."

There was no such place as Dewey's, which didn't stop Jack from replying, "I was just there an hour ago and it was jumping. The sign said 'Open Twenty-four Seven."

Because the conversation had gotten out of hand, she demanded, "What were you doing there at −" Checking the bedside clock, she irritably continued, "three thirty-nine in the morning?"

Like a good detective careful not to get caught in a lie, he suavely responded, "Two thirty-nine. Remember, I said I was there an hour ago. I was pickin' up chicks."

"I'm hanging up now, Jack."

"OK, then. He'll have to read about the murder in the paper."

"That's where normal, decent people are supposed to read about murders."

"Then, put him on the phone because he ain't neither."

Poking Hugh in the pillow, she ordered, "Take this call. Jack just murdered someone and he wants to tell you all about it."

The pillow came off faster than she thought possible.

"Jack just murdered someone?"

"You needn't sound so hopeful. Business isn't that grim."

Handing him the receiver, Ellen slipped out of bed to retrieve the baby. Jacqueline in arm, she settled into a chair, determined not to leave and thus relieve the party of the second part from the squall.

"Hello?" Hugh shouted. "Who did you kill?"

"I don't know."

"You don't know who you killed?"

"I mean, I don't know who killed him."

"Him, who?"

"Stanley Wexler."

The end of sleep as he knew it vanished up the proverbial chimney.

"Oh, no."

"Oh, yes."

"When did this happen?"

"A few hours ago."

"How did you find out?"

"I was with Dad when he got the call."

"What were you doing with Dad?"

"Playing penny poker."

Without bothering to put his hand over the mouthpiece, Hugh turned his attention to Ellen.

"Are you and this telephone a dream?"

"Better hope not or you'll have a hard time explaining Jackie. What did he say?"

"He was over at the Wade's playing poker when Dad got a call about Stanley Wexler being murdered."

Responding with legal instincts older than the profession, she quipped, "Hang up now and we'll deny ever having taken the call. He's obviously drunk or calling from a locked ward."

Sadly, Hugh had gone to a different law school.

"They don't have telephones in mental institutions."

Fortunately, her degree had been issued by the School of Protecting Your Derriere.

"Ask him who was winning. If he says he was, he's delusional and you can hang up. If he says Dad was, I'm calling Mary for eyewitness testimony."

Because the clock read 3:45, he responded as though it were 9:30. *Ante meridiem.*

"Who was winning?"

As though it was a perfectly normal question to ask, Jack responded in like manner.

"Dad. He cheats." After a pause, he added, "Like father, like son."

Absorbing the insult, if such it was, Hugh snapped, "You're his son, too."

"He cheats better'n both of us."

If the first statement had not been an insult, the second surely was.

Shoulders slumped, Hugh shook his head in Ellen's direction.

"It must be true."

Accepting the inevitable, she tried another approach.

"Has Jack been arrested for the murder? If so, he can bail himself out. He's had enough practice."

Hugh eagerly spoke into the phone.

"Are you in jail?"

"I'm at the jail."

"That's a relief." To Ellen, he elucidated, "He's already bailed himself out."

"Then, why is he bothering us?"

Somehow hearing the question over the baby's crying, Jack snapped, "I'm not a suspect."

"Then, why did Dad arrest you?"

"He didn't."

"You could be guilty. Is he holding you on the grounds you might escape? Did he ask you to turn in your passport? Don't make any confession until you've spoken to a lawyer."

"I am speaking to a lawyer."

"At the moment, you're speaking with a sleep-deprived father."

"Hugh, will you quit fooling around?"

It was almost too tempting to answer the statement with its dual meaning, but he didn't feel it appropriate to speak lewdly in front of his wife.

"Someone murdered Stanley Wexler. You went down to the precinct with Lieutenant Wade to get the scoop. You immediately suspected Bill Boerner and you wanted to warn me he might need a lawyer. Is that it?"

Jack's audible sigh reached Sacramento.

"Yes."

"What do you expect me to do? I can't call him. That would appear as though I suspect him."

"He's your client."

"He's a man who came into my office consulting me about a business contract, not a homicide. We made no legal agreements. I merely offered him some free advice. That doesn't constitute an attorney-client relationship."

"OK, but I told you he said he was gonna get Wexler."

"Hearsay," Hugh snapped.

"You mean, you won't represent him?"

"We don't even know if he needs representation, Jack. How was Wexler killed?"

"Autopsy pending. Some suspicion of poison because the guy was in perfect health and he puked over the floor before he died."

"Jack, I'm sorry the man's dead. If it was murder, I'm sorry someone felt that was their only avenue of redress. But, at 4:00 in the morning, I'm even sorrier you woke us up."

"I thought you might be interested. You used to be," he added as an afterthought in a hurt tone.

"Now, you make me sound like an ambulance chaser."

Jack had the audacity to laugh.

"I'm gonna tell Wade you're not interested. That oughta make him happy."

"That makes one of us. Good night."

Groping for the receiver and failing to reach it on the first try, he settled for dropping the handset onto the bed.

"Are you going to go down there?" Ellen asked in resignation.

"No."

"Good. Then get me two aspirin and a glass of water."

"Are you going to drug the baby?"

He sounded more hopeful than he should have.

"I'm going to take them, myself. And during the exchange I'm going to hand Jacqueline to you. You walk her around the living room while I try to go back to sleep."

"What about my sleep?"

"You can doze at the office."

Which made him sorry he asked.

The day dawned bright and sunny without a drop of rain in sight which further dampened Hugh Kerr's outlook on the morning. Regretfully deciding that rushing back to work instead of taking his pre-arranged "baby holiday" off might not have been the best idea, he entered his office with the enthusiasm of a high-schooler facing finals.

"Good morning, Mr. Kerr," Geraldine greeted. Being a linguist, he translated the first two words of her sentence into, "You look terrible," therefore replying, "I feel terrible." Likewise, she answered without realizing he had read his mind. "Did the baby keep you up all night?"

"No. Jack Merrick did. If you see him, tell him I'm not entertaining this morning."

"Too late. He heard me come in and popped over."

Glancing around the office with heavily-lidded eyes, he determined it to be empty.

"Has he now added invisibility to his repertoire of sleuth accomplishments?"

"He's waiting in your office."

"Why?"

"Because he brought two cups of coffee so I thought you were expecting him."

"Good deduction."

Removing his hat and carrying it in his right hand while maintaining control of his briefcase with his left, he trooped down the corridor. Fortunately, the door had been left ajar, merely requiring a soft kick to widen the entranceway. Not seeing Jack in his accustomed place on the barstool, he glanced over toward the picture window and found him lounging on the couch smoking a cigarette and reading the newspaper.

"Business must be slow," he sourly observed.

"I was just reading up on Wexler's murder. Made the headline. It's the top story all across the state and the second or third lead throughout the country. A neat trifecta," he chuckled.

Whether from curiosity or as a challenge, he demanded, "How do you know?"

"I have a shortwave radio. I always tune in to whatever stations I can get as soon as I wake up. That way, if there's anything pertinent, I'm not caught by surprise."

"You expect to be called in on a federal case?"

"No, but you might." He grinned. "As a P.I., you ask me the darndest things."

"Which puts me on the level of a kid," Hugh grunted in reference to the television show hosted by Art Linkletter. "When do you have time to watch daytime TV?"

"He's funny as all get out." Tossing the paper aside Jack got up and wandered over, a paper coffee cup in hand. "Here. Thought you might need this."

Before accepting it, he asked, "Does it go on your expense account?"

"Yeah, but only one. I paid for mine on my own dime."

"I'm relieved to hear it." Glancing at the morning edition Geraldine had set on his desk, Hugh scanned the first few paragraphs of the featured article. "Doesn't give much detail." Removing the lid, he pursued, "It doesn't even mention he was poisoned."

"That hasn't been confirmed. It's P.I."

Hugh offered him a blank stare.

"It's… private investigator?"

"Privileged information."

"You can't use the same initials in the same conversation to mean two different things."

"You got it, didn't you?"

"Not without asking." Then, with measured exasperation, "I suppose 'Dad' let you tag along when he went to investigate?"

"Hell, no. But, I ambled down to the precinct to catch the early morning buzz. Prelim suspicion seems to be centered around a massive heart attack because Wexler was in perfect health. It could – or it couldn't – explain the vomit, leaving open the window for murder by poison. If he was poisoned, the coroner will have to identify the substance on a toxicology report." Flipping open his black pocket notebook, Jack checked for details. "First spotted at his office at the track around 10:00 P.M. by the janitor. He thought he was asleep in his chair and didn't want to disturb him so he went back around midnight. This time, he went in, determined he was dead and called an ambulance. The original diagnosis was heart attack but when a famous man croaks without being under a doctor's care the cops are always brought in and the body sent to the coroner. Over the objection of the family, I might add."

"Oh? Why was that?"

"They didn't want any scandal attached to his death. Besides," he added somewhat more kindly, "most people don't like to think of their loved ones being cut up after death."

"I would think most people would like to know the truth."

Jack stared at him in wonder, slowly shaking his head.

"Hugh, this guy was big. Bigger than big. The flags around the Sporting World – that's capital 'S,' capital 'W' – are already flying at half-mast."

"I'm missing the connection."

"Because we're a country that runs on sports. Guys check the baseball scores before they shave in the morning. They take a gander at the track results, too. Team owners and blue-blood thoroughbred breeders are celebrities. One of them pops off, it's lower the standard for a full month. A ball player or a horse, maybe a week. A pitcher or a jockey at least a day."

"You mean, similar to turning off the lights on Broadway when a theatre luminary dies. As a gesture of respect."

"That's the ticket."

"An actor has talent; all an owner has is money."

"Oh, baby, you'll never get it, will you? Americans love guys with deep pockets."

"They're enamored by gangsters with machine guns, too, but I wouldn't lower the flag for Big Al or Bonnie and Clyde."

"A man out standing in his field," Jack sighed, making an obvious break between "out" and "standing."

Hugh sipped the coffee in resignation.

"Need I remind you, we don't have a client, yet? All this early morning extracurricular activity of yours may be for naught."

"Naught? You're reverting to your Harvard days, pal."

"I didn't get any sleep last night. That has a tendency to make me loquacious."

"Work on it. Well, I'm off. Things to do, places to go and all that. I'll let you know if I hear anything else."

"You do that."

Whistling a merry tune that went unappreciated by his listener, Jack slipped out the back door. Before Hugh had time to catch his bearings after that somewhat unappreciated interview, Geraldine appeared at the door.

"Your first client is here, Mr. Kerr."

"Who is it?"

"I left the reservation card on your desk."

Glancing down, he saw a dozen file cards.

"Which one?"

"The one on top."

Picking it up, he scanned the handwriting.

"This doesn't tell me anything more than name, rank and serial number."

She looked confused.

"Name, address and phone number. Are you looking at the right cards?"

"What-does-he-want?"

"I suppose he'll tell you. Shall I send him in?"

As she left, he consulted the ceiling.

"This is no way to run a law office."

The client who passed the receptionist found his attorney talking to himself. It was not a good way to begin a legal relationship.

The call came in at 11:55, just as Hugh finished with his third client of the morning. Standing at the door rather than using the intercom, Geraldine waited until the lawyer glanced up to speak.

"I'm about ready to take my lunch break, Mr. Kerr. Are you available for a telephone call, or shall I have the party call back?"

Reacting to the first of her statements, his hand jerked up.

"Just a minute." Snapping the two clasps on his briefcase, Hugh withdrew the envelope Ellen had prepared. "Will you drop by the bank on your way back and deposit these checks?"

"I wasn't planning on going out. I brought my lunch. I was just going to sit in the break room."

Ellen had not prepared him for that denial.

"You're not going out?"

"No. Eating out is expensive and I only indulge myself once a month on payday . I could do it on my way home, but the bank is in the opposite direction of my bus stop. And besides," she added before he thought of an answer, "I don't get off until five. The bank would be closed before I got there."

"The deposit slip is made out for today. How is it going to get there if you don't take it?"

As the solution was obvious, she readily supplied it.

"You can take it on your lunch break."

"And stand in line? At noon? Behind fifty women?"

She surprised him by responding, "I should think you'd find that proposition intriguing. Being a man," she unnecessarily added.

"I'm married."

"You have not carried your point with the jury, sir."

"Who – who are you?" he stammered.

"Geraldine Sterrett."

"You've changed."

"Working alone in an office with irate clients filling the waiting room and refusing to believe you won't come in just for them; having the phone ring off the hook; and being unable to leave my desk for the necessities of life has had that effect on me."

"Can you revert to what you were when Mrs. Kerr returns?"

"I doubt it, sir."

He slapped his forehead.

"I'm doomed."

"I shall return promptly at 12:30. Will that be all?"

Unable to counter, she took his silence for an affirmative and departed. It wasn't until he had returned the envelope to his briefcase, slammed it shut and shoved it out of his way, incidentally knocking off his marble pen holder, that he remembered the phone call. Secretly hoping the caller had grown weary of waiting and hung up, he snatched the handset and growled, "Hello?"

"Mr. Kerr, thank goodness you answered!"

Foiled from the outset.

"Who is this?"

"Bill Boerner. You remember, I met you in your office several days ago? It was about a contract for a miracle cream —? With Jack Merrick and —"

"Yes, yes, I remember."

"I've been taken downtown for questioning, sir."

Because his mind was on lunch, he missed the obvious reference to "downtown," meaning "police station," and his reply came out sounding something like, "Why are they questioning you at the deli? Can't you make up your mind?" instead of, "Why are the police questioning you? Don't say anything before consulting a lawyer."

Fortunately for him, as was often the case, the listener heard what he expected the attorney to say rather than what he actually articulated.

"They think I may be involved with the murder."

Hugh's stomach growled.

"Are you?"

"No, sir! I'm as innocent as the driven snow."

Mentally correcting the expression to, "I'm as pure as the driven snow" for no better reason than he was annoyed, Hugh glanced at his watch.

"It's 12:05."

When he failed to follow up on the statement, Boerner guessed, "Does that mean you can get down here by 12:30?"

"No, it means it's lunch time."

"I need help, Mr. Kerr. I don't know who else to call. You said you were my lawyer."

Although he could have argued the point, Jack's early morning conversation had already sealed the deal.

"All right. Sit tight."

And do not let the bedbugs bite.

Not especially appropriate, but it rhymed and a man was likely to think anything when his stomach was empty. A similar reference to what his receptionist had meant about standing in line with fifty secretaries.

Dropping the phone down in defeat, he strode to the coat tree, grabbed his hat and left the office.

As luck would have it, homicide detective Hank Wade was waiting for him as he made his appearance at precisely 12:30.

"You made good time," he greeted the lawyer. "I had you pegged for 12:35."

"The parking lot was empty. All the staff must be out to lunch. Why didn't you go with them?"

"I've eaten," he replied with a smugness Hugh found irritating. "At 11:00. Mary packed me a tuna salad sandwich, cheese sticks –"

"What kind of cheese?"

"Sharp cheddar. Your favorite, by the way. Six oatmeal-walnut-raisin cookies and a banana. Sounds more like she was making it for you, doesn't it?"

"You-ate-my-lunch," he accused. Hank smiled. "And, why did you eat so early? No one has lunch at 11:00."

"I've been up all night. I skipped breakfast. Any more questions, Counselor, or do you want to get down to business?"

"Can you call Mom and ask her to bring down a duplicate order for me?"

"That would be consorting with the enemy. Word has it you're not at your best when starving."

Looking around to make sure no one was listening, Hugh snapped, "I'm your son."

"I tend to forget those niceties when I'm working."

"All right, let's get this over with. Are you charging my client with murder?"

"Nope. Just want to have a friendly chat with him."

"He's innocent."

"Is that so? How do you know?"

"Because I don't defend guilty people."

Hank chuckled and stepped away from the wall upon which he had been leaning.

"I'll pass that tidbit along to Mr. Bond. The D.A. will be glad to know he needn't bother charging any of your clients. Save everyone a lot of time and expense. Won't do much for your reputation, though."

"How's that?"

"No courtroom theatrics. That's what draws the crowds."

"I should think being exonerated for a crime they didn't commit would be enough to satisfy most people."

"You'd be surprised. How's my granddaughter?" he chatted as they walked toward the interrogation room.

"Loud."

"Good lungs. Glad to hear it."

"You didn't warn me."

"About your client being guilty?"

"Babies."

"Wouldn't have stopped you. It never does. When's Ellen coming back?" he asked, guessing the true cause of Hugh's irritation.

"Not-soon-enough."

Opening the door, Wade held back, allowing the attorney to enter before him. Bill Boerner popped up and rushed forward.

"I'm glad to see you! I've never been arrested before and –"

Wade clucked his tongue.

"Come now, Mr. Boerner, a lie is a bad way to start an interview. We've run your record. Two D&Ds and a barroom brawl –"

"Those were after big racing wins –"

"They still count. Sit down," he added in warning. Boerner complied and took out a pack of cigarettes. Offering one to Hugh, who refused, he lit one and shrugged.

"I don't know why I'm here. I didn't have anything to do with Mr. Wexler's death."

"We generally like to have a chat with recently fired employees. That makes for a good motive."

Bill slapped his hand on the table.

"OK, so he canned me and I was sore. But, not mad enough to kill him."

"Let's be careful what we say, Bill." Stepping between the officer and his client, Hugh used his body to make the point. One chuckled and the other pouted. "I'd like a few minutes alone with Mr. Boerner."

"Come on, Kerr," Wade cajoled. "On a full stomach, I'm not in the mood to charge anyone with murder. In fact," he added, taking out a roll of Life Savers and studiously peeling away the top foil, "we're not even calling it a murder at this stage. May very well have been a natural death. They happen, sometimes."

"Do tell." Noting Hank did not offer him a candy, Hugh's eye narrowed. "What flavor is that?"

Rolling the ring around in his mouth, Hank determined, "Cherry."

"Five Flavors," Hugh disgustedly identified the roll. "I had you pegged for a peppermint man."

"Spearmint, actually," Wade corrected. "But the precinct vending machine doesn't carry them. Only Five Flavors and peppermint."

"You carry a lot of weight around here. You ought to complain."

Hank blew air through his cheeks.

"Not as much as you think. Or, perhaps," he reconsidered, "not as much as I should. Considering I'm Hugh Kerr's greatest nemesis." Holding up a hand to indicate the banter was at an end, he stepped away. "I'll be back in ten. That long enough?"

Hugh nodded, waited until the door closed behind the detective then instantly morphed into an entirely different persona.

"All right, you heard him. They haven't determined the death to be at the hands of another."

"Then, why am I here?"

"They saw something they didn't like. He didn't say and I don't know. Something suspicious in the room where the body was found; the position of the body, perhaps. Jack mentioned Wexler vomited. That might indicate poison. Skin coloration; splotches. Lieutenant Wade doesn't overlook anything."

"He didn't seem to like you."

"Looks can be deceiving. We bring out the best in one another. Take it from me, he wants to know the truth as much as we do. And," he added with meaning, "he doesn't like to be lied to. He picked up immediately on your statement about never having been arrested. He'll hold that against you."

"It was a slip of the tongue. I meant I'd never been arrested for a major crime."

"When you've been pulled in for questioning in a murder case, you can't afford to take anything for granted. A slip of the tongue can tip the scales between being dismissed as a suspect and being charged."

"But, he said it wasn't a murder… yet."

"It was," Hugh grimly stated.

"How do you know?"

"I have the same gut feeling Wade does. And you have the most obvious motive."

"How do they know that already?" Bill demanded, wringing his hands in nervous agitation.

Hugh held up a finger for attention.

"Pay attention. Nothing I ever say is meaningless. While it may seem I'm having a little verbal jousting with him, I confirmed he had been up all night working on the case. That means he's had you checked out and memorized your rap sheet. That he's already interviewed the janitor who found the body, spoken to Wexler's secretary and had a look at the victim's appointment book for the last two weeks. He's traced the man's whereabouts on the night of his death and made a list of those who may have had an interest in his demise. By the end of today he'll know Wexler's financial status and he'll have put word out on the street asking whether he was involved in any... unsavory dealings."

"What does that mean?"

"Fixing races – that's always good for blackmail. Betting over his head – that brings out the loan sharks. A messy divorce. Any one of those little 'indiscretions' tells Wade where to look for suspects. In your case, you were fired. If you ran off at the mouth with Jack Merrick and I have his statement that you did, you probably blew off steam to others, as well. A bartender; a cab driver. Your landlady."

"I didn't kill him, Mr. Kerr! I swear to you. I was sore, but I've known the man for years."

Taking out another cigarette, Bill had it in his mouth as Hugh offered a flame from his lighter. Accepting the gesture, Boerner lit the smoke and puffed madly away.

"You've known the man for years," the attorney repeated, "yet you seriously misjudged him. You thought he'd sell you a horse and stand idly by as you and your associates got wealthy on a miracle cream. But, no sooner had you left the room than he picked up the phone and double-crossed you. That's two motives and brings you to the top of the class. Where were you last night?"

Boerner dropped his head.

"I wasn't anywhere."

"Where were you last night?" he repeated in the same monotone.

"Do I have to say?"

"Not if you want to be convicted." He let the statement sink in before adding, "Perhaps you'd feel more comfortable speaking with another attorney."

"No! You. I want you."

"Then, don't hold anything back. What you say to me is in confidence. If you did kill him, I need to know now. This instant. In which case, we discuss how to handle the situation. If you weren't involved – and by that I mean even peripherally – either as an accomplice or merely as someone who knew what was going down – I need to develop your defense."

"So, I was there last night," Bill begrudgingly admitted.

"You were where?"

"In Wexler's office. But, he was alive when I left."

"What time was this?"

"Around 7 P.M."

"Then, I ask you again: did you murder him?"

"No!"

"I'll accept that on face value for the moment. Why did you go there?"

"He invited me."

"Invited, or summoned?"

"Asked me to drop by. I hoped he was going to offer me my job back."

"Did he?"

"In a manner of speaking. So you see," he blurted, "I had no reason to kill him."

"What does 'in a manner of speaking' mean?"

"He wanted me to change sides. Instead of working with Mrs. Pazel and Jack on the spray deal, he asked if I'd help promote it for him."

"What did he offer you in exchange for betraying your partners?"

"You don't have to put it like that."

"That's how the D.A. will look at it."

"Why?"

"Because juries don't like suspects who play the rat."

The bluntness of the statement sobered the man. Pushing away from the table, he got up and walked to the window of the small room.

"Mr. Wexler could ruin me. Being fired was bad enough but he held sway around the entire racing world. He bad-mouths me and I'll never work again. Then, what do I do? Horses are all I know. So, I told him yes." He turned back, eyes hard. "The lady and Jack are no more hurt than they would have been if I had never said anything. It was my idea to take that spray, or cream, to the big time. She wasn't doing anything with it but curing her neighbor's dog," he added in bitterness. "The patent belonged to Mega Enterprises, not her. And Jack was just along for the ride. So, I figured I might as well get something out of it. Then, if I hit it big, I'd slip them a few bucks as a thank you."

Hugh casually strode toward the door, opposite his client.

"I put it to you that Wexler did offer a deal. Come along for the ride, as you say. Play up the 'miracle' aspect. Train Barrister's Baby, get her ready to race. When she wins, make a big deal out of how the horse was being put to pasture when this product was tried on her. You tell the press all the wondrous cures it can effect and then step back and let Wexler take it from there. He's the one who developed the cream. He's the one who ordered you to use it. He's the one who bought the patent and put his name on it: let's call it 'Wexler's Miracle Vanishing Cream.' That has a certain appeal, doesn't it? Like the vanishing cream women keep on their nightstand. Apply at night, works wonders during the hours of darkness, and they wake up with fresh, radiant skin. A panacea for the racing world and for horsemen everywhere. You get a small bonus. Let's say $500 and you get to keep your job. Wasn't it something like that?"

"Maybe."

"Maybe," Hugh repeated. "You expected a great deal more than that. The offer insulted you. You wanted a partnership. Fifty-fifty was it? Or, even thirty-seventy. Whatever the percentage, you demanded your fair share for discovering the cure. Maybe even wanted your name on it. He laughed in your face. You got angry and killed him."

"How?" he jeered.

"You already guessed the man who had betrayed you once was going to do it again so you came prepared. Assuming he was poisoned, you brought some with you. Slipped it in his drink. With Wexler dead, it's back to business. You bring your former partners together and tell them the plan's still on." Crossing his arms, Hugh smiled, assuming a disarming, almost charming expression. "I've just made the case for the prosecution, Mr. Boerner. And it's a *damned* good one."

"Maybe he won't think that way."

"Never underestimate the opposition. That's exactly where Mr. Bond will take it. And on the strength of what I've just outlined, he'll get a conviction. There's no defense for airtight logic."

"But, I didn't kill him!" he screamed. "You've got to help me."

"Keep your voice down! You think Wade isn't standing outside listening?"

"That's illegal, isn't it?"

"Not when you're shouting for all the world to hear."

Boerner slumped against the window sill, completely deflated.

"How do I prove my innocence?"

"I don't know."

"But... you're supposed to know everything."

This time, Hugh laughed.

"No one knows everything."

"You have to catch whoever really killed Wexler."

"That's the job for the police and I suspect they feel they're close to 'solving' it. Presuming, of course, they can prove Wexler was murdered."

"Am I going to be charged?"

"Not today."

"Tomorrow?"

"I don't speak for Lieutenant Wade. A lot will depend on whatever else he discovers. For all we know, he may find a better suspect. Stranger things have happened. In which case, you're off the hook."

"And if I'm not?"

"We'll take it from there."

"But, you will help me?" he pleaded, hands extended. "And, Mr. Kerr... I'm sorry I was a rat."

"I'm not the one you need to apologize to. And, yes, I'll do what I can."

Boerner crossed over, arm extended.

"I appreciate it." The two men shook as Hugh prepared to leave. "Mr. Kerr?"

"Yes?"

"One question. You told me nothing you ever said was meaningless. Then, what was your point when you asked Lieutenant Wade about his roll of Five Flavors Life Savers?"

This finally prompted a sincere grin.

"Merely to establish that he can take what he's given and run with it."

The reply failed to elicit a return expression of amusement.

CHAPTER 13

Hugh inserted his key to the apartment and was in the process of turning the lock when the door opened from the inside. Expecting Ellen, he did a double-take when identifying the woman as Mary Wade.

"Hi, Mom!" he greeted with enthusiasm. "Are you here to stay?"

Readjusting the baby she held in her arms, she stepped aside to let him enter.

"We were just going out."

"Out?"

"Not 'out' out, as in outdoors" she clarified, "but out into the corridor. It's almost like a park in here with all the lovely plants you've set along the corridor. I walk her up and down and then we stop at the windows at the end. She appreciates a different view." Cuddling Jacqueline, she swelled with pride. "Her eyes are so bright, Hugh, and I've forgotten how fast babies develop. She grasps and yanks and kicks like a wrestler and the interest she shows in her world is amazing. I believe she actually comprehends the street below one window is actually different than what she sees from another."

Taking Jackie's outstretched hand, the proud father squeezed it, then kissed her forehead.

"She also knows a good thing when she sees it. Grandma makes a pretty good rickshaw."

"I suppose I do and it's a delightful thing to be. Good exercise, too."

"Rover's loss is Miss Jacqueline's gain. How's the old fellow doing, by the way?"

"He's perfect. His coat is as thick and shiny as ever. He's gotten quite fond of Mr. Forsch but when he sees Hank coming, you'd think he was a four-legged puppy the way he runs up to him, yipping and tail wagging a mile a minute."

"Sometimes, adoptions work out just fine."

"Sometimes?"

"Had a nice chat with Dad down at the station."

"Nice as in 'nice,' or nice as in 'not nice'?"

Hugh chuckled before putting on his lawyer's face.

"He ate my lunch. The one you actually packed for me – with all the oatmeal-walnut-raisin cookies. And the banana." She waited for it. "And the tuna sandwich."

"Ah. He ate your lunch. I suppose that means he didn't use the paper napkin I put in there for your special use," she teased. "I hope he brings it home with the bag home so I can re-use it."

"Better ask him. I wouldn't want my lips to touch anything his have."

The baby grew impatient and kicked her feet. In the process a sock flew off. Hugh retrieved it, made a futile attempt to replace it then abandoned the effort.

"We better get going. Her Majesty's just stepped on the gas pedal."

"I was wrong, Mom. You're not a rickshaw, you're a Rolls Royce."

"Better save your flattery for your father."

"Never that."

He watched as the happy pair began their stroll before slipping inside the apartment and tossing his hat on the end table by the door.

"Hi, honey, I'm home!"

Ellen laughed as she came out to greet him.

"Too many comedies for you. I'm afraid exposure to television has radically altered your speech. You've gone from a stiff upper-lip Canadian to a cliché-riddled United States-American."

"Thank you for clarifying that. Which do you like better?"

"You're perfect either way."

"Oh, flattery will get you everywhere. Mom just told me to try it on Dad."

"I asked Mom to come by so I could have some help around the house. There's so much I've let go and I really need to catch up on my sleep before I consider going back to work."

"More pleasant words I have never heard," he sighed. "When? How soon? Has it really been three months?"

"Not yet, but I'm trying to prepare myself. In a way, I'm almost sorry and on the other hand, I'm excited. I miss the office. And sharing your life with you."

"Has being home been easier or harder than you expected?"

"Both. But, I'm glad I took the time, Hugh, and I appreciate your patience."

"Mine?" he asked in wonder. "You're the one doing double duty. But the baby has changed our lives, hasn't she?"

"That, more than anything else caught me off guard. Looking back, I don't know why. I guess I just presumed she'd be a happy addition without realizing everything we did, from waking and sleeping to our own relationship would have to be adjusted."

"I thought the same thing, so we're both guilty of being naive. But, we're happy, aren't we? We made the right decision to have a baby?"

"Yes, Hugh. The absolute right decision. And we are happy. I'd like to think happier than we've ever been. We've worked through the rough spots and that's made our love stronger."

"Counsel for the defense rests. I love you, Ellen."

"And I love you, too, sweetheart. But tell me, why did Mom ask you to try flattery on Dad? Did you have a run-in with him?"

"Not a bit of it. It seems we're sharing Bill Boerner."

"Does that mean he's been arrested? Was Wexler murdered, then?"

"Looks like a heart attack but Wade's suspicious. And where he smells smoke, he usually discovers fire," he added for good measure.

"It would be sad if Mr. Boerner did kill that man. He and Amy and Jack had such high hopes for her cream. It was a dirty trick Wexler pulled. I suppose you're going to take the case?"

"Looks like it." Crossing into the kitchen, he sniffed appreciatively. "What's for dinner? I'm starved."

"Breaded chicken breasts, steamed carrots and artichokes. You want a salad before it?"

"Yes, please."

"Fix yourself a drink and I'll make it. How does Boerner's case look?" she pursued, opening the refrigerator to get out the lettuce and other vegetables.

"He had a clandestine meeting with Wexler the night he died. Sold out for his job back and a pat on the head."

"Then, why murder him?"

"Resentment. Opportunity. With Wexler out of the way, he could still get the product up and running before the estate was ever settled. And, there's no saying whoever inherits would bother with the cream. It would be nothing more than a chancy sideline."

"That's the contention of the prosecution."

"Yes," he agreed, mixing two Manhattans. "I've already worked out Bond's strategy. I like it better than mine."

"You think Boerner is guilty?"

"No."

"Then, who killed Wexler? Or, was it really a heart attack?"

"If they don't identify the poison, that's where I'm going with it. Here," he offered, crossing back into the kitchen with a glass for her. Accepting it, she touched rim to rim.

"Here's to natural deaths."

They both sipped the alcohol before turning as a loud knock on the door was followed by the appearance of Hank Wade, closely followed by Mary and Jacqueline.

"The gang's all here," he announced. "When do we eat?"

"With that large lunch you had, it's a wonder you can even think of food," Hugh greeted in return.

"That was at 11:00." Hank checked his watch. "It's six o'clock, now. That's seven hours ago. I'm a growing boy and need my nourishment."

"Won't be a minute," Ellen promised.

"I'll just go and put the baby down and help," Mary offered. The baby, however, had other ideas and started squalling. "I'll just hold Jacqueline and supervise," she quickly amended.

"Want a drink Dad, Mom?"

"Don't mind if I do," he agreed.

"No, thank you," she declined. Scowling at her husband, she decided, "You hold the baby and I'll assist in the kitchen. I wouldn't want either of you men to perish from hunger if dinner is delayed."

Raising an eyebrow at Hugh, Hank accepted his charge without complaint.

"You can see who runs my house."

"But, you run homicide. Identify the poison, yet?"

"If I did I wouldn't tell you."

"I'll have the coroner's report before you do."

"That's probably true," he growled. "Must be a nice sideline for Grindley. How much do you pay him?"

"Oh, not me," Hugh innocently protested. "That old grump wouldn't give me the time of day off a ten cent watch."

"Too much television," Hank growled to the women.

"I was just telling him that," Ellen agreed.

"Then, where do you get your classified information from? No, don't tell me. But, don't think you're not guilty by association. That Merrick character spends more time at the precinct than most cops. Passing out your hard-earned money."

"You admit so much? That my money is hard-earned?"

"It will be this time."

"You're going to arrest Boerner?"

"I don't talk shop at home. And considering I've been spending more time at your home than mine lately, this place qualifies."

Flopping down on the couch, Hank began playing with his granddaughter. Half an hour later they were called to supper. Jackie was put to bed, the adults shared their meal together in peace and then, by mutual consent, spent the rest of the evening listening to Hugh's record collection. As the Black Forest grandfather clock chimed nine o'clock, the Wades both yawned.

"Time for bed," Hank announced. "You two can stay up and do whatever young married people do when their parents hit the hay. Just be quiet about it."

"Don't tell us you've forgotten," Hugh tried, but Ellen saved Hank from answering by quickly announcing, "Oh, no. We're right behind you."

Saying their good-nights, the couples separated, going their own ways. By nine-thirty the house was dark and the Sandman had done his work.

At six o'clock the following morning, Hank was up and dressed. Hearing him in the living room, Hugh emerged, tying the belt of his robe as testimony to the fact he had just awoken.

"Why up so early?" he asked with a yawn.

"Duty calls."

"Can I make you some coffee?"

"Mary made it half an hour ago."

"Oh. Tough, being a cop's wife."

"She always say so. She also made your lunch," he added, hefting a brown paper sack. "The same as mine so we don't have to quibble over it."

"Does that mean I'll be seeing you this morning?"

"It might just be we exchange a few pleasantries downtown."

"Shall I bring doughnuts?"

"If you do, you'll be a popular man at the station. For as long as it takes for the boys to eat them. Then, it's back to business as usual."

"They hate my guts, too?"

"You're only charming at home, dear boy."

"And I try so hard."

"Like hell you do. You're an irritant, Hugh. Like a cinder in the eye. No matter how hard you work on it, you can't be gotten rid of."

"Try eye drops."

"In your case it will have to be crocodile tears. See ya."

Grabbing his hat and coat, Wade waved and hurried off. Slightly depressed at the presumption Wexler's death had been ruled a homicide, he went into the kitchen and prepared himself a cup of coffee. Once finished, he decided it was too late to go back to bed, so he dressed, whispered good-bye to Ellen, kissed his daughter and left for the office.

The morning was unusually hectic and he had almost forgotten about the reason for his early morning arrival. It wasn't until two o'clock when his phone rang and Geraldine's voice announced, "Mr. Merrick on line one," that he remembered. He picked up the receiver with resignation.

"Hello, Jack. Don't tell me, I know –"

"You know about the arrest?" the detective asked in almost breathless wonder. Taken aback by the other's surprise, Hugh nodded.

"Wade spent the night with Ellen and me. He was up at the crack of dawn so I presumed he got the results of the toxicology report."

"Who could have believed it?"

A cold chill ran down Hugh's back.

"Believed what?"

"That the cops would arrest Amy Pazel for the murder of Stanley Wexler."

Sinking back in his chair, Hugh closed his eyes. Jack's shocking information meant two things: he had a new client and he would not be bringing doughnuts to the precinct.

By the time Hugh arrived downtown, his client had been photographed, fingerprinted and issued prison garb to wear. Looking smaller, thinner and paler than he remembered her from their former interview, she stood up as he arrived and smiled, something else he hardly expected.

"Hello, Mr. Kerr. I appreciate you coming down. And, I'm sorry you have to be inconvenienced at the end of the day."

"I'm sorry you're here," he countered, working on his own grin. "Does that make us even?"

"Only if we could exchange clothes, but I'm afraid I'd have to cuff the trousers and I don't have needle and thread with me. Unless," she hopefully suggested, "you could arrange to have my pocketbook returned."

"You carry a needle and thread with you?"

"Of course. It's often been noted I ought to have a revolving door replace the standard one at my office."

"Why is that?"

"I'm a woman working in a man's world. In fact, I'm the only female chemist Mega Enterprise employs. When one of my co-workers experiences an embarrassing rip, tear, loss of button, stuck zipper, or stain, they come running to me." As he digested the statement, she added, "When you're out and about with your wife and need a tissue, who supplies it?"

"She does," he replied, catching the implication.

"Spare change, matches, tweezers to remove a splinter?"

He bowed his head in respect.

"Point made, Counselor."

"I also happen to be a seamstress and a quilter."

"When do you find the time between work, home, children and husband?"

"One doesn't 'find' time, one makes it."

"I see. You don't sleep."

"Not very much," she admitted, silently judging him on the order in which he phrased his question.

Indicating she take a chair, he waited until she was seated before settling in beside her.

"Where does murder fit into your schedule?"

"Figurative or literal?"

His shoulders shook as he silently appreciated the rejoinder.

"Let's concentrate on literal for the moment."

"It doesn't."

"You did not kill Stanley Wexler?"

"In my own way, I try to improve life, Mr. Kerr. Not take it."

"I'm glad to hear it." He glanced around the room, lips curling. "I'll arrange for bail so you can get out of here. But, we have a lot of work ahead of us. Do you have any idea why you were arrested? I was under the assumption your nominal partner, Bill Boerner, was the prime suspect: if, in fact, it was murder, which I now presume the police have determined. At least to the district attorney's satisfaction."

"I had means, motive and opportunity," she replied in earnest. The answer took him aback.

"How so?"

"I had a meeting with him the night of his death."

"At what time?"

"Eight o'clock."

Hearing a second unexpected statement, he confessed, "I'm glad you're not defending yourself, Mrs. Pazel."

"Why? I'd only go after the truth."

"Unlike chemistry, I've found there are few absolutes in reaching that point. The truth, as they say, is in the eye of the beholder."

"No, that isn't correct. Perception may be in the eye of the beholder but truth is absolute."

He made her a slight bow. "I beg your pardon, madam. Your statement reminds me I'm becoming a little too jaded. You're right, of course."

She grinned at him.

"Like you, in my lab I've occasionally worked my way around several 'absolutes.' It's all in... how you play the game."

"You should have been a lawyer."

"I actually considered it. But, it's critical to do what you love, Mr. Kerr. Putting a dream away until tomorrow is the same thing as not having one."

"What do you do in your spare time, Mrs. Pazel?"

"Aside from raising a husband and three children? I sew, I bake and I am aleader in the Episcopal Church."

"That makes me feel lazy." Waving off further digression, he stood, studied the jail garb she was wearing, then stated in a more formal tone, "Eight o'clock at night is very late for a man to ask a woman for a business meeting." On second thought, he asked, "It was a business meeting, wasn't it?"

"Yes. It was."

"Was anyone else present?"

"No."

"A receptionist in the outer office? A secretary present to take notes?"

"No."

"Anyone see you go in the building? Did you have to check in with security? Speak with a guard?"

"Yes. On both counts."

"That explains how Lieutenant Wade got on to you so fast. What was Wexler's excuse to ask you to his office so late?"

"He said he was leaving town the following morning and what he had to say couldn't wait."

"You didn't find that unusual?"

"Of course I did."

"It didn't give you second thoughts? Did you ask if you could bring your husband along?"

"Yes. And no."

"Why not?"

"Because I'm used to late night business meetings. I've traveled all over the world and been involved in numerous conferences. I've been taken to production plants, had to speak with suppliers at their convenience rather than my own. Met other scientists in airport waiting lounges. Had to attend advertising photo shoots in a lab coat and high heels."

She finally made him chuckle.

"Yes. I've had a discussion or two about dress with my wife. So: you weren't frightened to meet Mr. Wexler alone?"

"I didn't know we were going to be alone," she corrected. "I assumed there would be other people present."

"But there weren't?"

"No."

"Forgive me for asking, but did he get smart with you? Make advances?"

"No. He was perfectly businesslike. Which is to say, he wasn't strictly formal but he never acted inappropriately."

"Did you see Bill Boerner there? Perhaps leaving the building? In the parking lot?"

"No," she said in surprise. "Although Mr. Wexler didn't say so, I actually expected him to be there. Assuming we were going to discuss the cream and he was a partner."

"And Mr. Merrick?"

"Yes, him, too."

"Was it Wexler, himself, who called you?" She nodded. "What time was that?"

"After dinner. I'd say about 5:30 in the evening."

"He didn't give you much time. Why didn't you call Bill or Jack and ask if they were invited? Perhaps, so you could all go together; present a united front."

"I didn't have their phone numbers."

Hugh paced the room as a dozen questions swirled through his mind, only half on the present interrogation and the remainder on constructing a defense. Finally forcing his thoughts back to the present, he stopped, stiffened a moment, then turned back to her.

"How full was the parking lot?"

"It was empty."

"All right: we've established means. You were – in the eyes of the police – the last person to meet with the victim before his death. Which, incidentally, exonerates Boerner. What did he want?"

"To hire me."

"As a chemist, I presume? Not as a partner in his new enterprise?"

"You're correct. To work in his lab and manufacture the spray. There being no need to convert it into a cream since he owned the original patent."

"Your presence in the production plant would be convenient for him, since you know the process –"

"And the suppliers. Some of the chemicals in the formula aren't readily available on the open market."

He raised an eyebrow in surprise.

"But, you had them. In your lab at home. Did you take them from work? By take, I mean, did you steal them?"

He expected a negative reaction and a harsh denial and was pleasantly surprised when she reacted with a calm demeanor.

"I purchased them."

"Even though they were not readily available? And presumably expensive?"

"Mr. Kerr, skin care chemistry is a very small field. Those of us who work in it know one another and if we're any good at our jobs, which I am, we get to know and usually become friends with the suppliers. It was a matter of no consequence for me to buy what I needed."

"Because you were friends with the supplier?"

"It wasn't illegal. We're not speaking of controlled substances, just uncommon ones."

"Could Wexler or his bevy of scientists buy them? Without you?" Folding her hands, Amy looked away as she debated how to answer. Seeing her hesitate, Hugh stepped closer. With his back to the window, he loomed in silhouette, tall, dark and formidable. "Whatever you say is held in confidence, Mrs. Pazel. I mean no harm to anyone and I would never break a confidence between you and your associates. At least, not without your permission."

"I appreciate you reminding me. I was just thinking how to phrase my answer. I suppose it would be difficult. There's a strong bond of loyalty between chemists and the people who sell to them. In the cosmetics field we're not working on secret government contracts or projects that have to do with national security, so the confidence doesn't extend that far. But, taking me as an example, I develop entire lines of skin care products. There's a great deal of money involved, from R&D to production, advertising and shelf space."

"That, I understand," he grunted without humor. "I became a quick-study in the production and sale of toys."

"Then, you understand the concept. A supplier, who is typically very knowledgeable in their field, can make a pretty good guess, based on what I'm ordering, as to the products I'm developing. When I ask for unusual chemicals, they want to know more, if only to be prepared for how much I require. My success is their success."

"But money usually speaks louder than friendship. If I offered them a higher price, I'd expect them to jump at the opportunity to make a better deal."

"If you sold to a competitor – one, Mr. Kerr, who's only interested in developing a single project – you'd betray me, who's a far better one. And one who's also a friend. It wouldn't take one of my suppliers five seconds to determine Wexler was going to manufacture my cream. They'd immediately determine he had bought the patent from Mega and they'd come to me for an explanation."

"And, to ask what the deal was."

"Yes. If I said he had stolen a personal project out from under me, I doubt very much they'd do business with him."

"How hard would it be for him to go somewhere else for what he needed?"

"In the case of my cream, it would be difficult because most chemical houses don't carry the requisite chemicals. A manufacturer would have limited choices. Loyalty means a great deal. I won't say without my approval, but... against my wishes, they would have to decide who is the better client. Me, who not only purchases chemicals for my own research but who buys in bulk for Mega Enterprises, or Mr. Wexler, who's only interested in limited quantities. He could offer them a great deal of money, or go outside the normal channels, but then you're speaking of expensive. You have to remember: he's developing a product with limited appeal. It may work 'miracles,' but only on animals."

"Because developing it for people would require extensive and time-consuming testing before it's approved by the government?"

"Yes. The more you pay for the 'ingredients' to make the cream, the less your profit margin."

"In which case, it might not be worth his bother. Without you."

"You could say that."

Re-taking the seat opposite her, he leaned forward.

"What sort of a deal did Wexler offer you?"

"A job with an excellent salary."

"No profit sharing? No incentives?"

She leaned back, sighed and shook her head.

"Nothing like that. But, it doesn't matter what he offered. I wasn't interested."

"Why not?"

"Because it would have been a betrayal to Mr. Boerner and Mr. Merrick."

Hugh held his own council a moment before finally blinking.

"We're going to need a better defense than that."

"It's the truth."

"Altruism very rarely goes over with a jury."

"I'm sorry to hear that."

"You'd better be." He let the statement stand, then shook his head. "How long did the meeting last?"

"Less than half an hour."

"After which, you got up and left?"

"Yes."

"Around 8:30?"

"That's right."

"Would it interest you to know Boerner had a meeting with Wexler an hour before you did? And that he sold you out? He agreed to go back to work and have Barrister's Baby serve as the 'poster horse' for his new product."

"He was in a bad position."

"And, now you are. The police have their motive. In their eyes, you killed Wexler to regain control of your reformulated cream. The prosecutor will argue Wexler had the money to go ahead with the project even without your help and I believe the jury will buy into that. The police also have opportunity. The last piece of the puzzle – for them – is the poison. What do you know about that?"

"Lieutenant Wade came to my lab at work."

"Did he have a subpoena?"

"I didn't ask. He wanted to look around and I didn't see any reason why they shouldn't."

"What did he do?"

"He introduced another man as a chemist. He went around writing down the names of all the chemicals he saw. He took a number of samples."

Hugh grimly nodded.

"The chemist then went back and gave the list and the samples to the coroner. Based on those, Grindley ordered a new set of toxicology reports and came up with the means of death. That's too bad."

"I had no reason to stop them. I didn't poison Mr. Wexler."

"Someone did. Until the real culprit is found, that's you."

"Innocent until proven guilty, Mr. Kerr." He started to reply, but she spoke over him. "That's the Pollyanna in me. I had that written on an evaluation, once. That I had a Pollyanna personality. Ever pleasant and hopeful."

He raised an eyebrow.

"Was it meant as a compliment?"

She laughed.

"No."

"Well, let's see if I can keep it up for you." Offering his hand, both the suspect and the lawyer stood and shook hands. "First step, bail. Then, the hard work begins."

"Mr. Kerr, I ought to ask. I don't know if I can afford your services. You're a very famous attorney."

He frowned as though the statement was of the gravest import and her answer to the next question would determine her fate.

"What did you charge Mrs. Wade for curing her dog?"

"Nothing."

"I'm very much afraid your altruism may be catching."

He started for the door when she stopped him.

"The jury won't like that."

He laughed out loud.

"I'll only practice it outside the courtroom."

She returned his laugh.

CHAPTER 14

Standing in front of the door, the woman wearing a smart business suit and stylish, low-heeled shoes, hesitated, then took a step back. Quickly assuring herself she was alone in the corridor, she permitted herself a moment to study the sign announcing the names and professional occupations of those who worked within.

> Hugh Kerr:
> Attorney at Law
> Ellen Thorne-Kerr, Associate
> Jack Merrick Detective Agency

A great deal had changed since those words had been inscribed in their place of prominence. As awe-inspiring as they were intimidating, she suddenly felt overcome by emotion, as though she would break a spell should she enter. Clutching her purse, she quickly came to a determination and walked around the corner. There, another door presented itself. With only a slight hesitation she latch-keyed it and walked inside. Supposing the room to the dark, she found it bathed in light as though she were expected, which could not have been the case, for her visit was unheralded.

Heart racing in a type of terrified excitement, the lady, whose name was so prominently placed between the lawyer and the private eye, crossed the room, put her ear to the closed door which led into the main office and listened a moment. Determining her appearance had gone undetected, she then turned to survey her kingdom.

It was as she remembered it. Her desk remained in place, the top neatly and efficiently cleared of pending paperwork. Her typewriter, covered the way she had left it, emitted the same aura of readiness it always did. A small crystal vase used to hold fresh flowers when the occasion arose, sat empty. A marble pen holder, situated opposite on the right side for ease of use, awaited her touch. Along one wall, a bookcase lined with general-use and legal dictionaries, a thesaurus, several reference books on Latin and a collection of worn, leather-bound law books, ranging in age from the late 1800s to the early 1900s filled the shelves.

Smiling in remembrance of what they signified, Ellen opened the bottom drawer of the desk, placed her purse inside, then removed the cover from the typewriter. Refreshing the supply of paper in the low-sided wooden holder, she gathered a steno pad and pen, quickly checked her appearance in a wall-mounted mirror, steadied her resolve and quietly opened the inside door.

As though walking into another world, she was immediately assailed by sights and sounds. From the reception area she heard Geraldine's voice, either speaking on the telephone or talking to a client in the waiting room. Another line rang with urgency. The low murmur of men's voices indicated others were waiting their turn to see the master. A commingling of coffee and cigarette smoke assailed her nostrils, while the sensation of refrigerated air offered both a relief from the morning heat and a slight, unnatural chill.

Without wishing to make an appearance and cause an immediate disruption to the normal flow of business, Ellen drew back a desk drawer, removed two items then slipped out of her office and glided left, down the corridor. Bypassing the kitchen and break room, she came to Hugh's office. Lightly knocking, she waited for a response, heard nothing, and opened the door a crack. Peering in, she found the room empty. Surprised and slightly disconcerted, though there were a dozen logical reasons why he would be absent, she walked inside.

"Hugh?"

The question was mere formality; she felt in an instant he was not there. That he had recently occupied the space was equally apparent. One glance noted the coffee cup. Using the liberty of one close to the subject, she dipped her finger into the liquid and found it still warm. Smiling at the audacity because it was so like Jack, she further copied his style by licking the coffee off her finger for good luck, then inspected the lounge, suspecting he might have stolen a moment to read the morning paper or smoke his pipe. While the early edition had been set out for him, appearances indicated it had not been opened. Nor, did she smell the aromatic blend of Cavendish.

"All work and no play makes Hugh a dull boy," she teased in a quiet voice.

Checking the private bathroom and finding that empty, as well, she mentally reviewed all the places he might have been. The most obvious was that he had gone down the connecting hallway to have a chat with Jack in his own suite of offices. Failing to picture him there, Ellen had almost decided to pull up her accustomed chair and sit by his desk until he returned when another thought occurred to her. Retracing her steps with equal care, she entered the law library. The imposing room that would have done any college library proud, was partitioned off by wall-to-wall glass-fronted lawyer's bookcases. Filled with every legal tome available and hundreds more covering myriad topics, the research room was his treasure trove where, at any given moment, he could discover ancient precedent, check the phases of the moon from decades ago, investigate religious rites, translate obscure symbols and languages, or investigate historical and fictional murders throughout history.

There, sitting at the long table, head in a book, she discovered him. With a leap of joy, Ellen absorbed the scene a moment longer than required, before speaking.

"You'll ruin your eyes, pouring over the pages like that."

"I know," he replied to the familiar voice without looking up. "But, it's how I enjoy what I'm reading; as though I can get more fully absorbed in the text. It... brings me closer. Speaks to me in a way a normal position doesn't allow for."

Suddenly realizing the incongruity of the situation he sat bold upright, took in her face and form, then leapt to his feet. Engulfing Ellen in his arms, Hugh planted a kiss on her lips before standing back in admiration.

"You're home!"

"I'm back."

"Oh, dear God, I missed you!"

Flattered, her eyes watered.

"You saw me two hours ago."

"Yes, but not here. You look different, somehow."

"I'm dressed and made-up for work."

"I like it."

"And not as the mother of your child?"

"Our child," he easily corrected. "I like that, too. In fact, I like everything about you. We ought to get married."

"We are married."

He laughed, then pointed to the pad and pen she held.

"And ready to get down to business. As much as things change, they stay the same."

"Is that good?"

"Perfect. But – where's Baby?"

"Mary's going to bring her here later this morning. We'll see how it goes, Hugh. I'm not sure I'm full speed ahead, yet, but I did want to try. Build back up to full time. Depending on how Mary and Jacqueline adjust."

"They'll be just fine. Sit down. I was just boning up on poisons."

"Planning on murdering someone?"

"Always. But, in this case, Jack just brought over the signed autopsy report on Stanley Wexler."

"They found the poison?"

"Carbon tetrachloride."

"Oh, good."

"Good and bad," he corrected. "They took samples of it from Mrs. Pazel's lab. That's how they knew what to look for. Otherwise, they would have missed it. It's not on your routine list of murder agents. Ingestion simulates a heart attack."

"Too bad. Amy might have gotten away with it."

"Not Amy," he grinned. "Think of someone else. Now that you're back, I need your insight."

"Who's leading the pack?"

"Bill Boerner, I'm sorry to say. The one Wade went after first – not without reason."

"Where would he get – or even know about – carbon tetrachloride?"

"We'll work on that." He indicated she take a chair as he resumed his reading. "Listen to this: it's from a 1917 fire engineering article." Finding his place, he read from the text. "'In recent years the use of carbon tetrachloride as a cleaning and solvent agent has considerably increased, owing partly to a decrease in its cost of production, and partly to a more widespread knowledge of its properties…. Carbon tetrachloride is a water white liquid, having, when pure, a pleasant, agreeable odor quite similar to that of chloroform.'"

He glanced up in satisfaction. She nodded agreeably.

"Everyone ought to be able to make that comparison. But, why was that article in a fire engineering paper?"

"Carbon tetrachloride is used in fire extinguishers because of its non-flammable properties."

"Wade found a fire extinguisher in Amy's lab?"

"We'll have to ask her. If so, the discovery hardly implicates her, as the public has easy access to them."

"That's a start. I'd hate to think we had to point the finger at Jack's friend."

"Better than implicating Jack."

"But, he wasn't really a partner, Hugh."

"Bond can make him out to be the President of the United States if he wants to."

Since she couldn't argue the point, she tried to soften the damning statement.

"He has too much hair."

"Good thought. Most presidents are a little thin on top."

Before he could resume his investigation a rap on the door alerted them of danger and both looked up. Coming in, Geraldine stopped cold before a radiant smile crossed her face.

"Mrs. Kerr! You're back. Thank God! I was beginning to think I'd never see you again!"

Giving her a quizzical look, Ellen shook her head.

"You two are beginning to sound like one another. That's exactly what Hugh said."

"Is that a positive or a negative?" he queried.

"Thumbs down," she demonstrated. "I want Geraldine to sound normal."

Taking that for the insult it was, Hugh stood.

"Duty calls?"

"Immediately, if not sooner. You have a room full of clients."

"All right. Give me a minute then send the first one in." To Ellen, he requested, "Please see who and what's on the agenda. I've sorely missed you."

Sneaking in a kiss on her cheek Hugh slipped away.

Ellen surprised herself by how easily she fell into the rhythm of the office and it was only after the intercom buzzed during the second interview that she was reminded.

Excusing herself to the client before answering the summons, she answered, "Yes, Geraldine?"

"Your... ten-thirty appointment is here, Mrs. Kerr."

Immediately recognizing the code, she cast an embarrassed look at Hugh.

"Oh. I'm sorry. I have to leave. I'll only be a minute."

"Must be someone pretty important," the man sitting in front of the desk guessed by the expression on their faces.

It took Hugh's laugh to ease the situation.

"It is. Perhaps the most important 'appointment' we've ever kept. Would you like to meet the lady?"

Guessing there was something peculiar afoot, the client readily agreed.

"Absolutely. Have her come in."

Ellen hurried off and both men stood in anticipation of receiving the woman. A moment later she made her appearance, although being carried in her mother's arms was hardly the appearance the client anticipated.

"Miss Jacqueline Kerr, meet Mr. Fred Rule. Mr. Rule, I am proud to introduce you to Miss Jacqueline Kerr, making her debut in the law office of her father and mother."

Greeting the newcomer with a smile, Rule made her a formal bow.

"Honored to make your acquaintance, ma'am." Turning to Hugh, he added, "Or, is it 'Princess'? My first daughter was called Princess until she graduated high school. But, I might add as a word of warning, never in front of her friends."

"One of many names she has earned," he acknowledged. "Her Ladyship being another, but I'm sorry to say we most often refer to her as 'Baby,' having referred to her that way before she was born."

"Isn't that terrible?" Ellen agreed. "But, he's right. Not knowing what we were going to be blessed with, that seemed the most... politic, and now it's hard to break the habit. Poor Baby," she added, squeezing one of Jackie's little hands.

"No harm," Rule chuckled. "As long as you revert to her given name before the next one arrives. I'm afraid my wife and I had three 'Princesses' and it got very confusing."

"Three daughters?" Hugh complimented. "Good for you."

"Only until they get married and I'm on the hook for three dowries," Rule sighed in exaggeration. "Terrible custom. It ought to be the other way around. I'm not gaining a son, I'm losing a daughter."

"We refuse to think that far in the future."

"Don't blame you. But, perhaps she'll go to law school and supply her own."

"Once she gets past the pony stage I'll put it to her."

"Is there a pony in her future?"

"Her Godfather seems to think so."

"Then, buck up, Kerr. That means at least one broken arm and numerous trips to the emergency room. With my three, I confess the staff at the local hospital knew my wife and me by our first names."

"I don't want to hear it." Making her excuses, Ellen backed away. "I'll just be a minute."

Her minute turned into twenty and by the time she returned the two men had completed their business.

"I'm so sorry." Turning to Hugh, she added, "I'll have your notes typed and ready by this afternoon."

"No hurry," Rule assured her. "Your husband was telling me you also serve as a consultant here. I can't wait to tell Mrs. Rule. I'm sure she and her friends at the Women's Circle will be calling on you. As an intermediary, you're just what they need. Not legal representation but someone to answer questions about the association. And they'll be thrilled you're a working mother. Not many of those around."

"More than you'd think. I'll have our receptionist give you several of my business cards."

Hugh ushered the client out, returning shortly with a broad smile.

"Your return seems to be a great success."

"I apologize for the delay, Hugh. Baby was hungry and I was only too glad to feed her. I forgot how pressing the need was. I hope I didn't embarrass or inconvenience you."

"Nonsense."

"Not all clients will be as understanding as Mr. Rule."

"Then, they're more than welcome to look for another attorney. There are lots in the book." Putting his arms around her, they hugged. "This is precisely what we agreed to. How's Mom?"

"Handling everything like a trooper. I thought I was organized, but she has me beat by a mile." Moving to the desk, she picked up her notes. "We can take a minute before the next client. Please fill me in on the details of what you discussed so I can catch up." As he took his seat, she hesitated before pursuing, "It makes me wonder, though, how Bond is going to react knowing Mrs. Henry Wade is our nanny."

"Yes, I've worried about that, too. I say we don't let the cat out of the bag."

"He'll get word somehow. Seriously, Hugh, now that I'm back and I see how this is going to work, I'm concerned."

"How will he find out? The Wades have been living with us on and off for three months and he hasn't caught on."

"I doubt Forsch called his office and gave him a hot tip. And I would imagine most of the other residents at the hotel don't have much to do with police lieutenants or their wives. But here in the office you're dealing with wealthy men who circulate in high places. More than a few of them probably know B.B. and may even recognize Mary. If not, when the four of us go to court, she'll surely be identified."

"You make her sound like a criminal. 'Calling all cars: suspect identified at the courthouse. Alert the D.A.'s office immediately.'"

"Something like that," she agreed without a smile.

"All right, she's with her grandchild. Nothing wrong with that."

"A granddaughter with the last name of Kerr? Would you like to rethink that, Counselor?"

"It's not illegal for Mary to take a job outside the home. Besides, it's not as though we're revealing client's secrets to her."

"That's an iffy defense, Mr. Kerr."

"Oh, I don't know. She overhears us talking and reports to Hank. What's not for Bond to like in that?"

"It's the opposite scenario I'm worried about. She hears Dad talking about his cases and reports back to you. That's how Bond thinks. He's paranoid. And we've given him cause."

Finally exasperated, Hugh slapped his hands on the desk, causing several papers to fly off. She retrieved them as he spoke.

"Wade hates my guts."

"That explanation has worn thin."

"All right, there's nothing Bond can do about it."

"Yes, there is. He can prohibit Hank from working on any cases you're involved with."

"Good for us! Wish I'd thought of it sooner."

"Stop it. It will hurt his career. And if not that, his standing in the department."

"What are you suggesting? The only alternative I see is to have Mom and the baby stay at home and we slink around like thieves in the night. That wasn't the plan. We want Jackie with us. Here, in the office. We created an entire nursery for her. You want to continue breastfeeding for at least another three months, maybe for as long as a year. I'm not going to change that. And, I refuse to have you stay at home, either. I need you here. I will not have my life revolve around Bartholomew Bond!"

More surprised at his outburst than she should have been, Ellen withdrew, carefully rearranging the papers she had retrieved from the floor.

"We'll let it go for now."

"We'll let it go, period."

Hardly reassured, Ellen went to the door.

"I'll get caught up later. Your next client is Mr. Steven Henshaw. He's facing a theft charge. I've briefly gone through the papers he submitted. I think you can help him."

He started to acknowledge the information, then frowned.

"When did you have time to put that together?"

She looked puzzled.

"Between your first and second clients. Why? That's my job."

He finally smiled.

"Welcome back, Mrs. Kerr. You don't know what a relief it is having you here."

She did and wondered, without saying so, how long it would last.

Checking his watch, then confirming the time by the wall clock, Hugh grimaced.

"Another late day. What do you say we go home, grab a bite to eat, put Baby to bed and then drive over to the Pazel's? I'd like to see the home lab Amy has there."

"I'll have to ask Mom. I don't know what her plans are. She may want to go home and fix dinner for Dad."

"Have him come to our place."

Somewhat reluctantly, she acquiesced.

"I'll ask if that's all right. But if she looks reluctant, you'll have to go by yourself. And put that lower lip back in your mouth, Mr. Kerr. We're taking liberties, as it is." She was back in five minutes, purse in hand. "All set. Dad's coming to dinner and they're going to stay the night."

Arrangements settled, they hurried out. Back at the penthouse, Ellen made a light meal before getting "Miss Reluctant" into bed.

"She was as good as gold in the office today," Mary offered as Ellen put Jackie into her tiny bed. "I suspect she'll sleep for a good three or four hours. Plenty of time for you and Hugh to go out and return before she's awake and hungry."

Ellen turned to the older woman with true sincerity.

"I can't tell you how much we appreciate what you and Dad are doing for us. But, you look all done in. It was a long day."

"I am tired. You forget how much work a baby is. But the nursery at the office is as good as any home, and at her age she sleeps a good deal of the time. You didn't hear us, did you? I was a bit afraid her crying would have been audible through the walls."

"Not a bit. Aside from her one grand appearance no one would have guessed we have a baby in the office. But the down time must have been a bit boring for you."

"I wouldn't mind a radio or a television set," Mary confessed. "But, other than that, I brought my knitting with me and read three chapters in my book. It's not as though I do anything different when I'm at home. In fact, I was hoping you or Hugh would have some work for me. Research, or telephoning, or filing."

"Gracious, you do enough for us, already."

"Feeling useful is the most important thing in the world. And getting paid for it −" She hesitated, then added, "You don't have to, you know. Grandmothers everywhere do this sort of thing." It's called being part of your children's lives. Something I sorely missed with Jessica and Peter's children."

"What does Dad say?"

"We're to stay here Monday through Friday and spend the weekends at our house."

"That's more than I expected."

"He's the frugal Irishman, my dear," Mary grinned, patting Ellen's hand. "He says you two are footing the bill for groceries, so he's in the den now making out menus."

"You're not serious."

"I thought I'd nip that idea in the bud by telling him that's exactly what his other son – Jack – would do, but he only chuckled. That frightened me." They laughed over the joke as they returned to the living room. "But, I'm a little worried about you, daughter. Working full time and then being dragged out on late-night expeditions. When do you plan on sleeping?"

"In catnaps. That part of my married life hasn't changed." Seeing Hugh standing by the door, she grabbed her purse and waved good-bye before calling across the room to Hank. "What are we having for dinner tomorrow?"

Pulling down the pair of reading glasses perched on his nose, he promptly responded, "Prime rib. I was going to put down steak and lobster tails but I decided that was more of a Friday meal."

"I thought Catholics only ate fish on Fridays. You'll have to abstain from the 'turf,'" Hugh objected.

"Since cops work around the clock and never know one day of the week from another, we're given a dispensation."

"Really?"

"Come on, dear," Ellen encouraged, guiding him out the door. He mulled the question in the elevator all the way to the bottom, finally asking as they emerged, "Is that true?"

"It's called practicing a living religion."

"You mean it isn't true?"

"It means God understands."

"I accept that."

Relieved that had crossed that hurdle, they drove to the Pazel's, arriving shortly after seven o'clock. Having been alerted of their arrival, Mr. Pazel met them at the door.

"Welcome," he greeted. "I'm Paul. I want you to know I appreciate everything you're doing for my wife. What a travesty. She's just trying to make the world a better place to live and this happens. Whatever your fee is, I'll pay it. Sell the house if I have to. I just want this mess cleared up so we can go back to living our lives."

"Pleased to meet you. Don't worry about it," Hugh dismissed, shaking his hand. "This is my wife, Ellen. Please call me Hugh."

"I hope you can explain this to me. None of it makes any sense and all Amy wants to talk about is your baby. We have three daughters, too, but I want to bust the D.A. in the face. My wife never killed anybody."

"That's what we're here to prove." Taking in the tall man, he added, "You're a big fellow."

"Thanks. It takes two of Amy to make one of me. Come in."

He stepped back and Amy came up to greet them.

"Everyone is a little jittery. The police were here this afternoon with a search warrant. They went through the house and took samples from my lab downstairs. We sent the children across the street to the neighbors."

"Not the Wades, I hope."

"He was one of the officers who came to the house so I didn't think it was proper to send them over there."

"Right. I'd keep that thought. I realize you're friends with the Wades but he's on the other side at the moment. It never helps to mix work with pleasure. Besides," he added after a glance at his wife, "Ellen and I are very close to them, as well. In fact, she's our nanny. They have been spending a great deal of time at our house. Something else we don't advertise."

Amy did a double-take as she put the statement into context.

"You're their adopted family! She mentioned something about that but she never gave me the names."

"That makes two of us in this room guilty. Now, let's see how we can clear you."

"My analytical laboratory is this way."

"Analytical?"

"That's what a professional lab is called. Indicating it conforms to industry specifications."

He nodded and she guided them downstairs, taking the couple into a neat, spacious laboratory. Hugh whistled in appreciation.

"Nice. This would do Frankenstein proud."

"He's a horror buff," Ellen explained.

"Although I am a seamstress, I've never sewed body parts together. But, I could string some Tesla lights together to give you the proper look."

"You're being put on my Halloween list."

"We're not doing Halloween this year. Remember what happened at our last party." On his crestfallen expression, Ellen added, "We're going to Lodi this year."

"We'll invite them up there."

"I'm afraid you can't," Amy reluctantly explained. "Knowing the Wades were going to be away, we took it on ourselves to give out candy at their house last year. So they wouldn't get their windows soaped. If it was your party they went to, I suppose we'll be doing it again this year."

"Then, I'm already in your debt." Moving around Paul, he inspected the laboratory equipment with obvious interest. "I've done some research on carbon tetrachloride but I'd like to hear it from you."

"Then, as you know, it's a powerful industrial solvent. It's most useful application is in cleaning airplane motors."

"Meaning it could readily be found at airfields. And it's also used in fire extinguishers?"

"I suppose it could be."

"What do you, as a chemist, use it for?"

"As a solvent." He winced. "Cleaning glassware. The beakers we use are extremely expensive. They may look like normal glass, but they're specifically designed to withstand sudden and extreme changes in temperature that would shatter ordinary glass. You may be familiar with Pyrex; it's nearly indestructible." Picking up a measuring tube, Amy held it out for inspection. "This is an example although lab glassware comes in all sizes and shapes. When using a variety of chemicals or formulating a new compound, there's always the unknown and unexpected to contend with: a sudden spill-over, or a gooey mess. You can't afford to throw out the container, you have to clean it."

"With carbon tetrachloride."

"Yes."

Turning the tube over in his hands, he felt the difference before offering it to Ellen who did the same.

"Where else might the compound be used?"

"Petroleum labs; gasoline distillation plants. Dry cleaners. You might find it in a hospital blood lab where they do chemical analysis, or even a food-grade lab. For that matter, Lieutenant Wade could ask for a sample from his own forensics expert who tests for gun residue. In fact, I wouldn't be surprised if the police scientists keep samples of most known poisons for comparison testing."

"That certainly eliminates no one," Ellen quipped. "Not even Hank."

"Which has its good points," Hugh pointed out. "The more suspects, the merrier."

"Just as long as you don't charge him," she warned, only half teasing. "That might disrupt Mary, and if that happens Baby and I stay home."

"You're testing my professional ethics."

Amy grinned at the repartee which eased her fears and made everything seem safer and more normal. Poking Ellen with his elbow, Hugh indicated Amy go on.

"It's a very valuable chemical."

"And safe?"

"Not if ingested," she deadpanned, causing both Kerrs a moment of surprise before they laughed.

"What else can you tell us about it? Other than ingestion, is it safe to handle?"

She negated the question faster than they had responded to her former observation.

"No. It's extremely dangerous. It has a low boiling point of 76.7 degrees Celsius. If you really wanted to kill someone and couldn't get them to drink it – and, of course, if you happened to have the means – you could boil it down to its basic components, creating hydrochloric acid and phosgene gas. Inhaling that combination is a great way to destroy your liver and kidneys."

"With fatal results?"

"It certainly can be deadly."

"Woe to the careless chemist who isn't paying attention to what he's cooking up over the Bunsen burner," Ellen quipped.

"Especially if he's been drinking," Amy added with a professional's humor. "Alcohol consumption greatly adds to the effects."

Hugh's head snapped up as his eyes glistened in attention.

"Was Wexler drinking the night of the murder?"

"Yes. He was."

"Were you?"

She made a face.

"No. I wasn't nearly comfortable enough for that."

"Why so you say that?"

"Because I was alone, first of all. Second, because I don't drink with strangers. I didn't really know him, Mr. Kerr, and when I found out what he wanted I was even less inclined to drink."

Moving apart from the others, he inspected the layout, carefully observing but not touching any of the apparatus. On her nod of approval, he did open one of the cabinets and inspected the chemicals stored there.

"I presume you keep this room locked? So no one can get in when you're not around? The children, for instance?"

"Of course. Household accidents are a leading cause of death. I'm a trained scientist. No one in the field can afford to be careless. If they are, they don't stay employed – or married – long."

"I see. Can you show me where you keep the carbon tetrachloride?"

"You can cut it to 'carbon tet' if you like. It's easier to say. Or, by its chemical name, CCl_4." She walked past him and took out a container, clearly marked with the traditional skull and crossbones to indicate poison. He took it from her and studied the contents.

"A clear liquid. Nothing suspicious there." Removing the glass stopper, he sniffed the contents. "I read that in its pure state it has a pleasant, agreeable smell likened to that of chloroform. This, then, is pure as that seems to be true."

"Yes, it is. When sold commercially, the manufacturer adds sulphur impurities to give it a more unpleasant small to lessen the chance someone might inhale too deeply."

"Which indicates that even without boiling, the fumes are dangerous?"

"Absolutely."

"All right. I think I've seen enough for now."

They walked back upstairs and crossed into the living room.

"Please sit down. Can I get you anything?"

"No, thank you," Hugh replied for both he and Ellen as they positioned themselves on the couch. "I realize it's late. Just a few more questions. Is there anything else I need to know about carbon tet?"

"I could write a pamphlet on it." Sitting opposite, Amy folded her hands. "Like benzene, carbon tet is composed of small molecules, meaning it's capable of breaking the skin barrier. In other words, it penetrates easily, making it more dangerous."

"The ideal poison," Hugh mused. "Lethal by inhalation, ingestion or contact."

"Even better," Amy helpfully supplied, "a person can build up an immunity to it by taking very small doses and working up to what would be a fatal dose. So that if you put it in a glass of scotch you don't have to remember which one is the doctored drink. If you happen to be dyslectic."

Hugh sighed.

"If nothing else, I'm working up my own case file on desirable poisons. One last issue before I let you go for the evening. How much carbon tet would it take to have killed Wexler as fast as it did?"

She started to reply, then changed her mind and rephrased her answer.

"I don't know how long it took him, Mr. Kerr. He was alive when I left. And he didn't show any signs of being ill."

"Perfect!" he congratulated, slapping his knee. "That's a trick question the D.A. is likely to try if he ever gets the chance to cross-examine you. I need to know I can rely on your quick wit and intelligence before I ever consider putting you on the stand. Now, for my sake, how much poison would it take?"

"The lethal dose in an adult is 5 to 10 ml. Possibly as little as 2 ml in combination with alcohol, or in the setting of pre-existing liver disease."

"Not much."

"No."

"And how fast does it work?"

"The larger the dose, the faster it works, obviously, but for all practical purposes I'd say almost immediately. The first reactions would be nausea, vomiting, dizziness. The victim would lose a sense of reality; become confused. He would have trouble breathing, suffer from an irregular heart beat and a precipitous drop in blood pressure. Sooner than later he would fall into unconsciousness. Unless help is at hand and resuscitative measures are taken, death follows."

Speaking his thoughts aloud, Hugh remarked, "The janitor saw him slumped in his chair and thought he was asleep. That, I presume would be the unconscious stage. When he checked again and he noticed Wexler hadn't moved, he investigated. All right, that answers everything I need for the time being. I'll be in touch."

The Kerrs stood and moved toward the front door.

"How long will it take before the trial?" Paul demanded. "Is there any chance this ridiculous charge can be settled before it gets that far?"

"If we find the killer, that would help immeasurably. Otherwise, the prosecutor will hurry things along as I presume he feels he has everything he needs for a conviction. If I need more time, I can always petition for a later court date."

"Amy knows everyone in the cosmetics business. We can bring dozens of witnesses to step forward and testify about her good character," he protested.

Hugh's grim expression settled the issue before he added the final touch.

"I usually save that for the penalty phase, Mr. Pazel. Good night."

Paul slammed the door behind them, not as a reflection of his dissatisfaction with the lawyer but in frustration for feeling helpless. Ellen shivered as they walked to the car.

"You might have been a little more hopeful," she offered as he opened the door for her. "So they can sleep better."

"The only way either of them is going to sleep better is when she's exonerated. And we're a long way from that." Getting in the driver's side, he started the engine, revved it a moment, then shifted into gear. "I'm afraid I can say the same for us."

Unable to disagree, Ellen made no follow-up to the unpleasant thought.

CHAPTER 15

"Bill Boerner met with Wexler first, so that rules him out as a suspect unless he somehow came back." Fiddling with a pencil, Hugh wound it between his fingers. "We need to find out whether he did. Someone may have seen him in the parking lot."

"I'll check that out. If not Bill, then someone else," Jack observed, averting his head because Hugh's machinations were making his stomach flip-flop.

"If not Bill," Hugh pursued, understanding Jack's reluctance, "we need to find someone else with a motive. Check and see what Wexler's plans were for that evening. Did he have a dinner date? Does he have a wife? Why didn't anyone call the office to see why he never came home? And see if Boerner has an alibi after he left Wexler."

"I already asked. He doesn't."

"Good for us, bad for him."

"I don't believe he's our guy, Hugh."

"Then, find me a better one."

"I'm gonna try."

Slipping off the stool, Jack uncharacteristically picked it up and set it out of the way, compelling Hugh to ask, "Does this mean you're not coming back?"

"I've got other cases I'm working on."

He hesitated, expecting a challenge. When he got none, he shrugged and left by the private rear door. Hugh started at the bar stool a long beat before dropping the pencil and redirecting his attention to the paperwork on his desk. After signing several documents, he got up and walked into the reception area.

"Has Mrs. Kerr called to say she was going to be late?"

Geraldine shook her head.

"I haven't heard from her this morning. Is Mr. Merrick gone? I didn't see him come out."

"He left the back way."

"I wish he wouldn't do that. Are you ready for your next client?"

"Send him in."

Retracing his steps, Hugh was standing behind his desk as the receptionist escorted in his ten o'clock, only fifteen minutes late. They got down to business without a private secretary in attendance. By the time Hugh finished with him and had completed his interview with the last scheduled client of the morning, it was 12:15. Escorting the man to the front, he noted Geraldine's empty desk. Only then realizing the lateness of the hour, he checked the breakroom and found her there.

"Why aren't you in the reception area?" he snarled in annoyance.

Startled by his tone, she put down the sandwich she was holding.

"I always go to lunch at noon unless I have special instructions not to."

"But, you saw I was still involved with a client." On her blank stare he pursued, "Who was here to answer the phones?"

"I always switch them over to Mr. Merrick's office at twelve. They run on a different break schedule so we cover for each other. Marie goes to lunch when I come back and then I answer her phones for half an hour."

"Did I know about this?"

Pushing back in her chair, Geraldine prepared to stand.

"Mr. Kerr, I'm sorry you're upset Mrs. Kerr didn't come to work this morning. If you want, I'll go back to my station. But, it's empty at this hour and the phones are covered."

Annoyed at being found out although the reason for his temper was ill-disguised, he shook his head.

"No. Stay where you are."

"Do you want me to call her and find out if she's coming in this afternoon?"

"I know the number."

Turning on his heels, he stormed off. Emerging into the hall, he heard noise in Ellen's office and jerked open the door, catching her by surprise.

"Hello, Hugh," she greeted. "I thought you'd be at lunch. I was just going to go in and see if you left any notes for me to type."

"Where have you been?"

Noting the absence of, *I've been worried sick about you,* she finished putting her purse away before answering.

"I forgot Jacqueline had a morning appointment at the pediatrician's. Mary drove me over there and, of course, we had to sit in the waiting room forty-five minutes before we were seen. By that time it was already late so we caught a bite to eat before she dropped me off here. Besides," she added, noting his facial features had not changed, "we had a late night and I was more tired than I expected. Exhausted, actually. It's going to take me awhile to get back in the groove and I certainly didn't mind an extra hour's sleep."

"You didn't think to call and tell me you'd be running late?"

Casually straightening the hem of her skirt as an excuse to look away, she asked, "Which are you more annoyed about? That you had to work without me this morning, or that I'm not dead on the highway and thus excused – if not forgiven – for failing to alert you of my plans? Honestly, Hugh, I meant to and in the rush I simply forgot. Besides, I did mention I wanted to get back into the fray slowly."

He slapped his hand against his thigh.

"I don't remember that."

"I thought Mr. Perfect had a didactic memory."

Which did not improve the situation but left her unrepentant.

"I'm going to lunch. I'll be back."

Ellen checked her watch.

"At what time, precisely, sir, so I may be in attendance when His Lordship is prepared to begin his afternoon work?"

"When-I-return."

"I see. There are different rules for the master and the help." Changing her mind, Ellen reached into the desk drawer, removed her purse and started for the door. "I have a better idea. I'm going home. Figure it out for yourself." She had almost slipped away before he spoke.

"Ellen." She froze, then slowly turned around.

"This is exactly what I was afraid of, Hugh. You want things to go back to normal and they can't. Not the 'normal' we used to have. I hoped you'd understand we need to create a new normal – one that includes *both* our responsibilities to Jackie – and to each other – but I see now we have a long way to go. You promised me no late nights and that was a fantasy to begin with. You said you'd understand when I was tired and you've 'forgotten' what we discussed about my taking things slowly when I came back. I told you to hire a secretary and you refused. I think it may be time you did, and I simply retire. A high-powered attorney like you needs someone full time. Since you're not prepared to slow down, the answer is obvious."

"Go home," he stated, but not, as she feared, in an icy tone. "Let us both contemplate our roles in the 'new order' and discuss them when we're not upset. I did break my word to you and for that I apologize. And appearances to the contrary, I was worried." He made an effort to soften his voice. "How long did you say before things return to normal?"

"Twenty-one years," she bravely tried. "Longer, if we expand the family. Better make it thirty to be on the safe side."

"About the time I'm contemplating retirement."

"You'll never retire." She offered a small wave. "See you tonight," and left by the private door. Closing his eyes, Hugh remained rooted to the spot for several seconds before turning on his heels and going out the main exit.

Tapping the man ahead of him on the shoulder, Jack casually stated, "Hey, bub, nice take."

Turning around, a fist of bills clutched in his hand, James Ewell pleasantly smiled.

"Thanks. I got lucky."

"No way, man. A guy who bet ten bucks on Cat's Yowl to win at 45:1 odds is a genius. Mind if I shake your hand? I'd like some of your moxie to rub off on me." He held up a ticket. "I thought I had this race down pat. I knew the favorite wasn't going to win; I watched his morning workout. He was dull. That left it wide open. Club Foot had a better track record and I gotta admit the odds on the Yowl scared me off. So, I went with what I thought was the better option. I got third place but I ain't gonna make my car payment with scratch from that."

Ewell flashed his money before caressing the paper against his cheek.

"You can rub my head, too, if you want, but it isn't bravado, Mister –?"

"Jackson. 'Jack' to friends."

"Jack," Ewell easily replied. "I'm Jim Ewell. Haven't I seen you around here before?"

"You've got a good eye as well as a fat payday. I hang around the track most days. Can't stay away."

"I know the feeling. Nice, if you can afford it."

Jack brushed away the denial.

"I work nights to support my habit. Although, I'd rather say I work nights to fool the IRS into passing me by when it comes to audit time."

Clearly interested, Ewell motioned Jack to cash in his ticket. He did and they stepped away from the line.

"A guy only says that when he's won a few big ones."

"More than my share but not enough." Stooping down, Jack started collecting paper.

"Looking for a winning ticket some fool forgot to collect on?" Jim chuckled. In contrast, Jack gave him a piercing stare.

"You know what I'm doing. What do you take me for?"

Hands extended, the other asked forgiveness.

"Yeah. I do the same thing. Getting proof you lose more than you win. Come on. I'll buy you a cup of coffee."

Stuffing the tickets in his pocket, Jack obligingly followed him to a small café. Sitting under an awning to keep out of the sun, Jim gave the order and they waited for it to be served. Jack offered him a cigarette which he accepted. Disinterestedly lighting both from a flashy lighter, Jim snapped it shut.

"What kind of night work do you do?"

"Gigolo," he deadpanned.

Clearly intrigued, Jim leaned forward.

"Really?"

Jack shrugged. Without bravado.

"Why not? Dames like a nice looking hunk. I keep three or four of them on a string. The pay's good and once in a while I get little gifts. Gold cufflinks. A nice lighter." Taking one out of his pocket, he snapped back the cover, rolled the wheel and brought forth a high flame. "When I'm done with the girl, I hock the presents. Not this puppy, though. She had my initials engraved on it."

Before the words were out of his mouth, Ewell grabbed the lighter and inspected it.

"Then, why does it have 'T. P.' on it?"

"Stands for 'toilet paper.' And if your name is Jim Ewell, I'll eat my hat."

Returning the lighter, Ewell smiled.

"You know your way around."

"Mebbe. It's you who's the question mark. You're new here. That means you're from outta town. You're playing some sort of game and it got too hot for you where you were – Saratoga?" he guessed, "So you moved on. I first spotted you about... three months ago? Maybe a little less. You usually have a girl on your arm."

"Jealous?"

"Just want to make sure you're not moving in on me."

"And if I was?"

"There are a few of us who work the 'husband's away' circuit. Me, I don't worry too much. But the others... we're a tightknit fraternity. They might not like it."

"Relax. I don't offer that kind of service. But, I'd never turn down cufflinks. Or, lighters, either."

"You're playing your clients for money? Selling a scheme?"

"You might say that, and although I use it, between us, I don't like the word 'scheme.' I have a system."

Sitting back, Jack waited until the coffee had been delivered, then gave him the skeptical eye.

"I can see how well it works."

"Yes. You can. I just collected $450 at the winner's window."

"Then, why do you need dames to stake you?"

"No one wins all the time, Mr. Jackson. You know that. I like to live high. I was born into money and I appreciate the good life. I spend what I make and when it's gone, I look around for a new source of funding. The ladies give me investment capital and life goes on."

"What's the enticement? Aside from your baby blues?"

"I mostly hit on women with good jobs who want to better their financial prospects. I run into them by 'accident,' establish a relationship – purely platonic," he emphasized, raising his cup in salute, "and sell them on the chance to better themselves. All perfectly legal."

"Except you forget to pay them dividends when you hit it big."

"No. Then I show them all the losing tickets. The same way you show the tax boys. Too bad they took a high flier that didn't come in." He shrugged. "It happens, sometimes."

"You and I play both sides against the middle."

"Neither one of us is honest but it's a dishonest world, Mr. Jackson."

Jack drank more coffee, then doused his cigarette in the remainder. The butt made a low hissing noise as it died.

"So it is. How about we exchange notes on systems?"

Ewell chuckled.

"What's in it for me?"

"I want to better my odds at the window. In return, I maybe can put you on to a few... ladies who might like to better themselves."

"Your clients?"

"We're not working the same circuit. Remember?"

"You may have something there. But, I don't want to talk here. Too dangerous. You never know who's walking by. Besides, I have a few more bets to place. What about later tonight? Unless you're working," he added with a wink.

Removing his black pocket notebook, Jack flipped through the pages.

"I'm open between four and eight this evening. That work for you?"

"Sure. There's a coffee shop on Hollywood across from the Cherokee book store."

"I know it. The Copper Penny."

"See you there at five."

They stood, Ewell dropped change on the table and the two men separated, both hoping they had found a golden goose.

Maneuvering the stately car into the parking lot, Hugh spied an empty space and pulled in. Disregarding the sign, "Executive Team ONLY," he got out, leaving the top of the convertible down. Reaching for his briefcase, he walked up the two steps to the main entrance, opened the left side of the double glass doors and entered. Approaching the elevator, he scanned the directory, over which a gold-plated plaque read, "Mega Enterprises: A Family Corporation."

Maintaining an implacable expression at the company mission statement, he found the floor for the "Executive Team," pressed the button and waited for it to arrive. When the doors slid open and the operator drew back the brass gate, he stepped inside.

"Penthouse."

"Do you have an appointment, sir? No one's allowed at the top floor without an appointment."

"I called this morning. Mr. Shaffley is expecting me."

"Very good, sir."

Flipping a switch preventing the lift from stopping, the attorney had a direct trip to the top. Offering the man a coin, he politely nodded and stepped out. Confronting him was a spacious reception area. Comfortable couches and padded chairs lined either wall, while an efficient steel desk devoid of personalization sat between. Private offices to right and left flanked the entire corridor.

Assuming an affable smile, Hugh approached the expensively-dressed and coffered middle-aged woman standing guard over the entire floor.

"I don't know whether to salute or to ask how you're related to the president," he opened when she didn't speak. The statement was clearly not what she expected, as a flicker of emotion crossed her otherwise stern features, and it required more than a moment for her to mentally page through the Employee Manual for a standardized reply.

Failing to find the prescribed "script," she lamely fell back on the generic, "Why would you say that, sir?"

"Everything looks so efficient here it's as though I walked into Field Marshal Shaffley's headquarters. And if not that, since I was warned by a prodigious notice over the directory that Mega Enterprises was a 'family corporation,' I wondered if you were a wife, daughter or cousin of the Shaffleys."

"I am the receptionist, sir," she replied in a tone between bewilderment and defense.

"With a rank or a bloodline?"

"Neither, sir."

Satisfied with the answer which stated, without words, *I am a nobody in the organization and none of the Shaffleys would be caught dead in such a menial position,* he moved on with the conversation.

"I have an appointment with Mr. Philip Shaffley."

Without glancing at the open book before her, the woman, now on safer ground, replied, "You are Mr. Hugh Kerr."

"Am I?"

"Yes."

"I beg your pardon, but have we met before?"

"Certainly not."

Unsure whether he was being insulted or she was denigrating herself, he opted for the latter.

"Then, how do you know who I am?"

"Mr. Hugh Kerr, of the Kerr Law Firm, has a two o'clock appointment with Mr. Philip Shaffley."

"I see. It is two o'clock. Ergo, I must be Mr. Kerr."

"No one is permitted ingress to the penthouse suites without an appointment."

Shifting the briefcase in his hand, he mildly shook his head.

"Did you have an appointment this morning when you reported for work? And must it be renewed daily, or are you permitted to be slotted-in for five days at a time?"

Slightly shocked, she fell back on company script.

"You were asked, were you not, if you had an appointment before being transported to this floor?"

"I was," he promptly responded. "But, mightn't I have lied? My credentials weren't checked. Nor, I'm rather surprised to state, was I frisked."

"Frisked?" she asked in horror, either because she did not know the meaning of the word, or from its crude connotation.

"Checked for deadly weapons. A knife. A revolver. A vial of poison." He held up his briefcase for inspection. "Might I not have one of those concealed within? Or, perhaps this is a sample case and I'm actually a Fuller Brush salesman."

"Mega Enterprises manufactures brushes so there is no need –" She stopped herself and squared her shoulders. "You are jesting, sir."

"Indeed, I am. And I apologize for the interrogation," he added with a wide smile. "As a trial lawyer, I occasionally use my courtroom techniques to get to the heart of the matter."

If his dialogue had caught her off-guard, the apology sent shivers down her back.

"No justification is required of you, sir. I am merely –"

"An employee," he finished for her. "Without rank or family connections."

"Just so."

"Then, I'm sorry for you, because under that prescribed demeanor I think you're quite wonderful."

For lack of a response, she whispered, "You are Mr. Kerr?"

"I am he," he admitted with a bow. "And you are Maddy?" he added, leaning over her desk to read the salutation on a note left there. "Short for Madeline?"

Embarrassed, she dropped a hand over the paper.

"Yes, sir. Madeline Daugherty. I do beg your pardon for my indiscretion." Fussing with the incriminating evidence, she finally opened the top drawer of her desk and slipped it inside. "I'm responsible for purchasing the coffee for the office. One of our... junior secretaries was reminding me we were... out."

He raised an eyebrow while scanning the room.

"You are to buy coffee without drinking any, yourself? I see no mug."

Attempting to regain her composure, she stated more flatly, "We aren't allowed to drink on the job."

The phrase inadvertently made him chuckle.

"I admit a slug of scotch between clients is generally frowned upon in most workplaces, but to banish coffee seems a bit extreme. My private secretary and I can't get through the day without a stiff 'cocktail'. I take mine with sugar and double cream. I regret to say when first I met her, she took hers black. But," he added, holding up a finger to make a point, "I'm bringing her over to my side."

Mrs. Daugherty appeared shocked, but quickly reassured him.

"Too many calories, sir."

"That's what she said. But I dismissed the objection as being out of order." Reappraising the desk, he inquired, "Where, pray, is your name plate?"

"Only middle- and upper-staff are accorded those, sir."

He scowled.

"I put my secretary's name on the outside of my door. Directly under mine. As a... 'family corporation,' I could hardly do less." His scowl deepened. "Nor, do I require my staff to purchase their own coffee. That comes out of *petty cash.*"

Slightly disconcerted, Maddy attempted to mitigate the damage.

"Mega Enterprises sells coffee. I get a discount at the company store."

"I don't imagine they sell much to employees, inasmuch as they're not allowed to drink it."

"On break, sir. Away from the public." Her voice lowered. "Are you representing Amy – Mrs. Pazel?"

"Indeed, so."

Her attitude abruptly altered.

"I read about it in the newspapers. She's wonderful, Mr. Kerr. Please help her. She couldn't have killed anyone. Everyone here loves her."

Intrigued, he raised an eyebrow.

"She doesn't adhere to the stand-and-salute mentality?"

"She recognizes people as people." Maddy debated how much more to say, then added in so low a tone he had to read her lips, "And I think... you're just the sort of attorney who can get to the truth. Please tell her we're all on her side –"

The intercom buzzed and she snapped to attention. The voice on the other end growled, "Is my two o'clock here, yet?"

The lawyer pointed to his wristwatch.

"Am I an hour rather than a man?"

Putting a finger to her lips, she bade him quiet as she spoke toward the intercom.

"He is here, sir."

"He's late. It's two minutes past two."

Catching Hugh's eye, she quickly demurred.

"He was detained. He was... misdirected, Mr. Shaffley."

"How is that possible?"

"I will send him right in, sir."

Disengaging the intercom, she stood and came out from behind her desk. Making a face, she grinned and he matched it.

"Shall I salute when I enter? Make the sign of the cross? Walk in bowing?"

"He loathes artifice," she stated in a flat, practiced tone.

Hugh's knees buckled and his shoulders shook in merriment. Allowing him a moment to compose himself, she guided him to the royal suite, ostentatiously labeled in raised, gold lettering, "Philip Shaffley, President, Mega Enterprises."

Reaching a hand up, he drew an imaginary line under the title and quipped, "Enter at your own risk," winked and entered. She followed, two steps behind.

"Mr. Hugh Kerr, sir."

Before the words were out of her mouth, the receptionist vanished, leaving the two men alone. Shaffley stood to greet the visitor.

"Philip Shaffley, Mr. Kerr. Pleased to make your acquaintance. Your name is often in the newspapers. Quite an outstanding reputation you have."

"The pleasure is mine. I do my best."

"Be seated."

Although that had been his intention, Hugh spited him by taking a moment to look around the room. A magnificent desk dominated one corner, with one leather-bound chair in place before it and a matching one set to one side. On the walls were dozens of photographs depicting various buildings, laboratories and products displaying the sunburst logo of Mega Enterprises.

"Surrounded by your work, I see. A 'mega' empire of business."

"Exactly right."

Stepping closer to several, he studied them with acute interest before speaking.

"I considered putting the portraits of clients I successfully defended up on my walls, but my wife suggested that would look more like a Rogues Gallery, so I settled for hanging my collection of 16th century artwork."

"Oh? You're an art collector? Very nice. I, too, am somewhat of a collector but I display mine at home. I have a Monet and a Van Gogh as the centerpieces."

"My home is decorated with my wife's paintings. Most of which," he confessed with a pseudo-sigh, "I had to purchase. Before we were married, of course."

"Oh? She's an artist? Do I know her work?"

He turned and took the seat.

"I have a corner on the market."

Uncertain exactly how that related to value, Shaffley resumed his own chair.

"How may I help you, Mr. Kerr?"

"I'm representing Mrs. Amy Pazel. One of your exceptionally fine research chemists."

"Yes. So I have been informed." On Hugh's sudden hooded expression, he hastily added, "That she has been arrested on a murder charge. Most unfortunate. We have, of course, suspended her until the matter is settled."

"That would be, suspended with full salary and benefits? On the legal assumption of innocent until proven guilty?"

"I did not go into details with my legal department."

"Then, I suggest you do so. Immediately. On that principle, of course, and the fact she is family."

"I don't follow your meaning."

Hugh pointed to the statement, engraved into a golden plaque on the desk.

"'Mega Enterprises: A Family Corporation.' I assume you stand by your word."

"That refers, sir, to the assumption we work together for a common goal."

"Assumptions, sir, are in the eye of the beholder. I'm positive I could convince a jury to agree it meant that all employees – from receptionists to the president – are protected by the ties that bind one like group of individuals to another. In this case, Mega Enterprises is expected to stand by Mrs. Pazel to the fullest extent of blood relations. Her continued employment and your financial support in the way of salary is expected, Mr. Shaffley. By your own words."

"I am not a lawyer, Mr. Kerr."

"Stand by her or look the hypocrite to your staff and customers, Mr. Shaffley."

"If that is all you came here to discuss, then I'm afraid the interview is at a conclusion. I will have legal investigate our responsibilities. Good day."

He stood. Hugh remained seated.

"Actually, that was not the reason for my call, but I'm glad we had the opportunity to discuss it. My concern is with the sale of one of Mrs. Pazel's patents by you to Mr. Stanley Wexler. The man who has so recently... expired."

"What of it? It was perfectly legal. I owned the patent, as I am sure you're aware. Whatever an employee creates while working for me belongs to me. My lawyers will be glad to review with you the employee contract she signed when we took her on."

"'Took her on' is rather cavalier, isn't it? Mrs. Pazel is one of the premiere chemists in the field of research and development for skin care lines."

"Hired her, then. I am not here to spar with you."

"Why did you sell the patent?"

"Because it had no relevance to the company. It was not a product we cared to manufacture."

"Is it a common practice to sell employee patents?"

"Company patents," Shaffley corrected.

"I stand corrected," Mr. Kerr suavely corrected. "Please answer my question."

"I'm not on trial here and you have no right to interrogate me."

"Did Mr. Wexler explain why he wanted the patent?"

"I hardly see why that is relevant."

"On the contrary, I consider it of vital import."

"Why is that?"

"I think you ought to run that by 'legal,' Mr. Shaffley. I imagine they can explain it to you." Picking up his briefcase, Hugh took another look around the room. "There is one thing missing here."

"What's that?"

"A photograph of yourself. Or, a painted portrait. Or, possibly, a full-length oil, flanked on either side by 'family.' Your wife; your son. 'Family,' Mr. Shaffley. And both on the payroll holding top positions in the corporation. That would suit nicely. Good day. I'll see you in court."

Ignoring the insult for the larger issue, the president stood, face turning red.

"Why, in court? I had nothing to do with Wexler's death! Are you threatening me?"

"Alas, another question for legal. I hope they're on salary because you're going to be keeping them awfully busy. Good day. It was interesting meeting you."

Turning his back on the man, Hugh walked away. The intercom was buzzing as he passed the receptionist's desk. He gave her a thumb's up which she hastily returned before answering the summons.

CHAPTER 16

"First of all," Jim Ewell began, placing his finger on the sporting paper Jack brought with him, "without knowing anything about you, you're using this rag all wrong."

Slightly offended, he demanded, "How's that?"

"You're looking at odds and bloodlines."

"So?"

"You start with the trainer and the jockey. I saw you hanging around with some of them down at the track. That's good. But, then you went against the grain by betting on Club Foot."

"He had a better record. One third place finish and one second out of five races."

"Those were his earliest times out. And in both he was ridden by Tim Southcott. The last three races he was ridden by different jockeys two steps above a stable hand," he dismissed in derision. "What does that tell you?"

"The owner went cheap."

"Why would he do that?"

Jack grunted. "He gave up on the horse?"

"He'd seen enough to know he didn't have a champion. He was hoping for something but didn't expect it. There's a big difference between expect and hope. They call that luck. I don't discount it, but I don't bet on it, either." He leaned forward, shoving the two cups of coffee out of his way. "The owner knows the horse better than you do. By going with Club Foot to win, you're actually betting against the owner's opinion." Placing his hand over the paper so Jack couldn't read it, he demanded, "Who is Club Foot's trainer?"

"I don't know."

"You should. You need to study these things if you're going to be a serious player. The trainer was Phil Dehner. He likes horses that break fast and hold the lead. Club Foot doesn't have that kind of speed. He's more of a start in the middle of the pack and move up runner. But, the jockey takes his orders from the trainer and he started fast, didn't he?"

"Yeah."

"And your heart was in your throat," Jim smiled without humor.

"And then he faded."

"That's because right from the gun you have a conflict. Not all trainers are suited for all horses. Each one has his own style. A good jockey plays off what the horse gives him. That's because he knows if he wins, everything is forgiven. But a run-of-the-will rider follows orders."

"Because he knows if he doesn't and loses, he's out of a job."

"Sure. We all gotta work for a living, pal. A jockey is no different than anyone else. Lots of guys who can follow orders want his postings. So, what do we have? A mediocre horse mismatched with a trainer and a jockey who isn't going to use his instincts – if he has any. Now, I grant you, the field was weak. It was a low purse deal to fill up a card. Your horse finished third out of six. That's what I call a flip-of-the-coin race. Heads, you finish third; tails, you finish third."

Effecting wonder, Jack raised his arm to summon the waitress.

"I want a piece of pie. You want some? On my dime?"

"Sure. I never turn down anything that's free."

The woman came over and Jack ordered two cherry pies before tapping his cup to indicate he wanted it refilled. She gave him a look before going to fill the order.

"OK, you made me feel like a jerk. What about Cat's Yowl? That nag was the long-shot and you made a killing. By putting down a sawbuck. A guy could live for a week on that if he was careful. Ten bucks is a lot to lose on a chance."

Jim waited until the pie had been placed before them and the cups refilled before speaking.

"Everything is a chance, my friend. You have to accept that before getting into the game or you're never gonna make it. If horse racing is your hobby, bet at the $2 window and be happy if you break even one day out of five and hit big every other season. That's entertainment. That's how the tracks make money. But, if you're a sportsman and a gambler, you take it seriously. You gotta live and breathe horses and racing."

"You do that?" Jack asked with skepticism.

"Every second of every day." His eyes hardened, belying what followed. "I love it." The look vanished as soon as it came. "Nothing in the world is more important to me."

"That's why it doesn't bother you to fleece dames?"

"They're looking for... pie in the sky," he stated, digging a fork into the cherry pie. "They want it easy. Life ain't easy. It's tough. They're not betting on a horse, they're betting on me. That makes them suckers. I'm a bad bet. Like Club Foot."

"How do you stay ahead of the cops?"

"The same way you do. I move fast. I won't be around here long."

"Where to next?"

"Who knows? I got a deal going down. I'm just waiting to cash it in. And maybe take your client – the one you're gonna give me – and run with it."

"Yeah, well, don't take her for too much. She's gotta pay me, remember?"

Jim laughed.

"When it comes to that, all bets are off."

"Great." Jack finished his pie and shoved the plate aside. "So, why Cat's Yowl?"

"You need to get one thing straight. The game isn't about winning races."

"If it's not, what, then?"

"It's about making money."

"What's the difference?"

"Four hundred and fifty dollars."

"Yeah, I see where you're going. A $2 bet on the favorite gets you pennies in return."

"I don't bet on every race. There's no percentage in it. You nickel-and-dime yourself to death. You need to go against the odds. And you need to have the courage of your convictions. Two dollars on Cat's Yowl would have netted me pocket change. Ten dollars was gravy. The odds were out of whack for a middle of the card race. Those are what you look for. You don't find them often. When you do, you sit down and put together the pieces. Yowl has an interesting bloodline. Not the kind that raises your eyebrows but one that had a ton of potential for someone who knows how to judge it. If his sire had been handled better, he would have been really good. I saw him run as a two-year-old. Not the big time, but on smaller tracks. There never was enough money behind him to let him race for decent purses. He passed out of sight and that was that. But when I saw his colt I liked him even better. I thought he had real potential. I've been following his career."

The waitress came back and Jack handed her a dollar.

"Keep the change."

"Thanks, handsome."

As she walked away, Jim snorted.

"You have to pay for compliments?"

"I like girls."

"If you like them better than horses, then stay in the business you're in."

Jack brushed the objection aside.

"You were saying?"

"He had some bad luck along the way. He wasn't handled properly. Never placed in the money. That's why the odds were so high against him. And maybe a little bad-mouthing, too. He was probably on his way to the glue factory when a spot opened up here. The trainer didn't travel with him so a new guy was brought in. I had a long talk with him over a few beers."

"I see. I get java and the 'new guy' gets beers."

"You didn't even get that," Jim pointed out. "You paid for the coffee and pie."

"You're an operator, all right." He checked his watch in disgust. "Now, finish the story. It's getting late and I gotta get some sleep if I'm gonna dance all night."

Jim grinned at the expression.

"We discussed bloodlines. I told him about Yowl's sire. The way he liked to run. He hated to be in the middle; other horses to either side upset him. Threw him off his game. But give him his head, let him get out in front where he was heads and tails ahead and he had enough stamina to put it away. I thought it was worthwhile to try the same strategy. He liked what I had to say and frankly, at that point he had nothing to lose and everything to gain. That's why I put a Hamilton on the horse. I'd have doubled that if I could have."

"That would have been a payday for the ages," Jack whistled. "OK, I'm off. I'll ask around, find a match for you with one of my ladies. Give me your phone number."

"We'll meet at the track. You can tell me then."

"This is gonna be an 'I'm ready now' transaction. When the husband is out of town on an overnighter, got it? They don't make dates in the future. Too iffy."

"Got it. I'm at the Sawley Arms. Ask for Mr. Ewell. Room 240. Evenings. I'll be expecting you."

Wondering why, Jack got up, thought about offering his hand then decided against it. Touching Ewell would have meant a shower and he didn't feel in the mood.

Waiting until lunchtime, Jack walked into the library and casually sauntered up to the desk. Miss Dwight looked up, saw him and gave a hopeful smile.

"Hello, Mr. Merrick."

"Hello, yourself. Going out for a bite to eat?"

"I thought I'd eat my lunch in the back."

"Not today. I'm taking you out."

"Please, you don't have to do that. It's I who should be treating you. Unless you have some... hopeful news?"

"I have some news. I don't know how hopeful it is. Anyway, I like to keep my clients updated on what their money is being used for."

"And your time, Mr. Merrick. You've already spent more hours on my case than you said you would. If you've really come about your fee, I'll willing to drop the whole thing and call Mr. Ewell a bad investment."

"You may call him worse than that. A... cad," he came up with and grinned. "How's that for a librarian's word?"

"I'd say it was pretty near perfect: if you can name me one from classic literature."

"Edward Rochester," he snapped. Dana did a double-take.

"You think Mr. Rochester was a cad? I see your point, but I would have suspected you of having a more modern interpretation of the character."

Jack coughed as a means of turning his head.

"Come on. Let's get a move on."

"Let's get the show on the road," she added to his surprise.

"That expression is from a book?"

"Librarians also go to the cinema. Although, in this instance, it may have originated from P. T. Barnum for all I know."

"Yeah. Good thought."

He offered his arm and they marched out together, laughing as they went. At the diner within walking distance of the library Jack ordered a hot dog smothered in onions and chili and Miss Dwight opted for the *soup de jour*. After it was delivered they spent several minutes trying to guess what it was before she returned to the subject of their previous conversation.

"Please tell me why you chose Mr. Rochester as a cad."

"OK, you caught me. I heard a friend of mine say, 'I'm no Edward Rochester.' Taking it in context, I figured 'Ed' was a bad apple."

She clapped her hands.

"Very good. But, why did you assume Edward was a character as opposed to... a politician, for instance?"

Jack choked on the iced tea he was sipping. Coughing for real this time, he swallowed, pounded on his chest to make the liquid go down, then cleared his throat.

"Say, you're all right." Flattered at the compliment, she bade him continue by offering a paper napkin. He wiped his lips then shoved it under his plate. "My friend is an egghead; he reads a lot. But I really deduced it from his tone of voice. If Ed had been a politician my friend would have sounded a lot angrier and I don't think he would ever liken himself to one, no matter what he'd messed up on. But a character in a book – that's right up his alley. Or, maybe some – scoundrel – from a horror movie. Or, a

Western. But, those creeps tend to be more... eclectic, and he wanted to be understood."

"Mr. Merrick, I think you're quite wonderful!"

"I hold the same opinion, ma'am, but I'm usually a man out standing in a pasture," he dismissed.

"You're the most successful detective in Los Angeles," she corrected. "So, I doubt you're alone in your good opinion."

Jack hesitated, considered, then shrugged.

"*Jane Eyre*. I looked it up. In the library."

"Did you read it?"

"I checked it out. Read a few pages, then flipped through the rest."

"You read it, word-for-word. What did you conclude?"

"My friend was right. He was no Edward Rochester." Leaning forward, making a point to put both elbows on the table, he adeptly changed the subject. "I've had several conversations with your 'investment partner.' He's an operator, all right. I don't think I can shake him down because he doesn't have a conscience. But, I'm going to try and set him up for a fall."

"How?" she eagerly pleaded, sliding the soup away.

"Give him a new mark."

"A sucker."

"Yeah, well, a pigeon. Have her drop some money on him. Then, when he makes a decent score – a big payday – he's got something going down – I confront him. Remind him it's time to make restitution to his clients. He'll brush it off, of course. That's when I bring in my big gun."

"The law?"

"Yeah, but not the cops. I already told you that wasn't going to play. A lawyer."

"Who threatens to sue him?"

"Same difference. No. One who's going to spread the good word."

"In this instance, not referring to the Bible?"

"Right. He knows people with money. Lots of them. One guy owns a baseball team or something. They'll put out what you might call a private wanted poster. Our friend, Mr. Ewell, or whatever he's going to call himself in New York or around the racing world, won't be able to show his face at any ticket window without being recognized. The track enforcers will shake him down for all he's worth and then some. After that, he'll be through with racing."

"Won't he be able to bet through a bookie?"

"He could. But he has to pay them a percentage. And besides, you're missing the thrill of winning. That's collecting at the window. Being a big man. Riffling his wad to the envious onlookers. That's part of the game. He won't be able to live with that."

"He'll believe the threat?"

"In a flash. So, my expectation is that he'll cough up what he's made – you're not the only one he's working – and get outta Dodge on the first stagecoach."

"You'll let him go at that?"

"You mean, you want him to have an accident? Fall down the stairs? Run into my fists? I did say you weren't paying for thug service."

"What I meant was, he'll just pack up and start a new 'system' somewhere else."

"At the risk of sounding callous, that ain't your problem, ma'am," he tried in his best Humphrey Bogart voice.

She pulled back in disappointment, then crushed a handful of crackers into the soup she suddenly decided to eat. After taking several spoonsful and waiting for him to swallow a bite of hot dog, she looked back up.

"Is it dangerous? To the woman you're going to use? I've... already written my money off as a bad investment and foolishness. Lesson learned. I don't want anyone put in danger." As he took a larger mouthful and chewed contentedly, she argued, "I mean it. And, to be honest, I don't want to throw good money after bad. I don't think I can afford to pay her."

"You don't pay her. I do. It comes out of what you paid me," he spoke with him mouth full. "It's on me to figure out expenses before I quote you a price. Besides," he swallowed, "I wasn't planning on paying her."

"Why would she do it without compensation?"

"Because she's Jane Eyre. Sort of like setting off into the wilderness without a penny for a crust of bread."

"I might point out Jane could have starved to death. Or died from exposure to... the elements."

"I'll be right there to protect her. You can count on that."

"I believe you." They ate in silence until both had finished their meal. "When is this going to happen?"

"When Ewell makes a score. Or, is close enough to smell it. She'll be the clencher. Added to whatever he's got going – another 45:1 race – he'll have enough dough to skip town and live high off the hog for months. Maybe longer."

"Yes. He'll go back to Kentucky and buy himself a horse farm," she added in derision.

"That, too. Here's to success."

He tapped his glass of iced tea to hers and they drank to a payoff at the "ticket window."

Checking his watch, although the precise time was hardly significant, Hugh hesitated as he worked up his nerve. Feeling a rivulet of perspiration run down his side, he waited for it to be absorbed into the fabric of his shirt. Had it been a river of sweat, he would have done the same because the issue was not one he gladly broached, and speaking proved difficult.

"Are you going to go with me to court tomorrow?"

"I was wondering when you were going to ask."

Ellen might have phrased her question, "I was wondering *if* you were going to ask," but in either case her meaning was clear.

"You haven't been to the office. I know it's difficult –"

"Difficult for you, not for me. I've had a delightful time with Jackie. I enjoy motherhood, Hugh. It's what I've always wanted." Supporting the infant's back, Ellen bounced her on her knee. "Interestingly, I've gotten over calling her 'Baby.' A few endearing names, but not what we got in the habit of doing. She's become a unique person to me. The time with her has been very special."

"I agree. We rushed things. That was my fault and I apologize."

"No need. We both underestimated the situation. No," she decided, switching Jackie from one knee to the other, "That's not the word I want. We're both guilty of misjudging. Not only the situation, but each other. And ourselves, as well. And, of course, the influence Jacqueline has had on our lives." She smiled without humor. "She's not a 'grab-and-go.' You know. Like the sign they post down at the car hop. She's a full course meal where you sit down and enjoy the ambiance as well as the food and the wine. Just as you wouldn't rush through that, I don't want to hurry through the meal, shoving a hamburger down my throat on my way to the courthouse."

He shifted weight from one foot to the other.

"You want to retire?"

Although phrased as a question, she understood the wiggle-room he offered.

"I haven't thought that far into the future."

Sitting on the arm of the couch opposite her, Hugh pursed his lips.

"Let's not deceive ourselves by complicating our original underestimation," he began, reverting to her first choice. "You've thought of little else. In my spare time," he grimaced with a touch of bitterness, "that's where my mind has turned."

"We do seem to have been playing a lot of solitaire lately. That's your game," she added with a sourness that matched his. "Won many hands lately?"

"No. The cards are cold." Her shoulder gave a slight hitch, but she remained silent. He held out his arms. "Let me hold – my daughter. If it's permissible."

"Hugh, we're not arguing parental rights. Of course it's allowable. I don't want to keep Jacqueline – you almost said 'Baby,' didn't you?"

"Yes."

She handed the baby over and he cuddled the child to his chest.

"I don't mean to keep her to myself. For God's sake, that's the last thing I desire. She has and deserves a mother and a father. And a grandmother and a grandfather. And a big brother," she added in exasperation.

"Then, perhaps we're discussing the wrong issue. It's not you who needs to retire. It's me. If you're going back to work has put a wedge between us, then I think we ought to reevaluate. I can sell my law practice. We can move to Lodi and grow grapes. Establish a Kerr vineyard. Sell Zindenfel wine."

"No," she snapped so fast it surprised him.

"Why not?"

He anticipated something but not the reply she offered.

"Too close to my mother."

A loud huff, between shock and amusement escaped him.

"You have a point there. We could send her back to Paris."

"We fooled her once. We won't a second time."

"Then, I'm out of options."

"We could murder her."

"No!"

"Why not?" she asked as though the idea was perfectly feasible.

"First of all, you've already collected your inheritance, so we have nothing tangible to gain. As for the second, I'd have to defend us. Lawyers are like doctors. They should never operate on themselves or their family. They tend to be… over cautious. Or, over ambitious. They lose their common sense."

"If we have nothing to gain, then we've complicated our motive. The D.A. will be running around in circles trying to find one."

"Do we care?" ·

"Not especially. But, it will force him to come up with something despicable."

"Like what?"

"Alienation of affection."

"That's a motive for divorce, not murder."

"Maybe someone saw you kissing her. You've been known to kiss strange women, you know."

Inexplicably, his eyes brightened in delight.

"Guess who I saw the other day?"

"Who?" she asked, supposing some trick.

"Sam Dodson."

"That's not particularly surprising, considering he works for the district attorney."

"Not in court. Coming out of Lem's Chinese Restaurant. Guess who he had on his arm."

"Geraldine."

His grin turned upside down.

"Why do you say that?"

"Because we seem to be keeping things in the family, lately."

"Not Geraldine. Guess again."

"I've already given you my best guess."

"Evelyn Wentz."

This time, it was Ellen's turn to be shocked.

"You're making that up."

Disengaging his right arm from around Jackie, he held it up as though he were taking an oath.

"I swear."

"Will wonders never cease." As quickly, her brows furrowed. "What were you doing outside Lem's? And who was with *you?*"

"No one. I actually went there to see him. I called the prosecutor's office and they told me where to find him."

"You wanted to kiss Sam Dodson?"

"I thought I'd ask if he was interested in doing some *pro bono* work. For Brother Manolo."

"You mean, to help that poor man who couldn't take his family to Missouri?"

"Exactly. I hoped I'd have the time but my calendar is full and I don't want to put it off. And if he found the work interesting, he might stay on at the Mission as a volunteer attorney. If nothing else, it's a perfect way to fill out a resume. I like him. He's got talent. Eventually, he'll want something better than assistant D.A."

"Considering he's never going to move up because B.B. Bond will be re-elected for the next twenty years."

"Exactly."

"Did you ask him?"

He made a face.

"Not when he had Miss Wentz with him. That would have interrupted a —"

"Perfectly innocent assignation," Ellen laughed. "Good for them."

Jackie yawned and her head drooped.

"Ugh oh. Someone's tired."

"Too much talk and no action. Give her to me and I'll put her down."

He obliged and followed her into the bedroom. Placing the baby into her cradle, Ellen tucked the blanket around her, then wound up the music box over the toy dangling Winnie the Pooh characters from slender threads. Immediately a tinkle-tune played as the tiny stuffed animals moved in response. Jackie's attention immediately turned to them.

"See how much she's developed, Hugh. She can already identify where the sound comes from. And she knows when the music plays the toys dance."

He squared his shoulders in pride.

"Getting closer to that pony all the time."

Putting a finger to her lips, Ellen led him outside, leaving the door open a crack so she could hear when the baby cried.

"Speaking of which, how is Jack getting along with that rat who stole the woman's money?"

"I don't know. I suppose she'll have to be satisfied by having Jack beat him up in the end."

"That's not exactly how the law is supposed to work." When he didn't answer, she sighed. "What about Amy Pazel?"

"I'm not sure how the law is going to work for her, either. Bond has a decent case. I'm going to have to pursue alternate theories."

"Bill Boerner?"

"I actually like Philip Shaffley better. The 'family man.' He sold the golden goose and then reconsidered his folly."

"That's a stretch."

He snorted in derision.

"Only so far as to question the value of the golden eggs. I'm working on that."

"But, he sold the patent. Killing Wexler wouldn't get that back."

"No. But if Amy could reformulate the chemical composition, so could one of the other scientists at Mega Enterprises. Without Wexler's heirs pursuing the option of putting the product on market, he's eliminated the competition."

"Using that logic, he'd have to murder Amy, too."

He negated her objection by a curt shake of the head.

"No. She and her partners don't have any money. It might take them years to find financial backing. By that time, Shaffley will have his cream on every shelf in the country."

"Do you think he really did kill Wexler?"

"I wouldn't put it past him."

"It's a pleasant thought."

"And you haven't met him," he grinned. "If you had, you'd be dancing on your toes."

Crossing into the kitchen, Ellen asked, "Would you like some lunch?"

"Probably. But, I have to get back to the office."

"I'll make you something to take with you, then." Opening the refrigeration, she contemplated her options. Which had nothing to do with making sandwiches. Taking out a jar of mayonnaise, she abruptly added, "No, Hugh. I don't think I'm ready to go to court with you. I need more time."

"All right."

"I'm sorry to disappoint you. I've disappointed myself, too. I'm just not sure of my place, anymore. Or, how to handle my priorities. I never imagined it would be this difficult. I really think you ought to hire a full-time legal secretary."

"All right."

Stung by the fact he had opted to repeat the same statement twice without elaboration or argument, she withered inside.

"I feel as though I've failed you."

She waited, dreading the idea he would try for a third. If the idea crossed his mind, he abandoned it.

"I never want to hear the word 'failure' in reference to our relationship, our baby or my law practice." Noting her wince, he hesitated, then rephrased the word of contention. "Our law practice. Whether you work in the office or not, you'll always be my associate. I want you to understand that. Your position will always be open. That's how we started our relationship and it can never change. No matter if I hire a secretary or a legion of… assistants. Is that clear?"

"It's clear for now. I think you should leave your options open."

"And I think you're being too harsh on yourself. And on me."

"Why do you say that?"

"Because you're making decisions based on emotion rather than logic. That's not like you. The pressure of this impending court case has placed you in a bind; forced you to judge too quickly when you weren't prepared for it. Let time heal the raw edges of the situation. And, if you eventually decide handling motherhood and a legal career are too much, then I want you to consider other options. Your painting, for instance. Or, photography."

Her face flushed as she bit the inside of her lip to quell her racing heart.

"No, Hugh. Never. Once I married you, they became hobbies rather than a career choice. I dedicated myself to *your* career and once you made me your associate, that was a dream come true. If I abandon those, I will never substitute anything else."

He tried to step closer but she backed away, effectively stopping him.

"Then, I suggest we table the discussion for the moment and we extend your three month sabbatical indefinitely. I'll hire a temporary replacement and we'll take it from there."

Without realizing, she used the same words he had chosen.

"All right."

Leaving a chasm a mile wide.

"I'll see you tonight. Don't bother making anything. I'll stop by the deli on my way to the office. Kiss Jacqueline for me."

Because you'll be here when she wakes and I won't.

A hurt, unintentionally inflicted.

CHAPTER 17

"How do you select a juror?" Amy asked, staring at the assembled group who had been brought in for the first round of questioning.

"That depends on a number of things," Hugh replied, following her example by critically examining the men and women as they settled into their seats. "Those with obvious bias, either I or the district attorney can dismiss for cause."

"Someone who says, 'I think she's guilty and I hope they fry her'?" she suggested.

"Let's try and be more optimistic," he encouraged with a low grunt of disapproval.

"Someone who says, 'I think she's guilty because she ought to be at home with her children instead of working with dangerous chemicals all day'?"

A look of angst crossed his face.

"Why do you say that?"

Surprised at the reaction, she supplied the requisite answer.

"Because I've heard it a thousand times. Did I upset you?"

"Yes," he confessed, causing her to move away from him. "It's a personal matter. I apologize for my reaction."

Redirecting his face toward the prospective jurors, he clenched his jaws in an attempt to close the issue. His action offered Amy the opportunity to study his face.

"I didn't mean to upset you."

"Actually, it's good you brought that up. It's something I have to account for. Men can be so cruel."

"Women use that expression more often than men."

He turned back in surprise.

"Why is that?"

"Because women feel their place is in the home."

"I can see why a man would say that. He's traditionally the breadwinner and wants to be the king of his castle and the sole object of his wife's attention. But why would a woman object to another working outside the home? Having a job is the key to..."

"Respectability? If you say 'yes,' you're denigrating motherhood."

"Can't she have both?"

"You know my answer. I've been working full-time since I graduated college."

"Even though you've been condemned for it?"

"I can't let other people's opinions rule my life, Mr. Kerr."

"I agree. But, how do you manage it?"

"By wanting to, first of all. By envisioning myself as both a wife and mother and a research chemist. By hard work and sacrifice. By financial necessity: I make more money than my husband. And by having a partner who shares parenting responsibilities. But, most of all, by looking in the mirror and asking what I want out of life. And by asking what God wants of me. I was bestowed with a gift. Making my small corner of the world better by what I do is not only Christian, it carries with it tremendous satisfaction."

"Did   you   ever   doubt   your   decision?"

"Of course. Everyone doubts. That's the human condition. We all want what's best but we don't know the Plan. We have to hope we've chosen the right path. That's called faith. In oneself and in God."

"How does one... convey this to another?"

"By being honest. And by respecting the decision of the one you love. By treating her the same way you would a man: by allowing her be an adult. Too often people think of women as children, better guided than forging their own way." She hesitated and he motioned her to continue. "Women weren't allowed to vote because it was presumed they didn't understand politics. They were expected to leave the workforce after the men came home from World War II so the 'better qualified' men could take their jobs. It's considered a universal truth that children need their mother in constant attention. None of that is true. Women are equal to men in God's eyes. They need and deserve equal rights and responsibilities. It's as simple as that."

Hugh twisted in the chair, then fingered the knot of his tie as if it were too tight.

"And, if they choose motherhood over a career?"

"Implying they have that option?"

"Yes."

"Then, they've found a different satisfaction. Like men, none of us are the same. If you love your wife, Hugh, you'll let her decide. And stand by her decision, realizing you're in a unique position."

"What is that?"

"You can't lose."

He finally smiled.

"That's what every defense attorney wants to hear. Was I that transparent?"

"No. I just happen to know your situation. Mary's discussed it with me long before I ever needed your services. I think she was aware Ellen was going to have a hard time making up her mind."

"What side did she favor?"

He asked too quickly and Amy grinned.

"She said there was no right or wrong 'side,' but she was afraid you'd both take it that way and come out swinging from opposite corners."

"Now, I'm twice embarrassed."

"If life was easy, I wouldn't be charged with murder and you wouldn't be a lawyer."

"What would I be?"

"A father."

He winked and they turned their attention back to the jury selection process. One with curious expectation and the other with a new set of questions to ask.

Hearing the knock on the door, Ellen hurried in from the kitchen to answer it. Although she knew from the selective five raps followed by a pause and then two more it wasn't Hugh, she tried to fool herself into thinking he had forgotten his key and was playing a game. Therefore, when she opened the door and saw Jack, her face fell.

"Is it as bad as that?" he asked. "Who were you expecting? The television repair man? You know they never come on time. They wait until you've given up and decide to take a shower before they show."

He made her smile, not an easy feat to accomplish.

"Come in. What are you standing on ceremony for? And if you're looking for Hugh, he's not here. He's in court."

"Jury selection. I heard."

Her voice turned angry.

"Then, you also heard I wasn't with him. He asked and I didn't go. If you're trying to change my mind, forget it."

"Whoa, Starlet. Don't put the carriage before the horse. I was glad to hear it."

"Why?"

"Because I need you."

"I won't help Hugh so you think I'll help you?" she cried in frustration.

"Yeah."

The simple acknowledgment nearly drove her mad.

"Jack, I'm so frustrated I want to scream and all you can say is, 'yeah'?"

"I need a classy lady and you top the list."

"I'm not feeling classy and I'm not sure at this point what being a lady means." Uncharacteristically, Ellen flopped on the couch, shoulders hunched inward. "I'm just plain down in the dumps."

"Good. I have just the thing to cheer you up."

She looked up without enthusiasm.

"Between a shot in the arm and a shot in a glass, I'm going with the whiskey."

He whistled.

"You are low. Get your face on and we'll go out."

"To a bar?"

"We can stop by one on the way back and get smashed if you want. I tried this new drink the other day; called a Blue Blazer. Wow, it rocked me back on my heels. You'll like it. It'd be swell having you for a drinking partner. I hate to drink alone."

"You don't suppose Hugh would mind?" she asked with obvious sarcasm. He hesitated just long enough for her to read the mad script writing behind his eyes and her heart went out to him. "What do you need a classy lady for? Because if it involves a slinky dress you're out of luck. I'm still working on getting my shape back. Baby fat is a bitch to get rid of."

Recovering from his shock at the off-color language, he wiped his forehead and grinned.

"I always knew you could, but hearing you cuss like a boy sends shivers down my back."

"Is that good or bad?"

"Oh, honey, it's the tops!"

She laughed and got up, good mood restored.

"You know I love you, Jack. There's no one like you in the whole world."

He feigned seriousness.

"I hope not. Otherwise, he'd be trying to steal my paycheck."

"And the cats," she offered.

"Well, maybe not them. When I forget to clean it, the litterbox smells to high heaven." He waited and when she didn't pick up on the chance, he shook his head. "If I said that to Hugh, he'd say –"

She got it in a flash.

"If there's a 'high heaven,' does that mean there's a 'low heaven'? Now, Jack, would that be the purgatory we hear so much about, but which is not precisely canon, or something else? Is heaven like Dante's *Inferno* with multiple layers?"

"And I'd reply, 'If there's an *inferno,* call the fire department. Why ask me?" he quipped.

They laughed together before she brought the conversation back to where it started.

"What do you want me to do?"

"I'll tell you in the car. The sports job, if you don't mind."

She started for the bedroom to put on her make-up when realization struck.

"Does that mean I wouldn't agree if you told me now?"

"Nah. I just don't want to give you extra time to ask how much I'm gonna pay you."

"And what about Her Nibs, Junior? Are we going to leave her here?"

"Mom's on the way over."

"You had this all arranged?"

"Sure. Only, I offered to pay her."

"On the assumption she'd turn down the offer?"

"Natch. And forget about the slinky dress," he regretfully sighed. "Better save that for His Nibs, Senior."

"I might as well. He hasn't had anything else."

Her shot struck Jack below the belt and his knees buckled.

"OK, I didn't hear that."

"Two Blue Blazers and he won't have any regrets."

"Right. He'll be on the floor."

She disappeared inside the bedroom and fifteen minutes later, after consigning Jacqueline, who had managed to pick up another nickname, to her grandmother, the two conspirators were on their way.

"So, here's the deal," Jack explained, checking his watch for the time. "I'm a gigolo and you're one of my clients."

She digested this information with a straight face.

"I see. Sounds feasible."

He gulped.

"Just pretend, of course."

"I could imagine it working out that way. It almost did, once."

A car ahead of him stopped for a traffic light. Failing to notice in time, Jack was compelled to slam on the brakes, propelling them both forward.

"That just made my stomach do flip-flops."

Rightly presuming he meant her statement and not the near accident, she let it pass.

"I'm your client and —?"

"Your husband is loaded —"

"Loaded with what?"

"Dough." He got the double meaning and nervously laughed. "Yeah, that, too. But, he's cheap."

"No Kerr jar."

"Right. You like your little pleasures –"

"That would be you."

He checked the rear-view mirror.

"You're not making this any easier, you know."

"When I'm out on a gig I like to have fun." She tapped him on the arm. "There's a motel over there. You could pull over."

"No dice. It's too cheap for the likes of you."

He said it so seriously it was Ellen's turn to blush. She recovered quickly.

"How-do-you-know? Even been in there?"

"I've cased it."

"Any bedbugs?"

"Not that closely."

"I see," she added with a degree of skepticism.

"So, you need bread – money. I told you about this guy and how he's got a system to double or even triple your investment."

"You're not talking about James Ewell, are you?"

"You catch on fast."

"Yes," she decided, rolling up the window so as not to have her hair blow. "I'd like to –"

"Go ahead," he pleaded. "Say it."

"Screw the bastard." He sighed in hedonistic pleasure. "I'm just one of the boys, remember?"

"I take that back, big time. You're as classy as they get, Mrs. Kerr."

"Ugh. Better not call me that."

"Yeah, right. Who do you want to be?"

Ellen Thorne-Kerr, mother and legal associate.

"You pick a name," she replied, instead, feeling better about her silent, unintended confession.

"Mrs. Jerome Kantar."

"Where did that come from?"

He pointed out the window.

"I just read it on a billboard. Real estate. Beverly Hills. 'Only the best properties.' He sounds like a snot."

"Why? Because the name sounds Jewish?"

"No. Because he's gotta suck up to his clients all day, so he plays master when he gets home."

"I sometimes think, Jack, we're all a little too worldly."

"That's why we got Jackie. To put our lives in perspective."

Awed by his statement, Ellen patted his arm, remembering for the thousandth time why she loved him.

"Is it the system you're trying to find out?"

"No, I got that. I want him to take your money and bet it on a horse. He's got something in the works."

"You hope he loses?"

"I hope he wins. Then, when he tries to skip town without paying back your principal as well as your dividends, I catch him before he escapes and you threaten to sue."

"Because my husband is actually a lawyer?"

"A bigger-than-big lawyer. A raging bull, even. One he can't ignore because he can ruin him. And he wants your money back plus all the cash he's stolen from other women."

"Like your client."

"That's the ticket."

"Otherwise – what's your client's name?"

"Miss Dana Dwight."

"Miss Dwight will have to settle for having you beat the tar out of him. Satisfying, but hardly sufficient for a retirement fund. That's what Hugh said and I couldn't disagree."

"Think you can pull it off?" On second thought, she added, "Natch."

He grinned in pure pleasure at her vernacular.

"You're the cat's meow, Mrs. Kerr."

"And you don't even have to change my litterbox."

The car hit a pothole he failed to avoid. Jack cursed. To keep himself on an even keel with his partner-in-crime.

Twenty minutes later they pulled up at the Sawley Arms. Parking a quarter of an inch past a fire plug, Jack reached into his wallet and took out a wad of currency.

"Two thousand smackos." Riffling the high denominational bills, he kissed them before handing them over. "Your stake for Mr. Ewell."

Accepting the money, she raised an eyebrow in surprise.

"Where did you get this?"

"I robbed the bank, otherwise known as the Merrick Detective Agency safe."

"You keep that much money there?"

"Have to."

"In case you need a fast getaway?"

"Oh, baby, two thousand bucks ain't gonna take me where I want to go. No. For schemes like this. Or, when one of my boys needs bail money in a hurry and the bank's closed."

"You're putting up your own money? You could lose it. Why would you do that for someone you hardly know?"

"Because she's a client. I said I would help her if I could. That's my word. I don't have much in this world, but that's sacred to me. Besides," he coughed, looking away, "If I lose it, I'll just pad my bill to Hugh. He never looks at my invoices."

"He reads every word."

"Really? He never barks about anything."

"He trusts you."

Jack groaned.

"Don't try and make an honest man out of me."

"Wouldn't think of it. Besides, I think he enjoys the games you two play."

"I never play games with money."

"Right. Just like you're not doing, now."

He rolled his eyes.

"I'm coming up with you. There won't be any funny business, but just to be on the safe side."

"All right. I would feel safer with you around."

He scrambled out of the car and hurried over to open her door. Acknowledging his gesture with a nod, she got out and they walked into the building. Depressing the alert button under Ewell's mailbox, the system buzzed and the front door unlocked. A minute later they were greeted by Mr. Ewell, himself.

"Welcome," he offered, stepping back. They entered his flat, climbed the steps to the second floor, then he went to close the door when Ellen stopped him.

"When two gentlemen are alone with a lady, the door remains open."

"Not when we're talking business."

"The door remains open. You may keep your voice down for security reasons. I am perfectly capable of hearing you. We will maintain decorum, Mr. Ewell."

His expression conveyed the idea she permitted the door to be closed during her dalliances with Jack, but by respectfully dropping his head, he made amends for his previous objection by playing the gentleman.

"You're right, of course. It's a pleasure to meet you."

"This is Mrs. Kantar," Jack belatedly introduced. "I've told her a little about your –"

"System," he hastily interjected before Jack could pronounce the word "scheme." "Please. Come in and take a seat. I realize your time is precious and I have a great deal to cover." Leading them into what passed for a living room, he indicated the coffee table. Numerous charts and graphs were neatly stacked there. "I won't bore you with the details, but –"

"Mr. Ewell, I came here with the understanding that if I liked what I heard I was prepared to invest two thousand dollars of my... hard earned money. While some may call it an allowance, I prefer to think of it as a tribute to my worth. I do not risk it lightly. 'Bore' me."

Falling naturally into a rhythm of a pitchman, Ewell's suave manner and easy grace quickly soothed the troubled waters. Offering more detail to her than he had to Jack, he discussed how odds on a horse race were calculated, then opened a hand-bound book.

"This is my bible, Mrs. Kantar. I've been keeping it for decades."

She leaned over for a closer look.

"A family album of horses?"

"Something like that. I have thousands of photographs. When I had the chance, I took pictures of foals as soon as they were born and then every six months or so after that."

"Toward what end?"

"Development; muscle mass. Stature. Breeders know about their own animals, of course, but that's a one-sided approach. I want to know about all racing horses. How they're trained and by whom. What's their fastest practice run; what's their slowest. And why. Was the track too sloppy? Too hard? Different feed; even something as obscure as the saddle or the weight. You wouldn't think a few pounds makes a difference but it does. Noise. I've known horses that won't run their best if it's too quite. They want to imbibe the excitement of the moment. Or, the opposite. They can run like the wind in the morning but by afternoon when the crowds spill in, they get nervous. All that adds up to precious seconds. And time, as you know, ma'am, separates a champion from a nag."

Indicating he place the heavy tome on the table, she carefully turned the pages, pausing a number of times to study the cramped, voluminous notes jotted under the photographs.

"I approve of your method and your detail, Mr. Ewell, but what about luck?"

He surprised Jack by pulling a straight face.

"Now, you've hit it. As a gambler, I'm as well versed as any card player in the caprices of Lady Luck. All the skill, care and dedication to the art of the sport of kings is vital, but it's not a sure thing. To be blunt, no one wins every time. Let me put it to you this way." Leaning back, his eyes glistened with the faith of a true believer. "You understand poker?"

"I am familiar with the game."

"A professional sharper sits down at a table. Let's say there are three other players: two have a skill roughly equal to his own. The last is a novice. He knows the basic rules but he's guided by his gut rather than probability. Over the course of an evening, the novice will actually win several hands. That's the luck of the draw. Which," he added, tapping the book, "can never be underestimated. The other three will divide the bulk of the winnings until it comes down to the final hand. This is the big one. The sky's the limit on betting. The odds favor the gambler with the best track record; the novice is the flier. Who wins?"

"Whoever gets the best hand," she promptly responded.

"But, how do you get there? Were you dealt four aces? Did you get an ace, king, queen jack and three and discard the three hoping to get a ten? Or, do you go with the odds and exchange four cards in expectation of receiving three of a kind? Do you end up with a pair of deuces and try to bluff your way through? Or, do you fold and save your stake for another day? The choices are endless."

"Personally, I'd use the king I palmed from the previous hand," Jack supplied.

"And get shot for your trouble," Jim grimaced.

"Or, find the king doesn't benefit the cards you hold," Ellen more practically observed. "What do you do?"

"There is no one answer. That's why I'm telling you all this. It's called informed consent, Mrs. Kantar. I'm the guy betting on the outcome of the last hand and you're the bettor laying her money on me. That's the game within a game. Maybe I don't bet at all. Ask me why."

Ellen turned to stare at Jack before answering.

"If one of the players is cheating, the chances of him being caught tip the scales. The big winner of the night has luck going for him but luck is fickle. You're good, so the odds between the three of you are roughly equal. Therefore, you have to consider the risk of betting big and losing what you've already won. The big question, therefore, is the novice. Is he up to it? Does he bet with his heart or his instincts? If you've observed him all night and the answer is his instincts, you don't bet."

Ewell whistled in appreciation.

"You've got it!"

"So, may I presume you have a dark horse in mind? A race where the odds are worth chancing two thousand dollars on?"

"More than that. Every penny I have in the world."

"If you lose, I lose. If you win, I win. At what percentage?"

"Twenty percent of my take."

"Twenty-five."

"Too much."

"Then, we're through here." She quickly got to her feet. "It's been a fascinating lesson, Mr. Ewell. I appreciate you taking the time to enlighten me. But, if I'm going to risk my money on a dark horse, I demand control. Not in the name of the horse. I wouldn't expect you to give me that because then I could bet on it without a middleman. But, I will have a say over my remuneration."

Ewell blew through pursed lips.

"Whew. You're a hard bargainer."

"Let's say I'm a novice who plays with her instincts, not her heart. Your call."

"Since I can't bluff, I'll meet you. Twenty-five percent."

She offered her hand.

"Deal. And may the best 'horse' win." Taking the cash Jack had given her, she handed it over. "Now, if you'll give me a receipt for my money, I have some shopping to do."

He quickly wrote the amount on a piece of paper and handed it over. She turned to Jack.

"I'll wait for you in the car."

Jack got to his feet, politely nodded and waited until she had left, shutting the door behind her before wiping his brow.

"That was a close one. I thought you'd lost her there for a second."

"Me, too. I've never given a woman twenty-five percent of my winnings, before."

"That, I can believe. When's the race?"

"I'll let you know."

"Yeah, well, keep in touch. We're square, right?"

"Right. Want to get in on the deal?"

"No."

"Sure fire, can't miss."

"We just beat that rabbit down the hole. My stomach's doing flip-flops. Way outta my league. Gotta roll." He checked the time, then groaned. "Oh, geez, will you look at that?" Holding out his sleeve, he showed Bill the ketchup stain. "Crap. Double crap! I didn't see that and I gotta look my best. Where I'm going, the butler is dressed to the nines. I can't show up looking like a slob."

Boerner chuckled and pointed toward the kitchenette.

"There's a can of spot remover under the sink. Help yourself."

Jack scurried over, found the Carbona Cleaning Fluid, liberally dosed the red splotch, counted to ten, then wiped it off with a paper towel.

"Wow. It worked. Good stuff."

"You ought to carry some for an emergency."

"Thanks. I think I will. OK, be seeing you around."

"Have fun."

"It's work, baby. Not fun."

"Right. Well, sweat a little for me."

Jack waved and slipped off into the sunset.

Surprised to find Ellen waiting for him in the driver's seat, he settled into the passenger's side.

"Feeling your oats?" he cheerfully inquired as she gunned the engine.

"As a matter of fact, I am. This is the first time I've felt really... invigorated in weeks."

"It's the novelty."

"No, it's being useful."

"I'll recruit you any time, doll."

"Call again. But, I'm strictly freelance, Mr. Merrick. I already have a fulltime job." Pulling the two-seater onto the road, she blew through a yellow light. "Good thing I decided against the slinky dress. I have places to go and things to do."

Without saying "court," she easily translated her intent to Jack. He signed in satisfaction.

Performing good deeds was becoming fashionable.

CHAPTER 18

Ellen marched into the courtroom with a new sense of belonging. Ignoring the stares of the curious, she walked down the aisle, pushed through the swinging partition separating the crowd from the participants and tapped Hugh on the shoulder. He looked up, saw who it was and grinned in unexpected delight.

"Hello, stranger."

"Hello, yourself." He stood and she slipped past him, temporarily assuming a seat between him and their client. "What have I missed?"

"Jury selection."

"How'd it go?"

"Swimmingly. I dismissed three old buggars for cause."

"On what grounds?"

He winked at Amy.

"Old fashioned prejudices."

"I can guess."

"Are we 'on'?" he asked, references one of his favorite Boris Karloff poverty row pictures.

"We're 'on,' Louie," she replied before addressing Amy. "I apologize for being late."

"No need. As my mother would say, I'm making memories."

"A wise woman."

"She was a nurse and learned how to make the best of any situation."

Ellen moved past her, taking the outside position. Removing a steno pad and pen from her pocketbook, she set them out on the desk. Allowing her that brief moment to settle herself, Judge Gillman addressed the court.

"Mr. Bond, are you prepared to make your opening statement?"

"I am, Your Honor."

Glancing at his papers, the district attorney habitually straightened his tie before standing and stepping out from behind his desk.

"Means, motive and opportunity," Bartholomew Bond began, addressing the jury with quiet but assured determination. "The prosecution contends that the defendant, Amy Pazel, is the only person who had all three of these vital elements required to callously, and in cold blood, murder the decedent, Stanley Wexler. Why and how, you ask, would a woman – a mother with three children; a reputable scientist – commit such a brutal act? What could she possibly have to gain that was more important than a happy home, the love of her family and the breaking of God's most sacred commandment – Thou shall not kill – to justify losing all that? I'm afraid the answer is even older than Moses' stone tablets. Greed, revenge and pride. All of which goeth before a fall: a judgment I trust you twelve jurors will pass onto her."

Shoulders back, eyes intent, he moved across the room, making eye contact with the assembled jurors. He liked what he saw. They were an attentive, well-matched group with a mixture of ages between twenty-five and sixty-seven. Between Hugh Kerr and himself, they had selected seven women and five men, plus one alternate serving as a backup should anything happen to one of the originals.

"Greed," he continued, following the sequence he had established. "This case revolves around a patent designed by the defendant for a formula holding the potential for great wealth. Revenge: the purchase of this patent by the decedent. After having its value explained to him by Amy Pazel, herself, he recognized its value and determined to eliminate her from its production and subsequent marketing, depriving her of what she held to be her sole province. Pride: as the creator of this remarkable spray, she felt it was hers, alone, to profit from its benefits. With her name prominently associated with this product, she had every right to believe the highest doors to customized skin care development would be opened to her."

Walking up and then back along the jury box, Bond continued his intense summary of the case he would present in detail.

"Amy Pazel is a scientist of great intelligence and acclaim, but she has seen men with perhaps lesser credentials rise above her. Why? Because she's a woman. Here was her chance to soar above the competition. Establish her name as a pioneer in the field of research chemistry. Prove, even to the most skeptical, her ability and her creativity. Her spray, developed to heal wounds with remarkable efficiency, has the potential to revolutionize the field of veterinary medicine and, taking it one step further, when applied to people, radically cure those injuries presently unresponsive to traditional methods."

He paused for effect, savoring the twelve minds of the jurors as well as those assembled in the courtroom, hanging on his every word.

"She had every right to expect such achievements, but when she discovered Stanley Wexler had bought her patent out from under her with the intent of marketing it under his own name, her expectations were not only shattered, her sensibilities were aroused. It then became a question to submit to a cruel fate or take matters into her own hands and put her ambition back on track. How to do that? She went to Mr. Wexler to plead her case and when that failed, she saw only one option: murder."

Moving away so that he stood in center court, Bond stared out into the audience, appeared to gather his thoughts, then resumed his speech to the twelve who mattered most.

"Premeditated murder. The prosecution contends and will prove that the defendant, Amy Pazel, brought with her an insidious poison to the private meeting she had with Stanley Wexler on the night of July 15th. Discovering him to be resolute in the determination to use her patent without including her in the development, marketing and profit-sharing of her spray, she opted to eliminate him. Eliminate, ladies and gentlemen, being a euphemism for death. She put the poison in his drink, waited long enough to see it begin to take effect, then left him to perish alone in the utter agony of prolonged death."

A murmur of low disapprobation swept the courtroom as those behind the partition expressed their shock and disgust. Bond savored it a moment, fully aware he was not alone in comprehending the judgment passed, then nodded respectfully to the twelve separated from the rest.

"Amy Pazel poisoned Stanley Wexler so that she might have the opportunity to claim what she erroneously believed to be hers. She did so with malice aforethought. If Mr. Wexler's demise was what it took for her to regain her formula, she had no qualms about committing God's ultimate sin. For that, she must be punished. A verdict of guilty of murder in the first degree will accomplish that and I trust you, ladies and gentlemen, will have no qualms about convicting this woman of her crime. I thank you for your attention."

Making a slight bow, he turned on his heels. Head thrown back, Bond glided toward the prosecution table, the silent applause following him as patent as though the onlookers had stood and clapped.

Hugh stood and without letting the moment devolve into a stirring condemnation of his client, purposely and with an equal determination, addressed the jury.

"Ladies and gentlemen, the district attorney began his opening remarks by reminding us all of the three basic concepts he must prove for a successful prosecution: means, motive and opportunity. I congratulate UCLA for instilling in one of their most... recognizable graduates, a formula recited by rote by every lawyer, policeman, crime writer, mystery fan and, more than likely, every criminal in and out of the jail system."

His opening remarks caught most in the court by surprise and those in the jury box smiled, while a number in the gallery outright chuckled. Acknowledging the levity by a slight smile of his own, Hugh walked across the apron toward the jury box.

"What my learned colleague failed to mention was the last component of a successful prosecution." He held up his hand, thumb tucked into the palm so as to reveal only four fingers. Enumerated them, pointer to ring finger, he dropped one for each word. "Means. Motive. Opportunity." With only his pinkie remaining, he stared at the twelve in front of him. "The last is character." Exchanging the fifth finger for the third, his smile widened. "Using this finger as an example, if I displayed it out a car window, you'd all know something about my character."

This brought an even more humorous reaction and guffaws of amusement circled the room. Judge Gillman hesitated, then, failing to cover a grin of his own, let the room settle without intervention.

"But, that is not the finger I left standing." He dropped the middle finger and brought back the pinkie. Tweaking it with his left hand, he visually made his point. "Character. In this case meaning, does the accused possess such a deviate personality that she is capable of murdering in cold blood? Of poisoning a human being and then, in the words of the D.A., 'waited long enough to see it take effect, then left him to perish alone in the utter agony of prolonged death'?"

Deepening his voice, Hugh strode forward.

"The answer to that is categorically, NO!" Voice thundering across the chamber, his eyes flashed with righteous indignation. "The defendant, Mrs. Amy Pazel, is not only a wife and mother of three girls, but, and here, again, I quote Mr. Bond, a scientist who has 'established her name as a pioneer in the field of research chemistry.' A creative and renowned scientist who 'developed a formula that healed wounds with remarkable efficiency, had the potential to revolutionize the field of veterinary medicine and, when applied to people, radically cure those injuries presently unresponsive to traditional methods.'"

Turning to the prosecution table, he made a slight bow.

"This Harvard attorney thanks the UCLA attorney for his stirring words." Caught without the opportunity to protest, Bond merely returned the acknowledgment but without matching his opponent's smile of recognition. Hugh turned back to the jury.

"'Facts,' ladies and gentlemen, are merely suppositions until proven without a shadow of a doubt. The defendant, herself, would tell you that. A researcher, or, in this case, the police, started with a fact: a man was dead. The first question became: did he die from natural causes or was foul play involved? Assuming the former, they came – as Mr. Bond will subsequently attempt to prove – to the conclusion it was murder. Who, then, might be the killer? Here, the equation becomes murky. As you listen to the case unfold, you will hear there were several suspects the police considered before assembling enough *circumstantial* evidence to charge Mrs. Zimmerman."

Making eye contact with each juror, he seemed to be transmitting his faith that they would follow the details and arrive at the conclusion he developed.

"I emphasize the word 'circumstantial,' because there were no eye-witnesses to Mr. Wexler's death. The district attorney is not going to 'pull a rabbit out of his hat,' as I have so often been accused of doing, and provide you with incontrovertible proof of her guilt. Therefore, you will be asked to judge this case on that oft-overlooked fourth word in the trilogy, 'means, motive and opportunity.'"

Satisfied he had established his goal, Kerr moved away, folding his hands in satisfaction as he came to a stop by the bench.

"Mrs. Pazel is a warden in the Episcopal Church. She has a strong faith in the Almighty: something else the prosecutor mentioned in his opening remarks. God. God and His Commandments. Almost as though he and I were arguing the same side."

The audacity of the defense attorney shocked even seasoned courtroom veterans and they leaned forward, captivated by the pronouncement.

"Amy Pazel created a formula: not for her job; not for money or a bonus. She developed it in her spare time, at home in her own laboratory. For what purpose, then, you ask? To save a dog – a poor, innocent three-legged dog belonging to one of her neighbors – from needless suffering from a skin condition that had proven unresponsive to traditional veterinary methods. Did she charge her neighbor for this product she created at home, with chemicals she purchased out of her own pocket? She did not. The issue of reward was never broached. You will hear from this neighbor so she can tell the story in her own words." Turning to Bond, Hugh pointed a finger at him. "In fact, I challenge the prosecutor to find one single person Mrs. Pazel has *ever* charged for her good, and I might even say *saintly* works. He cannot."

Pausing, he waited for his words to be digested before continuing.

"'Greed' is not a word in Amy Pazel's vocabulary. Nor, is revenge. And pride? The last of his other three words? 'Pride,' meaning satisfaction in personal accomplishment, or pride in its more biblical interpretation of 'excessive self-promotion'? Of thinking yourself superior to those around you? I could bring this trial into the next century with character witnesses testifying to her self-effacing good works."

Taking a deep breath, Hugh again walked closer to the jury box.

"Evidence that does not point directly to a defendant is circumstantial. 'Maybe she did this.' 'She could have done that.' And, 'perhaps this is what happened' are hypothetical. No more than guess work. 'Maybe,' 'could' and 'perhaps' are actually the three words the district attorney has in his playbook. Mine are love, respect and honor. 'Love your fellow human beings.' 'Respect the sanctity of life.' And, 'honor God by using the gifts He gave you.' That sums up the defendant and what you will actually be called upon to judge. I thank you for your attention."

Nodding politely toward the twelve, he stepped back, paused a moment to glance at the audience, then resumed his seat. The courtroom fell silent before Judge Gillman broke it in his official tone.

"Mr. Prosecutor, you may call your first witness."

With a bland, professional expression that belied the fire burning inside him, B.B. Bond stood and called, "Leo Mattingly."

An elderly man wearing an ill-fitting suit reflecting the fashion of twenty years earlier, made his way from the prosecution's side of the courtroom, through the half-door and to the witness stand. After swearing to tell the truth, he took his seat. Bond, standing apart from the proceedings, quickly approached with a spring in his step.

"Mr. Mattingly, what is your occupation?"

"I'm the night janitor at the main office building at the Santa Anita racetrack, sir."

"Were you on duty the night of July 15?"

"Yes, sir."

"As part of your duties, was it your responsibility to empty the trash from the office buildings?"

"Yes, sir."

"Did the decedent, Mr. Stanley Wexler, have an office in that building?"

"Yes, sir."

"Did you go into that office at any time during the night of July 15?"

"Yes, sir."

Determining the witness was not going to add any details, Bond prompted, "Once, or more than once?"

Looking slightly confused, Mattingly wrung his hands.

"I don't remember how many, sir. Do you mean, including when the ambulance came? I was called in –"

"Let me be more specific. When was the first time you entered the office?"

"Ten o'clock, sir."

"Was this to perform your normal cleaning duties?"

"Yes, sir."

"Did you see any person in the office?"

"Yes, sir."

"Who was it?"

"Mr. Wexler, sir."

"What was he doing?"

"Sitting in the chair behind his desk."

Slightly perturbed, Bond pursued, "Did he speak to you? Was he awake and alert?"

"No, sir."

"Could you explain how he was, then? Was he sitting up? Did he make offer small talk?"

"Objection. Leading the witness," Hugh called.

"Sustained."

Bond rolled his eyes.

"Can you please tell the court what, if any activities, Mr. Wexler was performing when you first saw him sitting in his chair at 10 P.M.?"

"He wasn't doing anything, sir."

"Was he sitting upright?"

"No, sir."

"Was he slumped over?"

"Yes, sir."

Heaving an inaudible sigh, the D.A. pressed harder.

"You entered the office at 10:00 P.M. and found the decedent slumped over in his chair. What action did you take?"

"I left, sir."

"You didn't speak to him? Go over and shake him, to see if he was all right?"

"No, sir."

"Why not?"

"I thought he was asleep."

Having finally achieved that point, Bond pressed on with obvious relief.

"Did you go back to the office a second time and if so," he quickly added to avoid another, "Yes, sir," "what time was it?"

"Around midnight, sir."

"What did you see?"

"Mr. Wexler was still sitting in his chair, sir."

"What, if anything, did you do, then?"

"I asked him if I could pull his trash, sir."

A low smattering of amusement filtered through the courtroom.

"Did he answer you?"

"No, sir."

"At this time did you approach him and if so, what did you discover?"

"He was dead, sir."

"He-was-dead. Thank you. What happened next?"

"I called an ambulance, sir."

"Did you stay with the body until the ambulance arrived?"

"No, sir. In my experience, I've found the dead generally like to be left alone."

"I see. Where did you go?"

"Down to the front door, sir."

"Why?"

"It was locked, sir. I wanted to be there when the ambulance arrived. To let them in."

"I see. Thank you. No further questions."

With a scowl implying the interview had been more taxing than anticipated, Bond took his seat and Hugh replaced him at the witness box.

"Mr. Mattingly, were you in the armed services at any time?"

The old man's eyes lit up.

"Yes, sir. I served in the army in both wars, sir."

"This court thanks you for your patriotism."

The old, gnarled hands slowly unfolded.

"There's not many who say that, anymore, sir."

Bowing his head, Hugh honored him before speaking.

"The world, sir, will never forget. Now, may I ask you several questions about the night in question?"

Shoulders squared, he nodded.

"Yes, sir. I am ready to answer anything I can, sir."

"The first time you entered Mr. Wexler's office – that would be at 10:00 P.M. – you testified that he was slumped over in his chair and you thought him asleep, as was the logical assumption. What I'm curious to know is whether he moved at all? Twitch in dream? Was he snoring, perhaps? Take your time. This is important."

"He weren't moving, but I thought I heard him breathing. Kinda light, sir."

"Shallow, in fact?"

"Yes, sir. That would be a word to describe it."

"Did you smell anything? Did the room have a peculiar odor?"

He scratched his head to summon memories.

"Yes, sir, I believe it did have a sourness to it."

"Now that you've remembered, can you put a word to what you smelled?"

Mattingly knit his fingers.

"Like maybe someone had been lightin' matches."

"Yes, I thought that be it. Excellent recall. And the second time you entered the office? That would be around midnight. Kindly think carefully before you answer me. Had Mr. Wexler moved? I realize he was still sitting in his chair, but had he changed positions? Fallen more to one side or the other? Dropped his head on the table?"

"Objection. Leading the witness," Bond sourly complained.

With a half-smile, Gillman ordered, "Sustained."

Matching one grin for another, Hugh reiterated, "Was the body out of position from your previous visit? Even slightly?"

"Yes, sir. I think it mighta been. One arm had fallen off the chair arm."

"I see. Thank you. Just a few more questions, sir. You mentioned that after you called the ambulance, you went down to the main entrance to wait. To let the doctor in. Because the door was locked."

"Yes, sir."

"Was, in fact, the door locked?"

"Yes, sir." Hugh started to frown when Mattingly cleared up the matter. "Because I locked it."

"You locked it? When was this?"

He shrugged and looked pained.

"I don't wear a watch, Mr. Kerr."

"When you first came on duty? What time would that be, by the way?"

"Seven o'clock, sir."

"What time do you get off?"

"Seven in the morning, sir."

"You work a twelve hour shift?"

"Yes, sir."

"Did you check the lock at 7:00 P.M.?"

"No, sir. I start at another part of the building and work my way around. I guess I would have noticed the front door was open about a little after 10:00 o'clock. After I came down from Mr. Wexler's office the first time."

"Is that part of your regular duties? To see the building is locked at night?"

"I do it from habit, sir. There's a security guard but after he makes his first rounds. That would be Mr. Egan. He starts the same time I do, but he mostly walks around outside. Checks the stables; makes sure no kids are hanging around the track. That sort of thing. I'm in the building by myself all night. If I see something not right, I call him."

"If the door is locked and someone opens it, does it re-lock automatically?"

"No, sir. It doesn't."

"Did you notify him Mr. Wexler was still in his office at 10 P.M.?"

"I made a pot of coffee after I locked the door. Mr. Egan came over to my cubbyhole – that's what I call my office – and I told him, then. He said that explained the unlocked door. That Mr. Wexler came in late and went up to his office. He's supposed to remember to re-lock it, but he didn't." The old man smiled. "Mr. Egan said, 'Good catch, Leo.'"

"I'm sure he did. Now, tell me, did you see or hear anyone else in the building that night?"

"No, sir. It were quiet as the grave." Dropping his head, he slowly shivered. "I beg your pardon, sir."

"That's all right. No one else was working late?"

"No, sir."

"And you didn't see or hear anyone come in? Someone who might have had a late night meeting with Mr. Wexler?"

"I'm in and out of the offices, sir. It's not likely I'd see anyone unless they come looking for me. To change a light bulb or something like that."

Hugh lightly tapped the witness chair.

"Thank you. No further questions."

Politely waiting for Mr. Mattingly to get up and work his way back to his seat, Hugh crossed to the defense table. Impatient to get on with his work, Bond scowled before calling, "Call Titus Grindley to the stand."

The physician, well-rehearsed in courtroom procedure and previously notified of his place on the witness stand, got up and strode forward. Raising his right hand, he took the oath then settled himself into what could have been his home away from home. Bond smiled as he approached. They were playing an old, familiar game, although it might have been noted that while Bond's successful prosecution was a feather in each man's cap, Grindley kept his glory for himself.

"Good morning," the D.A. greeted. "Please tell this court your occupation."

"Los Angeles County Coroner."

"Did you, on or around July 15, perform an autopsy on Stanley Wexler?"

"I performed an autopsy on July 16."

"What did you find as the cause of death?"

"He was poisoned by a substance known as carbon tetrachloride."

"How did you determine that?"

"I discovered the substance, which is extremely toxic, in the victim's body."

"By what route was the poison administered?"

"There are three basic ways a victim may be exposed to this chemical: inhaled as a gas, absorbed through the skin or taken orally. In this case, I determined it had been ingested."

"Swallowed, you mean."

"That is correct."

"How did you make that determination?"

"If the victim had been subjected to a gas, the perpetrator would have had to heat it. This particular agent has a very low boiling point of 169 degrees Fahrenheit. As it decomposes, it creates phosgene gas and hydrochloric acid which would have spread into the room. I ordered the office furnishings swabbed for traces of such gas, but that was merely for protocol. None were discovered."

"Explain why that is."

"Two very simple reasons. Number One, the person heating the substance would, of necessity, be required to have the means to bring it to temperature. It is unlikely one was assembled in an office without arising the suspicion of the intended victim. Number Two, that same person would need to wear a mask to protect his – or herself – from the noxious fumes. Again, not the most subtle way to commit a murder."

A low wave of amusement rippled through the spectator's area.

Appreciating the reaction, Bond offered, "Go on."

"The second method would be by absorption through the skin. The same logic applies. The victim would have had to dip his hands into the chemical or have it applied to his body. In either case, awkward and unlikely. However, I did have the hands and exposed areas of the decedent's body tested and in no place were large concentrations of the chemical discovered."

"A very thorough examination," Bond flattered. "Which brings us to the third method –"

"That of ingestion. I did, in fact, conclude that to be the method of administration."

"Administered in what?"

"Alcohol. Traces of the chemical were found in a glass on the decedent's desk. One," he added, staring across the room at the defense table as if to challenge his right to add a pertinent fact, "which had his fingerprints on it."

Acutely aware of the silent scene being enacted, Bond hastened to add, "Yes. The prosecution will have that fact confirmed by a fingerprint expert. Thank you." Stepping back to give the jury a better view of the witness, he pursued, "Kindly explain what symptoms, if any, the victim would have suffered before his demise."

"Carbon tetrachloride reacts on the central nervous system. Depending on the dose administered, if left untreated the poison would eventually destroy the liver and kidneys, resulting in a prolonged evolution toward death. The initial symptoms would be nausea, abdominal distress, dizziness and a mental disorientation. Given in larger quantities, the effects would quickly worsen into a marked drop in blood pressure, cardiac arrhythmia and difficulty breathing. In combination, death is considerably quicker."

"Did you determine how long it took the decedent to die after he drank the poisoned liquor?"

"That requires a multi-part answer." Bond swept out his hand, indicating time was not a concern. "If the victim is predisposed to liver or kidney disease, the effects are more startling."

"Did you determine, on autopsy, if such were the case with the decedent?"

"I did. He was in the early stages of liver failure, brought on by alcoholism."

"Meaning the poison would act faster?"

"Correct."

"What, then, did you establish as the time of death?"

"Based on the testimony of the night janitor who stated the body had moved somewhat between his first and second visits, we may assume the decedent was alive but likely unconscious at ten o'clock. Therefore, I place the time of death between 10:15 and midnight."

"At what time, then, do you calculate he drank the poison?"

"Considering the fact he had liver disease and taking into account the concentration of poison found in the glass, I would place that event as occurring somewhere between 8 and 9:00 P.M."

"After ingesting the poison, how soon would the effects have been felt?"

"Almost immediately. To that point, I conclude the victim's restoration to full health and vigor was unsalvageable in a very short time: as little as twenty minutes."

"Meaning that if Mr. Mattingly had acted immediately upon first discovering the decedent at ten o'clock, he would not have been able to save his life?"

"That is correct."

From a row behind the prosecution table, Mattingly gave a low moan of relief and slumped forward, head in his heads. The effect was stunning and Bond let it sink in a moment before continuing.

"Granting that death by poisoning is a difficult process by any standards, how would you describe this method of... execution?"

Adding a second shock to those listening with rapt attention, he succeeded in compounding the horror.

"Extremely difficult, to the point of torture."

A woman in a rear seat cried in dismay, furthering the miasma of tension which filled the courtroom with its own brand of poison gas. Again, Bond waited a full moment until it had been absorbed into the consciousness of the listeners before continuing.

"Torture, cruel and unusual," he stated for the record. "Cold blooded, without compassion or mercy." Catching Hugh twitch out of the corner of his eye, he hurried on before he could object. "How much of this ungodly poison – carbon tetrachloride – would be required to bring on this type of death?"

"A very small amount; less than a tablespoon."

"Easily placed in a man's glass. While he was distracted; looked away?"

"Yes."

"Objection," Hugh announced. "Calling for a conclusion."

With the damage already done, Gillman reluctantly agreed.

"Sustained."

Smiling at his small victory, Bond nodded.

"No further questions."

Already standing, Hugh passed the district attorney on his way to the witness box.

"Before I address the larger issues, I'd like to clarify one point, Coroner Grindley. You said just now that the decedent, Stanley Wexler, was suffering from the early stages of alcoholism which had already begun to damage his liver."

"I did."

"Were the symptoms acute enough that Mr. Wexler would have been aware of them?"

"Objection," Bond called, playing tit-for-tat. "Calling for a conclusion."

Without revealing his awareness of the game the two dueling attorneys played, the judge shook his head.

"I think in this case I'll allow it, based on the witness' expertise in the field."

Grindley nodded and continued before Hugh had a chance to thank the judge.

"Based on my long experience, I would say not. Alcoholics tent to minimize their discomforts or seek some other explanation for their ills rather than attribute them to the consumption of alcohol."

"I see. Based on that statement, it is unlikely, therefore, the murderer could have known about his medical condition."

"Without stating it as a fact, I would tend to follow that reasoning."

"Yes. Now, let me delve further into the details of the autopsy." Returning to the table, Ellen handed him a paper. Returning with it, he held it out to Grindley. "This is a copy of the preliminary report. Do you recognize it as such?"

A brief glance and a nod accompanied his terse, "I do."

"Request it be entered into evidence."

"So ordered."

Having it marked, Hugh returned to the witness.

"This states the cause of death as a heart attack. Please explain how the conclusion was altered to death by poison."

Greatly annoyed by what he presumed to be a slur on his professional assessment, the coroner scowled.

"The symptoms of carbon tetrachloride closely mimic that of a myocardial infarction. I had no immediate reason to suspect foul play. Especially considering the fact the victim had evidence of coronary blockage."

Hugh waved away the objection.

"Am I correct in assuming it was not until given a list of routine chemicals discovered in the laboratory used by the defendant that you went back and looked for an alternate cause of death? In fact," he continued, raising his voice, "you did not even have the contents of Mr. Wexler's glass tested until the police lab identified the well-marked vial of carbon tetrachloride. Did you?"

The answer came in a surly, "No."

"I might even go so far as to point out that a body, poisoned by carbon tetrachloride, often has a yellow, somewhat jaundiced appearance. You noted that in this preliminary report but drew no conclusion from it."

"I presumed the coloration of the skin had more to do with liver disease than poison."

"Yet, you just stated the decedent was in the early stages of that disease. Persons suffering that early condition do not appear jaundice, do they? The whites of their eyes are not the tell-tale yellow, are they?"

"No."

"Yet, you identified both those facts and drew no other conclusion than the man died of a heart attack. Perhaps if you completed a third autopsy you might come up with an entirely different cause of death and we wouldn't be standing here today!"

"Objection!" Bond screamed, face red in anger. "Badgering the witness!"

Judge Gillman smiled thinly.

"Mr. Kerr, please modulate your tone. Overruled."

"Yes, Your Honor." Holding up the preliminary autopsy report, Hugh faced the jury while ostensibly speaking to the witness. "I submit that you did a poor job on this autopsy. Presuming, by your own words, you had 'no reason to suspect foul play,' you were careless, if not negligent in your duty, making both reports suspect."

Getting to his feet, Grindley waved a hand at Kerr.

"I resent that! When I had cause to go back and re-examine my results, I was thorough and meticulous. There can be no doubt as to my ultimate conclusion. They call it a 'preliminary report' for one very good reason, Mr. Kerr: because it was not finished!"

"That, sir, becomes an issue for the jury to decide."

Behind him, Bond turned to his assistant, Sam Dodson, and furiously whispered something in his ear. Dodson nodded, got up and hurried out of the courtroom. Fully aware of his assignment, Hugh resumed his calm, superior demeanor with the witness.

"Let us talk about the supposed poison. Carbon tetrachloride. Had you ever heard of it before the police laboratory mentioned it in a report?"

"Of course," Grindley snapped in extreme agitation.

"What is it?"

"An industrial solvent."

"Used for –?"

"Used in the manufacture of fluorocarbons, but primarily known to me as a cleaning agent."

"In your autopsy room?"

"In any chemical laboratory. It dissolves animal and vegetable fats. Blood. Oils, varnishes, waxes, resins, mineral oils, paraffin and tar among other substances. It is commonly employed to clean expensive testing equipment which has been contaminated by such substances."

"Do you and other scientists use it in its pure state or is it typically diluted with other chemicals?"

"Both."

"Kindly explain the difference."

"It's extremely expensive and dangerous. Manufacturers typically add sulphur impurities."

"To make it less costly?"

"To give it an unpleasant odor. So women and children won't be tempted to smell it for any length of time."

Hugh reacted with an exaggerated double-take.

"How many women and children of your acquaintance work in autopsy rooms?"

The question elicited another round of amusement. Grindley's scowl deepened.

"When sold commercially."

"Good to know." The sarcasm did not go unnoticed. "What does sulphur smell like?"

"Rotten eggs."

"In your experience, might the odor also be described as the residue of 'someone striking matches'?"

"It might."

"That's how the janitor described what he smelled upon entering the room. Would that indicate to you the carbon tetrachloride used to kill the victim was not laboratory quality, but a commercial solvent?"

Grindley stiffened in the chair.

"The same description might also be used to describe vomit."

"Did you detect sulphur impurities in the poisoned glass which bore the decedent's fingerprints?"

"No."

"Was the carbon tetrachloride taken from the defendant's laboratory pure, or was it adulterated?"

"It was pure," he snarled.

"Meaning the poison which killed Stanley Wexler did not come from the defendant's laboratory. No further questions."

Shooting the defense lawyer a hateful stare, Grindley walked away with the tacit promise that the next time their swords crossed he would come away with a different outcome. Judge Gillman shuddered.

"Mr. Bond, call your next witness."

Standing, Bond stared contritely at the judge.

"At this time, Your Honor, the prosecution would like to ask for early lunch dismissal to allow me time to develop the testimony of a new witness. Once who, unfortunately, was not in court this morning."

Checking the time, Gillman granted the reprieve.

"Very well. Court will reconvene at two o'clock."

Including Amy in the conversation, Ellen whispered, "He's going to have the assistant coroner review Grindley's conclusions. You made a fool of him, Hugh."

"Not easy to do."

"What did it gain us, Mr. Kerr?" Amy asked with excited interest.

"Ultimately, the result will be the same: Wexler died from 'carbon tet' poisoning. But, not from your lab. That was significant. My other point was to create a doubt that will linger in the minds of the jurors. If the D.A. presents a perfect case, they're more likely to believe everything he says. But, if I can prove even one of his witnesses is less than reliable, it casts a shadow on the whole. Out of one hundred facts, if even one is tainted, it tends to spoil the rest."

"One bad apple," she interpreted with a smile.

"Doubt is one of the strongest tools I have. It recurs over and over again. Consider a chemical formula for a new product. You test it and everything turns out right – or, almost right. One small component is slightly askew. Not what you expected. Everyone passes on it but you're not sure. It starts weighing on your mind. You wake up in the middle of the night realizing you've been testing and re-testing that experiment."

"And each time I'm convinced something's actually wrong," she readily agreed.

"Exactly. So, you go back to the beginning and re-work it, trying to explain or eradicate that nagging doubt." He snapped his fingers. "And then you see it: that which was more than a slight deviation. Something that would occur down the production line and turn into a major...." He trailed off his words, then winked at her. "Miscalculation of justice."

"You instill doubt in one juror and they influence the rest."

"That's the hope, at least. Bond is working with a circumstantial case. He doesn't have any eyewitnesses. He doesn't have any hard evidence – such as your fingerprints on a vial of poison found in the decedent's waste can. His job is to make castles in the air: not that he'd agree with that assessment," he added, holding up a hand, "but that's what he's doing. Creating a scenario of what might have happened in the expectation his logic will carry the jury. Mine is to explain away his circumstantial case by other credible explanations. Or, by destroying it all together."

"I never realized. How much of your defense is extemporized?"

"That depends entirely on the witnesses. Technically, Grindley went through all the steps in a precise, logical manner. I could and did argue he was a little careless by not identifying the poison the first time, but carbon tet isn't a substance a routine blood test would identify. You have to know what you're looking for or you probably won't find it. And, when given further information, he did go back and correct his initial impression."

"The point about the jaundice was sloppy, Hugh," Ellen interjected, determined to give him his due.

"I agree. But he did have a –"

"Credible explanation," Amy supplied.

Hugh arched an eyebrow.

"Aren't you nervous? Frightened?"

"Actually, I'm fascinated. I've never followed a trial from start to finish before."

"But, you're the defendant," Ellen pointed out. "Your freedom is at stake."

"I have faith. And," she winked back at Hugh. "I don't lie to my attorney. One of the basic tenets, I understand, of being a good client."

She made him laugh, not an easy emotion to elicit when he was in court. Without wiping out the smile, he patted her on the arm as the matron approached to take his client away.

"Keep that faith. It will sustain us all."

Amy waved and went quietly with the officer. Ellen sighed in disbelief.

"She's a remarkable woman."

"And then some."

"She's right about getting her off, too. You have to."

"For reasons other than justice?"

"She's the one who makes the spray for Irish Rover. If she's behind bars, you'll have to face Mom and Dad when the dog starts itching again."

"A fate worse than..." He quickly reconsidered his original thought. "Worse than not having any ice cream for dessert."

They left the courtroom laughing. Those trial-watchers who regularly followed the Kerr-Bond confrontations noted the light-hearted emotion and promptly altered the odds they had bet on the outcome, changing them from 4-1 Bond to 3-2 Kerr.

CHAPTER 19

With lunch over and court reassembled, Bond stood and addressed the judge.

"Your Honor, at this time the prosecution would like to add a witness to our list and call Andrew Raintree to the stand."

"No objection," Hugh called, nodding to the women sitting beside him.

"That's the assistant coroner," Ellen whispered in explanation. "It's a blow to Dr. Grindley's ego, but you saw Mr. Dodson run out of the court while he was testifying? Bond sent him to have the autopsy results confirmed by a second expert."

"That's what I thought."

Ellen patted her hand.

"Good girl."

"If I were a juror, it wouldn't dispel my doubt."

"That's our plan."

The assistant coroner testified that he had reevaluated the test results and reconfirmed the original determination that carbon tetrachloride had been the instrument of death. Hugh did not bother following up with any questions and a somewhat chagrined D.A. called his next witness.

"Lieutenant Henry Wade to the stand."

Wearing his court suit and tie and with his chin jutted in firm assurance of what he would say, the lieutenant took firm steps toward the box, swore to tell the truth and assumed his familiar seat. Directing his eyes on Bond, he made no effort to appraise either the jury or those at the defense table.

Resuming his normal aplomb, and feeling on safer ground, Bond addressed him with curt professionalism.

"Lieutenant Wade, you work for the Los Angeles County police in the homicide division?"

"I do."

"And you were assigned to investigate the murder of Stanley Wexler?"

"I was."

"Please explain what you did in pursuance of this end."

Without referencing notes, he sat back and spoke in a loud, unemotional voice.

"My first duty was to report to the scene of the crime. That would be Mr. Wexler's office at the Santa Anita racetrack. There, I discovered the body of Stanley Wexler. It was positioned in a chair, slumped forward, the face resting on the desk."

"Please describe what else you found."

"The victim had apparently vomited as there was emesis on the floor by the chair. There were no marks of violence on the body. There were two glasses containing what smelled like scotch on the desk and an open bottle of scotch nearby. The glasses and the liquid were sent to the laboratory for analysis."

"What was the result of that report?"

"The liquid proved to be scotch. The decedent's fingerprints were on the glass closest to him. The other glass had no fingerprints."

"Indicating it had been wiped clean?"

"That was my determination."

"Was anything other than scotch found in either glass?"

"Yes, sir. In the glass with the decedent's fingerprints, a substance known as carbon tetrachloride was discovered."

"The same chemical that was determined by chemical analysis and autopsy to have caused the decedent's death?"

"That is correct."

"Indicating the victim had been poisoned by drinking the tainted scotch?"

"That was the conclusion I drew."

"What else did you do?"

"I investigated who might have cause to murder the victim. I began by checking with the decedent's secretary; a Miss Bradshaw. To determine who had recent appointments with him. I obtained a list and had them checked out. Two individuals stood out from routine business associates."

"Please give the court their names."

"Amy Pazel and Jack Merrick."

"Amy Pazel. That would be the defendant?"

"Yes."

"And Jack Merrick? The detective who often works for my esteemed colleague, Hugh Kerr?"

"The same."

Bond bounced on his toes as though he had uncovered a relevant connection.

"They met with the decedent together or separately?"

"Together."

"Was there anyone else present at this meeting?"

"William Boerner. An employee of Stanley Wexler."

"What is his position?"

"Horse trainer."

"Did you determine the purpose of this meeting?"

"I did. It seems they were planning on marketing a spray or a cream Mrs. Pazel had developed. As I understand it, the compound has a unique ability to heal wounds."

"What type of wounds?"

"In two instances I have been able to confirm, a dog and a horse were healed by her spray. The dog had open sores from scratching and the horse suffered from an irritation caused by a bridle."

"Did you subsequently interview the defendant?"

"I did. Both at her work and in her home."

"Concentrating first on the initial interview, where was this?"

"At Mega Enterprises, where she is employed as a research scientist."

"What, if anything, did she tell you?"

"She confirmed she and her partners met with Mr. Wexler at his office to discuss a business proposition. She stated Mr. Boerner wished to purchase a race horse from him. The same horse I mentioned as having benefitted from her formula."

"Toward what end was this... partnership interested in purchasing a thoroughbred?"

"To use as proof of their claim that the spray was far better than any presently available on the market."

"Was there more to her request?"

"That, I believe, was the substance of the conversation."

"Did she tell you the result of that demand?"

Changing positions, Wade scowled.

"I did not say any of them made a demand. It was my impression it was put as a request."

Hiding his annoyance, Bond shrugged.

"Demand; request. Did she tell you the outcome?"

"Yes, sir. She stated Mr. Wexler asked for time to consider the proposal and subsequently informed Mr. Boerner he would not sell the horse."

Bond inched closer, eager to emphasize the issue.

"The decedent refused to sell the horse, thus depriving her of the proof she needed to market her product. That must have been very annoying."

Hesitant to turn himself into a hostile witness, Wade nevertheless shook his head.

"Whether it was or not, she did not give me the impression she was 'annoyed.'"

Clearly surprised, Bond tried harder.

"What impression did she give you?"

"That the matter was over and done with."

"But, of course, she was at work. And that was hardly the place to show her emotion. Nor, I imagine, was she going to display anger to a policeman interrogating her."

"Objection!" Hugh called, rising to his feet. "Counsel is drawing a conclusion not substantiated by the witness' testimony."

"Sustained. If you have a question, please restate it, Mr. Bond."

The D.A. dipped his head in less than a contrite indication of wrongdoing. Walking away from the box, he stopped several steps away as though distance would elicit better answers. The symbolism was not lost on the detective.

"While you were in the defendant's laboratory –"

"Objection," Hugh charged a second time. "Nowhere in his testimony did Lieutenant Wade state he was in a laboratory. He merely confirmed she was 'at work.'"

"Sustained."

Bond glowered, whether from the pettiness of the objection or the fact he had been brought to the point of suffering two objections from the dithering of a witness for the prosecution.

"Very well," he gracelessly conceded, "you stated the defendant was at work. Please describe in what specific room you questioned her."

"A laboratory."

The succinct reiteration of the word elicited a round of light amusement from the audience who appreciated the unexpected clash of swords. Unlike the jury, none of whom smiled, these devotees of courtroom procedure and back-and-forth wordplay appreciated the contest as much, if not more, than the verdict of which they had no personal stake.

Without physically acknowledging the judgment, Bond smiled. Not playing for the jury, the facial gesture was meant to convey to those who would eventually re-elect him, his mastery over the affair.

"A laboratory. Please describe it in detail so we may all envision that to which you refer."

Wade, whose job was not held at the whim of the public, settled in for a siege.

"I found Mrs. Pazel in a somewhat smallish room with four walls, a ceiling and a floor. The tiles were bare; there was no rug or carpet of any sort. Several long tables comprised most of the open space, with walkways in between for easy passage by an average-sized male. The countertops were black. I am uncertain of their composition."

"Go on," Bond encouraged, determined to play his hand to the full extent of his power.

"There was, as I would describe it, laboratory apparatus on these tables. Beakers; test tubes. Bunsen burners. Timers. There was also," he noted, "a clock on the wall. There were also charts and graphs, depicting, I supposed, work in progress. There was a notepad with writing on it: a chemical equation if I'm not mistaken. Or symbols and numbers to that effect. A pencil rested by the book – to the left side. The defendant, I noted, is left-handed."

Eyes bright with success, Bond bounced on his toes as he altered his position to stare at the defense table.

"Most thorough, Lieutenant Wade. You have permitted us to envision the laboratory clearly. And knowing my esteemed colleague's fondness for the horror genre, I can almost imagine Dr. Frankenstein, clad in a white lab coat, mixing various concoctions for the eradication of his enemies."

Hugh might have left the obvious mistake go, but for Bond's conclusion. Standing to address the court, he politely inquired of the judge, "May I take a moment to address my *very* esteemed colleague's summary, in as much as it was spoken for a light-hearted jest for my benefit?"

Glancing at the D.A. who nodded, a cautious Judge Gillman made a point of staring at the wall clock presumably similar to the one the witness had mentioned in his *detailed* summary of the laboratory.

"With the permission of the prosecutor I grant you leave. If you keep it brief, Counselor. After which I expect both *esteemed colleagues* to return to the subject of this trial and not waste the court's time on spurious... chit-chat."

The spectators sighed in silent relief, absorbing the contest as high and mighty farce.

Which it was. But on a deeper level, both men were skillfully playing for the sentiments of the jury who, in the ultimate determination, were the critics of their play.

"Being an aficionado of the horror genre, as Mr. Bond granted me, I feel obliged to state, for the record, that the common assumption of Victor Frankenstein being a doctor, either of medicine or philosophy, is in error. He dropped out of college before completing his formal education. Call him a scientist – a mad scientist, if you will, but not a doctor. And, perhaps more to the point, his goal was not to destroy life but to create it. Thus, we have it, ladies and gentlemen," he added, directly speaking to the jury, "his desire was to make a perfect human being."

"And we all know how that worked out," Bond quipped, salvaging the argument.

Hugh grinned in acknowledgment.

"Yes. And it made an international star out of the great Boris Karloff. For we must never," he added on a serious note, "confuse fact with fiction."

Dipping his head in polite respect, he resumed his seat. Bond copied his expression before returning to the witness.

"Let us see what *facts* we can learn, Lieutenant. In your very thorough inspection of the defendant's laboratory, did you find anything else?"

"Yes, sir. Many storage containers of chemicals. All properly labeled."

"You say, 'properly labeled.' Explain how you can be so certain."

"I had one of the police technicians remove samples from those which were readily in view. I also personally examined the storage area where I asked that various samples be collected for analysis."

"And were they subsequently submitted to the police laboratory?"

"They were."

Dodson stood and Bond took a paper from him.

"Is this the finding you received from the police chemist?"

Wade glanced at it and nodded.

"It is."

"Request this list be submitted into evidence for the People."

"No objection," Hugh called.

"So ordered."

The document was marked and the D.A. returned with it to the witness. Handing it to him, he asked, "Is there any chemical in particular that has relevance to this case?"

"Yes, sir. In one of the containers found near a sink was the substance called carbon tetrachloride."

A hushed intake of breath underscored the importance of the discovery.

"I see. You found what was identified as the poison that killed the decedent in the defendant's laboratory."

"By the sink," he reiterated.

"Interesting. Thank you. Now: you stated you also interviewed the defendant at her home?"

"I did."

"Please describe that home."

"It was neat and well managed. An ordinary home. Comfortable, within the means of the defendant's income I would judge."

"Did you also find something the average person would consider extra-ordinary?"

"There was a laboratory in the basement."

"Ah! A laboratory in the basement. Yes, I think most of us would agree that was not the run-of-the-mill cellar most of us have; typically used for housing an in-law's guest bedroom or to store junk." The joint reference to in-laws and junk elicited smiles from the listeners. Wade let it pass as beneath his dignity. "How would you describe this laboratory?"

"Similar to the one the defendant used at work, only smaller."

"Did you investigate it? Look around?"

"I did."

"What, specifically, did you find as pertains to this trial?"

"A container marked carbon tetrachloride."

Again, the fact solicited an acknowledgment by those in the visitor's seats.

"Indicating the defendant had easy and ready access to the poison used to kill a – I won't say 'perfect human being,' as we acknowledge only one, but a man who claimed and had the right to expect a full measure of life, liberty and the pursuit of happiness?"

"Yes, sir."

Bond sighed in satisfaction.

"Proving she had the means of murder," he stressed, "readily at hand. Thank you. No further questions."

Hugh stood and walked forward. Holding out his hand, he took the list from the witness, scanned it and nodded to himself.

"Lieutenant Wade, did you have a search warrant when you went to Mrs. Pazel's place of work?"

"I did."

"Did she ask to see it?"

"She did not."

"Did she put up a fuss? Demand to call her employer? Call her attorney?"

"No, sir."

"Was she, in fact, cordial?"

"I would describe her demeanor in that fashion, yes."

"Helpful, even?"

"She answered every question I put to her."

"And when you interviewed her a second time at home?"

"Her demeanor was the same."

"I see. Did she attempt to hide from you the fact she had a lab in her basement?"

"No, sir."

"And, she took you there, herself?"

"She did."

"Did it appear to your trained eye than any attempt had been made to 'clean up' the lab? Hide chemicals?"

"I saw nothing that gave me that impression."

"Indicating she had nothing to hide?"

"Objection!" Bond called. "Asking for a conclusion."

"I believe Lieutenant Wade is capable of providing a professional assessment. Witness may answer the question."

"I drew that conclusion, yes, sir."

"The defendant had nothing to hide," Hugh repeated, nodding in agreement with the assessment. "You stated you found a container of carbon tetrachloride. This was after that chemical had been identified as the poison used to kill a man? Meaning, you were looking specifically for it?"

"I was looking for it."

"And you found it in plain sight?"

"I did. On the table."

"I believe," he smiled, "the proper term is 'bench.' A workbench. Did you take a sample of the substance?"

"I did."

Hugh held out the list, indicating a specific line.

"Does this item, marked as having been removed from the home, reference the sample you took?"

The detective read the words and nodded.

"Yes."

"Please state out loud what it says."

"Carbon tetrachloride."

"That is all it says?"

"Yes."

"It does not say, 'carbon tetrachloride with impurities? Thus conferring the fact it was a pure compound and not diluted by additives?"

"It merely says carbon tetrachloride."

"And this item? Marked as being taken from Mrs. Pazel's laboratory? It also reads, 'carbon tetrachloride.' Without impurities?"

"There is no mention of anything else."

Holding up the paper for display, Hugh showed it to the jury.

"Pure, unadulterated carbon tetrachloride. In neither instance could the compounds removed from the defendant's possession have been used to poison Stanley Wexler because they are not, in fact, the same substance."

Crossing to the jury box, Hugh handed the evidence to the foreman. He inspected it and passed it on. When all twelve had confirmed the fact for themselves, Hugh took it back, left it on the evidence table and returned to the witness stand.

"Did you hear a previous witness testify that when used as a cleaning solvent outside the laboratory it is mixed with other chemicals to give it an unpleasant odor? One 'women and children' would find offense?"

"I heard that testimony," Wade replied with a straight face.

"Would that indicate to you the substance might be readily available to the public at large? Meaning it is not unique to scientists working with chemicals that may contaminate lab beakers and test tubes?"

"Objection!" Bond shouted. "The witness is not an expert on this subject."

"Sustained."

"Thank you, Lieutenant. You are not an expert on the subject. But, you are, perhaps an in-law. If you were mine, I assure you I would not put you and your wife in my basement."

The courtroom broke up in laughter, requiring the judge to bang his gavel. Hugh had not yet reached his table when he ordered, "Mr. Prosecutor, call your next witness."

"Call Mr. William Boerner to the stand."

Noting the look of surprise on his client's face, the defense attorney nodded.

"Yes. I know."

"I thought he'd be on our side."

"The D. A. got to him first. Since he was the original suspect, I imagine Bond threatened him with being an accomplice if he didn't cooperate."

In horror, she asked, "What about Jack?"

Looking slightly amused, Hugh sat beside her.

"I got to *him,* first, or I daresay Bond would have served him, too."

He made her smile and she leaned forward to listen to the testimony, quietly remarking, "It's amazing, really."

"That Hugh prevented Jack from having to thrash the D.A.?" Ellen inquired.

Amy shook her head in denial and took the liberty of speaking while the witness was being sworn.

"That, too. But, I wouldn't want him to. Violence can't be the answer. I mean, this entire trial. How different it is, studying it from a new perspective. How Mr. Bond can take two relatively simple and uncomplicated visits from Lieutenant Wade and turn them into...

compelling testimony. How he can put a dire interpretation on the most innocent comment. I was involved in both encounters and I can tell you, I wouldn't have thought to describe either in the way they were presented to the jury."

Patting her hand, Ellen worked on a comforting affirmation.

"As Jack would say, that's why they pay him the big bucks."

Appreciating the effort, Amy turned to Hugh.

"And you. How you picked up the slightest nuance and attacked it as though it were tremendously significant, and by doing, put an entirely new interpretation to it. Considering myself fairly intelligent, I felt my brain going back and forth like a ping-pong ball trying to remember it."

Reaching down, she began fussing with her skirt. Feeling their eyes on her, she forced her hands back to her lap and apologetically remarked, "The prison dress I'm required to wear. It isn't very well-made. The hem was fraying on one of them and it bothered me to the point of distraction. I'm a seamstress, you know. If I had needle and thread, I could have repaired it. It sounds silly, but the loss of that ability upset me. I was actually looking forward to my court appearance so I could put on my own clothes."

"As good a reason as any."

"I think, after this, you'll be entitled to an entirely new wardrobe," Ellen seconded.

"I just want to go home," Amy snapped and they turned their attention back to the witness stand where Boerner had settled it to face the interrogation.

"Explain to this court your occupation."

"I'm a professional thoroughbred trainer."

"For whom did you work?"

"Mr. Wexler."

"The decedent," Bond clarified. "How long did you work for him?"

"I'd say about four years."

"Always as a trainer?"

"I was hired after his former trainer retired. It was a good job, so I didn't have any reason to murder him," he added with a snarl.

Judge Gillman leaned forward.

"Simply answer the questions put to you. No addendums are necessary."

Bill sullenly shrugged and Bond hurried on.

"Where is this farm?"

"In Kentucky."

"How would you describe your relationship with the decedent?"

"We always got along."

"How did you know the defendant, Amy Pazel?"

"I met a fellow at the race track during morning workouts. We got to talking about the horse we had just seen and I told him I had another I thought had more potential. I took him to see her."

"What was the name of the horse you took him to see?"

"Barrister's Baby."

"Was this an especially exceptional horse?"

"I thought so. But she couldn't be raced."

Effecting interest, Bond moved closer.

"Why is that?"

"She had particularly sensitive skin. Her muzzle kept breaking out after contact with the bridle. You can't race a horse with an open wound. It's against the rules."

"I assume veterinarians were called in to assess the problem?"

"Of course. The horse was a very valuable piece of property. The vets tried all the usual remedies but nothing worked."

"Meaning, this 'valuable piece of property' was useless."

"As a race horse, yes."

"Put out to pasture? That's the expression, isn't it? Sold to the glue factory?"

Boerner winced before shrugging his shoulders.

"It was a damn shame because that filly was special. So, this fellow says —"

"What is his name?" Bond interrupted.

"Jack Merrick."

The second time the name was mentioned it elicited instant recognition and those in the gallery turned to whisper to one another in excitement, indicating the trial had taken on a new and perhaps more powerful significance.

"Jack Merrick."

"Yes."

B. B. rubbed his hands together as if that juicy bit of information was of vital import by somehow casting aspersions on the lawyer. Having successfully played that card, he returned to his examination with renewed vigor.

"What did Mr. Merrick say when you explained 'Barrister's Baby's' medical condition?"

"That he knew of a spray that could maybe solve the problem."

"How would a private detective know more than a trained veterinarian?"

"His Mom's dog had an itching problem and a neighbor of hers developed some concoction that healed the sores it got from scratching. He thought the same thing might help B.B."

"B.B.?" Bond demanded in irritation as though he suspected the witness of playing a joke. The attention of the audience achieved an even higher level of interest.

"That's what I call the horse. All racers have nicknames. Who's gonna call a horse 'Barrister's Baby'? Too long; too complicated. They get registered with all sorts of fancy, high-sounding names because you can't use the same name twice. But no one call's 'em that. An animal wants something simple it can recognize."

Recovering quickly as if he were in on the "joke," the D.A. smiled.

"I thought, perhaps, this valuable thoroughbred was named after me, 'B.B.' being my nickname." Allowing a moment for his humor to be absorbed, he hurried on before the witness could make a further comment. "Did Mr. Merrick subsequently obtain this wonder spray?"

"He did."

"Did he say who, specifically, created the formula?"

"A scientist named Amy Pazel."

Pointing toward the defense table, he reiterated, "Meaning, the defendant?"

"Yes."

"Was this spray subsequently used on... 'B.B.'?"

His choice of name did not go unappreciated by the spectators and even those on the jury nodded in approval.

"It was."

"Kindly describe where and how this was achieved."

"At the barn at the race track. Mrs. Pazel came down with Mr. Merrick and she put it on the horse. She explained how it worked. I didn't understand much of what she said. But," he signed, "the stuff worked like a miracle. The wounds healed up right away. I had the horse taken to the track for a workout and then inspected the result. No irritation; no open sores. I kept using it and so far there hasn't been any reoccurrence. The horse is cured."

"Meaning it can be raced, again?"

"That's right. Presuming the spray passes track approval. Mrs. Pazel promised me it would."

"Do many horses suffer from the same condition as Barrister's Baby?"

"Not many, but a few. And if they're as valuable as this horse, the spray is worth any price. And Amy said it could be used on all sorts of animals. Like the dog. That's a gold mine."

"Yes. I can see why you say that. What, if anything, did you propose to do with this 'gold mine'?"

"I thought we ought to manufacture it. Put it on the market."

"By yourself?"

"No. Of course not. Me and Amy and Jack formed a partnership. We even went to Mr. Kerr over there to write up a contract."

"And did he draw you a contract?"

Boerner made a sour face.

"No. He said there were too many complications."

"He said this directly to you? While you were in his office, so that the testimony you're about to give is not secondhand?"

"I was there."

"Objection, Your Honor. Violating attorney-client privilege."

"The witness is offering to dispense with that privilege."

"There were two other people in the office with the witness when a contract was being discussed. Neither are willing to abandon their rights."

"Mr. Kerr, do you speak for both your client and Mr. Merrick?" Gillman inquired.

"I do, Your Honor."

"Motion is sustained."

Bond scowled before quickly reworking his questioning.

"You did not establish a contract. What, then, did you do? Without specifically revealing what Mr. Kerr advised."

"I went to see Mr. Wexler."

"The decedent," Bond clarified. "Toward what end?"

"I told him about the spray. I wanted to buy Barrister's Baby from him."

"Why?"

"To use as proof the medicine worked."

"What did he say?"

"He'd think it over."

"And did he subsequently give you an answer?"

"Yes. He said he wouldn't sell the horse."

"Did he give his reasons?"

"He was intrigued with the idea of the miracle cure. I didn't think he'd be interested in it as a sideline but he was. He contacted the owner of the patent and bought it from him."

As if hearing some new detail he had not been aware of, Bond pressed closer.

"The defendant – the woman who formulated the spray – did not own the rights to it?"

"No. She had already gone over that with me. She said she made it while an employee of Mega Enterprises and that meant they owned whatever it was she did, even if it was on her own time."

"Then, what made you think you could market the spray in the first place?"

"She said she could alter the formula enough so she could get a new patent on it."

Raising his voice, Bond turned to the jury.

"But not while she was still employed at Mega Enterprises. That, ladies and gentleman," he pursued, walked toward the box, "is clearly specified in the terms of her contract. Anything she developed, whether at work or at home in her private laboratory, belongs to her employer."

Getting to his feet, Hugh raised his own voice in warning.

"Objection! Citing facts not in evidence."

"Withdrawn," Bond quickly stated. "The prosecution will call a witness from Mega Enterprises to speak on the subject." Turning back to Boerner, he resumed his questioning. "The defendant told you she would have to reformulate the spray."

"She said she would make it into a cream."

"But not while she still worked at Mega Enterprises, because that would mean they would own the new formula as well as the original one."

"Objection. The question draws on facts of the contract not in evidence."

"Your Honor," Bond argued, "considering the defendant admitted this to the witness, I ask you to allow it."

"Then it becomes hearsay and I object on that ground," Hugh snapped.

Gillman considered before shaking his head.

"I think it best, Mr. Prosecutor, you firmly establish the terms of the employment contract before pursuing this line of questioning."

In a rare display of disrespect, Bond shrugged before continuing with the testimony.

"Your two partners lost out on a gold mine. Your words, Mr. Boerner. That couldn't have been easy to reconcile. How did Mrs. Pazel react?"

"Calling for a conclusion," Hugh called.

"Overruled."

"She was as upset as we were."

"'We,' meaning you and Mr. Merrick?"

"Yes."

"As anyone might be, seeing a potential fortune go down the drain." He moved closer to the witness, bearing down on him.

"This partnership you envisioned. Was it to be evenly divided? Thirty-three-and-a-third percent for each of you?"

"She would have gotten the bulk of the deal."

"Meaning she had more to lose than either you or Mr. Merrick?"

"I suppose so."

"You don't suppose so, you know so."

"All right. She would have lost out a lot more than me or Jack."

"In more ways than one, Mr. Boerner. It was her formula – her brilliance, shall we say – that was being… stolen right out from under her nose. A formula she devised, tested and proved its worth. She did not make it for Mega Enterprises, she designed it for her own purposes. Not to make a company wealthy but for herself –"

"Your Honor, counsel for the prosecution is making a soliloquy, not asking a question."

"Sustained. Mind your role, Mr. Bond. The jury will disregard the district attorney's last statement."

"Yes, Your Honor." Hardly contrite, Bond turned to the witness. "You had not anticipated Stanley Wexler buying the formula from Mega Enterprises?"

"No."

"Speaking only for yourself, were you upset? Angry?"

"Yes."

"And you only lost a portion of the potential profits. Imagine what it would be like to lose the bulk of it?"

"We are not here to 'imagine,'" Hugh stated in growing annoyance.

"I'll withdraw the question. Now, let us consider this proposition you three had. Before Stanley Wexler blew it up in your faces. Before I establish the fact the defendant did not own the patent, may I ask if the basis of your partnership was based on a re-formulation of it as a cream – one that would be as effective as the spray purchased by the decedent?"

"Yes."

"Assuming for the moment that to be a true statement, it was the understanding of the partnership that she could not be employed by Mega Enterprises and achieve that goal?"

"That was my understanding."

"Then, logically, the three of you would have to wait until she retired, some years down the line, before you could put your plan into operation.

And, by that time, it is also logical to assume the decedent would have beaten you to the punch and had already put a proven spray on the market. Therefore, what point in pursuing it at all?"

"We doubted Mr. Wexler could succeed without Mrs. Pazel's help."

"Did you discuss whether she was financially sound enough to wait out a year without an income?"

"She said she couldn't."

"What, then?"

"We hoped to locate a financier to pay her."

Bond raised his eyebrows in surprise.

"That would require a considerable investment on speculation. Did you have anyone in mind?"

"No."

Bond hesitated, debating how to work with that answer without impeaching his own witness.

"Let me go about this a different way. On the night of July 15, did you receive a call from Mr. Wexler inviting you to a meeting at his office?"

Boerner knit his fingers and began sweating.

"Yes. I did," he whispered.

"Please speak up so the jury can hear you," Judge Gillman ordered.

"Yes, I did," he loudly reiterated.

"Did he tell you why he wanted to see you?"

"No."

"Did you speculate?"

The witness finally brightened as he recalled the rehearsal the D.A. had put him through before being called to the stand. Flattening the palms of his hands on his thighs, his head raised.

"Yes. It occurred to me that he had reconsidered my proposal."

"That being?" Bond prompted.

"Either he was going to abandon the idea of marketing the cream and was going to sell me
the filly, or he was going to seek some sort of a deal."

"Did you keep the appointment?"

"I did."

"What time did it take place?"

"Seven o'clock."

"In the evening?" he patiently drew out.

"Yes."

"Was anyone else present? One of your partners, perhaps? A secretary?"

"No. It was just Mr. Wexler and me."

"No one else was there to witness the conversation?"

"No."

"What did Mr. Wexler say to you?"

Before re-knitting his hands, Boerner wiped a rivulet of sweat from his forehead.

"He said he was going to pursue the idea of selling the spray and he wanted me to me on board to show the horse; prove how it worked. Because I was the trainer and knew her better than anyone."

"And because you have an excellent reputation in the field? That the owners of these expensive animals would respect your word?"

"Yes, sir."

"What sort of a deal did he offer you?"

"A bonus and a cut of the profits."

"Generous. Did you accept?"

"Yes. I did."

"Did the decedent mention your other two partners? Involving them in manufacturing and marketing the product?"

"He did not."

"Even though you and your partners – the defendant and Jack Merrick – had discussed the possibility it couldn't be done without the oversight of the defendant?"

"He apparently thought otherwise."

"Making you the more valuable of the three?"

"I had the inside knowledge of horses and racing."

"So you did."

Thoughtfully nodding and stepping away to give the jury a clear view of the witness, Bond modulated his voice to make a salient point.

"The chemist might be dispensed with but not the trainer." Shaking his head, he slipped into an easy cadence. "Aside from the remuneration, did you have any other reason to accept? Considering that as far as you knew, the defendant and Mr. Merrick were not going to be involved?"

Boerner leaned forward, hands on the top of the witness box. Turning to the jury as he and the D.A. had practiced, he articulated in a soft voice.

"Yes, sir. I knew Mrs. Pazel's formula was a miracle. It saved the career of one horse and it had the potential to do that for other race horses. Not only them, but many different animals. I told you it worked on dogs. The poor beast was suffering and with a few days it was healthy and happy again. That spray was a gift to the world. It deserved to be available so dogs and cats and horses could be relieved of their misery. I truly mean that. Amy didn't create it to make money. She did it for mercy. If my working with Mr. Wexler helped achieve that end – no matter who profited – I felt it was worth it."

"Very commendable. That explains your perspective. Yet, I seriously doubt it expresses the feelings of the chemist who had created the spray and was being dismissed from its very profitable sale. No matter her altruistic feelings when formulating it, it was her brilliance that was being... stolen. That couldn't have been easy to reconcile."

Before Hugh could stand, Judge Gillman spoke.

"I have warned you once, already, Mr. Bond. Do not summarize the thoughts, feelings or emotions of the defendant. The last statement will be stricken from the record and you may consider yourself in contempt of court. Now, either conduct yourself professionally, or I shall demand you be replaced by your colleague, Mr. Dodson."

"I beg the court's pardon, Your Honor." Clearing his throat, he returned to the witness.

"When you left this meeting with the decedent – what time was that?"

"I'd say approximately seven-thirty."

"Did Mr. Wexler appear to be ill? Suffering in any way? Complaining of being nauseous, perhaps?"

"He did not."

"Let me ask you bluntly: when you left, was he alive and in the same state of health as you first saw him upon arrival?"

"He was."

"One further question, then. From your perspective, how would Stanley Wexler's death affect the manufacture and sale of the miracle spray?"

"My first thought was, no one who inherited his property would go to the trouble of marketing it. The horse farm was going to be hard enough to handle. Or, if they did, it would be years down the line."

"Time Mrs. Pazel time to find financing to put the cream on the market?"

"Yes."

"So, his death was, in that way, opportune to the defendant?"

"Yes."

Having achieved his goal, Bond nodded toward the jury.

"Thank you. No further questions."

Amid a low murmuring from the spectators, Gillman checked the time.

"Mr. Kerr, it grows late and I presume you have a lengthy cross ahead of you. Rather than break it up into two parts, I suggest we dismiss court and reconvene in the morning."

"No objection."

"So ordered. Court will reconvene tomorrow morning at ten o'clock."

Bond and Dodson were the first up. Moving quickly down the aisle well satisfied with the days' work, Hugh and Ellen waited for them to leave before assembling their material. As the matron stepped forward to get her, Amy asked, "How'd we do?"

"Bond had to trip over himself to get to the motive. More than a few times I thought he made a better case for Boerner committing the crime than you. He'll have to correct that as he goes along. All things considered, we did just fine."

"Thank you."

"Try and relax," Ellen encouraged as Amy was escorted away. When she had gone, she turned to Hugh. "Speaking of relaxing, I nearly melted into the floor when Boerner quoted Jack as saying his Mom had a dog with an itch. Surely, Bond knows he was referring to Mary Wade."

He chuckled.

"What does that say for us, that we're more worried about revealing a relationship than defending a client?"

"I didn't say more worried."

"You win on a technicality."

He took her arm and they left together, once more on the same side.

CHAPTER 20

"Mr. Boerner," Hugh began, casually pacing in front of the witness stand. "It's a matter of public record that you were the first person the police suspected of murdering Stanley Wexler. Isn't that true?"

Face reddening, Bill pointed a finger at the moving target.

"You can't say that! You're my lawyer. That's confidential."

"What you told me in confidence shall remain between us. But my point is – and I think the jury will react the same why the police did – by considering you had means, motive and opportunity to commit the crime. The fact the prosecutor chose to charge your partner instead of you doesn't clean your slate."

Rising out of the seat, the witness pointed into the crowd.

"I knew it! I knew that rat, Jack Merrick, would tell you I threatened to kill Wexler. But that was nothing more than... than big talk. I didn't mean it!"

"I appreciate you bringing that threat out into open court, Mr. Boerner."

Amid the twitter of voices, a clearly upset Bond stood and faced the judge.

"Counsel is deviating from what was established by my questioning. I request the witness' last statement be stricken from the record."

Gillman looked from the D.A. to Kerr as if judging not only the merits of the objection but the propriety of the defense lawyer's approach. Picking up a pencil that rested by his hand, he used it as a delaying tactic while gathering his thoughts.

"On the wider objection I am in favor of ruling for the defense. Mr. Kerr did not actively solicit the statement, the witness offered it of his own free will. However, on the narrower issue of whether the original intent was to get to that point, the issue is open to consideration. Counsel for both sides will approach the bench."

Having already won the point, Hugh stepped up, Bond snarling behind him. Gillman leaned forward and spoke in an undertone.

"I believe, Bart, you should have offered your objection after Hugh's first question. That you didn't tends to make me favor the defense. That said, I believe you're on dangerous ground, Hugh. Not only in straying from the prosecution's lead, but from the fact you obviously know more about the witness's involvement in this case than was brought out in testimony before this court. Having previously represented him when he was first brought in for questioning, you must guard against crossing ethical lines."

"I made it clear I was relying on the account of a second witness."

"No, sir, you did not. The witness inadvertently made it for you. And while what he stated may be true, you put him in a position to incriminate himself without benefit of counsel. Nor, sir, do you speak for the police or the prosecutor. I seriously doubt they consulted you before evaluating the evidence. How do you reply to that?"

"I will further develop the witness' involvement by the testimony of other witnesses, Your Honor."

"Thank you." The judge motioned them away. "Objection is sustained. The jury is instructed to disregard both defense counsel's remarks and those of the witness."

He banged his gavel to underscore his point and Hugh returned to face Boerner.

"Let us discuss your relationship with the decedent, Stanley Wexler. You testified you were on good terms with him?"

"Yes. I was."

"Please describe what you mean by that."

"I was his trainer. I served in that capacity for a number of years. I judged, worked with and supervised his racing thoroughbreds. That's a position of great responsibility. He trusted my judgment and we had a cordial relationship."

"As employer-employee, or a closer one? Were you a personal friend? Invited to social gathering unrelated to the business of racing horses?"

"I would say somewhere between the two."

"More than an employee but less than, shall we say, a close friend. I see." He stepped back to consider. "Being 'somewhere between the two,' I assume you had latitude to use your own discretion when it came to the horses. What would that entail?"

"Judging the quality and potential of an animal. Arranging its workouts; assessing progress. Overseeing care and treatment; feed, equine maintenance. Coordinating with others what races the horse might be entered."

"And veterinary care?"

"Yes. If I thought the horse needed to be examined, I would summon a vet."

"What was the name of the horse you mentioned in your previous testimony? The one with a wound on its muzzle?"

"Barrister's Baby."

"Ah. Yes. Affectionately called B. B. This was the horse on which Mrs. Pazel's spray was used?"

"Yes."

"Was this a valuable horse? One with... potential?"

"Yes."

"Considering it was at the race track, may I presume the object was to race it?"

"That was the plan."

"How did that work out?"

"She couldn't be entered until the open sores on her muzzle were healed. They occurred during her first workouts at the track."

"Did they heal under the care of your known and approved veterinarians?"

"No."

"Leading to what conclusion?"

"The horse couldn't be raced."

"In other words, Barrister's Baby's career was likely to be over before she ever established herself as a contender for the top prizes?"

"Yes."

"As her trainer, how did you feel about that?"

"I was upset."

"Prompting you to allow the application of an unknown substance to be placed on the animal? A substance obtained through the intervention of a casual acquaintance you hardly knew?"

Boerner stiffened in the chair.

"It was that or lose her."

"Not your loss, surely?"

"Not financially. But in here," he indicated, tapping his chest.

"Did you have permission to try this unknown substance on the horse? Notify the owner, perhaps? Get permission?"

"No."

"Had you ever done anything like that before?"

"No."

"Would it be fair to say you had it applied on the sly?"

Slapping his hand on the witness box, Boerner's eyes narrowed in anger.

"I did what I thought was best for the horse. That's my job!"

"What would it have cost you to ask?" When no answer was immediately forthcoming, Hugh pressed the issue. "Or, did you fear denial?" Again, no answer. "Or, did you have another reason for not asking?"

"What would that be?" Boerner demanded in pique.

Hugh smiled placidly.

"I'm not here to answer questions, just ask them. Since you don't appear to have an answer, let me try something else. "What happens to thoroughbreds when they can't race?"

"They breed them –"

"Please don't be ingenious with this court. Do horses with no proven record of success – ones, in fact, that are predisposed to a fatal flaw, such as thin or easily irritated skin – often get bred?"

The witness sat back in the chair.

"Not often."

"If not bred, what, then?"

"They get sold. Or, destroyed."

"Sold for a great deal of money? The same money they would bring if they were champions? Or sold for a fraction of their potential value?"

"Depending on their blood line, sold for next to nothing."

"Was Barrister's Baby's bloodline such that the horse would have commanded a hefty price tag?"

"No."

Hugh spoke as he walked toward the jury.

"Do I understand the situation correctly? That you tried to save the horse – its career as well as its life – by using some medicine of last resort?"

"Yes."

"In your experience, knowing your employer-friend as you did, would Stanley Wexler have approved of such use?"

Balling his fist, Boerner shouted, "Yes!"

Hugh spun to face him.

"Yes? You can state that unequivocally? Then, why didn't you ask him? Just to be on the safe said?" The witness shrugged. "That is not an answer. I suggest you didn't ask him for reasons of your own. That it occurred to you if the spray worked, you'd be in possession of a miracle cure. One no one knew about but you. And if the owner wasn't aware you had cured the horse, you would be able to purchase it for next to nothing. Racing it, using it as a showcase for the product you hoped to market!"

Having heard enough, Bond got to his feet.

"Counsel is getting too far afield. None of this has anything to do with the subject at hand."

"Your Honor, the questions I am asking relate directly to the final meeting between Mr. Wexler and the witness on the eve of the decedent's death. A subject directly covered by Mr. Bond."

"Sustained."

Bond sat and turned his head away. Hugh resumed his cross examination.

"I have already established you were less than open with Mr. Wexler on the subject of the miracle spray. Did you eventually report to him on its success?"

"Yes."

"Did you give him a detailed explanation? Who formulated the spray, for instance?"

"Yes."

"Did you mention the fact she did not own the patent?"

"Yes."

"Did you ask to purchase Barrister's Baby?"

"Yes."

"What did he reply?"

"He said he'd get back to me."

"Did he?"

"Yes."

"What was the answer?"

"No."

"No – what?"

"No. He wouldn't sell the horse."

"What else?"

"He had bought the patent from the owner."

"Who was?"

"A Mr. Shaffley."

"Who is –?"

"Someone associated with Mega Enterprises where Mrs. Pazel worked."

"Was that all?"

"Yes."

"Was that all?" Hugh repeated.

"He fired me."

"Mr. Wexler fired you?"

"Yes."

"Why?" No answer. "Because you had deceived him? Tested a medication on one of his horses without permission? Because you committed a grievous breach of your responsibilities by using an unknown substance on a race horse? An act that might have gotten both you and him in trouble with the racing commission? Because he thought you'd get in the way when he tried to market the product, himself?"

"I don't know! He didn't say!" Boerner screamed.

Letting the moment pass and allowing the witness to compose himself, Hugh stared at the jury to indicate they gravely consider what they had just heard.

"Mr. Boerner, you were fired. Your career was in tatters. Why, then, should Mr. Wexler turn around and re-hire you? We have only your word for that. We have only your word for the fact the decedent called you in the first place. Isn't it more likely you went to see him on your own, found him resolute and poisoned him?"

"No! I swear it wasn't like that. He did call me. He did offer me a job. I had no reason to kill him! It was her!" he screamed, pointing at the defendant. "She was the one. She knew about poisons! She murdered him because he stole her idea!"

Bond, who had been on the edge of his seat, settled back as the cross-examination unexpectedly came around his way. Hugh stormed the witness box.

"You were the one out on your ear. The one without a job. Listen to your own testimony. You stated, quote, 'My first thought was, no one who inherited his property would go to the trouble of marketing it. The horse farm was going to be hard enough to handle. Or, if they did, it would be years down the line.' End quote. Your first thought, Mr. Boerner. Not that of the defendant, Amy Pazel, but yours. No further questions, subject to recall at a future date."

He strode back to the defense table, perspiring heavily. Taking out a handkerchief, he wiped his face as Bond popped up, eager to underscore the witness' accusation while burying that of his opponent's final statement.

"The prosecution calls Philip Shaffley to the stand."

While the witness was making his way forward, Ellen leaned behind the defendant to speak to Hugh.

"You convinced me. And the jury, too, if I'm not mistaken."

Replacing the linen in his pocket, Hugh smiled. It was a theatrical gesture, knowing he was being watched.

"I'm not sure about my timing, but it'll have to stand for what it is."

"Do you think Bill really killed him?" Amy whispered.

"That's not my business. I'll call my own physician to testify that the poison could have been administered by him and only started working on Wexler after your visit. If the jury decides that's a viable point and we win, I'm satisfied."

"Do you think he's guilty?" she reiterated.

Wisely, he didn't answer.

Turning their attention to the front of the room, Amy shuddered. Ellen looked at her in surprise.

"That's your boss coming to the stand, isn't it?"

"He owns the company I work for. He doesn't know a thing about chemistry. He doesn't have to."

"How well do you know him? If you know him at all?"

"I've met him at parties – employee functions. And a number of times when I've won professional and company awards."

"What do you think of him?"

"I don't."

Ellen hid a smile behind her hand and looked back at the witness box as Shaffley was getting seated. Bond, being eager to show him off, made sure the jury was watching as he began the questioning.

"Mr. Shaffley, please state your occupation for the record?"

"I am the president of Mega Enterprises."

"Do you own it, sir?"

Shaffley stiffened as he gave his reply.

"It is a family-owned corporation. We're proud of that, Mr. Bond. I may be the principal shareholder but everyone is involved. No employee contribution is too small and all are appreciated."

"Very commendable. Could you please briefly explain to the jury what Mega Enterprises is all about?"

"Certainly." The speaker turned toward the twelve men and women as though he were offering a prospectus to interested investors. "Mega Enterprises was founded on plain, simple principals. Simply stated, we produce, market and sell a wide range of quality products at a fair price through a private salesforce rather than third-party department stores. I trust you distinguished people are not only familiar with our brand names, but have purchased our products."

Hugh stood, but the judge was ahead of him. Motioning him down, he spoke for the court.

"You have established your witness, Mr. Prosecutor. Please move on to the 'contribution' he may make to your case."

The point, if not the droll humor, struck home and the D.A. smiled.

"Your company employs the defendant, Amy Pazel?"

"It does."

"What is her position in the company?"

"A research scientist."

Crossing to Mr. Dodson, he accepted a set of papers and returned to the witness.

"Is this the contract the defendant signed before becoming an employee of Mega Enterprises?"

Shaffley briefly examined it before nodding.

"It is."

"Request this contract be entered into evidence for the People."

"No objection."

"So ordered."

The document was registered and Bond returned with it to the stand.

"Please tell the court if there is a clause in this contract that categorically states any formulas developed by employees of Mega Enterprises while in the company employ, whether done on work or leisure time, belong to you?"

"That is a standard inclusion."

"And does it also state –?"

Hugh spoke from his chair.

"I object to the prosecutor's word 'also.' The witness did not answer the question, he merely affirmed the clause was routine. Not that this specific contract included it."

"Sustained."

Bond deeply exhaled, glanced at the jury to imply the suggestion the defense had so little to offer it was forced to resort to trivialities, then asked of the witness, "Was this stipulation *also* included in the contract signed by the defendant?"

"It was."

"Thank you for clearing up that salient detail. Does it *also* state a specific time frame that is required to elapse before a former employee may sell a formula to a competitor or use it for private purposes?"

"It does. One year."

"What is the purpose of that inclusion?"

"To prevent employees going to a rival lab and revealing proprietary secrets."

"Nothing illegal or unusual in that, is there?"

"It is standard business practice."

"As you say. Thank you. This country was built by such entrepreneurs such as you, Mr. Shaffley. Let us further develop this idea. To your knowledge, did the defendant attempt to patent a formula under her own name while in the employ of Mega Enterprises?"

"Let me be specific, sir."

Bond raised an eyebrow.

"Please do. Clarity is the soul of a good prosecution."

The statement brought several nods of approval from those favoring that side.

"All patents are registered with the United States Patent Office under the creator's name. That, sir, is the law, by which we assiduously adhere. However, the ownership of such patent is concurrently registered."

"Oh. I see. In this case, the patent is registered to Amy Pazel but it belongs to Mega Enterprises."

"Precisely."

"Meaning, she could not legally sell it without your permission? Even if redesigned on her own time and at her own expense?"

"Yes."

"I will return to this subject with another witness." Finally stepping back, Bond faced the jury. "Was Mrs. Pazel allowed by the U. S. Patent Office to patent her new formula and keep the rights to it for herself?"

"She was not, those in charge recognizing that she was an employee of Mega Enterprises."

"What happened? Was she punished, censored by the company?"

"She was advised by the legal department of Mega Enterprises that the parent would be accepted by the Patent Office but the ownership of it would revert to Mega Enterprises. Our legal department advised her of such." He stared at the defendant across the open courtroom space. "She was not punished. We do not treat family in such a manner. It was considered an honest mistake and there the matter dropped."

His statement was received with a sympathetic response from the audience.

"Very commendable," Bond replied, responding to the reaction. "Now: did you receive a telephone call from the decedent, Stanley Wexler?"

"I did."

"What was the nature of this call?"

"He wanted to purchase a patent from me."

"What specific patent?"

"The one created by Mrs. Pazel. The spray designed for use in treating recurring sores in animals."

"The same spray she attempted to patent for herself and was rebuffed?"

"Yes."

"Did the decedent state why he wanted it?"

"He did. He saw a market for it and had ideas about developing a product for the racing business."

"Did you sell it to him?"

"I did."

"By selling it, that means you permitted him to legally transfer the ownership of the formula from Mega Enterprises to Mr. Wexler or one of his business concerns?"

"Yes."

"Could he then sell the product without being required to recompense the creator – in this case, the defendant – from any profits derived from the sale?"

"Most certainly."

Sighing, Bond slowly shook his head.

"That hardly seems fair."

"Mrs. Pazel was well-paid for her services. That, sir, was her reward."

"Then, I'm afraid I have to agree. No further questions."

Hugh and Bond exchanged places. Hugh smiled pleasantly. Shaffley did not respond.

"Mr. Shaffley, as president of the family corporation known as Mega Enterprises, were you aware one of your employees attempted to register a patent as the developer and owner of a new formula?"

"I was not. I run a corporation. I am not involved in the day-to-day details of minor transactions."

"You say a 'minor' transaction. This, then, was not a major issue?"

The witness waved it off as inconsequential.

"It happens all the time."

"Meaning other research scientists have attempted to privately patent formulas?"

"Yes. They don't understand the restrictions placed on them by their contracts."

"You would agree, then, this was a common mistake?"

Growing annoyed, Shaffley curled his lips.

"I have already said she wasn't reprimanded."

"And the formula she attempted to patent was subsequently registered under the ownership of Mega Enterprises? Is that always the case in such matters? Ownership is transferred to the employer?"

"When you refer specifically to those companies who pay for and market such chemical formulas, yes."

"Did Mrs. Pazel's formula have value?"

"I told you before, I wasn't involved, so I cannot say."

"When brought to their attention, would your legal department, then in possession of the formula, have turned it over to other scientists in the company for evaluation?"

"What they would have done, Mr. Kerr, is evaluated the description of the formula – that submitted by the patentee – to determine whether it had any value to the company. If they determined it to be something we could market, they would have done handed it over to development. In this instance, as I have *lately* been informed," he stressed, "they made the determination it was not a product line which would have fit it with what we sell and therefore, they filed it away with all the other patents we own but do not use."

"You have many of those?"

"Thousands."

"Meaning, clarity being the soul of a good defense," he quipped to a low outpouring of amusement from the gallery, "it was consigned to the dust bin?"

"Meaning, Mega Enterprises had no use for it," Shaffley rephrased, not appreciating the colloquialism.

"And so, when Mr. Wexler called and asked if you'd sell the patent, you didn't hesitate?"

"Why should I? I was getting something for nothing."

"You signed a legal contract with Mr. Wexler?"

"Naturally."

"And there your interest ended?"

"Upon receipt of his bank check."

A twittering of bemused humor could be heard as those appreciating the stipulation registered their acknowledgment. In response, Hugh walked toward the half gate, bringing him nearer the spectators. Allowing them a long moment to study his face, he suddenly turned and strode back the way he had come.

"And there your interest ended, Mr. Shaffley? I wonder. Did you, or did you not, belatedly check with your marketing department, questioning exactly what you had so cavalierly signed away? Did it occur to you, after the fact, that perhaps you had made a mistake? That the formula which had garnered the attention of one of thoroughbred racing's established owners might have true value? That Mr. Wexler was onto something big? And by big, I mean lucrative?" His voice rose as he spoke, nearly to the level of shouting. "Did you, Mr. Shaffley? Ask around? Discover that you'd made a mistake?"

The sharp retort of a flattened palm striking wood electrified the room for a moment, preceding Bartholomew Bond's angry declaration.

"Objection, Your Honor! Badgering the witness! Mr. Kerr has gone off on one of his famous meandering tangents in order to discredit the witness by innuendo and accusation!"

Judge Gillman allowed a moment for the room to settle, fully aware the district attorney's objection was meant to mitigate damage to the prosecution witness rather than make a point of law. Acutely aware his position was not to jeopardize either case, he made eye contact with both men before speaking.

"I believe, Mr. Kerr, you have made your point. The objection is overruled, but next time, consider using your courtroom voice. The witness may answer the question."

Red-faced and insulted, Shaffley glowered at the defense attorney from under hooded lids.

"I-did-not."

The flat denial sent waves of electricity through the air. Hugh's expression hardened as he put a hand to his ear.

"You did not? Did I hear you correctly?"

"You-did."

With instincts honed from many battles, Hugh edged closer to signify he was coming in for the kill.

"I have given you a chance to retract your statement, President Shaffley. And you have stood by your word. That is your choice because I trust your attorneys from 'legal' have adequately advised you that telling a falsehood under oath is a crime punishable by fine and imprisonment."

Rising to his feet, the corporation executive wagged a finger at his accuser.

"How dare you? Who do you think you are?"

"A man in search of justice, Mr. Shaffley. That's who I am. Someone who believes money and power do not shield an individual from just punishment." Bond got to his feet, prompting Hugh to hurry before another objection could be launched, breaking a second time the mood he had created. "And if I were to say to you, Mr. Shaffley, I will subpoena Mrs. Madeline Daugherty, your executive secretary, and ask if she put through for you a call to 'legal' at any time after you spoke to Mr. Wexler. Answering in the affirmative, I will subpoena your entire staff of attorneys and question each one under oath to ascertain whether you discussed Mrs. Pazel's patent. An employee of a 'family corporation' may do much to keep his job, but not, I seriously doubt, lie for you under oath. And if you did question the validity of your judgment, I shall have you charged with perjury."

Shaffley remained stoical but his head listed to one side.

"I have many reasons to consult with my legal department."

"Then, I ask again, was one of them to ask about Mrs. Pazel's patent?"

"As a matter of routine, I may have mentioned it. Merely to inform them I had approved the transfer. I hardly keep assiduous records of my consultation with company attorneys."

"You should, Mr. Shaffley. To refresh your mind from time to time. Especially when you are called to testify at trial. Appearing unprepared reflects poorly on your legal counsel."

"Is there any good reason for Mr. Kerr's circumlocution, Your Honor, or is he just wasting the court's time?" the D.A. demanded in pique.

"Mr. Bond wishes to know whether you are making a point," the judge translated.

"Yes, sir. I wish to know, Mr. Shaffley, whether your legal department consulted with your team of research scientists to re-evaluate their initial consideration of the patent. And if so, what was their conclusion?"

That was too much for Bond. Getting to his feet, he shook his head.

"Defense counsel is getting too far afield. Delving into areas not covered by my examination."

"Your Honor, the district attorney specifically questioned the witness on the subject of evaluation. The answer was, they did, in fact, evaluate the spray and determined it had no use for the corporation. Asking whether the team was subsequently ordered to re-evaluate the product is merely following up on the initial testimony."

"I will allow it. Overruled."

Hugh turned back to the witness.

"What was their conclusion?"

"They confirmed their initial report. That the product had value on a limited basis. Not suitable for Mega Enterprises."

Taking a stroll around the room with the casual intent of being unconcerned, Hugh spoke with his back to Shaffley.

"Not suitable for Mega Enterprises. I see." Spinning around, he demanded, "But, might it have been suitable for Philip Shaffley?"

"I don't know what you mean."

"Speaking in generalities, knowing the formula was a potential cash cow —"

"Objection!" Bond called again. "The value of the formula has not been established!"

"Sustained."

Hugh nodded and smiled pleasantly.

"Knowing the formula to be unique and had the potential to be marketed to a very wealthy clientele, might you not have been interested? For your own profit?"

"I am the corporation! I do not freelance."

"But might you? I'm asking if it's possible you could have purchased the formula for your own benefit? Not in the name of Mega Enterprises, but for some other company you either own or could establish? To make a private killing in the market?"

The question elicited a shocked reaction from the onlookers.

"I resent your implication. No. I would not have purchased the formula."

"Would not, or could not?"

"It would have been against company rules."

"But you just told this court you are the corporation, Mr. Shaffley. Recalling it is a 'family' business and your board of directors support you for the common good, might not they have permitted such a transaction?"

"That is preposterous. Toward what end?"

"Keeping a valuable patent in the family but out of the reach of the shareholders."

"I would never –"

"Let us dispense with hyperbole." Hugh strode closer, eyes narrowed as he attacked. "Isn't it true that you realized, too late, you had been hasty in your judgment? That you 'got something for nothing' but lost the big prize?" Reaching the witness box, his hand slapped down on the wooden cross-bar. "Too late to rescind the deal, what was your option? Might it have occurred to you that with the purchaser, Stanley Wexler out of the way, no one would market the product for years, if at all? Giving you time to have one of your own scientists reformulate it enough to be patented in your name? So you and your 'family,'" he added in derision, "might have the opportunity of establishing the product and benefiting from its potentially lucrative sale?"

"No! No! No," Shaffley screamed as Bond shot up, pointing at the defense attorney.

"Couldn't you have gone to his office, shared a drink with him while discussing… the weather, then poisoning him with carbon tetrachloride you could have obtained from his own laboratories?"

"Objection, Your Honor!" Bond screamed. "Counsel is completely out of order!"

Hugh made a slight bow to the judge.

"I withdraw the question."

Leaving him in total control of the mayhem.

CHAPTER 21

Slipping easily into his chair, Hugh maintained the grin he had cultivated on the way back from the witness chair.

"Brilliant," Ellen whispered. "You turned the tables completely. But, how did you know Shaffley had asked his staff to re-evaluate the worth of the formula?"

"Sheer guesswork," he admitted with a shrug. "Knowing the avarice mind."

"Not from personal experience," she countered.

"I've had my moments. No one likes to lose out on a fortune. Especially from a lapse of judgment. It tarnishes the image and after money, Mr. Shaffley is all about self-image."

She smiled in triumph for him.

"Now, you've raised the spectre of two potential murderers. If I'm sitting on the jury, I'm ready to go into deliberation right now, exonerate the defendant and be home for supper."

"A happy thought."

"But, you don't think so?"

"We have a ways to go."

"Why? I don't think Bond can shatter the illusion you just created. In fact, it wouldn't surprise me if he asked for a continuance so he can offer you a deal."

"He may, but whatever he came up with short of complete exoneration would be unacceptable. Amy's name must be cleared absolutely or she'll never be able to work in her chosen field again. Much less face her husband and children. Am I right?" he asked, turning to the woman at his side.

"I had nothing to do with Mr. Wexler's death. I want to be free to hold my head up."

"Good girl. That's the plan. Besides," he added, pushing away the legal pad in front of him. "Bond will finish out the prosecution and let it go to the jury. He has his own self-image to worry about."

"Even at the expense of convicting the wrong person?" Amy softly inquired.

Hugh debated before answering.

"Bartholomew Bond believes you're guilty. Otherwise, he would never have pressed charges. Don't fault him there. His problem is, that while the case appeared strong on the outside it was filled with holes. He was too aggressive without thinking it through. I don't believe he once considered

Shaffley as a potential murder suspect. And he went a long way toward proving Wexler was alive and apparently well after Bill Boerner met with him. Which, of course, we knew, but Bond had to carry the point without your testimony. In his eyes, you were the last person to see Wexler alive. He went on that assumption, thinking the jury would follow his logic. I put a... monkey wrench in his argument but I haven't closed the deal."

"You mean, we have to find the real murderer?"

"That would help us enormously."

He smiled and she returned it.

"I guess we're all in the business of re-formulating."

As if divining her thoughts, B.B. Bond stood and addressed the judge.

"Considering the lateness of the hour, I suggest we adjourn for lunch."

"No objection," Hugh offered.

Gillman banged his gavel.

"Court is in recess until one o'clock."

"Keep up the brave front," Ellen encouraged as the matron came for Amy.

"I've been told I have a unique capacity for creating coping strategies. As a scientist, I put such assumptions to the test on a daily basis."

"I like her, Hugh," she sighed as they watched their client walk away as though nothing on earth troubled her.

"A wonderful woman, I'm surrounded by them," Hugh agreed, slipping his hand in hers. Ellen pretended to slap it away.

"You are forgetting yourself, sir?"

"Never," he grinned, turning around to view the few remaining spectators who had lingered in the courtroom. Having taken in the loving gesture and thus been rewarded for their patience, they retreated, leaving the couple with a brief moment of privacy. "What's your pleasure?" he pursued, helping Ellen gather in the few remaining items from the desk and packing them away.

"My pleasure would be for a nice easy lunch with a glass of wine for a stimulant, then home for a hot shower and a nap. What would your pleasure be?"

"To shadow you in everything you just described."

"That, too," she winked while casually running a hand across her breasts. "But, I should have added, Baby comes first. And then I'll settle for soup, salad and a glass of iced tea."

"There's a comedown."

Suddenly growing serious, she caught his eye.

"Not feeding Jackie, Hugh. I can't tell you what pleasure that gives me. If I'm going to have both motherhood and a career, I want everything that comes with both. Come on. Let's go find Mom. She should be waiting outside. Probably wondering what became of us."

"Not wondering," he laughed.

Taking the briefcase in one hand and extending his elbow for her with the other, they walked out. True to form, Mary was there with Jacqueline but she wasn't alone. A man in a cheap suitcoat was standing in front of her, blocking her path toward the courtroom.

"Ugh oh," Hugh groaned. "I know what that is."

They waited while an indignant Mrs. Wade accepted a piece of paper from him, then pushed past with an angry scowl. Having already seen Hugh and Ellen, she clutched the baby tighter as though shielding her from unpleasantness.

"I've just been subpoenaed," she groused in extreme annoyance.

"I expected as much."

"What does 'Barrister's Baby Number Two' want with me?"

"Oh, no: Bartholomew Bond has to be Barrister's Baby Number One. He's older," he quipped as Ellen grabbed her child.

"I have a lot worse to call him. And I hardly think an hour and a half is sufficient warning to appear in court. If he wanted me – and felt he had to go to the trouble and waste city dollars having some rude person serve me – he might have just asked Hank to relay the request. Yesterday. Or last week sometime. This way, I'm ill-disposed to think kindly of him or his case."

"Do you, anyway?" Ellen asked, trying to break her temper.

"I do not. I never liked the man. I think he's a pompous ass. One, I might add, who has never given Hank his due." Her eyes narrowed as her ire flared. "I'd vote for him if he ran for governor just to get him out of the county."

"But think what he'd do to the state."

"California's big enough to take care of itself."

"And Los Angeles County isn't?"

"Apparently not."

"Counsel for the defense concedes the point."

"Please, Hugh," Ellen interrupted as the baby started to cry. "I need a private room. Sooner than later."

"I'm sorry." He led the three through the halls, found an unoccupied room and indicated they go inside. Letting them pass, he started to close the door behind them. "I'll stand guard."

If anyone questioned why the famous defense attorney was holding up a courtroom wall, they wisely didn't inquire and twenty minutes later the solitary soldier had disappeared, keeping his secrets to himself.

At 12:55 the Kerrs hurried into the courtroom, passing Mary Wade, who had arrived minutes before and seated herself on the prosecution side. Making no attempt to acknowledge her presence, they settled in at the defense table. Hugh remained standing as their client was brought in, allowed her to sit and then leaned toward her for a private conversation.

"Bond is going to call Mary Wade as a witness."

She gave grim acknowledgment.

"I thought he would."

The clerk sang out that court was in session, Judge Gillman appeared, settled down, then nodded familiarly at the D.A.

"Call your next witness, Mr. Bond."

"The prosecution summons Mrs. Mary Wade to come forward."

The lady in question stood, marched forward with decorum, raised her right hand and swore to tell the truth. Once she had settled, Bond approached, wearing a pleasant attitude.

"Good afternoon," he began. Receiving no return salutation he cleared his throat. "Mrs. Wade, do you know the defendant, Amy Pazel?"

"I do."

"How do you know her?"

"We're neighbors."

"Are you well acquainted? Attend social gatherings together? Are you familiar with her husband and children?"

"Objection. Asking about facts not in evidence."

"Sustained."

Unruffled by the outburst, Bond suavely let it pass.

"Do you have a dog, Mrs. Wade?"

"Yes."

Attempting to establish a more amenable report, he politely inquired, "What is its name?"

"Irish Rover."

"Have you had it long?"

"My husband and I adopted it after the horrible tragedy last year when twelve jurors were brutally murdered. The dog had belonged to an elderly Irish lady who was one of those who lost her life. As she had no family to care for the animal, we took him in."

Clearly surprised by the information, Bond took a step back.

"How generous of you. Dog lovers everywhere appreciate your kindness. As do those of us in the legal system who were affected by that terrible event." Clearing his throat a second time, he recovered quickly. "Did this dog have a condition that caused him to scratch away patches of hair, sometimes breaking the skin and creating sores?"

"He did. He doesn't any longer."

"Why is that? Was he treated by a veterinarian?"

"We brought him to the vet but nothing he tried worked."

"Did you happen to mention Irish Rover's condition to the defendant?"

Inwardly cringing at hearing Bond pronounce her beloved pet's name, she clutched her pocketbook.

"I did."

"What, if anything, did she say?"

"She thought she would be able to help."

"At that time, did you know she was a research chemist?"

"Yes."

"And you took her up on the offer?"

"Most certainly."

"What did she provide you with?"

"A medicinal spray, I think you'd call it."

"Did she tell you anything about it?"

"She said she had developed it in her laboratory at home."

"Did that surprise you?"

"Of course not. She's brilliant."

"What makes you say that?"

"I've seen her patents. She has them framed in her house. Beside them are commendations from various professional societies and awards she's won at work for being the Employee of the Year."

"She showed these to you?"

"No. She's too modest for that. I happened to see them when I went to her house one afternoon. She had just made a batch of chocolate chip cookies and wanted to send some home to my husband."

"I'm sure he appreciated it," he tried, but she cut him off before he could apply a smile for the sake of the jury.

"It's more than Lieutenant Henry Wade ever got from Mrs. Bond. And he's known you and your wife far longer than we've known the Pazels."

More than surprised to hear defiance from his own witness, Bond nevertheless found the smile Mary had prevented a moment ago.

"Mrs. Wade, if my wife ever baked chocolate chip cookies I wouldn't let them out of the house. In fact," he added, playing to the audience. Craning his neck to glance over at the prosecution side of the room where Hank Wade sat, he quipped, "I might be tempted to call your husband and have him investigate whether an imposter had invaded our kitchen." Giving the joke no more than a second to sink in, he grew serious. "Mrs. Pazel is brilliant. Then it is fortunate we have even more brilliant officers on the force who can see through their deceit and make them pay for their crimes."

Placed in a difficult position, Mary clamped her jaw shut. Bond stepped back to put some distance between them.

"Did you use this spray on the dog?"

"Yes."

Unlike men, Mrs. Wade felt free to leave off the obligatory "sir" at the end of her sentence.

"Were you the one who applied it?"

"Amy did it."

"Were you present when this transpired?"

"I was."

"What happened?"

"While I hesitate to personify an animal, I'd say Rover sighed in satisfaction."

His arm made an arc encompassing the jury.

"What subsequently happened – as pertains to the medication?" he clarified to prevent her from offering a vague generalization of world affairs.

"The dog stopped itching and his wounds cleared up as though by magic."

"In other words, it worked?"

"It did, indeed."

"How long did the effects last?"

She thought a moment, then made a slight gesture with her shoulder.

"Amy gave us the bottle. Hank and I used it whenever we saw the need. Rover has been perfectly fine since then."

Drifting away, Bond glanced at the defendant before turning his attention toward the jury.

"Did Mrs. Pazel ever mention, even in passing, whether she intended to market the spray?"

"No."

Detecting a slight hesitation, he turned back.

"Did you ever mention it to her? Saying, perhaps, she had a 'gold mine' on her hands?"

Mary paused a moment before admitting, "Something to that effect."

"What did she say?"

"She was glad it helped Irish Rover."

Drawing his eyebrows into a "V," Bond pressed the issue.

"After a comment like that: something 'to the effect' she had a gold mine on her hands, that's all she said? I ask you to think carefully before answering."

Acutely aware of the tacit warning, Mary conceded, "She may have said, 'That would be nice.' Who wouldn't?" she blurted, hurt and angry.

"Who wouldn't, indeed?" he readily agreed, having elicited the answer he sought. He returned his attention to the jury. "A woman develops a medication that works 'magic.' The witness' own word. For those of us with beloved pets – or more specifically, those who own extremely expensive and valuable race horses – who wouldn't pay a king's ransom for 'magic'? A dog is cured, a thoroughbred's career is resurrected. Instead of the glue factory, the animal goes on to win the Triple Crown. The prosecution is not arguing the fact the defendant is brilliant. Far from it. It is our contention she may be at the top of her field. For which, as her employer stated, she was 'well paid for her services.'" Catching Hugh out of the corner of his eye, he hurried on. "But, Mrs. Wade, 'well paid' is not a gold mine. Would you agree?"

"Being married to a policeman, I have no familiarity with gold mines."

The tart rejoinder elicited a chuckle from a man sitting on court left. The D.A.'s ears reddened.

"Mrs. Wade, you testified the defendant lived in your neighborhood. Is that correct?"

"Yes."

"A neighborhood of... how would you describe it? Pertaining to its value."

Failing to see where he was going, she debated how to answer and settled for, "Middle class, I'd say."

"Hardly Beverly Hills. Not on a policeman's salary, I presume."

"It is not Beverly Hills."

"Three bedrooms, one bath. A quarter acre of land?"

"We have two bathrooms, now," she defended.

He ignored the addendum.

"A ranch style. A small yard."

"Yes."

"With a mortgage?"

Growing annoyed, she snapped, "Yes. Like most people, we have a mortgage."

Ellen touched Hugh's arm to get his attention. Noting the questioningly raised eyebrow, he read her thought and demurely shook his head, silently transmitting the fact to interrupt would only make the situation worse. She leaned back in resignation.

"Having visited there at least once that we know of, would you say Mrs. Pazel's house is similar to yours?"

"I suppose so."

"An average, middle class house. In fact, a house that typifies the American dream. But, is it?" He held up a finger for emphasis. "The American dream, if I may be so bold, is to advance one's status in life. To move up; not only in society but in life style. A scientist may be 'well paid' and be satisfied, but one who has developed a 'magic' formula likely dreams higher than 'average.'"

Finally growing annoyed, Hugh interrupted.

"Is the prosecutor going to ask a question, or is he through with this witness?"

Bond immediately went into his prepared dialogue, saving the judge the opportunity to rule.

"Knowing the defendant as you do, was there ever a time when you discussed her future plans? Specifically, after seeing how her magic spray worked? If properly marketed, might it not have brought in a substantial reward? Allowing her to move into an upper class neighborhood? Perhaps even allowed her to quit her job at Mega Enterprises and work for herself? Send her children to private schools? The best collages? Wouldn't that be the logical outcome of a successful business enterprise? And as such, how much more bitter the pill to swallow when learning she cannot have those dreams?"

Hugh slapped his hand on the desk.

"By my count, that was eight questions! Which does the D.A. wish the witness to answer?"

"I will re-phrase." Pressing closer to Mary Wade, he demanded, "To lose everything over a technicality. Not only tragic but embittering. Enough of a devastating blow to prompt the defendant to murder? Murder with a chance of regaining her own work for her own profit?"

"Objection!"

Judge Gillman cringed.

"On what grounds, Mr. Kerr?"

"Putting words in the witness' mouth."

"I cannot rule in your favor on those grounds."

"Asking multiple questions," he spat, caught off-guard by the denial.

The judge turned to Bond.

"One question at a time. I won't warn you again."

Bond made a slight bow before turning back to Mary Wade.

"Would anyone, under those circumstances, be tempted to commit the ultimate crime to regain what they perceived was stolen from then?"

"I can't speak for everyone!" she cried in frustration.

"No," he graciously conceded. "You can't. That is for the jury to decide. No further questions."

He walked away, leaving the shattered witness to his opponent. He stood, rapidly debating where to take his line of questioning. While it had not been his intention to cross-examine, Bond's triumph left him little choice. He began speaking from behind the desk.

"Mrs. Wade, the prosecutor has ably demonstrated your relationship with the defendant. Therefore, I feel confident you can answer this one question. Did, or did not, Mrs. Pazel ever express to you bitterness, anger, despair or murderous intent over the discovery that she could not legally manufacture and sell her magic formula?"

"Never. She created the formula specifically for Irish Rover. It saved his life, for without it, he would have been so miserable we may have had to put him down to spare him unnecessary suffering. She said that had been her intent and she was satisfied."

"Thank you. No further questions."

Bond popped up, a smirk on his face.

"One further point on re-direct. However altruistic that statement may have been, she did, however, see a golden opportunity and form a partnership to market the product? Implying, of course, she was well aware of its potential value?"

Mary's mouth grew taut.

"I cannot answer a question that pertains to an inference, Mr. Bond. No one but God is in a position to read her mind."

"Then, we shall let actions speak louder than words. Thank you."

When Hugh indicated he had no follow-up, Gillman ordered, "Call your next witness, Mr. Bond."

"The People rest, Your Honor."

"In that case, court is dismissed until Monday morning when the defense may present its case."

He concluded by slapping the gavel on the desk and rising. The jury followed his example and filed out. The first to leave, Bond and Dodson made their way down the aisle without a glance at the defense table. In deference to protocol, Hank Wade did not speak to his wife as she hurried out ahead of him, holding a handkerchief to her face. Ellen stared angrily at Hugh.

"I hate that man."

"Bond?" he clarified without necessity. "He was only doing his job."

"He's a vicious..."

He held up a hand.

"Don't say it."

"Bastard."

To cover the transgression, Amy changed the direction of the conversation.

"I feel sorry for Mary. It's my fault."

"It would only be your fault if you killed Wexler and put her in the position to be grilled under examination. You didn't, so no blame can be, or is attached to you," he gently argued. "She'll be all right. Besides," he tried, "she did get in that dig about the chocolate chip cookies."

"For which he'll make Hank pay," Ellen spat in derision. "Bond hardly expected Lieutenant Wade's wife to be a hostile witness. I almost thought at one point he was going to declare her as such."

"So did I. But he didn't dare. Hank can handle it. Come on," he urged Ellen. To Amy he added, "We'll be all right."

"I'm not worried," she bravely asserted.

"I'll talk with you before court resumes."

Smiling for their sake, she went with the matron. They watched her go, head held back, arms relaxed at her sides.

"I'm glad *she's* not worried," Ellen remarked, shaking her head.

Before he could answer they heard the strident wail of a baby. Responding to the call, they hurriedly gathered their papers.

"Jacqueline! In all the excitement of Mary being called to testify, I forgot about her!" she cried. "Who has her?"

"I don't know."

The last to leave, they emerged into the corridor, frantically looking around. An arm raised above the crowd caught their attention and they shoved past several lingerers in their eagerness to reach the other side.

"Jack!" Ellen gasped in surprise.

"Who'd you expect?" he grinned, shifting the baby from one arm to the other. "But, I'm sure glad to see you. I didn't think Bond was ever going to shut up. Pretty rough, huh?"

"Buzz saw," she acknowledged. "How did you get Jackie?"

"Mary transferred 'ownership' to me."

"You should have come and gotten me."

"The thought did occur to me. But, I didn't want to get you out of court." He toothily grinned. "We did all right. Only one small injury." Extracting his left hand he held it up for inspection. A small red welt immediately caught their eyes.

"You jabbed yourself with a diaper pin," Ellen diagnosed as reality struck. "Why were you using a pin?"

"To fasten the diaper."

"You... changed her diaper?" she gasped, taking the baby from him.

"Well, I had to do something." He crinkled his nose. "Or else the guard wouldn't let me stand by the door and listen."

Of the two parents, Hugh was the more shocked.

"You didn't even attend Mrs. Mrs. Millwood's class!"

"Didn't have to," he dismissed.

"Where-did-you-learn-how-to-change-a-diaper?"

"The Philippines, where else? I told you. The locals brought their kids to the nurses for medical advice. Too many kids, not enough nurses. I was impressed into service. Not happily," he added with a wink, "but it earned me hero points. A fellow can never have enough of those. I cashed them all in before I left."

"For what? Or, shouldn't I ask?"

"The ladies got to take me out to eat instead of the other way around." The adults chuckled in unison as he licked his sore finger. "I'm out of practice, but the operation, as they say, was a success."

"Meaning, the patient lived?"

"Meaning the doctor lived."

Growing serious, the attorney asked, "Are you up on your tetanus shots?"

"Geez, Hugh, I suppose you're asking that from a legal standpoint? Don't want to be sued?"

"In case you lose your arm," he agreed. "I don't see how I could put up a defense. Unless I argued neither Ellen nor I specifically asked you to take charge of Jacqueline."

"Yeah, well, I'd counter the Good Samaritan rule and take you for a bundle. Maybe invest it in a formula for curing dogs and horses."

"We're not going there. Come on." He attempted to guide him away. "I did mean what I said. About the tetanus shot."

"Brother, in my line of work I get one every few years. Now, bedbugs –"

"Never mind bedbugs!"

"Just sayin' –"

"You've said enough. And you have more stories about your service in the Philippines than Carter has liver pills."

"All of them gospel." He reached into his shirt and withdrew a medallion. "I got the St. Christopher medal to prove it."

"I thought you weren't wearing it, anymore."

"I wasn't. But, then I got to thinking. It's a new one."

"Thinking – what?"

"You know the stories. Of how guys carrying pocket Bibles got their lives saved when the bullet meant for them landed in the Good Book."

"You believe a St. Christopher medal is going to deflect a bullet?"

"Stranger things have been known to happen."

"Where did you get it?"

"Yeah. That's a story for another time. Come on. Are we gonna eat?"

"Only if the nurses pay."

Two out of three adults laughed. Jackie remained the deciding vote and she kept her own council.

CHAPTER 22

Tapping his finger on the arm of the couch, Hugh reflectively shook his head.

"We're missing something here."

"Yes," Mary agreed, coming in with a tray of coffee cups. "Poison."

His head snapped up in sudden interest.

"You mean, Wexler wasn't poisoned by carbon tetrachloride?"

"No. I mean to put a few drops in Bartholomew Bond's coffee. I will never forgive him for what he put me through this afternoon."

"You gave more than you got," Ellen reassured her, passing around a plate of frosted vanilla cookies. Hugh took three, Hank reached for two and Mary passed. Taking one for herself, Ellen nibbled on it while turning the conversation back to Hugh. "Missing what?"

"Why was Wexler really murdered?"

"What are you saying? You don't believe he was killed over the formula?"

"We certainly have presumed that, but I wonder now if we haven't put the cart in front of the horse."

"What do you mean?"

"Fit the motive to suit the crime instead of the other way around. The finger of guilt is always pointed at the last person to see the victim alive. Since that – purportedly – was Amy, and Amy is a chemist with a formula – it was logical to assume they nicely tied together. Bond's argument is that she had to stop Wexler from manufacturing the spray. She needed a year of retirement before she could reformulate it, find a backer and put it in production. That may sound reasonable on paper but frankly, it's ridiculous."

"Why?" Hank inquired, feigning indifference while dipping his cookie in the coffee and watching the frosting melt off in the hot liquid.

"There are too many variables."

"Such as?" Mary put to him when Hank failed to follow up.

"Those I'm going to have an accountant elucidate in court on Monday. Bypassing all the minor points, let's concentrate on the only one that matters: the belief that Wexler's heirs would be too consumed running the horse farm to have the time or interest to pursue a side business."

"You think it was an inside job?" Jack asked, coming out from the bathroom air-drying his hands. Crossing to the tray, he stared at the cookies in annoyance. "I thought you were going to make chocolate chip."

"We'll save those for Christine Bond," Mary huffed.

"That means I'll never get any."

"It means no one will ever get any."

"Oh, I don't know," Ellen countered with a smile. "Once B. B. relays to her what was said in court, I think she'll be forced to whip up a batch."

"He won't tell her," Hank corrected both observations.

"I think you're right there," Hugh seconded. "But, I'll wager she has spies at court. She'll hear about it, all right. I suspect 'B. B.' will have a long, silent weekend."

"Good!"

All eyes turned to Mary before Jack spoke and returned the attention to himself.

"Wager, is right. I'm going to the track tomorrow. Barrister's Baby is running. Jim Ewell said he had a deal going down; a fat payday. My hunch is that he thinks B. B. is gonna win big. I want a piece of the action. It's also when I step in and make my move." He winked at Ellen. "For my clients."

Noting the silent communication, Hugh demanded, "What clients?"

Jack dismissed the question with a wave of his hand.

"Ewell's got another dame on the string. Maybe two. If I can help them along the way, I'm... wonderful."

"He's been reading his press clippings, again," Hank supplied.

"You know it, Pop. See ya."

Helping himself to the rest of the cookies, he casually dropped them into his jacket pocket.

On cue, Hank snapped, "Don't call me Pop, whippersnapper."

The private detective laughed all the way out the door.

Saturday afternoon Jack caught up to Ewell at the ticket window. Looking at what he held in his hand and reading the denomination of the wager, he whistled.

"Two thousand smackos?"

Ewell shrugged.

"The odds aren't what I hoped for but at 5:1 I'll make $10,000."

"That's a payday and a half." Moving to the window, Jack passed through a hundred dollar bill. "On Barrister's Baby to win." Taking his receipt, he frowned. "Damn! I only got 3:1 odds."

"That's because there's a lot of excitement. People are betting on her. I was the first here as soon as betting opened. Got in before the crowd. You should have gotten up with the chickens. Is a hundred bucks all you have to bet?"

"It's all I dare bet."

"Coward."

"This is my sideline, not my job. And if we win, the coffee and pie is on you next time."

"No, sir. It's steak and champagne."

"That, I'll hold you to. See you back at the window."

"You bet," Ewell agreed, flashing teeth.

The two men separated and went to watch the races. Barrister's Baby ran in the fifth. Buying a hot dog at the concession stand, Jack inadvertently squirted a stream of yellow mustard on the sleeve of his jacket. He cursed. A small boy behind him in line giggled. Jack accidentally-on-purpose stepped on his foot as he went in search of a seat.

By the time the bugle had announced the start of the fifth race, Jack had been to the men's room twice and a half, the partial trip excused because he needed it as an excuse to search for Jim Ewell. While not expecting to find him in the restroom, he had hoped to catch a glimpse of him from a higher elevation. He did not.

Cursing that he hadn't thought to bring a slew of men with him in order to cover all the pay windows, Jack hurried to his seat to take in the start of the race. Binoculars to his eyes, his heart leapt as the gate went up and the horses broke. A far better judge of horseflesh, racing and gambling than he had let on to Ewell, he set aside his personal stake for a grim, studied analysis on the ongoing contest.

Barrister's Baby, wearing number 5 and her rider the royal purple and green colors of Wexler's stables, came out in the middle of the pack. Running that way through the first turn, the jockey positioned her on the outside and gave her the whip. She responded with speed, bypassing the other fillies as though they were purposely holding back. Half way through, the jockey maneuvered closer to the inside, finally taking the last turn on the rail.

"Go! Go! Go!" Jack hissed, leaning forward, then abandoning the glasses to stand and shout. "Go, baby, go!"

Before the words were fully out of his mouth, he felt something give. It looked like, from his perspective, the horse coming up on the right struck Barrister's Baby. Not a full hit, but a touch. Enough to throw her off her stride. The horse on the outside surged past and then a second, close behind. By the time the tape was broken, the filly nicknamed B. B. had finished third.

Stunned, Jack tore his eyes from the track toward the big board, expecting to see a challenge. If a review of the tape showed contact, the winner would be disqualified. It wouldn't give his horse the laurel wreath, but at least it wouldn't condemn her to a dismal third place finish among an undistinguished field.

No challenge was made. His face flushed in indignation.

"Son of a bitch!"

A man to his side patted his arm.

"Thought you had it," he tried. "But, she's a nag."

Bitterly pulling away, he forced himself to grin.

"Yeah. She's a nag. What was I thinking?"

"There's a better race in the 7th. Put your dough on Tinker-Taylor. He's gonna take it by two lengths."

"You think?"

"I know," he winked. "Bet whatever you got left."

"I ain't got nothin' left."

The man hesitated, then reached into his pocket. He offered Jack two dollars.

"Here. I been where you are. Don't go home with nothing."

Unable to comprehend the generosity, he numbly shook his head.

"This one got to my heart."

"Can't let it, pal."

"Did you see? I swear, that horse on the outside – the 'winner,'" he bitterly added, "bumped my horse."

Mine, by dint of having bet on her.

"Never happened."

"She broke stride."

"She hiccupped. Didn't have it."

Jack waved away the money.

"Thanks," he said. "Decent of you. Good luck in the seventh."

Pushing away, he made his way through the crowd, no longer interested in checking the payout window. Heart hardening as he walked, he went down to the stables. Bill Boerner wasn't hard to find.

"I was expecting you," he said as Jack approached. "How much you lose?"

Taking in the man's demeanor, the detective's lip curled.

"You might have warned me."

"Of what?"

"Your horse is a nag."

He flushed in anger.

"She's not a nag!"

He didn't bother arguing.

"All right, then. You fixed the race."

"Why would I?"

Shifting his attention to Barrister's Baby as the animal was cooled down, he sneered.

"I see you got your old job back."

"I told you..." He let it go with a shrug. "The new owner didn't say anything when I showed up. And, besides, he wasn't in a position to make changes. Not right away."

"Jolly good for you, old man."

Boerner's eyes narrowed.

"I resent that. Get out of here. Go sulk over a beer. Drown your sorrows."

"Alone. Yeah, I get it. You don't have any."

"My horse just lost a race she shoulda won. I got plenty of sorrows."

"You arranged it so you could buy her. Wadda ya think, I was born yesterday?"

Bill stomped his foot, then walked over to the horse. Putting a hand on her neck, he left it there as though taking her pulse.

"I'm outta that business. I got no magic cream. Why would I want to buy her?"

"You just said it. The new owner don't know nuthin'." Letting his grammar slip to match the company he was keeping, Jack used his height to tower over the trainer. "She's a nag so he'll sell her cheap. That was always the plan. An' he's so overwhelmed with his inheritance, he won't have time to think about a damn formula. You hung around the office, saw Amy go inside and figured you had your patsy. After she left, you went back in, poisoned the old sot and knew the cops'd nail her. I wouldn't leave town because Hugh Kerr's gonna have a field day with you."

"You're crazy!"

"Crazy like a loon. See you in court."

Balling his hand into a fist, Jack took one last look at the "nag," then turned his back and slithered away.

"I screwed up, Hugh. I haven't done anything right from the beginning." Head in his hands, Jack sunk into the couch.

"Well, at least you're not the only one," Ellen tried, inflecting a cheerful note into the doom-and-gloom of the apartment. "Think about Jim Ewell."

"Oh, brother, I'm thinking about him, all right. And how I messed that up, too." She nodded, realizing he had cleaned up his language for her. "I thought I had it all figured out. He needed money for a sure thing on a horse race. I gave it to him, figuring when Barrister's Baby came in on long odds he'd be loaded. Then, I shake him down for what he owed Dana Dwight and you."

"'You' who?" Hugh asked in surprise.

"What he actually means is, for what Ewell owed his client and *him*," Ellen clarified.

The effort failed.

"Now, I'm doubly confused."

"Jack asked me to play a pigeon. He gave me $2,000 and I invested it with Ewell. He makes a killing at the track and before he escapes with the loot, Jack either digitally extracts it from his person," she grinned, "or you use your authority to scare the – shit – out of him."

Jack cringed and Hugh laughed at the crude word she had used for just such a purpose.

"Did I know about this?"

"No."

"Why not? It sounds dangerous."

"Unsavory, perhaps," she guardedly admitted. "But it worked."

"I thought you just said it didn't work."

"For me. I was feeling very down about my life, ready to – chuck the whole thing in," she tried in the vernacular. "I wasn't happy with the choices I faced and didn't feel equal to either. Going out with Jack on a 'caper' made me feel alive, again. Useful. Capable of facing the world. That's why I –"

"– met me in court!" he exclaimed, finally seeing the picture. "I wondered what happened. But was – damned – glad it had." He offered his hand to Jack. "I owe you."

The detective refused to take it.

"That was a happy circumstance. A mistake. Don't try and make me feel better." He got up and moved away from them. "I'm $2,000 in the hole, my client lost her investment – OK, which was a crap shoot from the start, but I mighta worked it out. And, Bill Boerner is a rat." He turned back, shaking his head. "But, he's also the murderer, Hugh. I got it all worked out."

"Yes. I listened to what you had to say. And I think you're close. But no brass ring, yet."

"Why not?"

"He might have thrown the race to buy the horse cheap. And he might have come back that night killed Wexler, but there you're stopped."

"How so?"

"Your theory hinges on the formula. With Amy in jail, he doesn't have it. And even if he concocted a story of how she could still support her family by the proceeds of the spray and she gave it to him, he'd still have to wait a year. Even putting that aside, he'd have to find a financier. How eager would someone be to invest thousands when the formulator is doing time on a murder wrap? No, Jack. It doesn't work."

"Then, why did he throw the race?"

"You're sure? Absolutely certain?"

"I... thought I saw what I saw."

"Then, before we take this any further, let's examine the tape. I can subpoena it for review. Would that make you feel better?"

"Nothing's gonna make me feel better, But, yeah."

"It'll take me an hour to find a judge on Saturday. What do you say we meet at the track at six o'clock?"

"Ohoo-kay."

Which was a far cry from "okey-dokey."

Leaning toward the screen, Hugh and Jack studied the tape for the tenth time. Finally, Jack sighed in resignation.

"So, I was wrong, again. B. B. wasn't bumped."

"No. She wasn't. It was close but there's just enough space between them to make out the separation. But, you were correct about one thing. Something did happen." Raising a hand, he indicated the film be replayed. "Take your attention off the other horse and fix it on Barrister's Baby."

The tape replayed. This time, Jack sucked air between his teeth.

"The jockey stopped using the whip."

"He stopped using the whip," Hugh repeated, "but he did move his hands. Was he reining in?"

"Criminy! I think you're right."

"Just enough to make the horse lose stride. That would have done it."

This time, Jack puffed air through his cheeks.

"I was right, but for the wrong reason. The damn race was fixed."

"But, why? Who benefits?"

"Bill Boerner."

"Someone else," Hugh prodded.

"A guy who bet on the other horse to win? Figuring B. B. was the horse to beat?"

"Why this race? If he was going to pick one, why not where the odds were better? 50:1? He would have gotten 5:1 but does that make up for the awful risk he was taking? I don't think so."

"Let's beat it outta the jockey."

"Yes. We could do that. In court."

"I was thinking of a back alley."

"I know you were. But, I'd prefer to do it my way."

"Then, I'll soften him up for you."

"That could be called witness tampering. Good for five-to-ten. Especially, with your reputation."

"At this point, I don't care. I need something to feel good about."

"Prison makes you feel good?"

"Three squares a day and a basketball court. I could do worse."

"By the time you get out, Jackie will be too old for a pony."

"I gotta do something to feel useful again."

"Talk to Ellen. She's been through it."

He puckered his lips, hesitated, then didn't spit.

"See you in court."

Waiting until he heard the door to the projection room slam, Hugh raised his hand.

"Another time, please."

For no better reason than to assuage his doubts.

Taking two separate cars, Hugh and Ellen met at the courthouse an hour before the doors opened to the public. Handing him his briefcase, she smiled.

"You forgot this."

"No, I didn't. I left it at home knowing you'd see it. And be compelled to bring it to court... in case you suddenly got cold feet."

"Fortunately for me, Jack's malaise isn't catching."

"For both of us. He'll be all right."

"I hope so. He's got it bad." Checking her watch, she asked, "How are we fixed for time?"

"We're all right. I've already spoken with Amy. She's doing fine." Putting a hand to his head as a pretext to stare into the rising sun, he frowned. Ellen wasn't deceived.

"She'll make a great witness for the defense."

"She'd better. In a circumstantial case, her testimony may prove crucial."

"The jury will like her. They'll believe her."

"Nailing whoever really killed Wexler would be better."

"You can't solve them all. Aren't you the one who always says that's up to the police?"

Guiding her away, they began a slow tour around the courthouse.

"No matter how I explain a defendant is innocent until proven guilty, juries tend to side with the authorities on the premise they believe there's enough evidence to convict," he stressed. "The defense counsel gets paid to represent his client; the D.A. is a public servant. I have something to gain. He doesn't. He's just looking for justice. No matter what the foundation of the law is, Themis never actually has her scales balanced. It's always an uphill battle."

Hugh stopped and held out his hands, palms facing up, the right higher than the left.

"I have to fight twice as hard. First, to even the odds, then to weigh the scales in my client's favor. Without a plausible suspect to take her place, I stand to lose the case."

"You've got Bill Boerner. And that fink, Philip Shaffley. No one liked him. You made both of them look shady. In your closing argument you can concentrate on them. That's reasonable doubt."

"It's iffy. I want better." Jamming his fists in his pockets, he resumed their trek. "Where's the joker in this poker game we're playing? There's a wild card in the hand that hasn't been dealt, yet. Who is he and why was murder the only choice he saw?"

"You have an idea," she guessed, goosebumps running down her back.

Hugh abruptly stopped and reversed course, cutting short their journey. He headed back toward the front entrance, lips tightly compressed.

"I have an avenue to explore. Nothing more. Nothing else," he corrected, finding the two rhyming words distasteful.

Ellen hurried to catch up without questioning why. A man who lived by the power of speech did not like his sentences to sound like grade school poetry. In the scheme of their present situation she felt it bode well for the power of his argument.

"Is the defense ready to call its first witness?"

Standing tall and confident, Hugh responded, "Yes, Your Honor. I call Janus McKinney to the stand."

A man wearing an expensive, three-piece business suit, stood and made his way to the front. Taking the oath, he sat in the chair, as though at attention. Rather than appear affected, his posture suggested he was well used to providing succinct, pertinent data to men who paid him well. Crossing to the evidence table, Hugh took a bottle and presented it to the witness, emitting a similar aura of authority.

"Mr. McKinney, what do you do for a living?"

"I am an independent accountant, sir."

"At my request, have you studied the financial aspects of marketing the spray the defendant, Amy Pazel, developed? This spray, already entered into evidence being ascribed with the ability to miraculously heal open wounds on an animal?"

"I have."

"Being as specific as you can, please detail your findings."

"My first order of business was to thoroughly examine Mrs. Pazel's contact with the company that employs her."

"That would be Mega Enterprises?"

"Yes. I confirmed that she is prohibited from patenting any chemical formula in her own name and retaining exclusive rights to it unless she had been separated from the company for a period of one calendar year. There would, of course, been no point going further without that stipulation."

"The defense grants that is the case."

"Legally, therefore, any plan to market the product for her own financial reward, whether as an aerosol, a spray or a cream, would have to be put off for 365 days."

"In other words, the defendant would have to retire or resign and wait a period of one year before moving forward."

"Correct."

"Go on."

"Mrs. Pazel earns $35,000 a year from her job at Mega Enterprises, exclusive of bonuses which I did not calculate into my formula, being subject to unknown variables."

"Understood."

The enormity of the salary elicited a buzz of respectful wonder from those taking in McKinney's testimony.

"I then examined, with your permission, the financial status of the Pazel family. Without taking into consideration the value of the Pazel residence which they would require to habitate, and exclusive of her retirement fund she would not be able to access until age 62, I determined the family had $10,921 of liquid cash on which to live. Adding normal living expenses for a family of five, including mortgage, utilities, food, clothing, transportation and education, I determined she would not be able to maintain her present domicile without substantial sacrifices."

"Would it be possible for her, as a scientist in possession of world-wide reputation, to obtain a similar position to the one she held at Mega Enterprises and thus offset her financial losses while waiting out a year?"

"I think it extremely possible she could find similar work, although as an established senior research scientist at her present job, her salary coming into a new company might be less than she is currently making. However, pertaining the subject at hand, such a move would not achieve her goal of patenting her formula."

"Please explain."

"It is standard throughout the industry – many industries, actually – that an employee signs away their rights to independent work for the duration of their employment. Which also includes the one year stipulation concerning such independent work."

"Specifically, you are stating that even if she were to change jobs, if she remained in the research and development field where her expertise and substantial remuneration lies, freeing herself from the prohibition of patenting a formula for one year is insurmountable."

"Absolutely."

"Point One," Hugh stated, holding up a finger. "She could not financially survive without a job nor could she change positions with the expectation of marketing the formula in less than a year. Is that correct?"

"Yes, sir."

"Let us move on. Given the formula for the patent, designed either as an aerosol, a spray or a cream, were you able to determine the expense of such a product?"

"I was. Pricing the chemicals required for mass production, the laboratory required for development and quality control, the production plant, the skilled staff needed to perform the labor and the packaging in which to put the product, I determined it could not be done for a start-up of less than $100,000."

"Far in excess of what Mrs. Pazel or her partners possessed?"

"Objection," Bond called, raising his hand for attention. "The defense is offering a fact not in evidence. No testimony has been given as to the financial status of the defendant's partners."

"Sustained."

"I will rephrase. Far in excess of what Mrs. Pazel, a horse trainer and a detective possessed?"

A ripple of amusement swept the room as Bond got to his feet.

"By any other name, Mr. Kerr. Same objection."

"Sustained."

Hugh gave the D.A. a polite nod.

"I'll withdraw the question until establishing the fact neither of Mrs. Pazel's partners – of which the detective was not officially included – had the financial wherewithal to supply the required $100,000. Putting a question mark by Point Two, let us move on to advertising. Mr. McKinney, did you research the expense of that necessary component of any successful business?"

"I did. Using such traditional promotional efforts as print ads, radio spots and salesmen canvasing likely users – in this case, those in the horse racing industry, veterinarians, breeders and animal shelters – I determined a modest effort would cost approximately $25,000 per year."

"Which does not include the question of purchasing a horse – one this ostensive team hoped to use as proof of the success of their product. An excellent idea, especially appealing to those who breed and raise expensive animals. I believe the name 'Barrister's Baby' has been mentioned in testimony concerning that connection. Disregarding the fact the horse recently lost a race and thus a great percentage of its worth as an advertising 'tool,' what did you determine its value to be at the time of its owner's death?"

"Somewhere in the neighborhood of $250."

"That seems rather low for a thoroughbred."

"According to my research, without the means of curing its condition, the horse couldn't be raced and was to be... put out to pasture, I believe is the euphemism."

"Specifically, because of the open sores from the bridle that wouldn't heal?"

"That was my understanding."

"But, if Mrs. Pazel's formula did work – which it did as evidenced by the fact the horse was able to be raced this past Saturday – then what?"

"If it had won, my research indicated it would be worth in excess of $5,000. Considering it lost but was still capable of racing, then I would put its value at $2,000.

"Bringing us up to $127,000. Which doesn't cover the cost of maintaining, conditioning and paying the track entrance fees for such a horse. That would be Point Three: without the question mark." He smiled and his humor brought on a like response from the jury. "A great deal of money, wouldn't you say? Out of the reach of most people?"

"I would say."

"In fact," Hugh continued, walking across the room toward the jury box, "as described and detailed by your research, what we have here is more of a dream than any possibility of reality. Three people came together and had a marvelous idea. But one hardly grounded in financial possibility. Would that be your conclusion?"

"I cannot see how it could be other than a wish."

Walking back and forth before the jury, Hugh directed his comments to them.

"Let us put these irrefutable points together. Using your detailed investigation and from the financial standpoint you have just outlined, what would the elimination of the decedent, Stanley Wexler, accomplish? Only that he wouldn't personally be able to market the formula he bought from Philip Shaffley of Mega Enterprises. Presupposing his heirs wouldn't be interested in following through with his plan – and we have no testimony presented by the prosecution to substantiate such a claim – what would Amy Pazel have to gain from his death? Considering the fact she had no fear of competition from the heirs because she never could afford to market her formula?"

Bond slapped his hand on the desk.

"Objection! Calling for a conclusion. The witness cannot read what was in the defendant's mind."

"No, but he is in a position to make that judgment based solely on financial considerations as phrased by defense counsel. I will allow it," Gillman decided.

"I see no point."

"Thank you. No further questions."

Glowing in triumph, Hugh took his seat as Bond marched toward the witness box, eyes gleaming and jaw set.

"Defense council has cleverly maneuvered you into drawing that conclusion, Mr. McKinney, but he has overlooked several salient details. Without the benefit of hindsight, which Mr. Kerr, himself, has argued against, let us suppose the horse cured by this miracle spray – Barrister's Baby – had been sold to the partnership of Pazel, Boerner and half a Merrick," he slyly interjected. "As they originally wanted and asked for. The defendant bites the proverbial bullet and resigns. Perhaps she borrows money from relatives; or takes a second mortgage on her house. Factors you did not take into consideration when making your one-sided calculations. Did you?" he charged, suddenly very angry.

"I did not."

"Of course you didn't, being paid by the defense." Letting the accusation sink in, he continued the attack. "The partnership cures the horse of its affliction and waits a year until they can patent the cream. Having achieved those ends, they use it on Barrister's Baby and race it under the new colors of Pazel-Boerner and 'Mer'" he presumed, eliminating the end of Jack's surname. "It not only wins one race, it goes on to win another. And another. In fact, they race it next season and it earns substantial purses. Are you following me?" he added with sarcasm.

"Yes."

"That not only covers the expense of its keep, but the track fees and goes a long way toward paying the defendant a decent salary so she need not live in poverty. Still following me?"

"I am."

"You added $25,000 to your supposed calculations for advertising. I put it to you, there's no better method of getting word around than success. The press loves a rags-to-riches story. They flock around the owners and ask how this horse, consigned to 'pasture' by its former owner, has suddenly become Black Beauty? They tell them about the miracle cream and suddenly it's on the front page of every sporting newspaper in the country. That's better than ten thousand magazine ads, radio spots or salesmen. So much for Mr. Kerr's Point Two. Everyone who has a dog with an itch or a cat with a sore suddenly wants – suddenly needs this cream," he clarified for emphasis. "Financiers come out of the woodwork begging to be let in on this gold mine. They put up the money – or, better yet, the partnership now has a product any bank would loan them money on – and they're in business. Using your financial expertise, would you say that was a likely outcome?"

"I would think a financier or a bank might take the success of the cream as collateral for a loan, yes."

"Using that same financial wisdom that helped you decide the defendant had no legitimate reason to murder Stanley Wexler, would you now care to reconsider? We know Stanley Wexler wanted to market the spray because he bought it from Mega Enterprises. He knew it worked. He knew he had a year before Mrs. Pazel could do anything to challenge him. With considerable wealth at his disposal, he could easily beat her to market. So, even if she had a rags-to-riches story, he not only has an established customer base, he could claim he has the original miracle cure. He undersells her product and puts her out of business. Making him the one who ends up benefitting from the positive press."

Pausing to take a breath, Bond pointedly stared at the jurors.

"In such a scenario as I've described, the defendant's 'wish' isn't a pipe dream after all, and the idea of murdering Stanley Wexler has more than merit – it's really the only 'point' we need to consider. Isn't it?" he concluded, running his voice up the scale.

McKinney shrugged. Although being a non-verbal reply Judge Gillman would demand he express aloud, the answer was clear.

"Point" for the prosecution.

CHAPTER 23

"No further questions."

With B.B. Bond's concluding words ringing in his ears, Hugh stood and watched his opponent walk slowly toward the prosecution table. A faint, almost wispy curve of his lips conveyed the impression he had been slightly amused by the other man's attempt to discredit his witness.

It was acting of the highest order.

Reluctantly tearing his eyes off the prosecutor, he trained them on Janus McKinney as he made his way down from the stand. Appearing to transmit a silent *Atta boy!* if such an expression could fairly be attributed to the Man from Harvard, he waited patiently for him to pass the swinging half door before announcing in a loud, almost triumphant voice, "The Defense calls Hershey Barr to the stand."

As if purposely seeking to rouse those in the courtroom from his mesmerizing talents, Kerr's officious pronunciation of the next witness's name shot a peel of almost raucous laughter through the enclosed space. Men and women slipped back from the edge of their seats, slapping their knees or turning to the stranger beside them and whispering with awe at the master's touch.

He planned it all along. Got the witnesses in the proper order to shoot Bond down.

In the excitement of the moment – and perhaps longer – the devastating testimony of the previous witness was all but forgotten.

Playing to his audience, Hugh strode across the apron of his personal stage, making a comical attempt to wipe an expanding smile off his face. Finding his mark, he waited patiently for the conclusion of the bit player's part to swear in the witness, then easily glided forward. Casually resting an arm on the top of the box, he gave the impression of delivering a dubious line of dialogue by raising the level of his voice.

"Please tell this court your occupation."

The impeccably-dressed elderly man with a head covered in shock-white hair, replied, "I am an attorney."

It was almost too perfect.

"Hershey Barr... at the bar?" Hugh innocently inquired for those prohibited from speaking.

"I'm afraid so," the man politely acknowledged, playing out a scene he had performed numerous times.

"If you'll excuse me for stating the obvious, it was rather... I hesitate to say 'indiscrete' – it was perhaps ill-disposed of your parents to bestow that first name on their son." Turning to Ellen, whom it was commonly known, was his wife, he added, "When we were expecting our first child, the first admonition we were given was to beware of... an embarrassing combination of names. With a name such as 'Kerr,' therefore, we shied away from choices such as 'Catherine' – Cat Curr. Or, Manfred, which children might shorten into 'Man-gy Curr.'" He cleared his throat. "Also avoiding an indiscrete combination of names like 'Bartholomew Lincoln Kerr,' making the initials 'BLK,' easily translated into 'blackguard.'" He waited while the crowd absorbed the statement. "The 'Lincoln,' of course, in acknowledgment of the revered 16th President."

Because he had made the point of signaling her out, Ellen rose to her feet.

"If I may be so bold as to address the court?" Gillman gave her leave rather than risk causing a riot. "As the mother of Mr. Kerr's child, I had the right to name it, and I assure you, had it been a son, *I* would have 'nixed' the idea of 'Bartholomew.' One," she added with verve, wickedly smiling across the aisle at the prosecutor, "is enough. And I certainly wouldn't want to take 'Bart' home with me!"

The house broke into genuine good humor. Being the butt of the joke, Bond could do no more than acknowledge the laughter, quietly seething that his previous work had been upended. Nodding respectfully toward her, he quipped, "No chocolate chip cookies for you, Mrs. Kerr."

The applause was deafening, finally forcing the judge to quiet them with a sharp rap of his gavel.

"We will call this repartee a draw and move on with the business at hand, gentleman – and lady."

Ellen sat and Hugh redirected his questioning to the witness.

"Mr. Barr," he began with almost a straight face, "you stated just now you are an attorney. For whom do you work? I am referring, of course, to an individual associated with this case."

"I was the decedent's lawyer. I now represent the heirs of Mr. Stanley Wexler, of Lexington, Kentucky."

Stepping away to give himself separation from the witness, Hugh pursued, "In that regard, you prepared the last will and testament for Mr. Wexler?"

"I did."

"Are you prepared to reveal the contents of that will to this court?"

"I have been given leave to do so."

Crossing to the defense table, Hugh accepted the document Ellen gave him and returned to the box."

"Is this a copy of the legal will?"

Barr glanced at it and nodded.

"It is."

"Request this will be entered into evidence for the defense."

"So granted."

The paper was marked and returned to Hugh.

"Kindly reveal to the court the persons who stand to inherit."

"The bulk of the estate goes to Mr. Wexler's son, Noah. There are a number of smaller gifts to Mr. Wexler's nephews; sons of his sisters, now deceased."

"What is the date of this will?"

"September 7, 1953."

"Have any codicils been added since that time?"

"No, sir. It has been unchanged since the day it was signed."

"Did Mr. Wexler recently communicate with you any desire to add, subtract or otherwise alter his will?"

"He did not."

Riffling through the lengthy document, Hugh nodded to himself.

"Considering this will has remained unchanged, I presume, then, no mention was made of the recent acquisition of a formula to be marketed as a cure for several animal health issues?"

"That is correct."

"Meaning that the formula falls under the general category of 'property' and the rights of the formula then transfer to Mr. Noah Wexler?"

"Also correct."

"Thank you." He started to turn, then thought of one more question. "May I ask you, sir, what nickname you go by among friends and personal acquaintances?"

"Candy. As in," he shared, "Candy Barr."

Leaving with the winning hand, Hugh smiled.

"None of us shall ever think of Hershey chocolate in the same light. No further questions."

"No questions," Bond announced from his seat, less than pleased with the outcome of the examination.

"Call Mr. Noah Wexler to the stand."

A man in his early 30s, dressed in a formal suit and tie, came forward. He swore to tell the truth and was seated.

"Mr. Wexler," Hugh began in a tone of noncommittal, "you are the son and principal heir of the late Mr. Stanley Wexler?"

"I am."

"First, let me express my condolences on the loss of your father."

"I appreciate that."

"You have been appraised by Mr. Barr of the contents of your late father's will?"

"At the time he signed it, my father explained to everyone mentioned in the will exactly what his wishes were. Since it was never altered, there were no surprises."

"Did your father speak to you of the formula he had recently purchased from Mega Enterprises?"

"Not directly. He did mention some sort of spray had been used on one of our thoroughbreds."

"Did he give you the name of the horse?"

"Barrister's Baby. He seemed quite excited about it."

"In what context?"

"That it appeared to cure the filly's long-standing problem with bridle irritation. He was very keen on that horse. That's why I decided to race her this past weekend. In his memory. I'm afraid he would have been very disappointed with the outcome."

"The horse came in third?"

"Yes. Show," he added.

"Did that outcome alter your own feelings toward the horse?"

"It did."

"In what way?"

"I no longer consider the filly a viable candidate for further consideration."

"You have no further plans to race her?"

"I do not."

"Meaning her value is considerably diminished?"

"Quite. It isn't uncommon," he added. "In defense of my father, many horses seem to have what it takes to be a champion and then, for whatever reason, fail to live up to expectations. That's what makes horse racing a sport, Mr. Kerr. If they were all winners, there wouldn't be any contest. No one would bet. Betting makes the horse racing world go 'round."

"I see your point. What does someone do with a horse that doesn't live up to expectations?"

"Dispose of it," he bluntly stated.

"Sell it?"

"If you're lucky. Put her in a claiming race. Up for auction. Even, sell her privately if there was any interest. You might make a few dollars. If not, there are other means of disposal."

"Is that what you plan for Barrister's Baby?"

"Yes. When I have time to think about it. At the moment I'm rather overwhelmed with the estate."

"Toward that end, you are now aware of the formula developed by the defendant, Amy Pazel? That you are, in fact, the owner of the patent?"

"I have been so informed."

"Have you given that matter any… consideration?"

"Frankly, most of what I've learned about it has been at trial. I'm surprised my father had anything to do with it. All I can suppose is that he planned to turn around and sell the rights to a third party, thus making a quick profit. That was his way. I can't see him bothering with it, personally."

"What about you? Now that you own it?"

"I imagine I'll do the same. Although, if it does what they say, I'm more likely to take a percentage of it and allow someone else to handle the manufacture and marketing."

"Thank you. No further questions."

Bond got up and walked toward the witness.

"Acknowledging the fact you suddenly find yourself in charge of a racing empire, how long would you estimate it would take to make a determination on whether or not to address the future value of the defendant's formula?"

"I have no idea."

"Six months? A year?" After a beat, he added, "Never?"

"As I said, I'll probably turn it over to a business associate. Someone who can handle the details for me."

"Can you be more specific?"

Wexler's eyes narrowed in annoyance.

"At high noon on November 1st, 1960. Is that specific enough?"

"Objection, Your Honor," Hugh growled. "Badgering the witness into giving a spurious answer."

"Sustained."

"I'll withdraw the question," Bond sighed. "But, you do find the prospect of marketing the formula daunting? You have no immediate plans to either sell it to a third party or assign someone else to oversee its production?"

"I will agree with that statement. I didn't expect to inherit a 'formula' and I haven't had the prospect of marketing it investigated." He waved his hand in growing irritation. "I may sell it for a dollar – like Barrister's Baby, for all I know. I'm a horse man, Mr. District Attorney, not a huckster selling wares on the street corner. If it has value, I'll eventually do something with it. If not, so be it."

"Thank you. That answers my question nicely. No further questions."

Smiling in triumph that he got what he wanted, Bond sashayed to his table. Hugh stood and addressed the judge.

"Your Honor, as it nears the lunch break –"

Taking his cue, Gillman signaled an end to the morning's proceedings.

"Court is adjourned until two o'clock."

Satisfied that he had achieved that much, Hugh turned in his seat to address Jack, who sat immediately behind the defense table. Leaning over, the detective put his arms on the bar in casual interest.

"I may call you this afternoon," Hugh began before noticing the yellow stain on Jack's sport coat and frowning. "And change your jacket. I don't want you to look as though you just came from an outing at a carnival."

Jack glanced at the sleeve and gritted his teeth.

"Rats. I forgot about it. I got that stain at the track – some crummy kid at the concessionaire bumped me and I squirted mustard on myself. That means I'll have to go all the way back to my house and get another jacket. This one's probably shot. I not only lost a hundred bucks at the window, I'm out a wardrobe. This case is costing me a fortune."

Grinning at his discomfiture, Amy attempted to improve the situation.

"It's not ruined. And you don't have to go all the way home. Just find a drug store and buy some Carbona cleaning fluid. It works wonders. It also contains carbon tetrachloride," she teased. "That way, 'this case' will save you the cost of a new jacket. There has to be some consolation in that."

His face blanched.

"What did you say?"

Mistaking his intent, she backtracked.

"It's perfectly safe –"

"No. I mean, what was the name of the product? The one with carbon tetra-whatever?"

"Carbona."

"Oh, shit." He struck his head with an open palm. "I think I'm gonna be sick."

"It does have an odor, but –"

"Listen, Hugh. You're gonna call me, all right, but not for the reason you think. I gotta get out of here. I got something I gotta check. I don't know if I can be back by two. If I'm not, tell the judge you have a toothache or something. Do anything you can to delay the trial. Trust me on this. If I'm wrong, all you wasted was your time getting a teeth cleaning at the dentist. If I'm right, we're gonna blow this thing outta the water."

"Tell me," he demanded, color rising to his cheeks in opposition to Jack's paleness.

"Can't. It was staring me in the face all along. Stupid, stupid, stupid."

He pushed away and disappeared into the crowd of spectators filing out of the courtroom. Hugh turned to Amy.

"When Jack says 'shit' he means –"

"'Got it'?" she guessed.

"Got it," he agreed. "Let's hope."

Ellen grasped Arm's arm, squeezed it for comfort, then gave her an encouraging nod.

"We'll see you at two. Try and eat some lunch."

"Shit," she tried with a brave expression. "And when Amy says shit, she means –"

"Inedible," Ellen laughed. "Well, if Jack's right, you'll be eating steak and mushrooms for dinner."

"And I'll make the chocolate chip cookies for dessert."

They smiled and watched as the matron came to escort Amy away.

"Amy's right. She does possess an amazing coping strategy, Hugh."

"I seem to be surrounded by smart. A nice place to be."

"You win the charm award, Mr. Kerr."

"I'll settle for winning this court case."

"And I'll raise the 'steaks'," she punned. "You win both."

"With a Hershey bar on top."

They laughed all the way out, secretly relieving the guard at the door that Bartholomew "Lincoln" Bond had gone ahead of them and not witnessed their merriment. It would have spoiled the D.A.'s lunch.

When court reconvened at 2:00, the smiles on the defense attorney and his associate had vanished. Apologizing beforehand, then pleading an excruciating toothache, Hugh asked for a continuum until the following morning. Judge Gillman granted the request and those with no further business slowly filed out, disappointed to have the trial delayed. More solicitous than might be supposed, Bond crossed the aisle, shaking his head.

"Sorry to hear about your toothache, Kerr," he began, holding a hand to his own cheek. "Next to losing a case, I hate a trip to the dentist most."

"I appreciate the concern, although I hope you don't mind if we split the difference."

"How's that?"

"I go to the dentist but win the case."

B. B. started to remark Hugh wasn't going to win before narrowing his eyes in suspicion.

"You don't have a toothache. You just claimed that as a delaying tactic."

Hugh's baby blues opened in innocence.

"Want to come with me? I always find the sound of the drill reassuring." His nostrils flared. "And that peculiar smell of the office: cold, clammy air with the scent of blood and spit."

"You're sick."

"I've been accused of coming from another planet. Maybe it's true."

Bond patted his pocket.

"I wouldn't doubt it. But no worry: I have a chunk of Kryptonite ready for you tomorrow morning."

Sniffing in indignation that he had been had, the D.A. stormed off. Ellen shook her head.

"You might have been nicer to him. He was only trying to be kind."

He made a disparaging noise.

"The 'Ks' belong to me. 'Kryptonite' and 'kind' aren't his style."

"He was actually giving you a compliment – Superman."

"He can save it for tomorrow – when he comes over to shake my hand. Come on. Let's get out of here. I want to be by a phone if Jack calls."

"There's one at the dentist's office."

"I'm-not-going-there."

It required a moment for her to digest the import of the statement.

"Don't tell me you and Bond have something else in common? A fear of the dentist?"

"Have you ever seen me go to one?"

"No, but I presumed you have... good teeth," she guessed. "I go every six months."

"And I've never offered to drive you, have I?"

"Actually, I never put two-and-two together. You have to go in for regular check-ups, Hugh. We can leave that argument for another time. But, you told Judge Gillman you were going and you are. I won't have you cited for contempt of court."

"I told him I had a toothache. Not that I was going to the dentist. I'll take two aspirin if that'll ease your conscience and we'll call it even." He took a step toward the aisle, then turned back. "What else do Bond and I have in common?"

"Arrogance."

"Two compliments in one day. I'm on a roll."

"You certainly are. Out the door and down the street. There's a dentist's office on Brand Street."

He looked sick. Fulfilling the D.A.'s prophesy.

"How do you know?"

"I looked it up while you were ordering lunch."

"Have I ever told you, you were too efficient, Miss Thorne?"

"No. And I don't suppose you ever will. If you know what's good for you. And five gets you ten Bond will have Sam Dodson following you. To see you really do go to the dentist."

"All right," he announced. "I'll go."

Suddenly suspicious, she was too well aware of his tactics to let the statement go unchallenged.

"You'll go – and then what?"

"You pull the car around to the rear exit. I'll walk through the office, go out the back and we can say honor is satisfied."

"Yes. Let's do that."

Ellen drove, let Hugh off in front of the single-story building, then pulled the car slowly away. When Hugh reemerged five minutes later, his ride was nowhere to be found.

He went back and had his teeth cleaned. It was a better option than sleeping on the couch.

The only one using a telephone was Sam Dodson. The assistant D.A. duly reported to his master then took the rest of the afternoon off.

Hugh was compelled to call a cab.

At first glance, the room at the Sawley Arms to be empty. Only the open suitcase on the bed gave Jack any reason to suppose the occupant lingered nearby. Tucking the burglar's tool he had used to open the lock in his pocket, he cocked his head, listening for noise. What he finally heard made him smile.

The sound of a man gargling.

Tiptoeing to the bathroom door, he kicked it open with his foot. James Ewell looked up in surprise, took the time to spit in the sink then tried a lopsided grin.

"Oh. It's you."

"Who'd you think it might be? The cops?"

"Why would I think that? My rent's paid until the end of the week."

"I was afraid I'd missed you. I had to make a short trip."

Ewell indicated the toilet by jutting out his elbow.

"You could have saved yourself the trouble. I have a john here."

"Not that kind of 'short trip.'"

Ewell carelessly let his hand linger over the straight razor he had recently used to shave.

"Trip the light fantastic? A trip down memory lane?"

"You're getting closer. You almost had me fooled. I knew you were a piece of garbage but I thought it was Bill Boerner."

"Bill – who?"

"When Barrister's Baby lost, I figured you got screwed, same as me."

"I lost a bundle on that nag!"

Jack ignored the protest.

"I couldn't see any reason you'd throw your money away like that. It all seemed to fit."

"I don't know what you're talking about."

Hands akimbo, Jack stared disgustedly at the man before him.

"You never bet a dime on that race."

"You saw the tickets –!" he cried, starting to sweat.

"I saw a handful of tickets. Like the fool I was, I never looked closely. You either had them from a horse you bet on and lost two months ago – another one of your schemes gone bad – or more likely, you scrounged them from a sucker who tossed 'em away when he didn't win his long shot. We all play that game. You kept them for a rainy day when the IRS boys picked you up after a real win. 'Look, gentlemen, see how I came up short? Don't shake me down, now, when I'm usually on the losing side.' We had that discussion."

Easing the razor into his hand, Ewell demanded, "What do you want, Merrick?"

"Interesting, you know my real name. I told you it was Jackson. Following the trial, are you?"

"What trial?" Ewell demanded, ignoring the larger issue.

But Jack was not ready to spill the beans. Not when he had a burning desire to play cat and mouse.

"The short trip I took. Down to Santa Anita."

"Have another hot tip?"

"You might say that. I coulda gotten what I wanted from that fancy pants in court today, but I wasn't sure I could get in to see him. My jacket," he explained, holding out the stained sleeve, "ain't gonna impress anyone."

"You're right about that. Just another… bum. Like me."

"Not like you."

"Better? Worse?" he attempting, trying to get past Jack and finding the way blocked.

"Put on a suit and tie. You have a date."

"What for?"

"To make a confession."

"To what? I never fixed that race. I wanted that filly to win."

"To get control of the magic formula."

"What does that mean? Something like magic beans I plant in the ground, then climb up the vine to find the golden goose?"

"I went to Stanley Wexler's office. Had a chat with the secretary. Gave her your description. Funny thing. She recognized it right off."

"I don't even know a Stanley Wexler."

"That's a dumb statement, coming from a track junkie who knows everything there is to know about the racing world. What does an owner think of his horse? How's the trainer gonna run him? It all adds up. That's how you say you work your scheme. Get to know the facts so you can beat the   odds."

"OK, so maybe I heard his name. But I'm hardly on friendly terms with... Mr. Fancy Pants. Isn't that what you called him?"

"I was referring to Mr. Noah Wexler; the 'decedent's' son. You know him, too."

"According to you, I know a lot of people."

Jack finally stepped back, allowing the man out of the bathroom. Ewell went to his suitcase and continued throwing items inside.

"I said, put on a suit and tie."

"I'm not going anywhere with you."

"Sure, you are." Jack removed a revolver from his pocket. "Now, do as I say."

"Mind if I change my undershirt, first? It stinks."

"It suits you. Leave it on."

"Look, pal, I don't know what your angle is, but –"

"It started innocently enough. I was hired by Miss Dana Dwight. That name ring a bell?"

Ewell rolled his eyes in disgust.

"Oh, shit. You're a private dick. I shoulda known. My 'red alert' must be slipping."

"All the way to your knees. Pal."

"So, she wants her $2,000 back. Tough. I ain't got it."

"Don't try the street language on me. You're a college boy."

"Yeah. I'm the Duke of Edenborough, too."

"Close enough. The bad sheep of a royal family, let's say. A royal racing family."

"Is that what Miss Bradshaw told you?"

"I didn't give you the secretary's name."

Ewell ignored the curled lip.

"I don't have the $2,000 clams your 'late-night dame' invested, either. What were you trying to set me up for? And who was she?"

"The wife of an attorney who's gonna roast your balls in court. And it was my money – I put her up to it. I told you. I read you wrong. I figured your 'scheme' was to win big on Barrister's Baby and clear out. I wanted you to make enough to pay off both ladies and maybe a few of the others you cheated. But, that wasn't it, at all."

"You gonna put that gun down?"

"I don't think so."

"You'll have to shoot me, then, because I'm not going anywhere with you. What's a dead witness worth?"

Jack smiled. Without warmth. An expression akin to the rattle of a snake's tail.

"Did you serve in the armed forces? In the war?"

"I was too young."

He leered in disdain at the obvious falsehood.

"Well, I did. I learned a lot. How to shoot a man so he's in exquisite pain but 'ain't' anywhere close to dying." He pointed the gun lower. "He'll just wish he was. I can make you squat for the rest of your life."

"You're too civilized for that."

"War strips that away from a fellow."

"The cops –"

"My dad's a homicide detective. I'm well-known down at the precinct."

"I'm not going with you. I don't know what your game is, but you can take a hike."

Selecting an undershirt from the suitcase, Ewell feigned removing the soiled one we wore. Using that to hide his intent, he tossed the fresh one in Jack's face, then lunged at him. Unfortunately for the assailant, his "unwary fly" anticipated the move, batted away the undergarment, then deftly kicked his hand. The razor Ewell had brought in from the bathroom went flying. Jack smiled, showing teeth.

"I was so hoping you'd do that." Tucking the revolver into his waistband, he went after him like a savage beast. Landing a fist into Ewell's face, he grunted in satisfaction as blood spurted from broken arteries. "You shoulda volunteered like I did, instead of getting your 'training' by watching gangster pictures."

His second assault went to the man's groin. As Ewell doubled over, Jack chopped him on the back of the neck, caught him before he fell and landed another punch to the face. Three more vicious blows nearly put out Ewell's lights, but Jack wasn't finished.

"I sorta promised Miss Dwight I'd take revenge on your hide if I couldn't extract dough from your pocket. Considering you didn't lose anything on Barrister's Baby, I figure you got a wad on you thick enough to choke a horse. I'll remove that for her."

Cocking his elbow, the track junkie weakly pleaded with watery eyes.

"Then, what's the beating for?"

"Me."

The knuckles landed just below the schemer's left eye. He dropped like a rag doll.

CHAPTER 24

The telephone rang. In the stillness of the night, it sounded like a medieval church bell tolling the hour. Loud, discordant and ominous, the noise would have had the effect of waking the household had it not been answered on the first ring. As it was, Hugh rolled to his side, waited for a repetition and when it was not forthcoming, slid off the side of the mattress. Wearily checking the bedside clock, he read 1:13. An unlucky number at any time.

Realizing the call had been answered from another extension, he grabbed his bathrobe, wiggled his feet into a pair of slippers and noiselessly crept away. He found Hank Wade standing by the phone in the living room.

Rather than asking the obvious, he demanded, "Why are you up?"

The detective shrugged.

"Couldn't sleep."

"You were expecting a call?"

"No." And then, "Maybe."

"Who was it?"

He waved Hugh off.

"Work."

"I gathered that."

"Why were you awake?"

"I wasn't." When Wade didn't challenge the statement, he pressed. "What did he want?"

"I have to go."

"That doesn't answer my question."

"Duty calls."

Hugh waited a beat too long. It conveyed his concern.

"Is someone dead?"

Wade's arms swung at his sides.

"Not that I know of."

"What did he want?"

"He didn't ask for you."

"Is he going to need a lawyer?"

"If he had, I suppose he would have used his first and only dime to ask for you."

The interrogation proved unnerving. Both men shifted positions.

"I'm going with you."

"This is police business." A beat, then, "You have court in the morning. Go back and get some sleep."

"How can I, if one of my witnesses is being held at headquarters?"

"Who said anything about being held?"

"I'll bring doughnuts."

Hank finally shooed him off.

"They're stale at this hour of the morning. Wait until 6:00 A.M."

"Is that a date?"

"Dating while on duty is against the rules."

"Like drinking?"

"Some things are worth making an exception over."

"I'll see you at six."

"Bring doughnuts. You might as well. It won't make the boys down at the precinct like you any better, but they won't hate you for it, either. Don't be chintzy. A dozen." He started for the bedroom, then thought better of it. "Two dozen. You can afford it. Sinkers. None of those fancy ones."

"I like jelly doughnuts."

"You won't be eating any of them."

Despite himself, Hugh laughed. He had to ask.

"Why not?"

"Lawyers have cooties. You touch one, you contaminate the rest. They'll be left out for the hoodlums. Be a waste."

"I'll remember that."

Dad waved him away.

"It's a pity they don't teach you manners at law school."

Ten minutes later, Hank Wade was dressed and out the door. Hugh sat on the couch and watched him go. When he heard the elevator doors open and shut, he picked up his pack of playing cards and dealt a hand of solitaire. He ran them, first time. That told him two things. He would buy two dozen jelly doughnuts, and luck at cards had absolutely nothing to do with the outcome of court cases.

Cops, he knew, would eat doughnuts off the sidewalk.

"The defense calls Mr. Jack Merrick to the stand."

Wearing a respectable jacket, white shirt and tie, the witness approached the front. Placing his left hand on the Bible, he raised his right. It was covered in a gauze bandage.

"Do you, Jack Merrick, swear to tell the truth, the whole truth and nothing but the truth in the matter now pertaining to this Court?"

"I do."

Jack took his seat, for all the world as composed as a cucumber. Hugh approached with a smile. In contrast, Bartholomew Bond appeared glum. Rather than watch the interplay, he stared at some papers spread out before him.

"Good morning, Mr. Merrick. I see your hand is bandaged. Not injured severely, I trust?"

"Just a scratch."

"May I ask how you obtained the injury?"

"On teeth."

A twittering went through the room at the anticipated answer.

"Anyone's teeth in particular?".

"You might say I was serving a summons on a reluctant witness."

"I see. Did you know that individual previously?"

"I did."

"What is your occupation, Mr. Merrick?"

"I'm a private detective."

"In what context did you know the reluctant witness?"

Jack stared across the room, making eye contact with Dana Dwight. She was sitting on the defense side, three rows behind the defense table. She nodded in approval for him to proceed.

"I was working a case. This man had entered into an agreement with my client to invest her life's saving in a scheme he promised was a sure thing. Nothing had come of it. She hired me to find out why."

"And did you?"

"He was a gambler. He bet on horses running at Santa Anita."

Those words elicited a murmur of recognition from those in the courtroom as they easily drew the parallel between racing and the charge of murder being argued.

"Not a particularly wise investment, would you say? As winning at the track is always... uncertain?"

"What he promised wasn't illegal," Jack agreed. "That part comes in when he wins big and refuses to pay off."

"Did this man win?"

"No."

"Did he lose?"

"No."

Hugh appeared to look perplexed.

"What, if anything, did he do?"

"He told me he was working a system."

"Was that his exact word? System?"

"It was."

"Did he reveal the nature of that system?"

"He did not."

"Did you draw any conclusions from his statement? Right or wrong?" he added for clarification.

"I thought he was waiting for a big race. One where he had every reason to believe his horse was going to win. At long odds. And put down a bundle. I mean, every dime he had."

His expression drew smiles from the audience.

"Was such the case?" As Jack hesitated, he clarified, "Were you correct in your assumption?"

"No."

"What did he do?"

"He fixed a horse race."

"Objection!" Bond hissed.

The judge glared over at him.

"On what grounds?"

Having no ready answer, he replied in a surly voice, "Defense counsel is delving into areas not connected with this case."

"I have every intention of trying them together, Your Honor."

Unconvinced, Bond added, "Coercing the witness into testifying on a subject he cannot possibly substantiate."

"Is that true, Mr. Kerr?" Turning to Jack, the judge inquired, "Were you coerced, Mr. Merrick?"

"No, sir."

"Are you prepared to substantiate the witness' statement, Mr. Kerr?"

"Yes, Your Honor."

"In expectation that you do, objection is over-ruled. If, by subsequent testimony you are unable to, I will re-address the subject."

"Thank you." Hugh returned to the witness. "You just stated this individual fixed a horse race. Please explain why this was done if he did not subsequently bet on the outcome?"

"He arranged to have it fixed so the horse would lose. In order to lower its value when the owner put it up for sale."

"Why would the owner put the horse up for sale?"

"It didn't win the race it was expected to. Therefore proving it had little, if any value, as a race horse."

"How did that benefit this individual?"

"He wanted to buy it."

"What was the name of the horse?"

"Barrister's Baby."

This caught the attention of the jury and they leaned forward in interest.

"The same horse owned by the decedent, Stanley Wexler?"

"The same."

"The same horse upon which was used the 'magic formula' created by the defendant, Amy Pazel?"

"Yes."

Hugh glanced up at Judge Gillman.

"That, Your Honor, is the connection."

"You may proceed."

"What was the name of this individual you allege fixed the horse race?"

"James Ewell."

"Thank you. No further questions."

"No questions," Bond muttered without interest as though acknowledging no new or pertinent facts had been revealed.

"Defense recalls William Boerner to the stand."

Reminded he was still under oath, the trainer slumped in the witness box. Hugh stood close, making his nearness uncomfortable.

"Mr. Boerner, it has been established you were the trainer of Barrister's Baby. Is that correct?"

"Yes."

"You were responsible for using an unauthorized medication on that horse. A medication which subsequently worked so well the horse was able to race again?"

"Yes."

"You were also a partner – along with the defendant, Amy Pazel and ostensibly Jack Merrick – who hoped to market this magic cream?"

"That's right! So, why would I want the filly to lose? I resent Merrick's accusation and I'm gonna sue him for libel for alleging that in court!"

"I think you mean slander and may I point out, your name did not come up in Mr. Merrick's testimony. He was speaking of an entirely different individual."

Clearly caught off-guard, Boerner hesitated, then clenched his fists.

"Well, I'm the trainer."

"Since you brought up the subject, let me ask you this for clarification. Do you know Mr. James Ewell, the man whose name was actually mentioned in connection with fixing the horse race?"

"I'm not going to answer that."

"Why not? If you don't know him and you didn't fix the race, what possible reason could you have to refuse to answer?"

"He… bets on horses. No one in the business wants to be associated with a gambler."

"But, you just heard that Mr. Ewell did not bet on Barrister's Baby. Either to win or lose. So, where is the harm?"

"How was I supposed to know that?"

"Then, let us put that aside for the moment, leaving it as you either did or did not know James Ewell – well. Barrister's Baby was entered into a race at Santa Anita. Do you happen to know whether the cream used on the horse to cure its recurring problem with bridle sores was approved by track officials?"

"It was."

"So, there was no impediment to racing the horse?"

"No."

"Who put up the entrance fee? Who made the arrangements?"

"The new owner."

"Who was –?"

"Mr. Noah Wexler."

"The son of the deceased? He, who inherited the bulk of Stanley Wexler's estate?"

"Yes."

"Calling upon your knowledge of horse racing, being an experienced trainer, answer this, if you will. What benefit would there be to the owner, Mr. Noah Wexler, if the horse won?"

Boerner appeared confused at the point of the obvious question.

"He'd earn the purse. And the value of the horse would increase. He'd be able to enter the filly into better races with higher purses. That's the business."

"Meaning, he would have no reason to fix the race so his horse would lose?"

"None, whatsoever."

"Who, then, would benefit from having the horse lose a race in all likelihood it should have won?"

"No one."

"Unless someone bet on another horse – one with better odds – to win?"

"I didn't bet on the race!" Boerner screamed.

"What did you bet on?"

Pulling away, the witness pressed himself against the back of the chair.

"What do you mean?"

"Winning money at the betting window wasn't the game. But, there was another way to come out ahead, wasn't there?"

"No! I don't know what you're getting at!"

"You saw another chance to buy this horse – the one you had originally planned to make your poster boy. The horse cured by the miracle cream. The *champion* horse. You couldn't have it the way you wanted, so you and your... new partner went in a different direction. With Stanley Wexler out of the way, you played on his son. 'Race Barrister's Baby. She's a winner.' He went along with your recommendation but the horse lost. What does one do with a 'nag,' Mr. Boerner? You sell it; dispose of it. Someone makes him an unsolicited offer and buys it from him. That's the first part of the plan. The second part is to market the magic formula. That's where the real money is: the pot of gold at the end of the rainbow."

Boerner shook his head. Dismissing that as poor play acting, Hugh stepped away, giving the jury a clearer view of the witness.

"You had originally planned on dividing the profits three ways. Dismiss Jack Merrick, who wasn't a real partner, anyway, and add a new player. One who *assured you* he could obtain the rights to the cream. One who *knew for a fact* he could wheedle the formula from Noah Wexler. That way, your original plan would work out nicely. Wouldn't it, Mr. Boerner? All you had to do was eliminate Stanley Wexler."

Shooting to his feet, face red with passion, Boerner screamed, "I didn't kill Wexler!"

Hugh finally withdrew, stepping back on his heels.

"No. But you know who did. And that makes you an accomplice." He turned to face Bond. "Your witness."

Being caught unawares by the entire testimony, the prosecutor had nowhere to go.

"No questions."

"Call James Ewell to the stand."

All eyes turned curiously toward the back. The first anyone had heard of this witness came from Jack Merrick's testimony, which court followers always anticipated with an eagerness akin to desire. Being Kerr's right-hand man, if the detective were called, it always meant either an exciting revelation or the dotting of the "i's" as the defense attorney wrapped up his case. Or, both.

The witness' appearance did not disappoint. Two black eyes, one a real shiner; sticking plaster on his jaw where the skin had been split, and a strip of tape over his nose that would not in any way affect whether the broken appendage healed straight or crooked, Ewell limped slowly forward. When he paused by the half gate as though he did not have the strength to push it, the court security guard crossed to him and held it back. Hobbling decrepitly to the box, he raised his right hand.

"Do you, James Ewell, swear to tell the truth, the whole truth and nothing but the truth in the matter now pertaining to this Court?"

"I do," he whispered in a weak voice.

Judge Gillman scowled.

"Mr. Kerr, is your witness in any fit condition to testify?"

"He is, Your Honor." Glowering at Ewell, he added, "I have a physician in attendance. Should he become faint or dizzy, a little ammonia under the nose should clear his head remarkably well."

Taking the comment more as a warning to the witness than a reassurance to the Court, Gillman gave assent.

"Very well. But, tell him to raise his voice so the court recorder and the jury can hear him."

"Speak up!" Hugh ordered in what could hardly have been considered a solicitous tone. "Repeat your reply under oath."

"I swear," he snarled.

"Be seated," Gillman completed, casting a questioning glance at the defense attorney. Hugh ignored it. When Ewell had seated himself, he approached, effecting a casual position to belie his previous sharpness.

"Mr. Ewell, what do you do for a living?"

"I'm a gambler."

"A card shark? Craps? Twenty-one?"

"Horses."

"How successful are you?"

"It depends."

"On what?"

"No one wins all the time. Sometimes I have more success than others," he replied out of the side of his mouth. No one watching him doubted his jaw hurt.

"When you string together bad luck, what, then? How do you – I hesitate to use the word – earn – enough to live, much less place bets?"

"I look for a partner."

"Or, partners?"

"As many as I can find."

"What is your *modus operandi?*"

Ewell's lip curled back in disdain.

"You needn't put it like that. What I do is perfectly legal."

Hugh mouthed an exaggerated "Ah" before verbalizing aloud, "You look for partners. Please explain how that works."

"In exchange for an investment in my system, I take their capital and bet it on a horse. One with good odds, so when I win, I make a substantial payday. They get their money back with interest and I *earn* my living," he stressed, finding no trouble articulating the word.

"That sounds risky."

"It is. I never hide that fact from them."

"What is your pitch? By that, I mean, how do you convince them you're a good risk?"

"I'm a horse man. I know everything there is to know about horses. I follow the sport *religiously*. Bloodlines, training, jockey; the competition of any given race. There's nothing I don't know for any given race. It's my... passion."

"Then, I repeat: how successful are you?"

"More successful than not."

"So, this... system, or scheme of yours earns enough to support a reasonable lifestyle?"

"Yes."

"But, not all the time. Which is why you occasionally require the financial backing of a mark?"

"Not a mark," Ewell snapped in greater annoyance. "A mark is a sucker; a pigeon. Someone taken in by a confidence man."

"Thank you for explaining that to the jury," Hugh smiled.

"I pay off. I'm honest as the day's long."

Leaning back, Hugh pretended to appraise the man.

"Underneath those bandages, I imagine you do cut a respectable figure. Nicely spoken, educated, well-dressed. Suave, I suppose, is the image you conjure. You talk a good game, Mr. Ewell."

Unsure whether or not he was being mocked, the witness let it pass. Bond, however, reading his opponent aright, turned to whisper something to Dodson. Hugh noted the action from the corner of his eye but let it pass.

"I am prepared to call two witnesses who willingly became 'partners' in your betting *scheme,* Mr. Ewell. Have you paid either of them off? By that, I mean, returned their investments with interest?"

"No."

"Why is that?"

"I haven't had any success lately."

Hugh clucked his tongue.

"That's too bad." Moving away, he started around the room before speaking. "You have been in court all morning?"

Ewell nodded.

"Witness will state his answer out loud," Gillman warned.

"Yes."

"You heard a previous witness, Jack Merrick, state you fixed a race in which a horse named Barrister's Baby ran."

"That's a lie! I play fair. I never fixed a race in my life. I never even bet on that race."

"So you didn't." His voice rose. "Do you know Bill Boerner? The trainer of Barrister's Baby?"

Ewell shrugged.

"I've met him a few times. I know most of the trainers on the circuit."

"A casual acquaintance? Nothing more?"

"We've had a few beers together."

"Discussing Barrister's Baby?"

"We discussed a lot of horses."

"I'm sure you did. And during one of these little chats, he told you about the formula. All his plans for fame and fortune. That rang dollar signs before your eyes. But, of course, there were impediments. His plan fell through. For him, perhaps. But not for you. You had an edge. One Mr. Boerner, who was actually, more than a casual acquaintance, knew. I suggest you two made a deal. In exchange for getting him rehired and a small remuneration, you created your own partnership."

"None of that makes any sense. How could I have done any of that that?"

Hands behind his back, Hugh strode toward the jury box. "Mr. Ewell, where were you born?"

"Kentucky."

"The home of thoroughbred horses. Is that where you gained your early knowledge of horse racing?"

"Yes."

"And, in fact, often volunteered that information to your prospective clients? That you were born and raised in Kentucky?"

"It was true," Ewell argued.

"Yes, actually, it was true. One of the few truths you told. And fortunate it was," he added, making the point to the jury before turning back at stare at the witness. "Because it enabled me to have you traced. Not easily," he confessed with a smile. "In the course of your professional life, how many names have you used?"

"I've used a few. So what? There's no law against that."

"But, there is a law against perjury. You recall I asked you to speak up when taking the oath. You swore not only to tell the truth, but to the name James Ewell. Was that completely true?"

"Yes!" he spat in triumph, thumping his hand on the arm of the witness box.

"What is your middle name?"

"Ewell," came the answer, lower and less assured.

"Ewell? Your full, legal name is James Ewell Ewell?"

"My name is James Ewell."

Across the room, the prosecutor shifted positions, then reluctantly abandoned the objection he was prepared to make over badgering the witness in the belief it would be overruled.

"James Ewell – what?" When he didn't reply, Hugh demanded, "Isn't it true your full name is James Ewell Wexler? And that you are the nephew of the late Stanley Wexler? The son of his brother, now deceased?"

A hush fell over the courtroom. Those who had been waiting for the bomb to drop nodded in anticipation of the fallout.

Hugh gave them their moment before continuing.

"It is a common truism that people who select aliases often use part of their name in their false identity. Typically, a first name. Which you did. And also a similar last name. Or, substitute a middle name for a surname."

"All right. There's no law against that."

"Unless such a deception is used to obfuscate facts. Why did you use a pseudonym?"

"I didn't want it known I was related to a famous family," he hedged.

"Why? In your... line of work, I would imagine being related to a racing baron would be a help rather than a hindrance. Was it because Mr. Stanley Wexler forbad you from using your real name? Because you were the black sheep of the family? Because you weren't worthy of the name?" He moved quickly toward the witness to punctuate his accusations. "You call yourself a horseman, but you weren't interested in the hard work involved in the day-to-day activities of the sport. Your interest lay in get-rich-quick schemes. Why did Stanley Wexler throw you out? Did he catch you trying to make a dishonest 'buck' on the side?"

"No!"

"But, you were dismissed from his family circle." Crossing to the evidence table, Hugh took a paper and marched back. "This is the last will and testament of the decedent, Stanley Wexler. While his son, Noah, it is primary beneficiary, two other individuals are specifically mentioned. One is your brother, John Wexler, who is to receive ten percent of the estate.

The other, James Wexler – you, Mr. James Ewell Wexler – are to receive a mere one percent. You weren't completely disinherited, but you lost your fair share of the pie."

Getting to his feet, Ewell shouted, "I didn't kill him for that lousy inheritance!"

The crowd murmured in disquietude. Hugh ignored them.

"No, I don't believe you did." The room grew quiet. "You killed him for the opportunity of achieving that 'big scheme' of which you bragged to Jack Merrick. He thought you were going to make a killing on Barrister's Baby by betting 'a bundle.' Every dime you had. But he was wrong, wasn't he? That wasn't your plan at all."

Hugh approached, eyes narrowed in anger. With the assurance of a man holding the winning ticket, he pressed the issue.

"You wanted the filly to lose, so you arranged with her trainer, Bill Boerner – who you somehow coerced, or perhaps sweet-talked your uncle into rehiring – to throw the race. Losing in a field she should have handily beaten reduced her worth to pennies on the dollar. That much, we've already established. Once her potential had been disproven, you could pick up your 'poster horse' in a claiming race. But, you still needed the formula: one Stanley Wexler wouldn't sell you. But, with him out of the way – with him dead, and his son the new owner of the magic formula – you planned on going to your cousin and offering a deal. Your one percent of the horse racing enterprise for the rights to Amy Pazel's spray."

"You're making that up! One percent is peanuts!"

"We can argue that another time. Its true, inestimable value lay in the fact it gave you a say in how the business was run. A small one, I grant. But enough to become an irritant, if nothing more, to the new owner. A man with your reputation is a bad apple. He casts aspersions on an otherwise untarnished business. One, where a sterling reputation is everything."

"He would have bought me out –!"

"Yes. I think that's true. But you wanted much more than what he would have offered. You wanted the Golden Goose: the rights to the formula. Assuming beforehand Mr. Noah Wexler would hardly be interested in a sideline: one that he would eventually sell or reassign to an outside firm, which, in fact, he has admitted to this court, you gambled that in exchange for your one percent he'd give you the rights to the formula."

Slapping his hand on the end of the witness chair, Hugh delivered his killing blow.

"You went to see your uncle, Stanley Wexler. Not at the office, where there would be a record of the meeting, but at his home. You asked for the rights to the spray, probably in exchange for your anticipated inheritance. He refused you. That meant putting Plan B into action. You put on a conciliatory face; proposed he rehire Bill Boerner; suggested he use him to promote the spray and then suggested he make a similar deal with Amy Pazel. Why cast her out when she could be useful? Wexler liked the idea, so he made an appointment to meet with both of them on the night of July 15."

Smiling with the cunning of a cat playing with a mouse, Hugh looked from the witness to the prosecution table and then to the jury as he laid out the actual events of "the night in question."

"The scenario I just describes has one... fatal flaw. It leaves you out in the cold. Already knowing your uncle wouldn't include you in the marketing the spray, the only way forward was to kill him and make your deal with the new owner."

"I don't know anything about poisons! It took a chemist to poison him."

"Shall I recall Jack Merrick to the stand? He will testify that you had a compound called Carbona Cleaning Fluid in your apartment. A product which contains carbon tetrachloride. In fact, you offered it to him to take a stain out of his jacket. The warning label on the product clearly states it is poison." Turning to the jury, he made eye contact with them. "Considering you had means, motive and opportunity, I think twelve men and women can readily deduce what you did." He took in a deep breath. "You waited outside Stanley Wexler's office until Mrs. Pazel left and entered the building through the unlocked door. You and your uncle shared one last drink together. When his attention was diverted, you put the carbon tetrachloride in his glass, waited until he had finished it, then quietly departed to await the good news of your inheritance. 'Peanuts'? Mr. James Ewell Wexler? I think not." Turning, he dipped his head toward the prosecution table. "No further questions."

Bond leaned back in his chair and stared ahead into space.

The closing arguments were conducted after the noon recess. Afterwards, as the jury was ushered into the deliberation room, Ellen turned to Hugh with a twinkle in her eyes.

"Shall we send Amy away with the matron and go to the office to wait?"

With great solemnity, he gave the question due consideration before checking his wrist watch.

"The jury went out at 3:15. Do you happen to know what they were served for lunch?"

Puzzled, Amy asked, "What does that have to do with anything?"

Using her claim on seniority, Ellen answered Hugh's question first.

"Vegetable soup with crackers served on the side, and toasted cheese sandwiches. With a beverage of their choice: coffee or water."

With a wink at his client, Hugh addressed her concern with another question.

"Between the two of us, you're the cook. Which also means you enjoy good food. Therefore, I put it to you: based on the evidence just presented by Mrs. Kerr, would you, as a member of the jury, prefer to hold out and have dinner 'in,' or would you rather take a vote as soon as the door shuts and be dismissed in time to be home for dinner?"

He meant the question to be rhetorical but she surprised him by giving both sides equal measure.

"That depends on how I'm going to vote. If I'm going to convict, then I'd just as soon linger over a discussion and eat in the jury room. That way, I won't associate condemning someone to life in prison with sharing a meal with my family. But, if I'm going to vote to exonerate, then I'd demand an early poll, find we're all in agreement and send word to the judge. That way when I get home, I'll feel as free as the defendant and want to celebrate."

"That means," Ellen interpreted, "we wait right here."

Hugh puffed air through his cheeks.

"Your decision was not predicated on the quality of the food."

"I have no problem with vegetable soup and toasted cheese."

"You may have just destroyed an entire line of legal thinking."

"I'm sorry."

"Don't be," Ellen grinned. "In five minutes he'll have forgotten all about it." She pointed to the clock. "That's when the jury will be coming back."

Indicating to the matron they would wait with their client, the three, as though by mutual consideration, stared across the aisle at the prosecution table. It was empty.

"Do you think Mr. Bond is expecting a verdict of guilty? He didn't wait."

Hugh shook his head.

"It would be unseemly if he banged his head against the courtroom wall. He went somewhere private to knock his brains out."

"Will he come back bandaged like Jack?"

"I don't think so. Jack had fun doing his damage. And I also imagine he was offering some stage theatrics. Bond will have a lump on his head as big as a golf ball."

"I could probably create a formula to help reduce the swelling."

Because she made the offer with a straight face, Hugh groaned.

"I'm afraid his condition is terminal."

"The injury will kill him?"

"Terminal, in that his ego is always in need of stroking. I pity the phrenologist trying to read the bumps on his skull."

They laughed, the clock struck 3:30 and the clerk gave notification the jury was coming back. The rear doors were opened to allow the spectators back in and B.B. Bond, looking the worse for wear, slithered down the aisle. Casting a sick glance at Hugh, he nodded his head before turning away.

"I think I saw the bump," Ellen chuckled.

"Poor man," their client offered.

Hugh finally grunted in exasperation.

"Don't you ever get mad?"

"Life is too short."

"Well, Ellen anticipated for the jury, "yours just got a lot longer."

Getting to their feet as Judge Gillman arrived, they waited while he questioned the foreman and received an answer in the affirmative that they had reached a unanimous verdict. He indicated it be delivered.

"Not guilty, Your Honor."

With a cry of pure joy, Ellen embraced Amy in her arms.

"Congratulations!"

Accepting the hug, Amy pulled away to take Hugh's hand.

"Thank you, Mr. Kerr."

"My pleasure, Mrs. Pazel. I have but one regret."

"What's that?"

"I couldn't nail Philip Shaffley with something more damaging than a blackened reputation."

"My husband," she winked, "Would agree with you."

"Go and get her sprung," Hugh requested of Ellen as Bond came over to him. The two men shook hands.

"Odd, isn't it," the prosecutor began, "how two unrelated cases merged into one. Without Merrick taking on the case of a woman cheated by this Ewell character, you never would have gotten her off."

"I was willing to take my chances that the jury couldn't convict on circumstantial evidence, but you're a worthy opponent. It could have gone either way."

"I appreciate you saying that. Justice prevailed. I can't argue with that. It also gave me the opportunity to try the real killer. As we speak, Lieutenant Wade is escorting 'Ewell' out to be booked." He hesitated, tried several words on for size, and then simplified his dilemma by abandoning all but one. "Dad?"

Hugh laughed, instantly making the connection.

"Yes, well, you know Jack. Always trying to get under Wade's skin. It's not... the first time you've heard him use that word in reference to Lieutenant Wade."

"I hope he kills him."

"Jack kills Wade?"

"No, the other way around, you fool."

"That means I'll have to defend Wade."

"Heaven help us. I take it back. On second thought," Bond added, pulling away, "he'd never ask you."

"Take comfort in that. He hates my guts," he added to Bond's back.

Which did not explain why he laughed.

"An acquittal, steak, mushrooms and homemade chocolate chip cookies! It hardly gets better than that!" Jack declared, smacking his lips and reaching for a cookie with his suddenly un-bandaged hands.

Mary slapped them.

"Steak and mushrooms first, cookies afterwards."

"Not for a boy."

Taking two, Jack stuffed them in his mouth, rolled his eyes and delight and took two more.

"Here," Hugh called, coming in from the kitchen carrying a tray on which sat an ice bucket holding a bottle and seven glasses. "– is something for you to wash it down with. Champagne."

Jack gulped and reached for a glass.

"The perfect host."

When they were all served, Hugh raised his in toast.

"May no good deed ever go... punished."

After sipping the sparkling wine, Ellen turned to Amy.

"What, now?"

She grinned in pleasure.

"Back to work – for Mega Enterprises."

"Won't it be hard working for that terrible Philip Shaffley, considering how he treated the whole affair?"

"Knowing he lost his chance to make – another – personal fortune is good enough for me. Besides, I love what I do."

"And the cream?"

"I think that can wait. Everything in the proper time."

"Then, here's to a bright and successful future."

Glasses clinked all around: Hugh and Ellen; Mom and Dad; Amy and Paul. Jack, being left out, finished his first and reached for the bottle.

"More for me," he explained. "The perfect ending."

No one could disagree.

Tuesday morning, Hugh arrived at the office at 9:00. Doffing his hat at Geraldine, he went into his office. Ellen was seated at his desk.

"A lovely morning to you, Mrs. Kerr," he greeted. "So nice to see you in your accustomed place." Dropping his hat onto a peg of the clothes tree, he stared at the pile of papers before her.

"What are you doing so bright and early?"

"Going through what amounts to three months of mail."

"Oh. That." He rubbed his hands together. "We missed you."

Her expression turned sour.

"I'm not all you missed."

"What does that mean?"

"There were seventeen checks in this stack."

"Well?"

"Six of them bounced."

"Bounced?"

"Big ones, too."

"Bounced?" he repeated as if not comprehending the word.

"Like rubber balls."

"Why?"

"Closed accounts. Moved, left no forwarding addresses. Insufficient funds."

"Well, I'll be damned."

"Probably not. But, it does mean one thing."

"What's that?"

"Next time I tell you to hire a secretary, you'll listen to me."

He dared smile in relief.

"No problem there. You're back. I won't need another secretary. Solved."

"Until the next time."

He was slow making the connection.

"Next time? What next time?" When the answer came to him, his face blanched. "Oh. Next time."

"By the time we're done, we may need a stable for all the ponies we're going to have."

"I thought you said... one to three."

"Seeing that look in your eyes last night, I may have been wrong."

His mouth opened. And then closed.

"Let me see those bounced checks. I'm going to need all the money I can get. I'll sue the bastards."

She laughed and he laughed and somewhere from behind her blindfold, Themis winked.

The End

GSFE

ALSO BY: S.L.KOTAR AND J.E.GESSLER
ALSO BY: S.L.KOTAR AND J.E.GESSLER

"The Hugh Kerr Mystery Series"..

- I   The Conundrum of the Decapitated Detective
- II   The Conundrum of the Absconded Attorney
- III   The Conundrum of the Sins of the Fathers
- IV   The Conundrum of The Two-Sided Lawyer
- V   The Conundrum of the Clueless Counselor
- VI   The Conundrum of the Loveless Marriage
- VII   The Conundrum of the Executed Defendant
- VIII   The Conundrum of the Jettisoned Jury
- IX   The Conundrum of the Perjured Pigeon
- X   The Conundrum of the Haunting Halloween
  - Party
- XI   The Conundrum of the Tuneless Tunesmith
- XII   The Conundrum of the Meddling Motorcar
- XIII   The Conundrum of the Blundering Bear
- XIV   The Conundrum of Shooting Fish in a Barrel
- XV   The Conundrum of The Girl with the Emerald
  Eyes
- XVI   The Conundrum of The Vanishing Cream
  -
  - To Be Continued!

"New Beginnings Series"

- I   The Believer
- II   The Heretic
- III   Arrow Song
- IV   Peas In A Pod
- V   The Agnostics

"the ReproBate saga"

- **I**   Beneath the Rose
- II   skull and cRossBones
- III   Redefining Bastions
- IV   thicker than Blood
- V   prioR Battles
- VI   Requited Blasphemy
- VII   The waR Between
- VIII   To Richmond or Bust
- IX   carrying Battlescars
- X   RamBlings
- XI   Retrieving Ballast
- XII   captain's RB
- XIII   wondeRous Backdrops
- XIV   ReproBate
- XV   time and tRouBle
- XVI   the Road Back
- XVII   oveR the Brink
  - To be Continued

"the Hellhole saga"

- I   First Draw
- II   Audition for a Legend
- III   Strange Bedfellows
-

"The Kansas Pirate Series"

- I   Pirate Treasure
- II   Strawberry Fields
- III   The Drinking Gourd

- <u>Catman</u>
-
- <u>ONE</u>
-
- <u>Shepherd of the Kingdom</u>
-
- <u>Wolf Eyes</u>
-
- <u>I Am the Ship</u>

Non-Fiction

"The Kepi Magazine," A publication specialized in the Civil War and 19th century life. An iconoclastic publication that specialized in the American Civil War and 19th century life. These two volumes reintroduce the ground breaking research, historically accurate timelines, period photography and an eye to the life and times of this unsettled period of American history.
:

- <u>**The Kepi Volume I and II**</u>
- <u>**The Kepi Volumes III and IV**</u>

Made in the USA
Middletown, DE
07 August 2020